ARC OF DIVINITY

Published by - Spines
ISBN: 979-8-89569-993-5

ARC OF DIVINITY

J.B. CURTIS

To Elle,
Eternally

Chapter 1

Watch your back, and keep your guard up.

Commander Ronnie Marcus scaled the smooth wall in the dark, vaulted room, his double-barreled laser handgun cocked and ready to fire with his aim directly in front of him.

C'mon baby, thought the perspiring Marcus, his stuffy black mask leached tightly to his face. *You've got to be around here somewhere.*

He hustled from the wall and quietly made his way into the oversized storage chamber. With the exception of a few enormous metal courier units, the room was mostly bare and uninteresting.

His heart began to thump more aggressively in his chest as he coasted towards the biggest unit near the center of the room that towered greatly over him.

Marcus leaned next to the unit, the glowing green lenses over his eyes serving as his greatest ally in the blinding game of cat and mouse in which he found himself deeply entrenched.

Come on out wherever you are. You know you want to.

Suddenly, he heard a step. His enemy had given himself away, much to his relief. He gazed up rapidly and spotted a dark figure standing above him on the unit, weapon in hand and prepared to fire at him.

The enemy wasted no time as he rapidly shot a laser toward Marcus, who had no choice but to sprawl to the floor in order to avoid a skull-piercing fatal blow.

The dark figure leaped from his respective unit and rapidly descended upon the fallen commander to officially finish the job.

Marcus quickly rolled onto his back and cocked his gun in an effort to beat his opponent to the punch. He acted on impulse and without the assistance of his target beam as his index finger pulled upon the trigger and delivered a laser that penetrated directly into the chest of his enemy.

Gotcha, you bastard.

The dark figure groaned in agony as his body, which hurled backward from the power of the shot he had endured, slammed wickedly onto the rock-hard, unforgiving floor. The enemy lay motionless on the ground and let out a pained moan that echoed against the walls of the spaced-out area.

Marcus rose to his feet quickly and ran towards his fallen combatant and stopped on a dime directly above him, his gun cocked and ready to finish off his enemy.

"Any last words?" Marcus snarled with bloodthirsty ambition.

"Okay, okay. I surrender," acknowledged the dark-clothed combatant, who gasped for air through the small air pocket in front of the mouth of his mask.

"Anything else you'd like to say?"

"Like what?"

"I don't know. Maybe, that I kicked your sorry ass again?" exclaimed Marcus with a brimming smile as he began to chuckle. "Lights!" he commanded aloud, his chuckling now converting to a snort as the room aboard their ship, the Beso de Maria, began to illuminate.

"Whatever, you cocky son of a bitch," groaned the still out-of-breath and pained figure, who gingerly pushed a small button that detached the uncomfortable mask from his face. The enemy, now identifiable as Lieutenant Thomas Byers, Marcus' lifelong friend from Earth and fellow comrade with the Space and Galaxy Exploration team, simply called SAGE, took a deep breath of the stuffy air in the storage room that suddenly felt so sweet and refreshing.

Marcus' laughter shook throughout as he pushed the button that detached his heavy mask from his unshaven face. He turned off his gun, securely placed his weapon into the holder adhered to his belt and looked down with delight at his defeated friend, who remained seated pitifully on the hard floor while continuing to nurse the physical and egotistical injuries he had endured.

He continued to chuckle as he extended his hand to help his friend to his feet.

Byers, although begrudgingly, accepted his friend's offer despite the feeling of pity that he understood was the reason for the help that had been offered.

The lieutenant stood upright as Marcus' large smile of satisfaction remained, his glistening face drenched in sweat. "I have to admit, I almost thought you had me there for a second. What does that make now, eleven times in a row, that I've beaten you at Night Watch?"

The incredulous appearance on Byers' face said it all. "You mean to tell me that you're actually counting? You've got to be freaking kidding me. I mean, I've always known that you were cocky, but now you're just being ridiculous. I bet you look at yourself in the mirror all day, too."

"Don't hate me because I'm beautiful and you're not. I'm just that good, baby."

Byers smirked and shook his head at his friend. "You're unbelievable, that's what you are." He deactivated his own gun and placed it in his own holder slowly, pain still throbbing throughout his body from the bone-crushing fall he had just absorbed.

Marcus wiped a wave of sweat from his eyes as he felt the need to address a beef he had with his buddy. "By the way, what was up with you trying to blow my head off back there? You could have killed me with that shot, you idiot."

Byers shrugged his shoulders and grinned wickedly. "Well, I figured if I couldn't beat you, I might as well just kill you."

"That's not right. I'm sure that you're pining for my job and all, but I didn't think you'd want to kill your best friend to make that happen."

"Trust me, your position is something I want no part of, so you can keep it. Anyway, you can relax. I had it on disabled the whole time, so the worst that would have happened was that you'd have had a splitting headache for a day or two. And, who knows? Maybe that could have helped deflate that big head of yours."

"Whatever. Just keep poking the bear because it'll just make that twelfth straight win even sweeter."

Marcus and Byers extended their arms and hit one another on the forearm, a friendly gesture that the two had kept since their childhood days. The two began to walk towards the shower room to get ready for the second half of their respective shifts.

Byers, however, still felt compelled to continue the trash-talking. "The only thing I know is that I'm breaking your shitty streak next time. Your winning ways are about to come to a crashing halt, my friend."

Marcus was more than amused by his friend's proclamation. "Uh-huh. Well, I guess we'll see if you're still running your mouth after I crush you again. And when I do, because I will, just promise me that you won't cry too much like you do after every time I beat you, okay?"

Their chiding was interrupted by an urgent message that was relayed over the personal intercom systems on the collars of their shirts by Victoria Jacobs, the ship's navigator.

"Commander Marcus, please respond. Commander Marcus, please respond."

Marcus peered at Byers curiously, worry instantly throbbing internally. The commander hit the button on his shirt to respond promptly to the message.

"This is Marcus."

"Captain Maxwell requests you to meet him in his chambers immediately, sir. He says that it's extremely urgent."

Marcus and Byers exchanged surprised glances over Jacobs' emergency request.

The commander batted his eyes blankly as he stared off into nothing, his mind beginning to fester with anxiety as he took a personal moment before answering.

"Okay, tell Maxwell that I'll be right there."

Marcus took his finger off of the button and turned his attention once more towards Byers, who adorned a poker face that gave no hints to the commander.

Byers suddenly smiled like a joker. "Uh-oh, Commander Marcus, looks like you're being sent to the principal's office."

"Shut up, Tommy."

Byers couldn't help himself but to further rub salt into Marcus' proverbial wounds. "All I know is that I'd hate to be you. I guess, though, that's why you're the second in command of the ship, and I'm not, so Amen to that."

"You need to shut that big mouth of yours before I do it for you."

Byers chuckled upon his commander's soured behavior as the misbehaved lieutenant patted Marcus on the shoulder blade to offer phony support. "I know you don't really mean that. You know that you love me, man."

He looked down at his wrist while pretending to gaze at an imaginary watch, his joking now officially reaching an all-time high. "Man, would you look at what time it is? I hate to miss all of the upcoming excitement, but I really should head to the showers because I'm starting to smell my funkiness, and it's definitely getting out of control. All I can say is good luck, and may God be with you. It seems like you're sure as hell going to need both right about now."

"Yeah, right. Thanks for your words of encouragement, asshole," bemoaned Marcus, who took no comfort from the words of wisdom, or rather stupidity, offered by his childhood friend.

Byers beamed without a care in the world and proceeded to

turn up the arrogance even further by singing an off-key tune that vibrated against the walls of the enormous room.

Marcus shook his head out of disdain but honestly expected no less from his jester of a lieutenant who waltzed his way into the shower room to his own amusement.

The commander could feel his blood still boiling out of irritation but gave himself a moment and took a deep breath before picking up his pace to carry on to Captain John Maxwell's quarters. He began to feel his worries migrate into the pit of his stomach, concern overcoming his mind as he himself knew that Captain Maxwell hardly ever requested closed door meetings with any member of his crew.

What could it be? Have I done something wrong?

His concerns rose further as he proceeded towards the ship's ancient elevator to make his way upwards to his superior's chambers, and his mind became boggled with endless possibilities of what was potentially on the horizon.

Marcus stepped into the empty space, pushed the button to the fourth floor to Maxwell's quarters, and took a deep breath. He exhaled deeply in a futile effort to ease the nerves that only pulsated with more intensity inside of him upon the cruel and slow close of the elevator door in front of his occupied face.

Chapter 2

Marcus stood gravely in front of his captain's closed-door quarters, anxiety riding over his body while he wondered what was waiting for him behind there.

He knew that Captain Maxwell requesting an urgent meeting was indeed rare, as the captain was the kind of man who would have no problem disciplining one of his crew members in front of others if need be. He was also a man who did not believe in talking in private, so to request a meeting in his chambers was bizarre, needless to say.

Marcus cleared his throat, ran his hand quickly through his close-cropped hair, and gazed at Maxwell's closed door, which was about to open upon his superior's request.

The commander took a moment and looked at his own reflection in the shined door, his face giving full exposure to the concern that broiled internally.

Get a hold of yourself. Maxwell will eat you up alive if you show any sign of weakness.

Marcus took a deep breath and pushed the orange button next to the door to summon his commanding officer.

"Yes?" the captain's strong voice asked through the speaker underneath the button.

A slight chill went down Marcus' spine upon hearing the inquiry, as he still needed moments at a time to summon internal courage when it came to dealing with captain. He gulped softly as he fluttered out a response that he prayed to be strong.

"It's Commander Marcus, sir."

"Ah, yes, Marcus. Enter."

The door to Maxwell's quarters slid swiftly open and exposed the captain seated behind his desk, who appeared diligent in his work, his attention solely on that of a journal that he continued to write in as if he were still alone.

Here we go.

Marcus picked up his deadened feet against his own will and moved towards his commanding officer, who still offered not even an acknowledgment upon his official entry into the chambers. He stopped before Maxwell but said nothing himself as the captain continued to write, the relics of an early 1900s feather pen in his right hand and late 20th-century spectacled glasses upon his nose serving as his greatest of companions as he continued to ignore his commander who stood quietly and internally frightened before him.

Another ancient relic of Maxwell's, a pipe that he had been puffing but was stationed for the moment on his desk, filled the room with smoke. Smoking had phased out from society long before either of their times, and the commander couldn't help but be curious as to how his captain had picked up on the dirty habit. Marcus choked and coughed from the menacing odor and carbon that filled the air, but the captain continued to pay no mind to his suffering commander.

The captain's office, in general, was consistent with his apparent fixation on the 20th century, an oddity considering that they were currently in the early stages of the year 2174.

A shelf containing many 19th and 20th-century novels stood behind him, the captain's love for older forms of literary master-pieces more than apparent to all who stepped into his quarters. A giant aquarium, meanwhile, gave a warm feel as the captain's personal collection of exotic fish swam gently in the clean water.

Maxwell's bed, located on his left side, was nice and neatly made. A digital map of the current galaxy they were exploring, the Sigma-10 system, hued the overall bland colors in his quarters to create a psychedelic look.

The captain's writing finally came to a stop, and he tilted his eyes upwards towards Marcus, who stood still in preparation for hearing his superior speak.

He turned his attention back onto his desk and put his feathered pen inside the ink bottle next to his pen stand.

"Are you going to just keep standing there, or are you going to have a seat?" Maxwell finally asked coldly, his sight still turned downwards from his commander as he reached for and took a couple of deep puffs from his smoking pipe.

Marcus said nothing before taking a seat in the ugly, burgundy-colored leather chair in front of him, the smoke from the pipe continuing to bother him.

The captain, in the meanwhile, placed his pipe back down and opened the drawer on his left side, quickly stashing the open journal inside, which Marcus guessed as a way to not only allow the ink to dry from his freshly written words but to also keep the information he had just documented private.

I can only imagine what he's written in that thing about us all.

A loud click came from Maxwell, who locked the drawer, took off his spectacles, and placed them upside down on his desk. He rubbed his eyes for a moment with both hands and exhaled deeply, smacking his lips in the process for whatever reason.

It was eerily quiet in the office, with the exception of the buzz from the aquarium that provided the lone soundtrack for the game of silence that still occurred between the two men.

A chill went down Marcus' spine as he eagerly awaited any sort of clue as to what was going on.

Maxwell, however, continued to offer nothing more than a straight look upon his aged face. He was a man in his early fifties who, at first glance, appeared to be closer to being in his mid to late sixties, perhaps a result of the stress of being a commanding officer for more than twenty years. The salt and pepper color of his hair and beard gave him a somewhat refined look, but the sagging wrinkles and droopy eyes, to the contrary, only screamed the notion of how tough his past two decades surely had become.

Marcus' anxiety continued to rise, his senses telling him that something of big proportions was preparing to make its debut. He longed badly to hear what the captain was going to tell him but continued to coax himself internally to not allow himself to crack with impatience.

Maxwell continued to offer nothing more than picking up a framed computerized picture of him, looking much younger and slimmer, along with his wife and children. He took his thumb and began to caress the edges of the digital frame before gazing endlessly at the photo before him.

Patience had finally run out for Marcus, who cared not about any potential consequences but rather felt the overflowing desire to end the awkward silence between them both.

"Sir?"

Maxwell laid the picture on its back and peered up at Marcus with lost eyes. "You have that suit on--I'm guessing that you must have gone Night Watching?"

"Yes, sir."

"You were victorious, I assume?"

"Yes, sir. I was."

"And you defeated Lieutenant Byers again, I assume?"

Marcus smiled cautiously for a moment before quickly taking it back. "Of course, sir."

Maxwell still offered no hints with his facial expressions as a stone wall remained. "You definitely always have been the best at that game, no question. With that being said, you should have gotten out of those disgusting clothes. In the future, I prefer that you be clean and in proper uniform."

"Understood, sir. In my defense, however, Jacobs told me it

was urgent, so I figured I should hurry and come up here as soon as possible and change afterward."

"I see. I suppose I shall let that slide in that case."

Marcus was shocked by the sublime response given as the captain got up out of his plushy black chair and walked towards the digital map that hung to his right on the wall, his back given to Marcus as he stared blankly at the colorful digital image in front of him.

There was a lot on the captain's mind, and it was more than obvious to Marcus, whose silence screamed his shock value.

"Commander, the reason that I ordered for you to come up here immediately was to inform you of something I have not shared with anybody on this ship. I cannot stress to you anymore that this is completely confidential, so I'm putting my trust in you that you will not pass this on to anybody else on this ship, and that especially includes Lieutenant Byers."

Marcus paused for a moment before answering the question to the best of his ability. "Yes, sir."

Maxwell turned and faced Marcus, who stared at his captain inquisitively and curiously, awaiting the news he was about to be informed of.

Here it comes.

"Marcus--"

The words from the captain's mouth seemed to be coming out in slow motion to Marcus but did little to affect him as his focus had never felt any sharper.

"--I'm stepping down as captain of SAGE after the completion of this mission. Assuming you do what is required, you will assume command immediately upon our return to Earth of the Beso de Maria."

The shock of lightning from Maxwell's announcement instantly hit Marcus, who felt paralyzed by the sudden news. "What? I mean--wow. If you don't mind me asking--why?"

The captain peered downward and took a deep breath before answering. "Well, the truth is that, in my over thirty years of being with this organization, I have been extremely fortunate to have seen and done so many different things and to have watched it grow from its original and, frankly, puny beginnings. I have explored so many various planets and systems in this seemingly endless galaxy and have gone on so many adventures that very few get to be a part of, let alone imagine."

Maxwell's focus remained on the ground as he sluggishly languished back towards his desk. "I always dreamed of being an astronaut as a child," he continued, "but after our original space program collapsed due to the economic downfall and SAGE was born, it provided a new calling and a career that I would have never imagined. And, to be one of the original two pioneers of this group is remarkable. But, despite all of my successes, I've also had to make great sacrifices along the way."

He stopped on a dime behind his desk and reached for the singular framed picture that occupied it. He turned the ancient relic of technology for their day and age towards his commander. Marcus focused his sight on the image before him that featured a family photo of Maxwell, his wife and their two children, the darkened hair and lack of saggy skin further giving away its age.

"This--has been my biggest sacrifice, Marcus," confessed the captain to his commander. "As much as I know how to lead a crew in space, I never learned how to be a loving husband or father."

Maxwell snapped his head upwards at the ceiling and sniffled quietly in a terrible attempt to hide his moment of weakness.

Disbelief flared through Marcus, who batted not even an eye in order to not miss a moment of what he was witnessing.

I can't believe what I'm seeing--Maxwell is on the verge of crying like a baby. Whoever thought this was possible?

The captain allowed himself a moment to regain his composure before continuing on. He turned the picture towards himself and focused intently on the image before him.

"I missed seeing Shelley give birth to both Rachel and Curtis," Maxwell continued once more, his usually stoic look replaced by the image of a broken man. "I've missed birthdays, graduations and wedding anniversaries, and it has cost me dearly."

He could no longer hold it in as a single tear streamed down his left cheek and implanted itself into his graying beard.

"Shelley--left me last year, and our divorce is to be finalized when I return home. I've begged her to change her mind and take me back since I still love her so much, but she wants no part of it. And my kids--well, that's another story in itself. I have never been close to either one of them, and now, with my divorce on the horizon, I suppose it gives them even more of a reason not to speak to me. It's like I'm already dead to them."

Maxwell's lip began to quiver as he had officially reached his emotional tipping point. He gently placed the framed photograph back on the table face first and grabbed a cloth from the breast pocket of his uniform.

"The truth is, I can't blame them for feeling the way that they do, Marcus," explained the captain while dabbing his watery eyes. "Deep down, I knew for so long that I was neglecting my family, but I still allowed this job to take priority over them all. I'm a goddamn fool."

Sadness filled Marcus' heart, who immediately rose to his feet and hurried to his captain's side for additional support. He did the first thing that came to his mind in this unusual moment of weakness for his captain and began to pat Maxwell's back.

Despite his captain's usual gruff exterior and behavior, Marcus had an ample amount of respect for his superior, who had been a part of his life since he first enlisted in SAGE, and he felt the immediate need to show some support.

"I'm sorry to hear about your family, sir. I want you to know that you have a lot of people on this crew who look up to me, especially included. And if you do indeed retire, sir, you will definitely be missed."

Maxwell sniffled loudly and nodded upon Marcus' reassurances, balling up his soaked cloth in his hand in the process. "Thank you, Marcus. I know you will be a great captain, especially with this young crew we now have. And, who knows? It might be just what they need instead of this old, broken-down man you see in front of you."

"Don't say that, sir. You know you're only as old or young as you feel."

"If that's the case, I'm damn near ninety then," joked Maxwell, who broke into a momentary smile and chuckled briefly before quickly returning to his serious form. "All joking aside, I do believe that I'm leaving at the right time. Perhaps this retirement will bring me some sort of vigor or zest that I lost somewhere along the way, and perhaps I will be able to find myself. As for my family--well, I guess I'll just have to wait and see. Only time will tell, I suppose."

Marcus offered another pat on his captain's shoulder in a further attempt to cheer him up. "I just hope for the best, sir. I hope that you find happiness with yourself and, possibly, your family."

"As do I, commander," Maxwell said in agreement as he placed the wet cloth back inside his breast pocket. He stumbled back towards his seat and could feel himself finally pick up his broken pieces. "Thank you again for listening, Marcus. I appreciate it."

"Anytime, sir. Glad to be of service."

Maxwell reached his destination and stood in front of his chair for a moment, his eyes nearing completion of complete dryness. The vulnerable man had officially vanished, while the stoic captain immediately took his place.

The captain completed his personal turnaround and placed the framed picture once more face down on his desk as the business had returned to being usual. "Anyways, it's time to go back to work, commander. I will see you up front at the bridge at 2200 hours for further instructions on our mission."

"Yes, sir."

Maxwell took a seat in his chair while Marcus turned his back in order to walk away. The commander took a brisk step before he was stopped dead in his tracks by a stern reminder from Maxwell.

"Don't forget, Marcus. I'm putting my trust into you that you won't tell a soul, and that especially includes Lieutenant Byers. I understand your two's friendship, but we must keep this confidential and as close to the vest as we can until the conclusion of our mission, when I will properly inform the crew. After all, the last thing we need on this odyssey is an unnecessary distraction on this crew because of what I've told you."

Marcus remained frozen in his stance, his eyes growing larger by the second as his captain's strong words and voice resonated down his spine.

Maxwell folded his hands and placed them on his desk to further drive home his point to the backside of his commander. "I warn you that if I hear any of what we have discussed come back to me, not only will I deny it, but I will also see to it that you do not get your promotion to captain upon our return to Earth. Do I make myself clear, Commander?"

A huge lump formed inside of Marcus' throat, who gulped in a futile attempt to wash his discomfort away. "Yes, sir. One hundred percent clear, sir."

The captain's face returned to normal color, along with the expressionless features on his hardened face. "Very well. That is all for now, Commander."

Maxwell wasted no time picking up where he left off, placed his glasses back onto his face and took a couple more puffs from his pipe. He exhaled the heavy white smoke from his crusty lips before taking his journal out of the desk drawer and arming himself with his feathered ink pen to continue on with his personal writing.

Marcus exhaled softly, the stress inside of him beginning to rise from a simmer to a boil.

That man is like a machine. It's almost like nothing even happened.

The commander could feel his internal clock ticking like a

time bomb as he departed immediately to avoid any possible punishment from his superior. He picked up his gait and marched out of Maxwell's quarters as the stench of his body odor, combined with the newly acquired smoky smell generated from Maxwell's pipe, increased the anticipation of taking a shower in his own quarters.

Multiple thoughts resonated through Marcus' mind. He worried about Maxwell. He worried about Byers and the rest of his crew, and he worried about himself and how he would respond on their journey, knowing, in a forced secretive nature, what was truly occurring with his lame duck superior.

His head violently began to pulsate from his thoughts, and he could not have reached his quarters at a better time as his brain felt as if it were ready to explode from its overloaded status.

He peeled off his sweat-stained black suit, put down his gun on the nightstand to the right of his bed and plopped himself onto the divine mattress that welcomed his mentally and emotionally brutalized body.

"Midnight," he commanded aloud.

The computerized room followed his command and emitted a soft blue hue that engulfed his weary self.

Ahhhh...

Marcus crossed his legs and placed his hands behind his head in an effort to further relax, while worries of the present and future kept that from being a reality.

What the hell is going to happen to us?

His thoughts continued to wander as his eyes began to get heavier. Although his mind was still going a million miles an hour, he could feel his body beginning to attempt a forced shutdown.

His heavy eyes could finally take no more as his mind floated away from worries into a peaceful slumber that was long overdue.

CHAPTER 3

Marcus' slumber was interrupted an hour later by the smooth sound of the door to his quarters opening. His eyes fluttered open upon the sound of footsteps creaking across his floor, his internal instincts automatically coming into action.

He rapidly rose from his bed, snatched his gun from the nightstand and flickered it on in preparation for firing at his uninvited intruder.

Who in the hell?

Before Marcus could instruct the lights in his quarters to come to his aid, the cold barrel of a gun touched his right temple. He closed his eyes as his unknown opponent had him literally beaten to death.

He prayed for some sort of mercy or that possibly he was about to awaken from a horrible dream as his heart rate paced into overdrive.

C'mon, wake up. Wake up, damn it.

"Get on your knees--" the intruder instructed.

Shit.

Marcus complied with the intruder's commands and did as he was ordered. He closed his eyes in horror, his realization coming into play that the bad dream he was involved in was indeed reality.

He could only hope against hope for some sort of mercy or unbelievable miracle to occur as his breathing became that of a soon-to-be-dead man.

The intruder chuckled out of relishing in the fright upon the commander's face.

"--and admit defeat, asshole."

Marcus opened his eyes, the voice of the intruder sounding all too familiar. "Holy shit," mused Marcus, who shook his head upon realizing that the intruder was none other than Byers, who had taken the golden opportunity given to him and ran with it completely. "You're an asshole. Lights!"

The laughter of Byers cascaded aloud, a brightness filling the room as he reveled in the sight of his friend kneeling helplessly on the floor whose Night Watch victory had seemed like ions ago.

He chortled in delight while Marcus' heart continued to quake through his chest. "Man, you set yourself up there, my friend," chuckled Byers, a joyous smile imprinted on his freshly shaven face. "I mean, you could have at least locked your door. You made it way too easy for me."

Marcus rose slowly from the ground, his body language showing the signs of a defeated and sleep-deprived man. He rubbed his eyes and got to his feet, his heart finally beginning to slow down from the frightening joke his friend had just completed pulling on him. "You're an ass."

Byers took pleasure in the insult and sat in the comfortable chair beside him. "Payback's a bitch, my friend. And that unbelievable stench seeping from your body is downright insulting. Ugh--don't you know there's such a thing as a shower? I mean, I could smell all of your funkiness before I even stepped in here."

Marcus shrugged his shoulders, and he walked towards the small bar area in his room. "Yeah, I guess that I kind of got sidetracked. After my talk with Maxwell, I guess that I just got tired and forgot."

"Well, do the whole crew a favor and at least clean up before you report upfront. By the way, how'd everything go with the old man?"

Marcus reached for a hi-ball glass in the cabinet over his head but was unprepared for the million-dollar question that had come his way. "Huh? Oh yeah--that. Uh, fine. Just fine."

He felt grateful to have his back towards Byers and cringed as he knelt down to scavenge for alcohol to make something to drink. He deeply despised lying to his best friend but felt it to be the right choice, especially after the harsh warning from his captain.

Byers' curiosity rose instantly upon Marcus' short response, a feeling coming over him that something was not quite right. "I see. Is there anything I should know?"

Marcus pulled out separate containers of vodka and tonic and prepared to mix the two into a drink that he hoped would some-what distract Byers from further questioning. "Um, not really. Say, how about a drink?"

The lieutenant could sense something was amiss from his friend's curt responses. "Yeah--sure."

Marcus finished making Byers' drink and pulled out a second glass to make one for himself, also. He copied the production, placing three ice cubes in the glass before slowly pouring the vodka and tonic.

Byers curiously looked on, his sixth sense telling him that there was more behind the uneventful answers he had been given.

"Ronnie?"

"Yeah?"

"Did something happen when you were in there with Maxwell? Is there anything important that I should know?"

Marcus could feel his friend's look, so he kept his head down as he walked towards Byers and handed him his drink. "No, just the same old bullshit as always."

"I see. I don't know, and I guess I'm freaking out because I found it odd that he called you into his quarters like that. That's very unlike him."

"Who knows, maybe he's getting senile and weird in his old age. I mean, the man walked the Earth with the dinosaurs, right?"

Silence was met for a moment before Byers cracked a smile and chuckled over Marcus' statement.

Whew.

A sense of relief came over Marcus, who could feel the tension begin to disappear from any other form of inquisition coming his way.

Marcus acted on the safe side as he decided to brighten the mood by lifting his glass towards Byers. "Here's to a great journey. At least, let's hope it's a great one."

"You got that right," Byers responded, copying his friend by lifting his glass as well.

The two friends tapped their glasses in cheers before taking a drink, their primary sips bringing great relief to them both.

Marcus' finger tapped his glass as he continued to savor his first sip. Byers, not as liberal in his drinking, continued to take sips and stared at the perfectly squared ice cubes that had begun to melt away in his fizzy alcoholic drink.

"I'm just hoping this shithole part of the universe gives us at least some sort of excitement," said Byers. "The first month of this adventure has sucked royally. I swear that this Sigma-10 system must be the most boring and uninteresting part of the galaxy, and trust me, we've seen some pretty dull ones, man."

"Yeah, it sure has. And you're absolutely right. It's definitely been a while since we had any sort of adventure."

"Mm-hmm." Byers hummed in agreement between his sips.

"It's funny because when we first joined SAGE, I had this idea that we would be part of this amazing group of space pioneers and that we'd get to explore planets and meet all sorts of different life forms that we could have only imagined. It's too bad that I didn't realize before I joined that most of the time would be spent looking for alien fossils, solar resources and other junk that's supposedly useful to our planet. Sometimes, I feel like we're nothing but wannabe archeologists, and truthfully, if I had known that in the beginning, I would have just stayed on our planet and probably still worked at the bar at DeAngelo's."

The glass in Byers' hand had become nearly empty as he nodded his head in agreement with Marcus. "I know what you mean. Picking up animal shit honestly would have been more exciting than this. All I know is I'm eligible for dismissal at the end of this mission, and at this point, I don't see myself re-enlisting."

Marcus choked on his drink out of sheer surprise. "Wait—what? Hold on a minute. Are you really saying that you're thinking about leaving SAGE after this mission ends?"

"Well, yeah. I mean, truthfully, unless something miraculous happens to change my mind. But with the way things are going, I definitely don't see that happening. I've told you before that I was thinking about this, Ronnie."

Marcus' jaw remained ajar out of surprise. "Yeah, you've talked about it, but I never knew you were truly serious. I honestly thought you were joking."

He paused for a moment and thought of a sneaky way to try to give his friend a thought without giving away the secret he had been sworn to.

"And--what about the commander's test you talked about taking for your promotion?"

Well played.

"Well, I did think about it for a moment. But truthfully, despite the pay raise, the more that I've thought about it, the more I've realized how miserable it's been to be on missions such as these. You and I have put in a couple of long terms on this team with little to no excitement, Ronnie. And, c'mon, you have to admit that you know what I'm talking about."

A simple shrug of the shoulders came from Marcus, who could say nothing more as Byers continued on his rant.

"And, honestly, a stupid promotion and increase in pay won't do anything to make me want to change my mind at this rate.

Besides, Maxwell isn't retiring any time soon, and you're not going anywhere, so what does it really matter?"

Byers finished his drink and put the glass on the table, which prompted Marcus to chug the rest of his drink in reaction to the breaking news he had just received.

"Besides, I have some serious catching up to do with our beautiful women back home, and they need some me," Byers continued jokingly as he attempted to break the serious mood.

Marcus felt shaken internally but tried to play it off as if everything were normal. "I feel you on that. Want another?"

Byers picked up his glass and held it in the air. "Yeah, I think we both might need it."

"Amen to that."

Marcus took both glasses and headed back to the bar to prepare their second round of drinks. He felt uneven, which he figured had to do with the empty stomach he had while consuming alcohol.

Byers' eyes were fixed on the two glasses while Marcus began to pour the vodka in both glasses. "What about you, Ronnie? Do you ever think about leaving SAGE?"

"I don't know," Marcus replied as he shook his head and poured the tonic water. "I really haven't thought about it very much."

"You should because of the way things are going; we're just going to waste away up here, my friend."

Marcus picked up the two full drink glasses and prepared himself for the short journey back. "We'll see, I guess," said Marcus simply as he made his way back to the table and delivered Byers' drink perfectly.

As much as he disliked being on most missions his friend did, Marcus also knew a promotion to captain was within his reach, which he believed gave him a legitimate reason to stay. Internally, he wondered at times what his own future with SAGE truly consisted of, but he didn't feel the dislike for the job that Byers possessed.

He wanted to tell Byers the truth about Maxwell, hoping that maybe the revealing of the secret would change the outlook and mind of his friend. The ringing warning of his captain, however, punctured his thoughts and disabled his brain from making any sort of attempt as he took a seat in front of his friend.

I'm putting my trust into you that you won't tell a soul.

He sat stone-faced, lost in Maxwell's stern words while Byers stared at him with confusion. "Ronnie?"

Marcus said nothing.

"Earth to Ronnie!"

Marcus finally came to and shook his head to shake off his lost moment. "Huh? I'm sorry--what happened?"

Byers shook his head at the caught-in-a-daydream Marcus. "It's okay, and I know you're going deaf. Now, this is the last time I'm going to ask you--what's stopping you from leaving?"

"I--don't know. I guess I just have to think about it more, that's all."

"Alright, I guess," shrugged Byers, who held his glass up high to prepare for a sarcastic and alcohol-influenced toast. "Well, here's to hoping you make a decision before you die on this ship, I suppose."

"Sure," Marcus replied sourly, which prompted the two men to tap their glasses and drink.

They both took large swigs as the commander wasted no time in turning the tables and taking the spotlight away from him and directly onto his friend.

"So, going back to the women back home you had mentioned. I wanted to ask you—-whatever happened to Kelly?"

Byers' confusion gave him the look of a man who had smelled something overly raunchy. "Who?"

"The girl that you met a couple of months back in North Angeles before we went on this mission. You know—-the brunette with the big saucers?"

Byers chewed on an ice cube while he silently recollected his thoughts. "Oh, yeah. Kelly—-that's right. Well, I was only with her that one night, and I honestly didn't even remember her name until you refreshed my memory right now."

Marcus was unfortunately unsurprised by Byers' nonchalance. "You're unbelievable. She was cute, though, and she sure seemed to like you a lot."

"Yeah, she almost liked me too much. That night we were together, she just kept talking and talking in bed after we had sex. First, it was about getting married. Then, it turned into having babies and a whole lot of other crazy shit. I don't know about you, but I'm just not ready for anything like that. Don't get me wrong, she was great in the sack and knew how to get down, if you know what I'm saying. But, after all of that overly emotional shit, that was a wrap for me. And, if I remember correctly, I think I may have called her Kathy the entire night. But she didn't say anything, so whatever."

Marcus chuckled and nearly choked on his drink upon Byers' latter statement. "Wow--I understand that, I suppose. Then again, we're all on our own time schedule. So, maybe you can meet someone good eventually down the line."

"I doubt that," Byers stated, swallowing the rest of his drink with only a remnant of an ice cube left to spare. "I don't see myself getting tied down anytime soon, Ronnie. I enjoy living the bachelor life, and I'm pretty sure that's not going to be changing anytime soon."

Marcus shrugged as he joined Byers in gulping down his drink. "As long as you're happy, I guess that's all that really matters."

"You're damn right about that. Hey, speaking of women, what's the deal with Monica Brackenridge? I see her checking you out on the deck all of the time."

A sheepish grin came over Marcus, who tried unsuccessfully to hide it. "Monica? Nah, you must be seeing things."

"I know what I see, Ronnie. I think that girl really likes you."

"I don't know about that," said Marcus, who attempted to downplay it even further. "I mean, don't get me wrong, I would love it if that was true. She's absolutely gorgeous, and I always go out of my way to say hello to her, for sure."

"I can't say that I blame you on that one. She is definitely the hottest woman on the ship, even though Jacobs is her lone rival. Who knows, maybe if you can get her back here to your quarters, you could show her how the commander is in charge, if you know what I mean."

Marcus felt slightly uncomfortable by Byers' piggish statement. "C'mon, have some respect, Tommy."

"I'm sorry. All that I'm saying is--don't be afraid to go for the kill. You can do this." Byers rose to his feet quickly but instantly felt lightheaded from the alcohol he had ingested. "Oh man--I think I had one too many. I guess I better take off before I really start saying some messed up shit."

Marcus laughed at his friend's foolishness. "Alright. See you at 2200 hours. And don't let Maxwell see you like that."

"Definitely not. Thanks for the drinks, by the way. Oh, and make sure Maxwell or anybody else doesn't know about my thoughts of possibly leaving. I mean, I know you won't tell anybody, but I just have to cover my tracks anyways, you know?"

Great, another secret.

"C'mon, you know I won't," Marcus replied, nodding his head out of reassurance, although he hated knowing that one more secret was placed onto his shoulders.

Byers smirked out of appreciation. "I guess that's one reason we've been friends for so long. You've got to have some real patience to be friends with me, as you know."

"Yes, you really do."

A smile grew on Byers' face upon Marcus' jab remark. "See you up front."

Byers exited the quarters without a care. The opposite took effect for Marcus, whose spine stiffened upon the closing of the door.

In the span of one night, he had found out that his captain was secretly retiring and that his closest friend was contemplating leaving as well. It felt strange to him knowing that two of the most influential people in his life were thinking about going their separate ways, and he couldn't help but wonder what the future held for him as well.

Marcus felt slightly lightheaded from the drinking and could feel his stomach growl intensely from a lack of food consumption. He didn't feel like he was going to vomit, but he definitely could feel the vodka tonic taking its action throughout his starved body.

More offensively and off-topic, Byers was completely right about his body stench, as Marcus got a first-hand whiff of the awful odor that penetrated deep into his nostrils.

It's time to do something about that. And maybe grab a bite to eat as well.

He went to his shower chamber and turned on the water, turning the dial to a slightly hot and comfortable setting while his thoughts began to run ragged yet again.

Marcus couldn't help but wonder what other surprises awaited in front of him as he stepped into the sauna-like environment that engulfed his weary self.

CHAPTER 4

Marcus played with the collar on his blue buttoned-up shirt to straighten it out, his personal grooming nearly at its end for his shift while he stared at himself in the mirror. He always took pride in his appearance and constantly wanted to look his sharpest, especially when reporting to the front deck, where Maxwell and the lovely Monica awaited him.

His mind had slightly calmed down from the thoughts running through his head, yet he still yearned to know what direction the mission was about to take.

Please, not another excavation on a desolate planet. Throw us a bone and give us something different, for God's sake.

He closed his eyes for a moment and said an internal prayer before opening them and staring blankly at his reflection. He smiled halfway in an attempt to cheer himself up but was suddenly interrupted by one of his top front teeth falling from the gums of his mouth and stumbling onto the sink in front of him.

What in the hell?

Marcus gasped loudly and dipped his head closer to the mirror to make sure he was not seeing things. He took his finger and placed it over the voided area while a new worry began to fester inside of him.

There was no blood in the open area, but the missing dark area in his mouth was enough to dial up his anxiety. He tilted his head downward, and his eyes fixated on the fallen tooth lying before him.

His eyes grew enormous as he picked up the ivory dental object and focused back on his maligned smile in the mirror. He took the lonely tooth and attempted to force it back into its original location with no success.

Fear came over the commander, who could do nothing more than stare at the gap in the mouth.

His worries, however, were far from over. His other top front tooth then followed suit of its predecessor and ungracefully fell from his mouth and onto the sink before him.

Marcus gasped once again, his breath becoming shorter and choppier upon the second act of horror he had witnessed upon himself. His fears continued to escalate as he helplessly watched one of his bottom front teeth succumb to the same fate, its companion quickly joining the suit, followed by another tooth after another.

The helpless commander could do nothing but swipe miserably at the ivory wonders that came cascading from his mouth as one after the other bounced harshly onto the sink.

"What--is happening to me?" Marcus asked aloud with a lisp that came courtesy of his toothless mouth.

"That," a mysterious and recognizable voice interjected, "is what happens to those who keep secrets."

Marcus' eyes scurried up at the mirror and onto the reflection of Maxwell, who stood directly behind him with folded arms.

"Didn't your mother ever teach you about not keeping a secret?" The captain further added, laughing hysterically while his flapped-gummed underling screamed bloody murder from the horror of his appearance.

"No!"

A white flash of light came across Marcus, who suddenly opened his eyes to a delightful surprise of a brimming and full-toothed smile upon awakening from the brief daydream he had immersed himself into unknowingly.

He exhaled deeply upon the normal sight and turned his attention to the sink underneath him that was free of teeth.

His focus shifted quickly back onto his mirror, which had now been voided of the sight of his prickly captain taking his rear. He turned his head for good measure to ensure that his eyes did not lie and was given the second source of assurance he desired.

Marcus bowed his head in sweet relief.

Whew--what a crazy nightmare.

He gave himself a quick second to re-compose and gave himself a quick last-second look before heading towards the open doorway and exiting.

"Close!" he commanded aloud as the door followed his order and quickly slid shut.

Marcus marched towards the elevator and passed the closed-door quarters of Maxwell, the nightmare he had just experienced beginning to flash once more in his memory bank.

Should I tell somebody?

His personal game of mind-numbing tug-of-war escalated once more as he reached the elevator and pushed the button for the second floor where the deck was located. He paid no mind to the bumpiness of the ride, his own thoughts numbing any sort of external feeling he may have usually experienced.

What the hell am I going to do? Oh, fuck my life.

The elevator came to an ungraceful halt upon its arrival at its requested destination, and Marcus waited not a moment too soon once the doors opened to burst onto the scene, his eyes focused squarely ahead and onto the business at hand to distract himself.

Just act normal, like nothing is wrong.

The commander allowed himself not even a blink of an eye's time to ponder his lava-flow of thoughts as he waltzed with false bravado onto the deck where his crew, minus the last-to-arrive Maxwell, awaited.

Byers, the first person he met eyes with, smiled and nodded

his head in acknowledgment to his friend and higher-ranked official. He generally stood with a slouch but straightened up out of habit whenever he prepared to introduce his immediate supervisor.

"Commander on board!"

Marcus smirked back at Byers and stood to the right of his lieutenant. The rest of the crew rose from their chairs and faced their commander, who acknowledged them with a salute that was reflected back onto him out of proper respect.

To the control panels on his right stood Officers Chester Rubidoux and Victoria Jacobs, the ship's co-navigators. Rubidoux, or 'Rube' as his crew referred to him, was the newest member on the ship and, at only 19 years of age, was entering his first tour of duty with SAGE. His nerves showed greatly on his baby face, while the unconfident posture he exhibited further screamed his greenness and inexperience.

Jacobs, the more seasoned of the two but still at the tender age of 23 years old herself, was on her third tour with the crew. She was a petite yet confident fair-skinned young woman, while her erect stature beamed off with much more confidence than that of her pupil directly next to her.

Marcus' vision glanced to his left, where Lieutenant Bryan Arraz, the ship's official operator of its lasers and torpedoes and unofficial 'weapons junkie,' stood gallantly. Arraz, at the age of 24, was already entering his sixth tour of duty, the result of enlisting early at the age of 17. The tallest of the crew with the body of a stick, he had a quick trigger finger, as was often demonstrated during training drills and was rearing to try it out during actual combat, which to that point had amounted to close to zero. It was no wonder that he gently stroked his own laser gun on his belt, as he was more than ready for any sort of reason to use it.

To Arraz's right was Dr. Desmond Jennings, the ship's lone scientist and physician who was on his fourth tour with SAGE. An extremely knowledgeable and intelligent man, he was also one of the oldest crew members aboard at the seemingly archaic age of

31. A former hospital physician on Earth, he had grown tired of the hospital game and joined SAGE to further explore and analyze extraterrestrial anatomy and get a taste of life in space.

Despite the molasses-slow activity for the other crew members, he was the busiest man on the ship and was extremely fascinated with the fossils and other forms they had witnessed along the way, which showed daily in his positive attitude.

Last, and certainly not least for the commander, stood Monica Brackenridge, the ship's main intercom communicator. If there was one person who made the SAGE uniform look good, it was her, especially in Marcus' mind, as it seemed to snug her perfect curves beautifully.

With piercing doe brown eyes, perfect caramel-colored skin and a luminous smile that lit up the room, the very notion of her looking his way gave him a warm feeling throughout his body, a sensation that only seemed to get more intense with each passing mission he spent working with her. A veteran of five space tours and still only 26, she was just as intelligent as she was beautiful.

She's absolutely perfect.

She smiled warmly at him, and Marcus couldn't help but be engulfed in her presence, which seemed as if it were a real-life dream.

Byers, noticing the eye interaction between the two, gave Marcus a slight nudge with his left elbow, a told-you-so type of message to his friend to further justify his hunch earlier about Monica's feelings towards him. Byers cleared his throat and grinned as Marcus did his best to maintain his professional composure despite the fact he felt ten feet tall.

He forced his focus to return to work immediately as Captain Maxwell entered through the door and onto the front deck, his traditional emotionless look etched upon his face.

"Captain on deck!" Marcus shouted straight-faced to the crew, who stood erectly in unison. Marcus joined the rest of the crew in giving his full attention to Maxwell, who stopped in the center of the deck and gave each member of his crew a long look.

He looked older than he truly was, and the light on the deck, along with the heavy bags under his eyes, only gave him a wearier appearance.

Being a part of SAGE for as long as he had definitely taken it out of him, Marcus couldn't help but notice how much his captain had aged in the past couple of years.

He just might be retiring at the right time.

The crew remained quiet and awaited the orders of their captain as Maxwell observed the room molecule by molecule. He stopped and stared at Byers for a moment, whose smirk vanished instantly once he felt the eyes of his superior locked on him.

He delivered an icy frown to his lieutenant before turning his attention to Marcus and delivering nothing more than a tired nod.

Why do I feel there's a hidden message behind this?

Marcus returned the favor by nodding to Maxwell, his arms folded behind his back in preparation for his captain's orders. Maxwell slightly scratched his scruffy beard as he cleared his throat in preparation for speaking to his crew, who remained in united silence.

"Ladies and gentlemen," the captain said as he began to address his crew, "it has been brought to my attention by SAGE headquarters that our mission has been dramatically altered. We will no longer be exploring the Sigma-10 system and will instead set our course for the Titan-6 system."

Marcus and Byers' jaws dropped simultaneously. It was rare that missions were changed on the fly, like in this instance, and the fact that it was now occurring made both wonder what was going on.

First, an emergency meeting occurred, and now, there is a change in plans. Hmmm...

"We have received notification from headquarters that there are unusual signs of life on a planet located in the Titan-6 system," Maxwell continued. "They believe it to be possible forms of alien life, but it is unknown at this moment due to the abnormal readings they have scanned thus far. Accordingly, our mission will be to explore this anonymous planet and see what we are dealing with so we can report it back to headquarters as either a threat or an ally. This is a blindsided mission, and we must exercise great caution at all times once we have landed."

Maxwell's sight caught that of the young Rubidoux, whose slouched body language screamed his nervousness.

"Rubidoux, it's time to take off the training wheels, my boy, because I'm throwing you to the wolves. Are you ready for this, son?"

"Sir, yes--sir," Rubidoux quietly replied, his voice cracking as he had trouble answering his superior as if he had soiled himself.

"I can't hear you, son. Once again, I asked you--are you ready?"

The rookie gulped heavily, the pressure from his superior becoming too much for him to take.

"Yes--sir."

A fiery look flared through Maxwell's eyes, and he stared deeply into the soul of his inexperienced young navigator.

"Don't let me down, maggot."

The captain was indeed a salty character to deal with, especially with his fresh and meaty rookies, who he enjoyed toughening up with his iron-fisted, my-way-or-the-highway dictator form of rule.

Maxwell turned his back to the freshly lambasted Rubidoux, who appeared ready to cry, and turned his glare to Jacobs, who knew her training session with the new navigator had ended quicker than either of them had anticipated.

"Jacobs," began the captain, "you're going to pull up a map of the Titan-6 system. I need you to investigate as much as you can about the unknown planet and its surrounding galaxy and assist your worthless, piece of shit companion in setting the right course. Is that understood?"

"Yes, sir," Jacobs strongly replied with focused eyes and outstanding confidence, although she internally did not care for the unnecessary and rather derogatory name-calling of Rubidoux.

"Very well, then. Rookie set course towards the Titan-6 system by shifting west at a 95-degree angle before accelerating. As for the rest of you, prepare for departure."

The rest of the crew took a seat at their respective stations while Maxwell made his way toward his plush black seat located in the center of the deck.

Marcus and Byers, meanwhile, remained where they were and tilted their heads toward one another while keeping their bodies straight ahead.

"Where is the Titan-6 system?" whispered Marcus to Byers.

"Beats the hell out of me. I thought you'd have known that already, Commander."

Marcus delivered an icy stare toward his smart-ass lieutenant. "Whatever. Well, at least it should be somewhat interesting, right?" Marcus asked, shaking his head along with Byers at the sight of the overwhelmed Rubidoux, who frantically attempted to figure out how to navigate through the computer panel on his own to get the ship in the right direction.

"Yeah, really interesting," answered a chucking Byers, who smugly grinned. He felt bad for the rookie but couldn't help but get a kick out of seeing him struggle like he did, even though he began to recall the hell he experienced as a new recruit with Maxwell himself.

Marcus himself felt pity for the puny rookie, who he could see with his own eyes continued to struggle.

That poor, helpless bastard. He'd better get a grip before he finds himself in more trouble.

Maxwell, on the contrary, sat comfortably at his chair in the center of the deck as he prepared to order the ship officially out of the Sigma-10 system. "I will provide the proximity of the planet once we have entered the system of desire. Begin the westward shift, rookie."

Misfortune turned its ugly head at Rubidoux, who still hadn't quite figured out the controls on his own. The young rookie bit his bottom lip and could feel the pain coming his way as the ship remained on the same course.

The captain began to tap his fingers on his armrests to show his frustration, while his beet-red face accompanied the notion. He had no mercy for incompetence, especially when his own orders were at stake.

"Are we having a problem?" asked Maxwell, his voice humming with annoyance.

"Uh--no, sir," Rubidoux shakily answered as he continued to fumble his way with the controls. "Just--a moment, please--sir."

The rookie continued to press buttons and could feel the burning stare from his captain piercing through his skull. The heat was on, and the pressure began to eat away at him. He made one final and feeble attempt to push whatever button on the computerized panel caught his eye, hoping that he would find the right combination out of mercy.

The captain could take no more as his anger began to boil over towards his still-learning rookie. "Rubidoux! Get us moving, maggot!"

As luck would have it, the more seasoned Jacobs mercifully intervened to assist her green and rattled trainee. She gave a look of tender care as she herself recalled being in his shoes during her rookie days. "Remember to start out like this," she instructed gingerly while pushing the necessary buttons to right the direction.

The ship began to veer to the west as Maxwell's order was finally fulfilled, and movement started to occur. Relief came over Rubidoux, who felt fortunate to have his friendly and helpful trainer come to his rescue.

"Well done, Jacobs," stated Maxwell, who glared at his rookie navigator in disapproval. "At least somebody knows what they're doing."

The rookie gulped upon the captain's verbal dagger. He said nothing, as he knew he was on Maxwell's shortlist, and stared down at his computer panel in preparation of stopping once they had reached the desired angle.

Marcus couldn't help but feel the heat between the heat between the captain and rookie navigator. Being on Maxwell's bad list was never an ideal place to be, and he couldn't help but remember his rookie days when his name was on it on a daily basis.

God, maybe Maxwell really is leaving at the right time. He seems to only get more brutal the older he gets.

Maxwell finally focused back on the space field in front of his face as the ship reached its desired angle of travel.

"Marcus," commanded the captain as he looked back at his commander. "Give the next directive."

Marcus was unready for the order as shock crossed his body. It was a first for Maxwell, a micromanaging control freak who never allowed anybody but himself to give a directive. The commander, however, picked up on the hint that it was the captain's cunning way of trying to get him one step closer to being his successor.

"Sir?" he could only ask.

Maxwell slightly nodded his head in reassurance. His face was ever so serious, but there was definitely a hidden agenda behind his request as he waved his palm toward his commander to further signal his intention.

Marcus, with the blessing of his captain, cleared his throat and prepared to take his first step as the captain-in-training. "Rubidoux and Jacobs," Marcus commanded, feeling awkward but loving the feeling at the same time. "Maximum speed to the Titan-6 system."

Rubidoux and Jacobs followed the directive of their commander and increased the ship's acceleration to its fastest possible speed to hurry up their arrival to their newly ordered destination.

Here we go. But to where?

A mystified feeling festered throughout Marcus' body as the ship glided towards its mysterious destination.

CHAPTER 5

Thirteen hours had passed since the voyage of the Beso de Maria's crew had unexpectedly changed course. The ship returned to normal speed while only Jacobs and Rubidoux remained on the deck and behind the controls. The rest of the crew members, sans Marcus, had been dismissed by Maxwell to prepare for their arrival on the unknown planet in the Titan-6 system in less than half of an Earth day.

Marcus rubbed his eyes as he prepared to depart himself but halted for a moment to observe the nurturing exchange between teacher and pupil, with Jacobs continuing her thoughtful counseling of the operations. Rubidoux, meanwhile, tried his best to listen intently to his mentor, although the glazed eyes suggested he was still struggling to keep up.

That poor kid. I bet anything that he didn't expect this when he enlisted. Thank God he's got Jacobs to show him the ropes.

Marcus remembered his early days with SAGE and how overwhelmed he felt at the beginning, as well as how difficult it was to constantly learn new skills, especially when it also came under the obsessive eye of the sharp-tongued Maxwell.

But then again, he had never experienced failing to get the ship to move as commanded when he first learned to navigate like

Rubidoux had, so, in his opinion, it was anybody's guess what the future held for the young trainee. It may have only been his first official day as a navigator, and while mistakes were expected, it sure hadn't gotten off to a good start for the rookie, which made the commander all the more nervous on behalf of his immediate and far future.

Marcus said nothing as he entered the spacious hallway on the second floor of the ship. His mind began to wonder once more but stopped quickly, thanks to the exhaustion he felt from the lack of sleep and the other unexpected surprises that had come along.

The bed is calling my name.

He reached the elevator and stepped into it to head to the fourth floor, where his quarters were located.

He waited for the doors to the elevator to close when he heard a high-pitched voice try to get his attention before it closed.

"Hold, please," requested the person as Marcus helped to open the doors by sticking his hand in between them. His generosity and chivalry had paid off with a surprise that stood behind the doors in the form of the lovely Monica Brackenridge.

"Oh--hello, Commander," Monica coyly said, a luminous smile plastered on her mocha-colored face.

"Hello, Monica," Marcus replied sheepishly, while the butterflies inside of his stomach fluttered upon his first glance of her.

"Mind if I catch a ride with you?"

Of course, I don't mind.

His smile turned coy upon her question. "Sure. Which floor?"

"Six, please."

Marcus pushed the button to the top floor of the ship, his finger rattling with nerves, and glanced back at Monica with a wide smile that only continued to blossom. He felt warm and gooey on the inside and could feel his heart pumping out blood at an alarming rate.

The doors closed rapidly to the rickety elevator, which began to make its way up the corridor slowly. The ride was going to be short and rather bumpy, but in Marcus' eyes, it was going to be enjoyable no matter what. He wanted to say something to her that was somewhat meaningful to break the ice but he didn't know where to start.

Alas, he realized that his short time with her was already coming to an end, and the large '3' on the computer screen assisted him in realizing that.

Damn, that was fast.

If there was ever a moment Marcus wanted time to slow down or stop, it had arrived.

His wish, much to his internal delight, was instantly granted on cue as the unreliable elevator stopped before it fully reached his destination.

As thrilled as he felt on the inside for the extra opportunity, he knew that he had to pretend as if he wasn't to be so obvious.

"Damn elevator," was the first thing Marcus could think of to say. "This has got to be the biggest piece of junk that we have on this whole ship."

"Yeah, it's pretty bad, sir," Monica said, still smiling even despite the unexpected holdup. "Oh well, I guess it is what it is, huh?"

He enjoyed hearing her positivity as he nodded his head in agreement. "I guess you're right about that."

Monica's attitude and smile were contagious to him, and she had a special gift of bringing him joyfulness, even if he knew very little about her personally. He longed for her attention and realized a golden opportunity had been given to him to get the ball rolling.

What can I say to help break the ice?

An awkward silence filled the elevator air for a few moments while Marcus thought of what to say next. He could have easily used his intercom to summon a crew member for help out of their small situation but decided to let the elevator's computer self-repair on its own to give himself a little more time with her.

Marcus only hoped, of course, that she wasn't catching on to what he was doing, as he still could come up with nothing productive to say. He had waited for this opportunity, and the last thing he wanted was to appear as though he were desperate or creepy.

He turned his head slowly towards Monica, trying his best to keep his cool, and turned his head towards her, saying the first thing that came to his mind.

"So, uh--how's everything going?"

You dummy! That's the best you could have come up with.

He was prepared to annihilate himself internally over what he deemed as a dumb question but was pleasantly surprised by her response.

"Fine, thank you, sir. And how are you, Commander?"

"Great, Miss Monica. I really couldn't be any better."

Okay, never mind. Good job.

Marcus couldn't help but smile at Monica. She had a candy-sweet demeanor about her that he simply could not ignore.

"And if Captain Maxwell is in a good mood, then things really can't be any better," he added on in jest.

She giggled upon his slight swipe at their enigmatic captain. "Yeah, I agree with you on that. I think it's safe to say we all feel that way sometimes."

Her polite laughter was just as warm and adorable, and it gave Marcus a warm internal feeling, especially knowing he was the source behind it.

She is so perfect and beautiful in every possible way.

Marcus felt lighter than air as he could feel the ice had been broken. Finally, on their sixth mission together, he actually got to have some sort of dialogue with the woman he had admired from afar since the moment he first laid eyes on her over five years ago.

I've got to take advantage and keep this going.

"You know, for a second there, I thought Maxwell was going to have a conniption with Rube on the deck," Marcus said jokingly.

Monica's giggle increased further over his comments. "I know,

I was afraid for him. I feared that we were going to witness Rube's funeral--that poor guy, anyway. I think he'll forever be grateful to Jacobs for helping to bail him out of that one."

"I'm sure he'll at least buy her dinner for that when we get back home," said Marcus. "And if I were her, I'd have him hook it up with a bottle of wine also."

"Oh yeah. Speaking of which, I could really use a good glass of wine myself after a day like this."

Marcus could see an opportunity unfold before him and decided to take advantage of the moment. "I take it that you're a wine drinker, then?"

"Absolutely. Now, don't get me wrong, I'm no lush, Commander. But at the same time, I sure do appreciate having a glass when I want to unwind a little."

Marcus couldn't help but smile more widely after hearing what she had just said. He also loved drinking wine, and it made him excited to know that they had a common interest they could talk about to help develop more a comfort with each other some more. "I know exactly what you mean," he said, nodding in agreement.

"Hmm, I take it you're a wine drinker yourself, sir?"

His smile finally broke from nervous to one of more confidence upon her question. "Yeah, you got me there. As long as it's not too dry, then I'm okay. So, needless to say, you won't see me drinking a red anytime soon."

"So, I'm guessing you must be into the sweeter wines, then?"

"Yeah, I admit it. What about you, Monica?"

"I'd have to say I actually like it a bit drier. But, I'm wide open, and I'll never turn down a good wine, Commander."

Well said.

Marcus' eyes remained fixated on her while he internally thanked the elevator for being its unreliable self for once. "I couldn't agree with you any more than that," he said, feeling absolutely beside himself over what had been happening for the past couple of minutes.

He had deeply liked her from the start but had never known how to get a conversation going, as his nerves had always gotten the better of him. It surprised him that he suddenly had the ability to hold a conversation with her, but he was definitely not complaining.

It was to his misfortune, however, that the elevator slightly shuttered and began to move once more back on its normal path and towards Marcus' floor, much to his chagrin.

Damn, it had to be just when the conversation was starting to get good.

Although disappointment set in upon reality setting that his alone time with her was coming to an end, Marcus was also more than aware that he had to continue to play it cool to not give himself away too much. "I suppose the elevator didn't forget about us after all."

"Yeah, I guess not," Monica replied.

The elevator ride couldn't have moved any quicker, especially in Marcus's mind, upon its jerky stop on the fourth floor. The doors opened in the blink of an eye to reveal the wide hallway that suddenly looked much gloomier and darker now that he was closer to leaving Monica behind. "Well, I guess this is my floor. And I guess that this is finally goodbye for the evening, Miss Brackenridge."

She smiled shyly at him. "I guess so. Thanks for keeping me company. It definitely made everything much easier."

"You're very welcome, and thank you as well for your company. Good Night, Monica."

"Good Night, Commander."

Marcus stepped out of the elevator and onto the fourth floor when an unexpected confidence inside of him kept him from going any further. He turned around and, in a surprising fashion, especially to himself, summoned up courage he hadn't even known had existed inside of him and held the doors from closing once more with his hand.

"I was thinking, maybe sometime we can have a glass of wine together and talk some more?"

Monica appeared stunned by his advancement, which immediately made him wonder about his sudden confidence boost and if he had taken it too far.

You blew it.

She offered nothing as she only batted her eyelashes. He could feel himself placed on internal pins and needles of regret for what he had attempted.

"I would really like that," responded Monica finally.

Whew.

A gigantic feeling of relief came over Marcus, but he maintained his cool exterior composure and did his best to contain the giddiness he felt. "Great. I look forward to it, then."

"Me too. Good Night once again, Commander."

"Good Night, Miss Monica."

The elevator doors officially closed fittingly as curtains to an unexpected great ending to the evening as Marcus pumped his fist in excitement.

Atta boy!

He turned around and skipped toward his quarters, an extra pep now in his step coming out as five years of waiting had finally come to a head. He felt as if he could walk on air, and he had to resist the urge to follow Monica to the sixth floor and perhaps ruin the start of something wonderful.

Take it easy. Quit while you're ahead because you're off to a good start.

Marcus did a spin move and a dance shimmy without care if anybody could see him. If there was ever a moment he was happy that the ship lacked a set of stairs, it had finally arrived, much to his approval.

He whistled a happy tune to himself while reaching the door to his quarters and prepared to enter until he was interrupted by a voice that came from behind him and startled him half to death.

"Commander Marcus!"

Marcus grabbed his chest and turned around to see Jacobs in front of him, who carried a grave look with her.

"Jesus--you scared the hell out of me!" he replied in a raised voice before taking a moment to regain his composure. "What--what's the problem?"

"I'm so sorry if I interrupted anything, but there's something of great importance that must be discussed immediately on the deck, sir."

CHAPTER 6

Marcus and Jacobs hurried onto the elevator and hit the button for them to head back to the second floor immediately.

Concern instantly grew for Marcus as he suddenly realized that his experienced navigator had tracked him down alone. "Wait—you left Rube there by himself?"

"Yes, I did," responded Jacobs with concern upon realizing what she had done. "I'm sorry, Commander, but I figured that he would be okay by himself for a few moments until we came back."

"Hmm, I sure hope that you're right."

Marcus shrugged his shoulders but offered nothing more when the elevator came to a rough stop on the second floor. Marcus and Jacobs scurried toward the deck, both hoping that Rubidoux hadn't done something wrong during his alone time.

They rushed through the sliding door and onto the deck, where the nerve-racked Rubidoux awaited behind the control panel, his once-soaked blue shirt now completely dry. "Si--sir," he said nervously, saluting clumsily after coming to his feet.

The commander waved his hand to refuse the gesture and get his rookie navigator to relax. "No, it's fine. As you were."

Rubidoux did not get the hint and continued to stand, his nerves officially on full display.

Marcus shook his head out of dismay and rubbed his forehead. "No, Rube. I mean--sit down, please. You're making me nervous, for God's sake."

A lost look came over the rookie, who finally understood the orders he was given. "Okay, sir. I'll sit down."

Jacobs stood to the right of the seated Rubidoux and put her arms behind her back, a look of seriousness remaining on her pale face.

The commander awaited her word as he tried his best to fight the tiredness that was settling into his body. "So, what did you have to talk to me about that was so urgent?"

Her face remained still before she sputtered out the right words to say. "Well, I have to talk with you about the coordinates that Captain Maxwell gave me, sir."

Marcus felt instantly puzzled by her statement. "Okay, but why do you need to talk to me about it? Why don't you just ask Captain Maxwell himself?"

Jacobs took a deep breath as further preparation before answering. "I tried to contact him about this, sir. But--he sealed the door to his quarters and wouldn't answer. And he also didn't respond when I attempted to contact him on the intercom."

An uneasiness came over Marcus upon Jacobs' statement. It was very unlike Maxwell not to respond, and nobody knew that better than him. "Wow, that is strange. Well, I can see why you came to me, and I apologize for your confusion. So, what's wrong with the coordinates, then?"

"Let me go ahead and pull up the map so we can view it as I explain it to you."

She touched the computer screen before her and slid her finger a few times while an image of the Titan-6 system began to expand and grow larger in the air space between Marcus and his two navigators.

"As you can see, there really aren't very many planets on this particular area of the galaxy. In fact, as I have examined this map more and more, there only appears to be two planets, or at least something that resembles them, that exist."

Marcus looked at the screen and pointed to a couple of areas that he thought proved otherwise. "What are these over here?" he asked, pointing towards the upper left-hand corner of the map.

"It appears to be a sun and moon, which is one of the interesting parts of this system that I have noticed. They have one sun and moon located in or close to every corner if you further examine it. Yet, there do not appear to be a lot of planets, at least from what I've researched."

Marcus began to rub his chin out of curiosity, a quizzical look implanted on him while his tired brain attempted to keep up with the complexities before him.

She rubbed the back of her pony-tailed neck as her serious appearance took a more frustrated approach. "It's very strange. I've never seen anything like it before, sir."

The commander could sense her feelings begin to swell, but was still in search of answers. "So, what does this have to do with the coordinates?"

Jacobs took her finger and slid it over to the left, starting at the northwest area of the map.

"Well, if you look closely, there is one planet located here along with a moon and sun, kind of like we have on Earth."

She moved her finger towards the northeast region and expanded the area she focused on.

"The same can be said for this corner, as well as the southeast corner also."

She slid her finger once more before stopping on the southwest region of the map.

"Here's where it gets interesting, Commander. As you can see here, there is a moon and a sun, but no planet to be seen in this region."

Marcus held up his palms, lost in confusion. "So, what does that mean?"

"Well, what it means is that our adventure has taken an interesting twist because, according to Captain Maxwell, these are the coordinates of where SAGE headquarters want us to explore, sir. And, if you are seeing what I am seeing, that takes us into the middle of nowhere."

Marcus was further confused and stared at the expanded southwest region of the Titan-6 system, which, just like stated by his navigator a moment prior, consisted of no such planet whatsoever. "No, that can't be right. It has to be a mistake on our part. That--just can't be. There's nothing there to explore at all."

The seasoned navigator shook her head. "It's no mistake, Commander. I've checked over the coordinates three times, and I get the same location every time. These are the exact coordinates our own captain gave us."

Marcus' jaw remained ajar upon the puzzling discovery. "No, something's not right about this. I mean, I'm definitely not saying it's your fault, but I also can't believe he, or headquarters for that matter, would be that much off on a location. They're as sharp as they come with things like that, and I'm sure it had to have been mapped out, either by headquarters or Maxwell himself, before orders were given."

"I don't know, stated Jacobs while removing the large map from the air with a quick stroke of her finger. "I'm positive that's what he told me, though, sir. I mean, unless I'm losing my mind because I'm never off like that, either."

Jacobs looked down and shook her head, her eyes tired from frustration and exhaustion simultaneously.

Marcus placed his hand on her shoulder to reassure his mentally drained navigator. "You're fine, Jacobs. You're a damn good navigator, and I believe you. Regardless of who's at fault, we do need to discuss this matter with Maxwell about this immediately."

The navigator nodded her head in agreement and slowly lifted her head as Marcus could feel a favor coming on.

"Would you mind speaking to him about this, please, sir?"

asked Jacobs, her voice tiring from her long night. "I think he would listen to you more, especially about something like this."

"No problem. Don't worry; we'll figure this out. In the meantime, just stay on course unless you're told otherwise by Maxwell or me."

She offered a look of appreciation with a weary half smile. "Very well, sir. I really do appreciate it. Thank you, Commander."

"No problem," Marcus nodded back in acknowledgment as he turned his back towards Jacobs and Rubidoux and headed out to exit the deck.

"Good luck, Commander," said Rubidoux, his voice cracking like an adolescent boy.

Marcus stared back at Rubidoux, who gulped loudly and attempted to add to his statement.

"I mean, with your conversation with the captain—-I just hope it goes well—-sir."

The commander chuckled to himself over the rookie's pure innocence and green nature. "Thanks," he stated as the door slid open and closed rapidly upon his exit.

Jacobs looked at her young trainee and shook her head in slight embarrassment.

"He's brave for going in there because the captain scares me," he shyly confessed to his teacher. "You don't think that the captain knows that I'm frightened of him, do you?"

Jacobs' face remained straight, although her interior notions felt sour from the dumb question she had been asked. "No, not at all," she half-heartedly replied with a touch of sarcasm.

The young rookie, oblivious to her actions, felt relieved. "Good. The last thing I want is for him to think I'm some sissy."

She rolled her eyes before looking out at the open space in front of them, her thoughts stewing in regard to where they could have possibly been heading.

CHAPTER 7

Marcus stepped out of the elevator on the fourth floor and headed down the hallway toward the quarters of his captain. He passed his own quarters and continued to head onward, thoughts running wildly through his mind as he prepared to speak with Maxwell.

The fact that the coordinates seemed so off just didn't make any sense to him. Maxwell was extremely sharp, especially with orders such as that. But then again, so was Jacobs, who was very intelligent and bright herself and rarely made any errors.

So the question remained in his mind: Who exactly was to blame here? And where would these coordinates, if they were indeed accurate, take them?

Marcus stopped outside of Maxwell's door and prepared himself to knock. Much to his surprise, the door immediately slid open as if his captain were waiting for him on the other end. A shiver came down his spine upon the sight of the darkness that awaited him.

What in the hell?

He stepped into and engulfed himself in the black matter, his right hand scaling the wall in an attempt to find his way blindly.

It's quiet in here. .It's way too quiet.

He was prepared to ask for his captain before being beaten to the punch in startling fashion.

"Yes, Commander?"

Marcus grabbed his chest for a moment, his heart rapidly beating inside of him from the scare he had just received.

A blue light came on above Maxwell, whose head remained unseen and draped in darkness while he lay atop his bed.

"You startled me, sir," Marcus finally responded as he turned towards his faceless captain. "I apologize if I woke you."

"No, I've been awake. I've just been lying here in the darkness, listening to my own breath."

A frigid chill came over him from the mysterious and strange response given to him by his captain. "I see, sir. Jacobs said she came up here a while ago to try to talk with you but your door was locked, and you didn't respond to her."

"That is accurate."

Another shiver went down Marcus' spine upon Maxwell's consecutively odd statement. His behavior was severely strange, and the icy tone in his strong voice did little to soothe any concerns he contained.

"What did she want?" Maxwell asked with disengagement.

Marcus gulped nervously. "Well, she wanted to talk with you about the coordinates you gave her--sir. She says there may be a problem with them--"

Maxwell growled as he interrupted his commander in between his speech. "There are no issues with them, Commander. I told her 132 latitude and 46 longitude in the fifth sector twice, and I'm not going to tell her again."

"Yes, that's the exact coordinates she has as well, Captain. But —-well--the problem is that there's nothing there, sir. There appears to be a moon and sun around there, but nothing more. Jacobs and I have both verified this."

Maxwell had officially grown tired of the resistance he felt from his right-hand man. His frustrations boiled over as he had finally reached his breaking point. "I don't give a damn, Marcus. We are following those coordinates, whether you or Jacobs like it or not because it is what we must do."

Maxwell arose quickly from his bed, and his face was finally revealed in the blue light. Despite the bluish hue, Marcus could see the fire in his captain's eyes while the tomato-red color of his enraged face appeared to glow in the dark.

"And furthermore, I will not be questioned about orders that I've personally given out," the captain angrily continued as the veins in his forehead began to pulsate. "When I tell you to do something, I expect you to do it because I said so. I'm in charge of this ship and its crew, and you, especially, are not in charge at this moment. Is that understood, Commander?"

The commander felt his manhood shrunken down to size upon the tongue-lashing he had just taken. "Aye, sir," he softly responded in despaired fashion, his head now tilted down like a child who had been reprimanded by his parent.

The captain felt more of a need to dominate further and did not waste the opportunity. "What did you say to me, boy?"

"Aye--sir," Marcus repeated in a raised voice.

He felt angry on the inside, and it took every bit of his will not to snap at his commanding officer, the flickering respect he still felt for Maxwell serving as his liaison from the rampage.

What the hell is his problem?

Maxwell refused to back away from his hardened stance. "You look pitiful and weak like that, Commander. Be a man and pick your head up."

Anger resonated throughout Marcus' mind. Maxwell had just stripped him down with his words, and he didn't care at all for the way his captain had just handled this situation. He felt he had tried to be helpful, but for whatever reason, Maxwell wanted no part of it.

Marcus did as his captain commanded and picked up his head to give the appearance that all was well, even though internally, he felt furious with his commanding officer. Externally, however, he gave the appearance of a cool and collected man and only hoped it would be enough to get Maxwell to cease from his drill sergeant stance.

Maxwell was brutal and downright nasty to deal with at times, but he seemed to be even older than usual on this particular night. He seemed to relish taking it out on Marcus, his right-hand man and accomplice, while a smirk now curled the corner of his mouth in the dark.

The captain's head finally came into view as the blue light cascaded upon it and gave the details of his bearded, ugly face. "That's more like it," the captain said to his commander with a growing smile of satisfaction. "Don't make me question your manhood, Marcus."

Don't make me punch you in the face right now, old man.

Maxwell's face disappeared back into the darkness, although his evil grin remained implanted. "And don't make me begin to question your leadership abilities. You need to remember that I have a lot of pull with SAGE regarding your promotion, and I refuse to commend a weak individual to replace me. Keep that in mind, Commander."

The commander swallowed his anger so as not to give his captain any further satisfaction. "Yes, sir."

Maxwell lay back down in the blue hue that draped his body. "That is all, Marcus," he stated, placing his hands on his chest.

Marcus turned and prepared to walk out of his captain's quarters, an irritated feeling flowing throughout his body. As much as he longed to release his anger, he didn't want to give Maxwell any further pleasure.

He could sense Maxwell staring at him through the dark, a sense coming over him that his captain was ready to get in one last barb.

"You may despise me, but without me, you are nothing. I, and only I, hold the key to your future, boy."

Boy, huh? I'll show you a boy, you bastard.

Marcus' rage boiled to its limit internally, and it took everything inside of him not to snap and give in to his captain's egging.

Unbelievable, he thought while heading out of Maxwell's quarters. *What an asshole.*

He headed down the darkened hallway towards his quarters, fuming and cursing along the way.

I ought to go back in there and give him a piece of my mind. That would show him.

Marcus could feel his anger boil over. Even though Maxwell and the crew were not present, he began to tell himself to calm down in an effort to salvage his dignity. He took a deep breath and closed his eyes for a moment as he stopped his gait in the middle of the hallway.

Just relax. Don't let him get the best of you. He'll be gone soon enough.

His body and blood pressure began to relax as his anger began to subside. He opened his eyes after a few moments only to discover Byers standing in front of him, appearing puzzled and inquisitive over his friend's relaxation technique.

"Uh--did I catch you at a bad time?

"No," replied Marcus with embarrassment. "Just saying a little mantra, I guess you could say."

Byers knew his friend well enough to know when he was lying. "Uh-huh. Well, mantra or no mantra, you have the look of a man ready to kill somebody."

"No, I'm fine. Just a rough end to the night, that's all."

The lieutenant felt the need to be nosy. "I see. Does it have anything to do with our beloved Captain Maxwell?"

"Lucky guess, but he's not so beloved at this moment."

Byers couldn't help but to find humor in the moment. "I didn't know you guys were having personal problems. Maybe some kind of counseling will help you both get through this rough patch. Relationships aren't easy, from what I hear."

Marcus was in no mood to play along. "C'mon, get serious. Does everything have to be a joke to you?"

"Wow, relax. Sorry if I hit a nerve."

Marcus realized that he had lost his cool and attempted to calm himself down by rubbing his temples, his pulse rapidly vibrating out of frustration. "It's alright. I'm sorry, it's just been a rough day overall, man. Maybe some rest will do me good."

"Whatever works, I guess," Byers said while shrugging his shoulders.

Marcus rubbed his tired eyes from the long day and a half he had endured, thoughts of his bed becoming all the more comforting, especially with his quarters a mere matter of feet away.

Byers, however, did not pick up on the hint. "Hey, before I let you go, what's up with these funky coordinates I heard Captain Maxwell give out? I heard there's nothing even there planet-wise. So, where in the hell are we going?"

"Beats me," Marcus answered in a sullen tone while scratching the back of his head. "I give up trying to find out, honestly. But if it's from headquarters, then there's really not much we can do anyways, right?"

"I guess. I know one thing, though, and that's that I can't wait for that old man to get off this ship for good."

Byers gazed around to make sure nobody was around in preparation for delivering juicy gossip through a whisper. "And between you and me, sometimes I just wish he would honestly just die. That man is unbelievably heartless."

For whatever reason unknown to even him, Byers' statement hit Marcus to the core and tickled a soft spot that he didn't realize still existed as he felt the need to correct Byers for what he had just said. "Wow, I would never go there. You're better than that."

"Hey, I'm just saying. You hate him, and so do I, so why not wish for the best?"

Marcus shook his head in disbelief and stormed past Byers, who stood by his lonesome out of confusion.

"I was joking, Ronnie," Byers pleaded in a futile attempt to pacify Marcus, realizing he had hit an unexpected nerve. "C'mon back, let's talk about it."

Marcus ignored his friend's request and disappeared into his quarters without offering a word. Byers, meanwhile, could only scratch the back of his head and wonder what had suddenly snapped inside of his childhood friend.

Chapter 8

Marcus stared at himself in the mirror as he finished getting ready for what he was sure to be an unusual day. He picked up his comb and began to slowly brush his neatly trimmed dark hair in zombie fashion, his sluggishness a result of exhaustion and unhappiness.

A solemn feel came over Marcus, who felt as if he were preparing for a funeral. He had the appearance of a man who hadn't slept for weeks, thanks in large part to the seemingly non-stop drama that had affected his work and personal being.

He knew this mission would be different from the previous ones he had. Previously, it would have been a reason to celebrate some potential excitement. At that moment, however, he felt full of empty confusion internally, combined with feelings of fright about what the future held for himself and the rest of the crew.

Where the hell are we going? And what the hell is going to happen to us all?

He stopped brushing his hair and put the comb down gently to his left on the sink in his bathroom, staring at himself deeply in the mirror as he placed his hands on each side of the vanity. Uneasiness crept through him regarding not only uncertainty but also the massive secret that clung to his soul.

Something just doesn't feel right about all of this.

Marcus closed his eyes in an attempt to relax himself. He was the kind of man who liked feeling like he was in control, and at this particular moment, he felt as if he were completely helpless. He didn't feel good about the way things were going with this new mission already, and the ship hadn't even arrived at their destination.

Relax. Just remember, it's the old man's last mission. He'll be gone soon enough.

Marcus took a deep breath, opened his eyes and looked at himself again in the mirror before taking his hands off of the vanity and straightening his shoulders to stand completely erect.

He felt a little better after the brief pep talk his brain gave him, although he still felt slightly unsure about where exactly the ship was headed.

"With any luck, maybe Jacobs will be right, and we'll get to head home early," he stated to himself, chuckling while he messed with the collar on his dark blue uniform shirt. "For once, maybe we'll prove Maxwell wrong."

A smirk came across his face upon the thought of an imaginary scenario he created of the crew reaching their destination, only to find nothing there. He pictured the look of confusion on Maxwell's face and the anger he spewed aloud towards SAGE headquarters for taking them to the middle of nowhere, especially with it being his last mission. He could imagine the veins on Maxwell's neck bulging and pictured the deep red hue of his face from anger and frustration, along with the probable tantrum to follow.

That would be so priceless.

Marcus straightened out his collar and patted down his uniform as final preparation for what he knew was going to be a very long day. The opening day of starting a new mission was always the longest of them all, and it was anybody's guess what this particular day would bring, especially with the uncertainty behind their unknown location.

Marcus checked himself out in the mirror one last time and

swayed his head left and right to take a final good look. He took one last deep breath, a slight case of butterflies churning in his stomach over the unknowns that the day would bring.

At least he knew he could rely on seeing Monica on the deck, which made him smile on the inside like a child on their birthday. If there was any consolation, at least he knew she would be present to help boost his morale.

"Here we go," he told himself as he turned and marched out of his room, turning left to head towards the rickety elevator.

Marcus walked down the fourth-floor hallway, which always seemed so lonely and bare, mostly considering that he and Maxwell were the only ones who held their quarters there. He couldn't help but look down the hallway to see if he could catch a glimpse of his commanding officer. As had been the case, especially lately, Maxwell's door was sealed shut, with no sight or sound of the captain.

Marcus' focus remained, however, on Maxwell's closed door, even as he reached the elevator. There was no possible way, especially in his mind, that he was going to get anywhere close to there, considering what had transpired hours ago.

What could he be doing there? And what's going through his mind?

He pushed the button for the second floor and suddenly smiled at the thought of seeing Monica on the deck, which alone was enough positive therapy to assist him in getting over the hell he had endured over the past day.

One of these days, you need to man up and ask her out.

Alas, Marcus' nerves always seemed to have gotten the better of him, especially in telling Monica how he really felt. He could sense that he was getting closer to making that leap but always seemed to find an excuse of some sort to justify his non-action.

He felt an upward sensation in his stomach as the creaky elevator stopped at the second floor and slowly opened its doors.

Marcus made his way through the ajar doors and began to make his way to the deck when he was interrupted by a voice.

"Ronnie! Wait up!"

Marcus stopped and turned around to see Byers, who was walking at a quick pace, attempt to catch up to him. "Don't forget about your lieutenant. You can't leave home without that."

"I don't know, I almost might want to, honestly," Marcus shot back, chuckling while his lieutenant caught up to him.

Byers chortled upon the low blow delivered by Marcus as he had officially caught up to his friend. "That's ice cold, man. At least you're bullshitting around again. I'm guessing the Ronnie from last night is gone?"

Marcus nodded his head and picked up his step along with Byers to continue to their destination.

"Yeah, I'm sorry about last night," Marcus offered apologetically. "It was kind of a rough night for a couple of different reasons, I guess."

"No worries. Just don't let it happen again, or I might need to crack some skulls. Or better yet, maybe I'll get Maxwell to do it for me."

Marcus only offered a shaking of the head as the two men entered through the door to the deck full of antsy crew members who awaited their arrival.

Byers' chuckling, meanwhile, morphed into hysterical laughter. "Commander and lieutenant on board," he shouted in between cackling, unable to contain his silly behavior.

Marcus poked his friend in the ribs with his elbow in an attempt to stop Byers' laughter, although Byers' contagious nature was affecting him as well.

"Settle down," whispered Marcus to Byers through gritted teeth in an attempt to keep himself from also falling off of the silly wagon.

The crew stood in acknowledgment and stared with confusion at Byers and Marcus, who were both struggling to put on the poker face that Maxwell mandated at all times during duty, or 'his time' as was often referred to by the captain himself.

Marcus sensed the incoming presence of his superior coming

through the doors soon and began to clear his throat in an attempt to settle himself down. "As you were," he commanded as the crew sat back down and resumed their duties.

Byers, however, continued to struggle as his chuckling vibrated his body. His eyes watered, and he closed his mouth in an attempt to shut himself up, which only resulted in him beginning to snort loudly.

"Knock it off," Marcus, now over his own silliness, firmly commanded. "You're going to get us all in trouble."

A single tear streamed down Byers' left cheek. "Sorry--I just can't help--but picture what I said about—-Maxwell--cracking skulls. I could—-see him--."

Byers, unable to finish his sentence, covered his mouth with his left hand feebly while his chuckle grew into full-blown laughter. He immediately cupped his hand over his mouth in an attempt to keep the noise down but did a poor job as Jennings and Arraz stopped their normal duties and stared with curiosity as their lieutenant erupted into laughter.

Urgency flowed through Marcus, who could sense that Maxwell was very close. "Tommy, settle down," he whispered to him more sternly, gazing around at the stares of the worried crew, who could feel the potential of a dead man walking. "For God's sake, please."

Marcus felt a hot sensation roll down his spine from the trouble he was sure they all would soon be in.

C'mon, not now. We can't start out the mission like this.

A loud gasp from one of the crewmembers helped affirm what he had feared.

Oh, shit.

Anger emblazoned the face of Maxwell, who appeared as mad as a swarm of bees that had lost their hive. Marcus gazed quickly at Byers, who placed his face into his hands while laughing deliriously, completely unaware that his captain had arrived.

This is not good. Not good at all.

Marcus felt scared, not only for Byers but also for himself and the rest of the crew. He could sense how screwed every one of them officially were was, and the rage resonating from Maxwell's body did little to quell that fear.

"Captain on the deck!" Marcus shouted loudly to salute Maxwell and inform Byers of his great mistake.

The crew responded and rose to their feet on cue. Byers, meanwhile, gasped and rapidly lifted his head from his hands. His laughter died a horrible death at the sight of his fuming captain, who had a visible fire that burned in his eyes of a man ready to kill.

Marcus, helpless as could be, could offer nothing more than concern over what his captain would potentially do. He veered his eyesight momentarily to Monica, who stood at her desk with a grave look of concern.

She even looks beautiful when she's worried.

He didn't want to lose focus on the happenings at the moment and returned his eyesight back towards Maxwell, whose death stare remained locked on his misbehaving lieutenant.

Byers remained frozen in place like a sitting duck as his captain prepared to unleash his fury. "What in the hell is going on here?" the captain angrily shouted while a single vein in his bright red forehead began to pulsate. "Are you really fooling around on my time, asshole?"

Byers felt frightened out of his mind. He knew he had been caught, and his violently beating heart helped to confirm that. He wished at that moment that he had listened to Marcus for once in his life. "No--no sir," he tried to explain, stumbling over his words. "I--I would never insult or disrespect you--sir. I--apologize, Captain. It'll never happen again--sir."

Maxwell offered nothing before turning his icy glare away from the scolded Byers and passing it on to the next victim. "And what am I to think of you, Commander?" he fussed at the unassuming Marcus. "Am I to believe that you find this kind of behavior acceptable, from the ship's lieutenant, no less?"

Marcus could think of no answer or excuse if his life

depended on it. "No, sir," he replied, his arms at his side as he gazed out through the viewing window ahead to avoid making eye contact with his furious captain.

Maxwell delivered an uncomfortable stare towards Marcus before placing his hands behind his back and trudging around the deck to address his crew. "Let me remind you all that tomfoolery such as this will not be tolerated on this ship," shouted the captain with complete command.

He glared with intent towards all parties involved on deck but paused especially for a long while towards Rubidoux, who unquestionably appeared to be the most frightened of them all.

Maxwell smiled with wicked enjoyment towards the rookie, who gulped nervously as the captain soaked in his moment of dictatorship. "And I remind you all as well that anyone who dares to challenge this will be at risk for the most dire and severe of consequences. Do I make myself perfectly clear?"

"Sir, yes, sir," the crew responded in unison.

The captain delivered a death glare to every member of the crew to further back his words while floating towards his chair. "Very well, then," he stated upon settling onto his cozy throne. "Now that we can get back to the business at hand--Jacobs, what is our status?"

The navigator immediately answered without delay, fearing another tongue-whipping for herself for not being timely enough. "We should be arriving in a matter of minutes, sir," Jacobs responded while staring deeply into her captain's eyes. "Everything is on point, Captain."

"Spectacular," said Maxwell with an expressionless gander before changing his focus to picking on his young rookie.

"Rube—-"

Rubidoux's head rose nervously from his control panel, his eyes slowly making their way towards that of his captain. He attempted with all of his might not to look frightened, even though he felt like jelly on the inside.

"—-are you prepared to land this vessel when we arrive at our destination?"

"Sir, yes--sir," Rubidoux stated, his voice cracking in between to further highlight his nervousness.

Maxwell fed off the young man's green behavior with insult. "You'd better hope you don't screw this up. It would be unwise to let me down, boy."

Rubidoux lowered his head in a weak attempt to hide from Maxwell and gulped heavily while the uncomfortable spotlight of his captain's stare remained firmly in action.

Byers and Maxwell stood behind their superior officer, still trying to recover from the verbal beating they both had taken.

"I told you to shut up," whispered Marcus. "You should have listened to me, you idiot."

"I'm sorry," Byers mouthed apologetically to his friend to avoid any further trouble from his captain.

Marcus rolled his eyes and turned his attention towards Monica, who sat at her chair and so happened to look his way at that exact moment. He moved his lips without speaking and mouthed *hello* to her, to which she, in turn smiled and returned the favor. He warmly grinned back but turned his head quickly to avoid any potential trouble for either one of them.

What a woman. She is so amazing.

Marcus' eyes suddenly focused out upon the open landscape of space ahead as his mind began to wander into a daydream. He pictured the two of them sitting together in the middle of a lush green meadow, watching an orange-red sunset as they sipped on glasses of sweet, sparking white wine together.

Ah, yes. The wine tastes absolutely refreshing. And the company and the sunset are so splendidly gorgeous.

A nice breeze slid across his face while he glanced over at Monica, whose shoulder length raven black hair flowed gently in the wind. The two of them lovingly gazed at one another and smiled as they took a sip together and continued enjoying the sunset that glowed spectacularly in front of them.

"This is so wonderful," she said as the reflection of the sun glistened in her doe-brown eyes. "It's like something you see in a dream."

Marcus leaned closely to her, unable to do anything else but smile at her beauty. "I think you're wonderful, Monica. And if this is a dream, I hope neither one of us wakes up anytime soon."

Monica turned her attention to him and smiled with welcome intent.

This is the moment you've waited for.

Marcus grinned and placed his wine glass onto the grass before leaning his head towards her to seal his feelings with a kiss. Monica, with her mostly empty glass still in hand, followed his lead.

His heart began to rapidly thump in anticipation of feeling the sensation of her lips against his own.

This is it...

"Commander--"

Here it comes...

"Commander!"

Marcus' daydream came to a crashing halt courtesy of Maxwell, who stared angrily at his right-hand man who had just been caught procrastinating on the job. He shook his head to get the cobwebs out and turned his attention to his captain.

"Yes—-sir?"

The impatient captain exhaled deeply to illustrate his growing frustration. "I've asked you twice already, Commander. Now that I've got your full attention, I will ask you once and only once more, and so may God help you if I need to ask again."

He cleared his throat before asking Marcus with a great deal of snarky sarcasm, "Are--we—-set—-up--with—-supplies?"

What an asshole.

"Yes--sir," he replied calmly while ignoring his own inner thoughts. "We are more than sufficiently prepared."

"Thank you for that scintillating update, Commander, even though it took you a year to respond."

I'll show you an update.

Maxwell grunted to himself before turning his seat towards the space in front of him.

Marcus stood silently, shaking his head while resisting the bubbling urges inside of him to unleash his anger.

At the rate he's going, he might get an early forced retirement courtesy of me.

Marcus turned away from the back of Maxwell's head and locked eyes with Monica once again, her soft gaze bringing a sense of tranquility to him somewhat. He smirked at her out of assurance, even though a feeling of rage still wandered around in his heart.

Calm yourself down. Don't let her see you angry.

Marcus took a breath and watched as Maxwell rotated his head to the left and began to force his wrath on Arraz, who sat frozen and seemed a bit shaken as well after watching his commander belittling before his eyes.

"What are you staring at, Slim?" Maxwell barked towards his latest victim. "Get to work and don't sit there like a worthless piece of shit."

"Yes--yes sir," replied Arraz, who turned quickly in his chair and nervously began to fiddle with the controls in front of him.

Maxwell twisted his head back to its normal position and peered ahead towards his next targets. A fire blazed in his eyes upon the sight of Jacobs and Rubidoux, who both were engulfed in their monitors. "Jacobs, Rubidoux, I demand a status report now."

"Two minutes to arrival, sir," replied Jacobs immediately.

Marcus turned his attention to Byers, who peered ahead and into the empty space that presented itself in front of them both. He still appeared rattled from the verbal assault he had endured, and the lack of joy on his face further pushed the notion.

Bet he learned his lesson not to do that again.

The commander joined his friend's side and stared out curiously into the dark space that continued to lack any speck of life.

Why haven't we seen anything yet?

The rest of the crew glared in unison at the space in front of them that continued to be devoid of the planet that was to have been close. A large sun and moon that could be seen in the far distance, along with clusters of shiny and sparkling stars that shone brightly, but yet the planet that had been promised by Maxwell was nowhere to be found.

Marcus attempted to hide his grin but failed miserably to do so as he turned towards Byers, who did the same at the sight of failure on the part of their bullish captain.

The commander turned his attention towards Jacobs, who appeared concerned and puzzled as she stared at the open space and wondered what was going to happen next.

Finally, Marcus turned his attention to Maxwell, whose stone face had begun to morph into a scowl.

"Status," commanded Maxwell in a monotone voice.

An eerie silence came over the entire crew as they turned their attention to the veteran navigator, waiting to hear what she would say even though they were all aware of what was ready to come out of her mouth.

"We're--here--sir," Jacobs stated in bits, feeling the heat from Maxwell's body begin to radiate. "These are the exact coordinates--sir."

Maxwell shot up from his seat and drifted towards the area where Jacobs and Rubidoux sat. The two navigators glared upwards at their captain, who lurched his way towards them, his arms behind him while his eyes remained captivated on the viewer window ahead of him.

He stopped at the navigation panel, put his hands on the dash area, gritted his teeth and scowled. He raised his right hand in a fist above his head and pounded the control panel with all of his might and great fury from his failure.

"No!"

Rubidoux gasped and fell over out of his seat and onto the

floor from the might of the scream, leaving Jacobs to feel his fury alone.

"What did you both do to screw this up?" Maxwell asked Jacobs in an attempt to void himself of responsibility.

The veteran navigator appeared insulted but firmed up her face to hide her frustration. "We have done nothing wrong, sir. These are the exact coordinates you gave us. You can check them yourself."

Maxwell raised his fist from the dash, gazed at the empty space before him and closed his eyes, talking to himself quietly. The crew curiously stared at their captain's odd behavior.

"What is he doing?" whispered Byers to Marcus.

"I have no clue," Marcus responded in a soft tone so his captain could not hear.

An awkward silence came over the room as Maxwell continued his own personal conversation.

What could he possibly be doing?

Suddenly, the captain's lips stopped moving, and his eyes opened at the speed of light. The crew stood silently, staring at him as they awaited his instructions.

"We're here," Maxwell suddenly declared to the puzzled crew, peering down at Jacobs in order to give her the next order up close and personal. "Prepare for landing."

Marcus and Byers joined their crew in baffling expressions as they stared out into the empty space once again before them, wondering if their captain had just lost his mind.

"Sir, with all due respect, what are you saying?" Marcus intervened as the tone in his voice began to rise. "Look for yourself. There's absolutely nothing here, Captain."

The captain was in no mood to be told of anything different as his tone turned even harsher. "Silence, Commander. You will do as I say, no matter whether you like it or not, and you will respect my orders. I will not tolerate any sort of insubordination like this."

"Insubordination? With all due respect, look out there, sir. There's absolutely nothing out there--"

Marcus' point was interrupted by the sudden appearance of a planet before his eyes out of the corner of his eye.

What—-in--the-—hell?

His jaw dropped upon the sudden and unexpected change of events, and a stunned look brandished upon his face as he stared blankly at the gigantic object in front of him.

The rest of the crew joined in stunned silence upon the unexpected surprise themselves. The jaws of Byers and Monica copied Marcus out of shock and disbelief at the sight of the suddenly visible planet that seemed to have magically appeared out of thin air.

Marcus' speech became impaired with the shock that rattled him while his body remained frozen like that of a statue. He was dwarfed under the presence of the blue and green colored planet that reminded him so closely to that of Earth.

A grinning Maxwell, with his hands crossed behind his back, lurched towards his stunned commander and leaned in close enough to whisper sweet nothings into his ear. "I'll save you the embarrassment this time. Don't ever cross me like that again, or I'll really make you look like the fool that you are."

Marcus offered nothing while the captain gave him a sly smirk that came with an I-told-you-so chuckle to boot.

Maxwell's slick smile remained from his accomplishment as he prepared to address the others. "We will prepare for landing immediately. You will need your supply pack and your gun, in case any of you geniuses didn't know that already."

He turned towards Rubidoux, who had just risen to his feet, and barked further orders. "Rookie! What do you think you're doing? Get in position and help Jacobs land this ship. This is no time to fart around. Get back on that panel now!"

Rubidoux stumbled his way back into his chair and nervously continued on with his assignment.

Maxwell turned from the navigation panel and stared out towards the view window upon their newest discovery.

Marcus picked up his jaw and finally blinked his eyes to show that he was still coherent. He turned his head momentarily and looked at his captain, who glared frostily back at him with a told-you-so expression that delivered a shiver down his spine.

He hated Maxwell being right, especially because his captain always seemed to find a way to save himself from ever being wrong.

The captain offered nothing else but to turn his head back towards the screen to take in the view of the glory that hung in front of him.

Marcus begrudgingly followed his captain's lead and turned his head towards the view of the planet, his thoughts beginning to get the best of him as they headed closer to the mass in front of them.

Here we go.

CHAPTER 9

A thud jolted the ship upon its completed landing the mysterious planet.

"We have officially landed successfully, Captain," Jacobs instructed aloud to the crew.

"Excellent," replied Maxwell, who flashed a rare smile of delight that momentarily erased his intimidating appearance.

Marcus stood by the captain's chair and scratched the back of his head in another attempt to figure out what exactly was going on.

How did that planet suddenly appear out of nowhere? And why does Maxwell look so happy?

None of what had just happened made any sense to Marcus. He couldn't understand how the planet mysteriously came out of thin air, and he had a hard time grasping the reason for his normally grouchy captain's feeling of jubilation.

Probably because he knows that he's right again. That bastard, anyway.

The captain, however, did not allow much time to dawdle in his internal glory and turned back on his tunnel-vision style of captaincy.

"Alright, you all know what to do," Maxwell commanded to

the crew while arising from his seat. "Grab your pack and weapon and head to the back docking area to disperse."

The crew stood in eerie unison and headed to the supply area located in the left hand rear corner of the deck to grab their packs and weapons.

Marcus, however, remained still and kept an eye on Maxwell, who joined the cluster of people in the corner in need of their supplies. A strange sense came over him, especially considering the grin that once again plastered the grumpy captain's mug.

Something is very wrong here.

He shook his head and closed his eyes for a moment while he attempted to wrap his head around the unusual circumstances that had occurred.

The crew began to file out of the deck before Marcus finally began to move himself. He immediately searched for Byers, who he knew for certain would feel the same way as him as he longed to further discuss the mysteries that suddenly surrounded their new mission.

Little did Marcus realize, however, that his friend had been one of the first ones to pick up their supplies and head towards the unloading dock.

So much for that, I guess.

He strutted towards the supply area and noticed Jennings, who appeared uncomfortable as he picked up his gun and pack.

He's better than nobody, I suppose.

"Hi, Dr. Jennings," said Marcus in an effort to be chummy. "Looks like we're the last ones standing here, huh?"

"Indeed," Jennings replied plainly. He flung his bag over his shoulder but held his weapon awkwardly as if it were an infected object.

The beginning of the conversation said it all. The two men had worked together for over five years, yet for whatever reason, never seemed to get to know one another well. Although they knew one another from being on the same crew, it seemed almost as if they were complete strangers in their dealings with one another. It also definitely didn't help that Jennings was as quiet as a mouse and seemed interested in nothing more than science and obeying his superior.

This is going to be a hoot.

Marcus picked up his gun and bag before continuing in his attempt to strike up a conversation. "So--are you actually going to be using a gun this time around?"

The doctor appeared baffled by the question. "Oh, no. Not that I can see, at least. I just do it because the captain tells us to. I've never even held a gun in my life, let alone fire one."

No shit.

"I see," Marcus stated, feeling quite dumb for asking such an obvious question.

Jennings was as squeaky clean as they came. He came from a wealthy background, as both of his parents were also doctors, and he went to an expensive private college to attain his Ph.D. He never cursed and was polite in almost everything that he did and said. He almost didn't seem to fit in with the salty environment the ship at times created, and Marcus couldn't help but wonder sometimes how a man like Jennings ended up on the crew.

It was all of no matter to the commander at this particular moment, however, as he continued to try to create some sort of productive small talk with Jennings to open up the conversation to more of his liking.

"So, how do you feel about this mission, Doctor?"

"I think it should be fascinating, Commander," replied Jennings with a bright smile. "But then, I suppose every mission has been."

You couldn't be any more wrong.

"Sure—-you bet," Marcus said in pretend agreement before pointing towards the door to help signal that it was time for both of them to leave. "C'mon, let's get out of here before we get in trouble."

"You're correct. We wouldn't want to upset the captain, would we?"

Marcus rolled his eyes while the two men began to walk side by side. They exited the deck and were met in an empty hallway towards the elevator that let them know that they were indeed separated from the others.

Marcus, however, still felt the need to give it one more shot as he delivered one more softball to the reserved Jennings. "I've always wanted to ask you. I know this seems random, but--do you have a girlfriend or a wife back home?"

"No, I don't have a special lady in my life besides my mom or grandma," replied a smirking Jennings, who was embarrassed by the question. "But I'm waiting patiently for my queen."

As nice as he thought the answer given was by Jennings, Marcus couldn't help but to again roll his eyes again at the corniness of it. Jennings definitely behaved like a man who never had a girlfriend in his life, and Marcus was convinced that he probably never even knew what it was like to kiss a woman, let alone be intimate with one.

Good God, somebody gets this man a woman.

The open elevator doors awaited the two men before they stepped inside. Marcus pushed the button to the basement and could feel his stomach prepare for the bumpy ride they had in store. The doors slid shut as the elevator began to deliver the experience the commander had anticipated.

"Well, hopefully, she arrives soon," Marcus said in an attempt to finish the current conversation and change the subject to the topic he had so badly wanted to discuss. "Speaking of arriving, I wanted to ask you about---"

His sentence was unexpectedly cut off by an apologetic Jennings. "I'm sorry to interrupt you, sir. But I do have something I would like to ask you of great importance since nobody else is around. Of course, if that's okay, Commander."

This better has something to do with this mission.

"Uh--sure," Marcus stated while hoping that he and the doctor were thinking alike. "What's on your mind?"

The elevator made an unwelcome stop on the basement level

as they stepped out and were about to make their way toward the dock.

Jennings, however, suddenly stopped outside the elevator and took a quick glimpse around to ensure nobody else was close enough to hear their conversation, even though there was no sight of anybody else.

Marcus halted his own step and moved towards Jennings, who grinned childishly.

"Just out of curiosity," the doctor began to ask quietly as if he were telling a secret. "Do you know anything about Miss Victoria?"

Huh?

"You mean--Jacobs? I'm not sure what you mean."

Jennings' coy smile remained. He appeared uncomfortable yet seemed to also contain the urge to spill his guts. "What I mean is-- I suppose I wanted to inquire if she was married or had a boyfriend that you were aware of?"

"I don't think she has a man in her life, although I don't know that for sure, so you'd have to ask her yourself on that one."

Disappointment came over Jennings, who had hoped that Marcus could have offered more. "I see. Well, I see you talking to her all of the time. Do you think you can ask her and put in a good word for me if she's not taken?"

Marcus was astounded by Jennings' request. "Why don't you ask her out yourself? I have to be honest--I'm sure she'd much rather have you ask her yourself. Plus, who knows, she might feel the same way and just be waiting for you to say something."

"I don't know. As much as I want to, I wouldn't even know how to start. It's amazing because she has this mystifying effect on me, even though we've hardly ever spoken to one another. It's like she has some sort of special power on me. Do you know what I mean, Commander?"

Marcus nodded his head carefully and stared dully ahead as Jennings' words made him think of Monica. The thought of her made him melt on the inside, and he could relate to what the virgin doctor had said.

"I completely understand where you're coming from, Doctor. One-hundred percent."

If there was any part of this mission that Marcus looked forward to, it was definitely the thought of possibly getting to work by Monica's side so he could possibly make his move and do what he had wanted to do for so long and ask her on a date.

Whether or not he would be able to conquer his fear, however, remained unknown even to himself, and he couldn't help but wonder if he would ever summon up the courage to complete the task he had given himself.

Jennings, meanwhile, continued on with gushing over his feelings. "I don't know. I guess I'm just nervous. I've never asked out a woman, so I don't even know where to begin."

The commander-turned-counselor felt the inner need to educate both the doctor and himself on what exactly to do.

"Just approach her and strike up a conversation. Keep it simple in the beginning. Something like 'Hello' or 'how are you' would be a good start. Just ease into it and let things flow, give her a nice little compliment on something and see if she would like to go out with you sometime."

Jennings smiled over the suggestion. "That's genius. It's so simple yet unbelievably well thought out. Those were some golden words of wisdom on your part, Commander. When you put it like that, it sounds so easy."

If he thinks it's easy now, just wait until he tries to ask her out. He's going to turn into a mountain of jelly.

Marcus and Jennings were close to the dock and could see the rest of the crew standing in formation, waiting for deployment.

The commander's stomach dropped upon the realization that he had lost his opportunity to discuss the strange happenings of the mission.

Better luck next time, I suppose.

Jennings, in the meanwhile, appeared happy and content over

getting to drain his emotional tank. "Well, here we are. Thanks for the company and the words of wisdom, Commander. I greatly appreciate it."

The doctor peered over at Jacobs, who stared straight ahead without the slightest idea that she was being watched and continued to take her in while he joined the back of the formation that had formed.

Marcus, on the contrary, stood behind for a moment, realizing he never got the opportunity to vent and make sure he hadn't lost his mind.

"Yeah, anytime. Glad to be of service."

He scratched the back of his head and began to move at the pace of molasses towards the rest of his crew.

Their mission was about to officially begin, and Marcus could only wonder what other mysteries awaited them all.

CHAPTER 10

Maxwell began to commence instructions at the opening of the dock while Marcus quietly tiptoed and slithered his way to the back of the line, hoping that his commanding officer hadn't caught his act of tardiness.

Just when he thought he had been deceptive enough, Maxwell stopped his instructions and glared at his commander.

Oh, shit.

"Nice to see my supposed right-hand man decided to finally show up. Perhaps next time, I should hold your hand to make sure you're on time, Commander."

The blood rushed to Marcus' face out of utter embarrassment. "Shit, man," he whispered to himself.

Maxwell read Marcus' lips and grew more frustrated. "You and I will have a serious discussion about your punctuality later."

Maxwell glared at Marcus, who closed his eyes and gritted his teeth out of feeling the wrath that would be imposed on him down the line.

The captain shook his head in disgust before turning back to face the rest of the crew. "Continuing on from what I was saying before I was so rudely interrupted--we will divide into two groups," he instructed, making sure to deliver a nasty glare once more towards his late-to-the-party commander. "I will lead the first group, and the fashionably late Commander Marcus will lead the other."

Byers, a couple of crewmembers in front of Marcus, stared back at Marcus. "What happened?" he mouthed to him.

Marcus shook his head. "Not right now," he non-verbally replied back, trying to get Byers to focus ahead before they both got in hot water with their captain once more.

The ever-so-sharp Maxwell cleared his throat and stared at Byers, who could feel the laser beams from his captain's eyes burn the back of his skull.

The lieutenant slowly turned his head forward and was met with a glare of annoyance as he realized that he had once again gotten on his captain's shit list.

"Well, I think I've just had a brilliant idea," declared Maxwell. "Lieutenant, since you and Marcus are so chummy and behave like children when you're together, perhaps a timeout will benefit you both. Because of that, you will be on my team, so I can keep an extremely close eye on you. Do I make myself clear?"

Byers' shoulders slumped from the punishment he had been assessed. "Yes, sir," he replied sullenly, like a child being punished by his father.

Satisfied with his own resolution, Maxwell focused back on the crew. A smirk crossed his face out of sheer enjoyment of getting to chastise both his commander and lieutenant in a matter of seconds. "Rubidoux and Dr. Jennings, you will also be coming with me," he commanded. "The rest of you, I regret to inform you, will be on Commander Marcus' team."

Marcus ignored the backhanded comment given by his grumpy captain and smiled upon realizing exactly what that was going to mean.

Monica's going to be with me on my team. Yes!

He quickly hid his smile to bottle up his joy, even though he suddenly felt on top of the world.

Could it get any better? I get to spend time with Monica and get away from Maxwell. Hallelujah!

"We will meet back here at the ship at sundown," continued Maxwell, whose focus shifted back onto Marcus. "And don't be late getting back here because we're closing the dock right at dusk. So, unless you'd like to spend the night sleeping outdoors on a foreign planet with unknown creatures, I would advise that all of you on Marcus' team make sure that doesn't happen."

Marcus stared back at Maxwell, who was locked and loaded with an icy glare back at him. It felt like it was starting to get personal, at least in Marcus' mind, and he didn't turn down the invite for a brief stare-down.

Maxwell bailed on the contest between the two of them and focused back on the rest of the crew to finish his instructions. "Stay focused on the mission at hand and report any kind of suspicious activity. Rubidoux, Byers and Jennings, let's head out. As for the rest of you--"

The captain stopped short of finishing his sentence as the three men he summoned disjointed from their tightly-knit line and huddled around Maxwell. Byers appeared to be the most pitiful of them all, even more so than Rubidoux, who seemed frightened out of his mind, knowing that he would be joined at the hip to his grizzly captain for the remainder of the day. On the opposite, meanwhile, it seemed like a walk in the park for Jennings, who smiled carelessly without realizing the tough assignment he had been given.

Byers turned back and rolled his eyes at Marcus to motion his disapproval of the punishment that had been bestowed upon him. Marcus could only shake his head and shrug his shoulders as his friend turned his head back around and picked up his pace to keep up with his group and avoid any further verbal barbs by Maxwell.

The commander felt bad for his friend, who was about to enter several hours of torture from their splintery captain, but at the same time, had tried to warn him about misbehaving while Maxwell had the floor.

If only that bastard had listened to me, all of this wouldn't have happened.

Maxwell's group had officially disembarked from the ship as Marcus gazed around at the three remaining crew members who stood there and awaited command. He felt an instant sense of relief knowing that Maxwell would, at least until the sun went down, be completely off his case.

First, he focused on Arraz, who appeared bored and already had taken his gun out of his bag and held it tightly against himself, waiting for some sort of action that involved any type of shooting at an individual or object. He definitely had some sort of gun addiction, undoubtedly, and a part of Marcus worried about the potential damage he was going to cause down the road.

Jacobs stood to Arraz's right side as she looked antsy and ready to get out and get some sort of fresh air, considering that a space suit wasn't required on this mission. Marcus felt relieved to have been given her and not Rubidoux, yet he wondered if perhaps the only reason he had gotten Jacobs was because she was a woman since Maxwell historically preferred an all-male crew on explorations.

That's his loss if that's the case.

Last but not least, there was Monica, who stood behind Jacobs and began to make her way to Marcus' right to complete the small circle that had come together. He couldn't help but smile as Monica stationed herself at his side and awaited his orders.

He raised his eyebrows to her as a way of saying hello while she smirked upon his gesture in return.

This is so great!

Marcus couldn't help but be excited about the prospect of having her in his group. At the same time, however, he knew he had a job to accomplish, so he decided it was time to put on his commander face for both Arraz and Jacobs. "Okay, folks--so, because of the fact that Maxwell's group headed east, we will head west and go from there, I suppose."

Marcus' attention turned towards Arraz, who began to play with and fondle his gun as if it were his most prized and beloved possession. "Arraz, please put your gun away. We haven't even left the ship, and you're already locked and loaded."

"Just want to prepared, Commander. You should always be ready for anything. That's my motto, at least."

The commander blinked his eyes blankly upon Arraz's foolish statement. "I guess if that's what suits you. Just be careful with that, okay?"

Arraz nodded his head and gave a thumbs-up out of approval. "No problem, Commander."

Marcus turned his focus onto Jacobs, who yawned and covered her mouth in an attempt to hide it. "How are you feeling, Jacobs? Are you tired?"

"No, just ready to get this started, sir," she replied, although the bags under his eyes suggested otherwise. "And I just want to get off this ship for a while."

"Understandable," said Marcus, who turned his attention and once again grinned upon the sight of the beautiful Monica. "And how about you, Miss Monica? How are you feeling?"

She appeared fresh and rejuvenated compared to the other two as her sweet nature continued to seep from her pores. "I feel great, sir. Thank you for asking."

He couldn't help but sheepishly smirk as the sugar flowed from her considerate answer.

Anytime, Monica. Anytime.

A warm sensation came over Marcus' chest. He felt so wonderful being in her presence, and he was completely smitten with everything about her. He loved her smile, and he loved her electric personality especially.

She was the sweetest mixture of brown sugar and honey, and

there was nothing he wanted more than to taste all of her goodness in its entirety.

Marcus' smile never waned as he cleared his throat to distract himself away and went back to the business at hand. "Well, in that case—-let's move out," he commanded.

Marcus headed towards the open chute, and Arraz, Monica, and Jacobs followed closely behind.

He stopped in his tracks upon his foot, hitting the ground on a lush, green surface that appeared and smelled a lot like the grass he knew back home on Earth.

What in the--?

It was completely gorgeous outside, almost like something out of a dream. A crystal blue sky hung perfectly in the sky and was accompanied by a large, yellowish sun that brightly shone to the northeast of them.

It felt extremely comfortable outside, while the air that the crew breathed filled their lungs with such goodness that they had never experienced on Earth. It felt so crisp, so refreshing, and uncannily clean, and it made them feel reinvigorated and reborn.

Majestically gorgeous and gigantic trees cascaded the descending hill before them that, gave off a forest-like setting that seemed like it came out of an old fantasy tale, at least in the mind of Monica, who could feel the stories she grew up became reality for that very moment.

The scenery was laid out nicely and neatly, almost like it had been organized in a certain way. A river in the distance sparkled in the sun as it cut through the heart of the land perfectly, and its crystal blue quality was unlike anything they had seen back home.

The crew gazed around in splendor as they relished in the visual treats before their eyes.

"Where are we?" asked Jacobs, her once tired face now full of vigor.

"I don't know," Arraz replied with his eyes stuck on the view while he stroked his beloved gun. "But wherever it is, I can't wait to see what else is ahead of us. What about you, Commander?"

Marcus nodded his head. "Agreed," he simply stated before turning back around and picking up his pace once again. "Let's go."

The crew followed the lead of their commander in the form of a disorganized cluster as they reached the pinnacle of the hill and began to take the slow descent down further into the mysterious yet picturesque land before them.

Chapter 11

The crew continued on their way as they began down an illustrious green pathway, which became more luscious and festered with trees the deeper they traveled.

Monica observed one of the trees to her left and saw a colorful bird-like creature sitting on a branch, squawking loudly to its mates in the other trees. She was amazed to see the multiple shades of colors that changed in the sunlight, shifting from a bluish-green to a fiery red in moments before her bewildered eyes.

"Look at that," she said in amazement, pointing up to the creature. "It looks like a giant, prettier parrot. And look how the colors change."

"Wow, that's incredible," replied Marcus upon her observation. "It's beautiful."

Their moment in nature was interrupted by a laser that cut through the branch and startled the creature, almost decapitating it in the process as the shot fired above its head. The creature flew off into the distance and squawked at the top of its lungs to signal to its friends the imminent danger they faced.

The branch fell to the ground in a loud thud as Marcus pulled his gun out of his bag in the blink of an eye and loaded it out of sheer reaction. Monica and Jacobs hit the deck and fell to the floor on their stomachs to prepare themselves for any additional gunfire that may have came from the mystery shooter.

"Damn, I missed it," Arraz bemoaned, holding his gun up high with his hand and hitting it with the other out of frustration.

Marcus turned around and stared at the lieutenant with a murderous glare. "What in the hell do you think you're doing?"

"Just trying to catch a bird," replied Arraz nonchalantly. "I thought it'd be cool to take one of those back home with us."

"Give me that!" Marcus shouted before ripping the gun out of Arraz's hand in the blink of an eye. "What in the hell is wrong with you? This is not a personal hunting trip."

"Sorry, Marcus," apologized Arraz. "I guess I got a little excited for a moment to finally shoot at something for the first time in forever. Plus, it may have been dangerous, so maybe you should be thanking me."

The commander shook his head at his new lieutenant's stupidity. "Well, I hope you enjoyed it because it's going to be the last shot you fire for a while."

Marcus put down his bag and stuffed Arraz's gun inside while the guilty culprit stared pitifully like a lost puppy.

Jacobs and Monica, finally realizing the coast was clear, picked themselves up off of the ground and dusted themselves off as pieces of the green grass-like substance fell from their clothes.

Marcus picked up his bag and flung it over his right shoulder while Arraz lamented, having his personal toy taken from him.

"Can I at least have a hand-held laser?" Arraz desperately inquired.

"No."

"How about an electro-blade, then?"

"You already have an electro-blade. And if you're not careful, you're going to lose that, too."

"Can I have yours, then? I like the one you have better."

Marcus delivered a death glare to Arraz, who got the hint and stopped his begging antics.

The commander shook his head and chuckled at the ridiculous antics of his lieutenant before heading back on the trail. Arraz was like a drug addict when it came to weapons, especially his prized guns. He always had to have one with him, and he almost felt helpless if he wasn't armed.

Monica and Jacobs followed their commander's lead back onward while Arraz remained stuck in motion from dejection.

Jacobs glanced at Arraz as she walked past him and couldn't help but to get in a shot at the hapless lieutenant. "Way to go, dumbass."

Arraz's face reddened from embarrassment. "You're lucky you're a girl," he lamely responded. "Because if you weren't--"

His voice trailed off once he realized Jacobs wasn't listening to what he was saying. He stood haplessly and placed his hands on his sides while the rest of his team continued to move on without him.

"Hey, wait up!" he shouted as he began to pick up his pace with the rest of the crew, who swerved collectively to the left to avoid walking in the river that now obstructed the middle of the road.

They formed a single-form line as they scaled the shore, with Jacobs, Monica and Arraz trailing in order behind Marcus.

Marcus stared down at the body of water that carried his reflection clearly off of the stream.

It looks so clear and incredibly clean, almost like it's been filtered throughout. We definitely don't see this back home.

He felt thirsty, and as curious as he was to try some, he wasn't sure whether or not to trust it, considering he was on soil foreign to him and his crew.

It does look tempting, though.

"Commander, do you think this water is drinkable?" Jacobs suddenly inquired as if she had read his mind.

"I don't know. It looks safe, but I wouldn't change it. So, just to be cautious, let's take a sample so we can take it back to the laboratory later and further examine it."

Marcus put his bag back down and grabbed a clear glass vial

out of it. He placed the vial in the water, filled it up three-quarters of the way full and closed the cap on top of it before placing it back in the bag.

"There we go," he said. "We'll check it out later when we return to the ship. In the meantime, I don't want any of us to try the water."

An internal feeling suddenly struck Marcus, who turned and saw Arraz bent down at the river with a full handful of water. He took a big swig, quickly dipped his hand back in the stream and filled it once again.

"No!" Marcus screamed, sprinting past Jacobs and Monica before smacking Arraz's filled hand. The water sprang out of the foolish lieutenant's hand like a rocket before crashing uselessly to the ground.

Arraz's head remained stooped out of the realization that he had just performed another act of insubordination.

Marcus could feel his frustration with him begin to boil over. "You idiot! Didn't I tell you not to drink from there?"

"Yeah--but I was thirsty, and I wanted a drink of water."

"You have water in your bag. What the hell's going on with you, anyway?"

Arraz stood up and wiped his mouth. "Nothing. It just looked so good, and I was curious. It tastes amazing, by the way."

Marcus shook his head at the stupidity shown by his lieutenant.

And to think, he's in charge of handling our weapons. What a scary thought.

"Don't defy my orders," Marcus commanded, channeling his inner Maxwell. "When I tell you to do something, I expect you to follow it. Do you understand?"

Arraz's focus remained downward on the ground as he felt unable to look his superior in the eye.

"Yes, Commander."

Arraz's immaturity began to expose itself. Even though his trigger finger was second to none and he was an excellent gunman, he was also a loose cannon and an extreme liability in terms of needing to be supervised, which could have also explained why Maxwell chose not to have him on his research team.

"Anyways, now that we've got that settled, let's get back on the road, everyone," Marcus ordered before picking up his pace along the river once again.

The crew continued on their way and broke up once more into an unorganized and relaxed cluster.

Marcus glared behind him to catch a glimpse of where Monica was. Much to his joy, she was merely a few paces behind, unaware of his stare, while she continued to take in the beautiful scenery.

He badly wanted to trail behind so he could catch up to her and be by her side to strike up another conversation, but he knew he had to stay in the lead as he was in charge.

If only I could get her attention somehow.

Before he could think of anything to grab her attention, Jacobs picked up her pace and moved to his side.

No! Wrong woman!

"It's gorgeous here, isn't it, Commander?" Jacobs asked.

Although he had a great relationship with her, Marcus wasn't fond of Jacobs at the moment for her bad timing. "Yeah, it's nice," he plainly stated.

"Nice? It's better than nice, don't you think?"

"I guess."

Marcus began to think about being back on the ship and seeing this beautiful planet they were now on mysteriously appearing. It still greatly bothered him that it appeared out of the middle of nowhere, and it seemed to be more of an issue that nobody in their right mind seemed to question what had happened on the deck.

Why hasn't anybody said anything about any of this?

The thoughts of the planet remarkably appearing and the odd antics by Maxwell that seemed to have had some part in making it appear ran through his mind, and he began to wonder if maybe there was a reason that his veteran navigator floated to his side to converse.

"Jacobs, can I ask you something?"

"Yes, sir—-"

Alright! Finally, it's time to get this off of my chest...

"--but I actually wanted to see if I could ask you something first, Commander?"

No! It'd better be about Maxwell and this damn planet.

He swallowed his thoughts once more and nodded his head to be a good leader of his people. "Sure. What is it, Jacobs?"

Jacobs turned her head and saw Monica. Still a few steps behind, engulfed in the scenery and beauty around her. Arraz, meanwhile, had gotten a hold of the electro-blade in his bag and began to play with and inspect it, looking ever so much the part of an addict that had been labeled upon him.

Marcus stared out of the corner of his eye at Jacobs, who looked at him unsurely as if she didn't know how to start.

"Jacobs?"

"Sorry, Commander," she replied apologetically, her voice beginning to lower into a whisper. "There's just something I want to ask you, but it's private."

Great, I guess we're ignoring the elephant in the room again.

"Okay, what is it?"

She swerved closer to Marcus' side while she prepared to spill her guts on what appeared to be a juicy secret.

Monica, perhaps not coincidentally, took her eyes off the scenery and focused on the two of them, wondering what was going on.

In the back of Marcus' mind, he could almost feel Monica's eyes piercing through the back of him. He was sure that she was wondering what was going on from behind as she watched with intent.

"Well, how do I ask this?" Jacobs shyly inquired. "I know you're my superior, but I've wanted to ask--"

Marcus' heart began to thump in fear that she was going to tell him something he didn't want to hear.

Dear God, don't tell me you're interested in me.

"--do you know if Dr. Jennings is seeing anybody?"

Whew.

"Dr. Jennings?" he asked with relief in his voice. "Are you saying that you like him?"

Jacobs smiled out of being able to discuss her secret crush. "Yeah, I guess I do. I think he's really cute."

Marcus' heart rate began to regulate, knowing that she didn't confess feelings for him, although it had nothing to do with looks since she was quite striking herself and was solely concerned about not wanting to ruin his chances with Monica.

He was curious about what made two of his crew members confess their feelings for one another on the same day and wondered why they had chosen him to be their mediator, considering he was their superior officer.

Maybe I should have been a counselor or relationship guru instead of the commander of a ship.

At the same time, it also made him feel good that he knew they both had feelings for one another, and he couldn't help but feel the inner matchmaker inside of him begin to bubble. And, of course, he was happy she had feelings for Dr. Jennings and not him, as his heart secretly belonged to the lovely Miss Brackenridge.

"I hope you don't mind me telling you this, Commander," said Jacobs. "I know this really isn't something I should be telling you, and I'm sure Maxwell would be furious if he knew this."

"No worries," Marcus told her in assurance. "I won't tell Maxwell any of this."

As much as he wanted to tell her what Jennings had just told him recently, he decided to keep it close to the vest and let them both find out on their own.

"Do you think he feels the same way?" Marcus asked, trying his best to make it seem like he knew nothing.

She sighed deeply upon his question. "I honestly don't know. Every time I look his way, it seems that he can't look at me. I want to go up and talk to him, but I guess I feel like that's something a man should do first."

Marcus nodded his head as he listened to her and started to wonder if Monica perhaps felt the same way about him. As glad as he was to finally start talking to her, he wondered if maybe she was just waiting for him to make his move. He wanted to ask her out, but the perfect time still hadn't presented himself, at least in his mind.

Or am I just making excuses?

"Maybe I just need to make the first move," continued Jacobs. "What do you think, Commander?"

Marcus blankly stared at Jacobs without batting an eye and began to process his thoughts of the right thing to say to advise not only her but also himself.

"I think you should let him pursue you," he finally suggested after a matter of moments. "Let him make the first move, but don't be afraid to maybe send a signal or two his way because sometimes we guys, need a little nudge to know that the ladies we're interested in feel the same."

You should really take your own advice on that one and do something about it. What if she's just waiting for you?

Jacobs smiled upon his input out of appreciation and appeared more than satisfied with his advice.

"Does that sound like a good idea?" he asked her.

"Yeah, it does, actually. I think I'll take your advice on that one. Maybe a little hint can get him going."

Marcus could only hope that he was right. He knew how inexperienced Jennings was when it came to dating, let alone approaching women, and he could only hope that he would take advantage if she indeed followed through on his suggestion.

And, of course, he couldn't forget about the presence of Maxwell, who would have had a conniption to have learned any romantic feelings were occurring within his air-lock tightly run crew.

"Thank you for listening, Commander," said Jacobs out of genuine appreciation. "I always have wanted to ask you as well, and I hope you don't mind me asking, but--do you have a special lady in your life?"

Marcus hesitated for a moment, unsure of how to answer the question as the lady she inquired about stood a matter of feet behind. He thought about what the correct answer to say should be, and said the first thing that came to his mind.

"Not yet, but I'm working on it."

Short and to the point--good answer!

"I see," Jacobs said, sensing he would not tell her much more than that. "Well, I wish you the best with that, Commander. I hope she knows how lucky she is."

"So do I," he stated, smirking upon the fact that Jacobs had no idea how close the special lady he wanted in his life truly was in terms of distance to them both.

Marcus turned his head and gazed at Monica trailing behind, who was staring at the ground before, appearing to be in a daze. He wanted her to turn her attention upwards so he could smile at her as a way to say hello and get another glance of her beauty, but his attention was suddenly sent elsewhere upon his realization that something was amiss.

"Where's Arraz?" he asked aloud to both of the ladies.

Jacobs and Monica collectively shrugged their shoulders in unison upon his question.

Marcus exhaled deeply out of bitter frustration. "Great. That's absolutely great. All I can say, I guess, is that he'd better be dead or close to it, because I'm going to kill him myself if he's not."

His frustration with Arraz began to boil over, and he was having difficulty keeping it inside. As cool and composed as he wanted to act in front of his crew of ladies, especially Monica, he had grown tired of Arraz's erratic behavior that now put them in an awkward position.

"It looks like our adventure is taking an unexpected turn, ladies," he announced with annoyance entangled in his voice. "Let's head on back to find our absent-minded lieutenant."

Jacobs sighed heavily out of despair while the team turned around and began to retrace their steps.

Marcus turned his head again towards Monica, who was trailing right behind him and appeared just as calm and composed as ever.

Even in times of craziness, she still maintains a great attitude. She's amazing.

He wanted to slow down so she could catch up to him, but was afraid to make it too obvious. He felt more motivated than ever to talk with her, with his pep talk providing the spark he perhaps needed for himself.

Marcus remembered, however, that they were not alone, and the last thing that he wanted to do was tell her how he felt when other people were around.

Just play it cool. Your time's going to come soon enough.

He closed his eyes momentarily to regain his focus on the mission. Although he wanted to talk with her so badly, he knew it was not the time, nor the place, to do so.

Marcus picked his focus back up and noticed that something was different about their surroundings.

It was quiet, almost eerily quiet as if the sound had suddenly been turned off. Gone were the sounds of the bird-like creatures that surrounded the air when they first arrived, along with any sort of added sound effects that had existed moments earlier. The river to their side even seemed like it had been tuned out also, and the leaves from the trees no longer rustled.

Marcus turned his head from left to right and gazed around, trying to figure out exactly what was going on and what had just silenced their lush surroundings.

Something is wrong around here.

Suddenly, a rustling could be heard in a bushy plant to their right ,made the entire crew alertly turn their heads to see what it could be.

"What was that?" Jacobs asked in a frizzled tone. "Is it Arraz?"

"I don't know," Marcus replied as he took his right hand and dug it into his bag to grab his gun.

He took out his weapon and turned it on, beginning to slightly crouch lower to prepare for whatever was about to come their way. "Stay here," he commanded to Monica and Jacobs quietly. "Arm yourselves, but don't move."

Monica and Jacobs followed his orders and took out their respective weapons, loading them and freezing them in place as commanded.

"Arraz?" Marcus asked. "Is that you?"

The plant rustled more, but no response was given to his question.

Marcus crept closer to the mysterious bush, his gun cocked and ready to fire at any moment. "Arraz, if that's you, you'd better knock it off."

The rustling grew more frantic, but no response was still given.

"Hey, I'm talking to you!" he shouted. "What the hell's your problem?"

The anger pulsated through Marcus towards Arraz. He almost felt compelled to shoot his lieutenant to teach him a lesson and was more than prepared to fire until he was greeted by an unexpected surprise that made the hairs on the back of his neck rise in fear.

Chapter 12

A loud growl from the plant shook the ground that Marcus stood on as fear and shock paralyzed the commander in his steps. His fear only rose upon the plant, beginning to take on a life of its own and lifting itself from the soil it had been rooted in.

Monica and Jacobs could do no more than witness the mutated plant to tower over the now pint-sized Marcus.

Arms and legs had suddenly developed from the plant, which took the form of a muscular giant close to four times their respective sizes.

Marcus gritted his teeth and finally showed signs of life as he pointed his gun towards the mutant, which opened its red eyes as its final transformation effect.

"You dare to threaten me?" the plant asked in a deep, scratchy voice.

It talks?!?

Marcus gazed at the creature in disbelief at what he was witnessing but put on a strong face to appear unfazed. He cocked his gun and took aim in between the plant's eyes, ready to fire.

"Don't move," he commanded to the plant, "or I'll shoot."

"Your intention is to threaten my being on my land, creature? You are creating an error to your being."

The plant took a step towards Marcus, who stood his ground and commanded his female counterparts to follow suit.

"Aim and fire!" he commanded to them before unloading an array of shots that penetrated right in between the plant's eyes. The ladies copied his example and fired their own round of lasers.

The mutant screamed in pain upon the shots and fell to the floor, creating an aftershock that violently shook the ground momentarily.

Monica and Jacobs followed Marcus' lead once more as he tiptoed his way toward the body of the fallen and motionless giant.

Marcus aimed his gun and prepared to fire another shot at its head.

He was a moment too late, however, as the plant quickly opened its eyes and delivered a haymaker punch from its backside to Marcus' chest that forced the gun from his hand and sent him soaring backward through the air and forcefully into the unready bodies of Monica and Jacobs.

The crew spilled onto the ground in agonizing pain while the plant sprang to its branchy feet and began to approach its sitting duck targets.

It growled viciously before grabbing Marcus by the neck with its sharp-leafed hands to hold him up like a doll.

"You will suffer violent consequences for your brash behavior," the plant threatened the helpless Marcus. "Beginning with the execution of your being, creature."

The plant's thorny hands began to squeeze mightily onto Marcus' neck.

Jacobs and Monica struggled to get up from the pain that paralyzed them momentarily and could offer nothing more than to watch their commander valiantly yet unsuccessfully kick his legs in a feeble attempt to pry the vice-grip hold that obstructed the airway he needed to survive.

"Commander!" shrieked Monica in horror. "Comma—-"

Her cries became muffled by Marcus, who could feel his soul

begin to drift. He felt dazed and lightheaded and could sense his body declaring a state of emergency while the hope of getting the fresh breath of air that he needed to survive began to fizzle.

His vision became darkened as his body and internal organs began to give up. He stopped his feeble attempts to free himself from the monstrous plant giant, which roared in the imminent victory it sensed was near.

Tears welled in his eyes in his final moments of life while Monica and Jacobs could only watch their commander prepare to die.

A strange feeling now came over him in preparation for his final seconds of life.

Until a miracle suddenly occurred.

"Halt!" the sound of a mysterious female voice suddenly screamed at the plant as a God-send.

Monica and Jacobs peered over and spotted a young woman with perfect olive-colored skin holding her hand up to the plant, which glared at the mysterious woman and growled in frustration upon the halting of his moment of homicide.

The woman's looks suggested that she was from Earth, but an aura about her screamed the fact that she was a different life form. "Cease, Ludan!" she ordered with great command. "Release!"

The plant angrily groaned and begrudgingly followed her command, throwing Marcus with great force to the ground.

The impact of the ground rattled Marcus' bones, who nevertheless was grateful for the long overdue huge gasp of air that never felt so sweet to his lungs. He coughed violently and attempted to catch up with replenishing the oxygen in his lungs while ignoring the excruciating pain his entire body possessed.

The mysterious alien woman, ever so composed, stormed towards the giant plant to conclude her orders. "Now away with you, Ludan. Away with you and to your belongings."

The plant followed her order and groaned loudly before making its way back to its original spot and mutating quickly to its previous form.

Marcus, still on his hands and knees, gazed up with blurriness in his vision at the woman, who made her way towards him with long jet-black hair flowing in the wind.

She arrived at his side and bent down, placing her right hand on his shoulder as he continued to labor in his breathing.

"Are you stable?" she asked, her hazel-colored eyes glimmering upon her question.

"S--stable?" inquired Marcus in between heavy breathing. "If--you're asking—-if--I'm alright, then--yes."

"I am grateful for this news. Thankfully, you are stable."

"I--suppose. At least--you speak--some form of English."

The woman was confused by his statement. "What is this English?"

"Never--mind. Who--are you?"

"I am named Samia. And what are you named?"

He took an extra long breath before finally answering. "Com-mander--Ronnie Marcus."

"It is of great pleasure, Commander Ronnie Marcus."

The air freshly traveled through his lungs and he could feel his respiratory system begin to normalize out. "No, no--you can just call me Marcus."

"Very well, Marcus," she stated, attempting to help him up but only to be rebuked for her effort. "Thankfully, I arrived on point. It was of preparation of Ludan to expire you."

He made his back onto his feet and began to dust himself off before rubbing his irritated neck full of cuts.

"If you mean that thing was about to kill me, I had a plan to escape," Marcus sheepishly said in a state of denial. "But thank you for your help, nonetheless."

Samia, despite being of a different species, smirked at the commander's false bravado while Monica and Jacobs finally made their way up from the ground and began to nurse their own aches.

"What in the world was that thing, anyways?" Marcus asked Samia.

"He is named Ludan. He is of the sweet nature and is the permanent keeper of this sector."

"Well, whatever it was, it's got to work on that temper. That thing could kill somebody."

Marcus stopped rubbing his neck and began to tend to his lower back before gazing over at Monica and Jacobs, who continued to wince in pain.

"Are you both okay?" he asked them both, even though he selfishly only cared for Monica's current state.

"Fine," Jacobs reported to him while Monica only nodded her head to answer. "Much better now that we know that you're alright."

Monica turned her head and stared at Samia, who genuinely appeared concerned about the state of her new acquaintances, sensing the genuine nature of her actions.

"Thank you for helping us," Monica said to her with great appreciation.

"It is my duty," replied Samia plainly. "You all appear to be of injured nature. I request your following to my habitation for tending."

Marcus immediately tried to rise to his feet but stumbled back onto his knees, his ego taking the greatest hit this time despite his hard-headed nature.

"No--that's okay," he said, his hardheadedness shining through. "Really, we'll all be okay."

"You are bloodied," Samia calmly stated to him. "And not to attempt to terrify, but the leaves of Ludan contain poisonous nature, and you are in need of the anecdote for it."

Poison? Just keeps getting better, doesn't it?

"With all due respect, she's right that you need assistance for your cuts, Commander," interjected Jacobs. "We still have plenty of time before dusk, and honestly, I think we could all use some therapy for our aches and pains after what we just went through."

Marcus delivered a what-do-you-think-you're-doing kind of glare for her statement. While he indeed felt unwell after his near-death experience with the sewlet and could easily peg it as the responsibility of the poison, he felt compelled to move on and was skeptical of receiving help from another being, let alone an alien of stranger status, when it came to his health.

He didn't like the idea of having an unknown source, albeit it came in the form of a dashingly beautiful young alien woman treating him for his wounds, even if she saved the life of himself and the crew. And he still didn't like the fact that the planet they were on seemed so perfect and beautiful, even after his horrific encounter with Ludan.

Something surely had to give, at least in his mind. Everything around them was so lush, so clean, and so gorgeous, almost like a dream.

It seemed so perfect. In fact, almost too perfect to be true, or so he thought.

"Sir?" asked Jacobs, noticing that her commander seemed to be off in another world momentarily.

He broke away from his daydream and continued to tend to his ailing neck, realizing that it was time to make an executive decision. "I suppose you're right," Marcus reluctantly obliged Jacobs before turning his attention to his new extraterrestrial friend. "We will take you on your offer, then."

"Understood," replied Samia mechanically as she nodded her head in acknowledgment. "Travel with me."

Marcus held up his hand to signal the ladies to stop as the thought of the MIA Arraz crossed his mind. "Pardon me, but before we go, I wanted to know if you had seen any more of us around here recently? There is a lanky young man with dark curly hair who broke away from our group a while ago, and I wanted to know if you possibly had seen him?"

Samia was confused by the question, as she did not quite comprehend what he was saying.

"About this tall?" he asked secondarily, hovering his hand upwards to the level of his eyes.

"My apologies, but I do not recall encountering a being such as that."

The commander cursed under his breath upon her confirmation. "I see. Have you seen any other beings such as us from Earth on your planet?"

"Negative. My pardons, but do I am of the assumption that you are from the Earth planet?"

"You guessed right, but how did you know that?"

Samia's eyes widened upon his answer and curiously shifted instantly to a lighter hazel color. She appeared as if she had been given great news based on the emotion on her face of excitement.

"It--was a guess of educational proportions."

Marcus' eyebrows rose up out of puzzlement at her reaction. Jacobs and Monica shared the same appearance as their commander while they themselves attempted to figure out what was going on with the young extraterrestrial.

"Are you alright?" asked Marcus to the statuesque Samia, who stood frozen in her spot.

"My pardons. It—-has been of great personal curiosity that my being has possessed about Earth inhabitants and whether your beings were of fictionalized nature. Our people have shared many myths of your kind, and it is of non-believable proportions that you are present."

"Well, believe it, sister," Marcus responded as his neck began to itch. It took everything inside of him not to scratch away the contaminated flesh, which felt like his neck was being carved into maliciously.

An odd purple hue began to flourish on the infected area of his skins as he gritted his teeth in attempt to get through the now unbearable torture he felt.

"Oh my God, Commander," Monica yelped in despair with a wide-eyes appearance. "What's happening?"

"Nothing--I'm fine," slowly answered Marcus in a futile attempt to ignore the torturous itching that began to engulf his upper chest. "I'm--"

A dire feeling suddenly engulfed his inner body. Pitch-black curtains came over his eyesight as he suddenly felt his body begin to give out.

"Commander!" Monica and Jacobs screamed in unison before running to Marcus, who crashed to the ground.

The ladies' passionate yells and screams started to become more muffled and muted as Marcus' heart rate slowed to a fatal crawl before he faded away into internal darkness.

CHAPTER 13

"--mander? Com--man--der?"

A woman's voice began to echo in the distance and rang through Marcus' ears, darkness covering his sight as he was unable to find the exact source.

Suddenly, his eyesight returned, and he found himself alone on a ledge, his mind now curious about where he was and how he had gotten there.

A circular platform a few yards south of where he was appeared like a mirage before him, and much to his horror, he found his crew tied up helplessly to imposing, frightening statues.

His eyes grew larger upon the sight of Maxwell, who stood freely with his hands behind his back and his chest puffed out proudly, the blue irises in his eyes now replaced with a frightening fiery orange of madness.

Anger immediately filled Marcus' heart, and his bitter feelings only swelled upon the sight of Maxwell beginning to torture the helpless crew, who were left with no other options than to face the brutal abuse of their monstrous captain.

The captain first made his way to Byers, who was unwilling to show his fear to the wickedly grinning Maxwell before spitting on his superior's boot. Maxwell's evil smile remained, despite the gesture, as he delivered a haymaker punch straight to the lieutenant's gut and followed it up with an uppercut below his bloodied chin.

Marcus felt a grueling pain in his own gut and chin upon the blows given to Byers while the taste of blood began to come across his palate.

Damn, why did that hurt me so bad?

Maxwell manically laughed upon the pitiful sight of Byers, who wiggled uncomfortably in discomfort from the body shots he had taken.

"Com—-man--der?" the female voice called once again in a muffled tone.

Marcus gazed around and tried to identify the source once again but was still unable to do so.

He grimaced upon recovering from watching and experiencing the hit given to Byers and, strangely, himself before quickly hopping down from his area and towards the platform of torture.

Maxwell smacked his lips before making his way to his next victim, Jacobs. He leaned close to her face and whispered something unpleasant into her ear based the look of disgust across her face.

Marcus, his gaze locked upon that of his neglected navigator and the abusive captain, continued on his descent to attempt to save his crew, but in the meanwhile, had no other option but to watch as Maxwell rubbed the right side of Jacobs' bruised face before unleashing a thunderous slap upon it.

A stinging hurt came across Marcus' cheek simultaneously with the hit that had been delivered to Jacobs. It was at that moment that he realized what was going on.

Dear God, I can feel their pain.

Hysterical laughter filled the air once again from Maxwell while tears streamed down Jacobs' face out of pain and humiliation. Marcus attempted to yell at his commanding officer as he had gotten closer, but nothing came out.

What in the hell?

"Com--mander?" summoned the woman's voice yet again in a clearer but echoed tone.

Maxwell's wicked grin curled into a smile of sheer delight as he began to creep towards Monica, whose usual luminous smile had been replaced by a frown of fear and despair in anticipation of her own punishment. A stream of blood adorned her lip, which further exploded the anger that resonated inside Marcus.

The commander once more attempted to scream to derail his captain from doing further damage, but his effort was to no avail as he was again unable to produce a sound.

I've got to hurry!

Marcus reached the bottom of the slope and was prepared to run onto the platform before being met, to his surprise, by a short rock bridge as his final obstacle.

Unfortunately for him, the bridge suddenly collapsed before he could begin to make his way across, leaving him stranded on the other side helplessly as the pieces of stone fell freely towards a large pit of red molten lava that stewed below.

Nerves began to hit Marcus, who realized that his task had become all the more difficult.

You've got to be kidding me.

A loud scream grabbed his attention instantly as Maxwell grabbed Monica by the neck and put a vice-like squeeze on her.

A lack of oxygen came over both Marcus, who began to now feel her pain and struggled to gain the air that both he and she needed for survival.

Maxwell turned his attention to Marcus and released the pressure from her before taking his thumb and caressing Monica's lips to further frustrate his sitting duck commander.

"She's beautiful, isn't she?" Maxwell yelled to Marcus. "Perhaps I should show you how beautiful I think she is."

The soulless captain swooped in towards her face and began to kiss her lips, sending Marcus' blood pressure to its maximum. It certainly didn't help that Marcus could also feel the kiss that was being forcefully planted, and he could sense his desire to kill increase rapidly by the second.

Maxwell stopped for a moment and intently stared back at Marcus with a toxic smirk.

"C'mon, boy," growled the captain as he began to tighten his grip on Monica's neck once more, closing off the airways for both Marcus and herself again. "Surely you won't let this happen to your precious love, will you?"

Marcus choked aloud and gazed at Monica, whose lips quivered in pain and fear as she looked at him in a plea for help. He could feel his emotions getting the best of him, and suddenly, the pit of lava before him did not appear to be as daunting as a matter of moments prior.

Marcus took a step back as he could no longer take the physical and emotional torture he had endured. He was going to jump and try to detour Maxwell from inflicting any further pain to himself, to the others, and especially to Monica, even if it killed him in the process.

"Com--mander?" the voice once again floated, now sounding slightly closer. It sounded almost like Monica, although he did not see her lips moving to call to him.

He took a few more steps backward and took one more glance at the obstacle, which spewed an orange flame from its opening to give Marcus a moment to pause and ponder his strategy even further.

Beads of sweat began to run down Marcus' forehead from the extreme heat of the lava. As hot as it was, however, he knew that a much more unbearable heat awaited him if he fell short of completing the jump.

Maxwell manically cackled uncontrollably before further tightening his grip even more on Monica's neck, who could feel the need for air become even more urgent.

Marcus, feeling the same as her, could feel he was almost out of time himself as he dashed towards the pit and leapt at its lip, floating towards the platform and standing lusciously before him.

Momentum was with him on his jump, and it appeared that Marcus was well on his way to reaching the other side successfully until a gigantic flame came out of nowhere and began to engulf his body.

His composure lost, he hit the edge of the platform and began to freefall down towards the lake of lava that awaited him as the ultimate punishment for his unsuccessful attempt.

Maxwell, who watched the entire incident, chuckled upon his shortcoming and impending death, his laugh bellowing throughout while his commander's skin began to deteriorate from his burning body.

"Commander?" the voice called again to him, suddenly much more clearly.

Marcus burned beyond recognition from the flame, felt the heat from the lava intensify even greater as he prepared to splash into the fiery substance and melt away instantly.

"Commander?"

He closed his eyes and prepared his best for the impending death that awaited him momentarily.

"Commander?"

Suddenly, Marcus opened his eyes and awoke drenched in sweat on a stone table, his vision blurry and unable to identify the figures that stood above him.

"Commander?" a familiar voice asked. "Commander, can you hear me?"

He gasped for air through labored breathing, his heart racing from the frightening nightmare he had just endured, and took a long moment before finally responding to the sweet voice that had been calling him.

"Mon--Monica?"

"Yes, sir," Monica responded warmly with a smile. "It's me."

Marcus exhaled deeply and began to rub the top of his forehead, a headache ringing through his brain. "Where—-am I?"

"You are in my lair," replied the voice of Samia. "You were altered due to the poison in your being."

Marcus tried to nod his head but could not get the strength to move it. "I see. Does that explain the gnarly nightmare I just had?"

"Correct. Hallucinations are common with the injection of poison in a being. The antidote was placed in your being to maintain a stable being."

Marcus feebly began to move and caressed his neck, which suddenly felt clean and free of the cuts he had prior to blacking out.

"The antidote also remedied your injuries," Samia further explained. "What is your state of stability?"

The commander batted his eyes rapidly out of confusion. He continued to have a hard time with Samia's usage of language but felt thankful that he could at least somewhat understand her.

"If you mean how I'm feeling, then the answer's great," Marcus answered quietly, his vision still slightly blurry while he tried to gaze into the glistening eyes of his alien nurse. "I feel tired, but overall, great, thank you."

"Positive. It will be of moments that you return to pure stability."

Marcus turned his head to the left and gazed at Monica, who, even in his altered state of vision, appeared relieved and happy to see he had regained consciousness. He struggled to use his facial muscles still to smile at her, although the joy filling his heart upon the sight of her suggested otherwise.

He felt ecstatic to see her, and the smile on her face let him know she felt the same way.

"I'm so glad you're okay," Monica stated, her eyes reddened by the tears that had filled her eyes upon his awakening.

"Me too," he said quietly in agreement, happy to see her beauty. "Where's Jacobs?"

"She's outside, keeping an eye out for Arraz. We still haven't found him, and there's been no trace of him, Commander. I'm beginning to worry."

He smacked his lips as the numbing in his face began to alleviate. "Don't worry, he should be alright. We'll begin to look for him in a few minutes."

"It will not be of necessity," Samia chimed in. "Our beings have begun to look for your friend. It is of suggestion that your beings rest."

"Are you sure about that?" asked Monica. "We don't mind, really."

"No, it would be unwise. Your unfamiliarity with our land contains fatal potential. We will find him on your behalf."

As crazy as it drove him to acknowledge what Samia had told him, he knew deep down internally that she was correct.

"I suppose," he stated in agreement against his will, his experience with Ludan still resonating through his mind and helping to shift his mentality. He gritted his teeth and felt the need to try to get up as the restlessness began to eat him up inside.

His back began to hurt from the stone material he laid on,, and he cringed while he slowly began to elevate himself from his uncomfortable surroundings.

"There are more of us, however," he continued, nursing his backside after completing his sluggish rise from the uncomfortable table. "So, if you're going to find our lieutenant, I would kindly ask that you attempt to find the rest of my crew as well."

"Of most certainty," Samia said, nodding her head in acknowledgment. "I will make it of vital request."

Marcus turned his attention to the open window in Samia's home and watched the sun, which began to set over a lush green hill to the east. "Appreciate it."

How interesting. The sun sets in the east here.

The sunset was beautiful, unlike anything he had ever seen back home on Earth. A glowing tangerine-colored hue radiated from the bright matter and flickered in his eyes.

Wow, a sun without the pollution and ashes to distort its appearance. Who would have ever imagined?

"Something the matter?" asked Samia to the mentally lost Marcus.

The sunlight warmed his dark irises and brought a warm feeling to his battered and beaten soul and body. "It's just so--different. I mean, it's so similar, but so different from ours back home."

Marcus could feel Samia's glowing eyes continue to stare at him from behind, the cutting feeling he felt in the rear of his skull being the tell-tale sign. He wasn't sure if she was attracted to him or not, but regardless, her stare and, most importantly, her beauty were enough to grab every fiber of attention that any man could possibly contain.

Marcus turned back and saw Monica cornered in the room, a strange look on her face as she turned away, almost as if she was trying not to pay attention to what was going on.

Oh, damn.

He began to worry that perhaps Monica would get the wrong idea from what she had just seen, and that was definitely the last thing that he wanted. As attractive and beautiful as Samia was, his heart secretly only belonged to Monica.

Then again, he still wasn't sure if she felt the same, and all he could do was hope until the right opportunity presented itself.

I wish I could just reassure her right now and show her how I really feel.

Monica walked through the open door and went outside to Samia's loft area, which overlooked the jungle they had just traveled through. A slight breeze made its way through the branches that gently swayed to-and-fro.

She placed her hands on a rock-like banister and gazed at the lush scenery, the sun giving an orange tint to her dark hair, which flowed gracefully in the wind.

She looks so beautiful.

Suddenly, before he could even approach her, his train of thought was interrupted by the presence of a young man who walked through the front area with great hostility.

"What is this meaning?"

Monica quickly turned her attention back inward, her eyes

expanding in size from fright. Marcus stepped closer to her, his internal instincts telling him that danger was possibly around the corner.

The man appeared to be in his early twenties, despite a thick dark beard that plastered his jaw. Long, wavy black hair came to his shoulders but did nothing to hide the menacing scowl etched upon his face. He was well built and chiseled like a sculpture, his arm muscles flexing as a means of intimidation to the strangers he had encountered.

"I have asked, what is this meaning?" questioned the man once again angrily, his attention now solely on the strange man he saw before him, violence clearly on his mind. "Speak now!"

Marcus could no longer hold his tongue as his backbone began to bristle in irritation. "I don't you an explanation, so calm your ass down."

Fire burned in the man's eyes from Marcus' response. "Regrets will come your way for your foolishness."

He made a giant leap towards Marcus but was immediately blockaded out of nowhere by Samia, who saved further damage from being inflicted onto the battered commander. "No! You will leave them be."

The man's anger only increased as he pointed towards the two Earthlings. "What is the meaning?" the man barked to her in question. "It is a requirement for an explanation."

"My pardons. I was unable to discuss this matter with you internally. I apologize for this occurrence, Father."

Marcus' and Monica's eyes grew in disbelief over the last word that left her mouth.

"Father?" asked Marcus, surprised in his voice, to the alien woman. "You mean to tell me that this buffoon is your father?"

"That is precise," her father responded with sheer anger still lingering in his voice. "I am most unhappy of this situation."

The youthful father stepped back and exhaled deeply, his blood pressure beginning to decrease. "And what is the name that belongs to you, foreigner?" he asked the commander.

"Marcus," was the response of the Earthman. "Commander Ronnie Marcus from SAGE, to be exact. And you are?"

"I am named Taark," said the father in a monotone fashion.

"Pleasure to meet you," Marcus stated sarcastically. "And this is Monica Brackenridge, a member of my crew."

Taark nodded in acknowledgment and gently stepped towards her. He smiled before stopping in front of her, picking up her right hand and kissing it in the act of welcoming, her surprise more than apparent from the alien man's ,completely charming turnaround.

"It is of great apologies for my behavior towards a being of such beauty," he smoothly told Monica. "It is my hope that I have not caused personal anguish."

Marcus was shocked by Taark's sudden attitude change as well but was happy nonetheless that he was not ripped into bits by the sturdily built extraterrestrial man.

Still, there was one part that greatly bothered Marcus.

He got to kiss a part of her body before I ever did. Unreal.

"Apology accepted," Monica calmly stated, her smile returning from the chivalry that he had exhibited to her.

The blood in Marcus' veins began to boil slightly out of jealousy.

He'd better not try anything funny with her, or I'll—-I'll--oh, forget it, who am I kidding? He'd probably rip the flesh off my bones and make a meal out of me. I just better hope he doesn't try to make a move on her.

Taark's smile faded quickly upon his gaze, fixating back onto Marcus, who glared back at him out of manly pride.

"We will discuss more at a future moment, Marcus," instructed Taark unemotionally. "I must talk internally with my daughter."

Samia appeared worried as she made her way towards the open door to walk out of her home and prepare herself for a most uncomfortable father-daughter discussion.

"Until our paths cross once more," concluded Taark, who

pedaled backwards towards the doorless exit, his stare fixated on Marcus until he turned around to make his way out.

He met his daughter outside their home and began to have an animated discussion with her, anger clearly oozing from his screaming voice and physical motions.

Marcus shook his head in bewilderment, amazed about what had just transpired with Taark and what had gotten him so angry. He especially couldn't get over the fact that Samia's dad appeared to be just as old as her and appeared as though they could have been siblings instead.

"Incredible," Monica stated while she observed the youthful appearances of both Taark and Samia. "I can't believe how young her father looks especially. We might even look older than him."

"Yeah," said Marcus out of agreement as he watched Taark storm away from Samia, who began to wallow in self-pity out of disappointing her father. "Maybe I should ask him who his plastic surgeon is."

Monica said nothing but smirked as he provided some brief comic relief to the presently tense moment.

Samia dawdled her way back into her home, her low-hanging head suggesting that she had just been scolded like a child. She paused before Monica and Marcus before wiping a tear from her eye.

"Apologies," she murmured out. "Father thought it inappropriate I did not discuss with him primarily of your arrivals. It did not assist matters that you are a foreign male being, Commander."

He knew it wasn't his fault, but the commander couldn't help but to feel somewhat responsible for what had transpired. "I'm sorry. We definitely did not want to get you in trouble, Samia. Especially with your--"

He paused for a moment, his mind still in disbelief over what he had witnessed. "—-father."

She raised her head in an attempt to brighten the spirits of them all. "Things will normalize," she said in an attempt to ignore the elephant in the room.

Marcus curiously observed her emotions and was fascinated by how human-like Samia truly was, especially in a moment of vulnerability. As much as he knew nothing about her species, he couldn't help but be amazed with her commonality with emotions.

"It is my suggestion to take advantage and rest," continued Samia. "My brother and some of our people are searching for your friend, so let your worries ease. Accept my pardon, for I must make myself momentarily absent."

Samia's eyes watered before she made her way to her personal quarters. Sadness began to overwhelm her once more, and Marcus couldn't help but wonder if her father had said something hurtful or if she was very sensitive.

An alien with human emotions. Now I've really seen it all.

Marcus scratched his chin out of thought. "It's sad, isn't it?" he asked to Monica, only to turn around and realize that she was nowhere to be found.

Where did she go?

He gazed towards the loft area and saw Monica standing there once again, her eyes fixated upon the now purple and orange swirl that occupied the sky. A refreshing breeze sailed through the air and swept through her shoulder-length hair, creating a further glamorous effect.

Marcus' attention fixated solely on her as he sensed a golden opportunity had presented itself.

This is it. This is the opportunity you've been waiting for.

He turned his head and checked around him to double-check that they were indeed alone.

It was quiet all around, almost like the moment had been perfectly scripted that way. Marcus was not going to complain, especially since he didn't have to worry about feeling the watchful eyes of his micro-managing captain, or anybody else for that matter.

Go for it.

He made his way towards the loft, his nerves beginning to set in, but his heart determined this time not to lead him astray as he set out on his personal journey of love.

CHAPTER 14

Marcus stepped onto the loft and behind the unaware Monica, whose eyes still gazed upon the gorgeous green paradise before her.

He could feel his palms begin to sweat as his nerves filtered throughout his body from head to toe. He felt warm and tingly, and he could feel the air he breathed in begin to feel heavier.

As much as he wanted to chicken out, he knew that he couldn't let this opportunity pass, especially with the rare chance of having nobody else around of any significance.

C'mon, man. This is your time to shine.

He began to think about what to say and what would be the perfect way to start the conversation with Monica, which he hoped would be eventful, although at the moment, he admittedly had nothing in mind.

Marcus said nothing and continued to stand behind her as her hair continued to sway gently in the breeze, an imaginative lump in his throat feeling as if it had swollen to the size of a watermelon.

She continued to be unaware of his presence behind her as she leaned against the stone railing and rested her arms to further take in the scenery.

What do I say? C'mon, say something.

He gulped heavily, his lips beginning to move as he uttered the first thing that came to his mind.

"It's beautiful out here, isn't it?"

There you go, buddy. Well done.

Monica turned her head and turned on a welcoming smile that sent a tingle down his spine. "Yes, it is, Commander," she said in agreement, her eyes glowing as warmly as ever. "Would you like to join me?"

Hell yes, I do.

"I would love to," he said to her gently, a giddiness running through him upon realizing that he had passed through his first personal obstacle.

Marcus slid to her left and joined her in leaning against the railing. He wanted to pinch himself since it didn't seem real that they were actually sharing a moment together. If this particular moment had been a dream, he did not want to wake up anytime soon, and he could only hope that what he was experiencing was indeed real.

"It's so gorgeous here," Monica said to him, her eyes brimming with happiness to match her smile. "Almost like something out of a dream."

"Yeah, it is," he stated in agreement, feeling like he wanted to brighten the mood a bit with some corny humor. "Besides the sewlet back there that tried to kill me, it's not too bad here, I guess."

She giggled loudly, picking up strongly on his intention. "That was really scary. I'm glad you can at least see some humor in it. But seriously, I'm so relieved that you are okay. I was worried about you, especially after you passed out."

Monica's concern blossomed with great satisfaction inside of Marcus. It made him feel good to know she was worried about his well-being, and he couldn't help but to beam externally and be unconcerned for the moment for showing his happiness to her.

"I'm glad to know you thought about me," said Marcus half-jokingly. "I'm not going to lie, I wasn't sure there for a moment if I was going to make it."

"Well, at least we don't have to worry about that, Commander," Monica stated, as her smile quickly faded. "Speaking of worrying, I feel so concerned about Arraz. I mean, he's out there on foreign land, and he's lost. I just hope he's okay."

"Don't worry, I'm sure he's fine. I wouldn't be surprised if we see him brought here shortly. Or knowing him, he may end up scrounging upon this place by accident at any moment."

"I hope you're right."

"Yeah, me too," he stated, downtrodden, concerned himself but also feeling his opportunity beginning to slip a tad.

"Can I ask you a question, Commander?" she sweetly asked, making the hair on the back of his neck bristle up.

Marcus began to wonder what the question was going to be.

Is she going to ask me how I feel about her? Or what if she asks me out? That would be embarrassing.

He began to drive himself crazy, wondering what her question could possibly be, although the warm and inviting look never vanished from her eyes.

What's she going to ask me?

"I've wanted to ask you this for a while," she began, "but I honestly haven't known how to, so here goes--"

This is it.

"--is it just me, or did you notice this planet mysteriously appear in space before we landed?"

That was not what I expected, but I'm glad somebody finally noticed!

Marcus picked his internal composure back up as the anticipation of her question came and went without impact. As relieved as he felt that she didn't ask him something about his or her feelings, he also felt disappointed that the moment he had anticipated still hadn't come to fruition.

Then again, he also felt a sense of relief, knowing that he hadn't gone crazy earlier on the ship and that he wasn't the only one who had noticed how the planet appeared out of thin air.

"I absolutely did," he stated. "I'm glad you brought it up because for a while there, I thought nobody else noticed it besides me. It's been driving me crazy for some time now."

She exhaled out of relief as her smile returned to her lips. "Me too. Thank goodness somebody else noticed it, and I thought I was honestly about to lose my mind over that."

"Well, I'm glad to know we both haven't," said a chuckling Marcus as his stare turned away from the scenery and solely on her.

"Yeah, me too," she stated in agreement while sharing in his laughter.

Their warm and gentle chuckling went on for a few moments, Marcus' stare never neglecting her throughout. She was so beautiful to him, and her warm personality certainly didn't hurt as the moment began to take a somewhat intimate turn, at least in his heart.

"I've been wondering, Commander," she suddenly said out of nowhere while turning off her smile. "Between you and I, there's something I've wanted to seriously discuss with you."

Oh God, could this be it?

Marcus paused in silence and attempted to hide his ever-so-rapidly-growing nerves. "What--is it, Monica?"

"Well, I'm not sure how comfortable you are telling me this, but I really want to know, so here goes—-"

This is it.

"--I'm sorry, but I'm not even sure how to ask this, so I'll try my best--"

Here it comes.

"--do you think that Captain Maxwell is beginning to go crazy?"

No, never mind.

Marcus was relieved yet disappointed yet again by her question. He began to question internally if she felt the same way about him that he did for her. They had been standing on the loft, watching as the sky began to change colors and get darker, yet no action or any sign of movement had taken place like he had hoped.

But then again, he himself hadn't made any sort of move as he had planned, so who was he to wonder about her when he hadn't done as he had promised to himself?

Maybe it's just time to temper my expectations a bit. Or maybe it's time to actually man up and do something about it.

Monica continued to stand by the railing, her eyes fixated while she waited for his response.

Marcus gazed back at her, appearing confused as he tried to answer her question to the best of his ability while not looking disappointed with how his opportunity began to fade, at least in his mind.

"Well," he began to answer while turning his attention away from her and towards the sky that had morphed into a darker shade of night-themed purple.

He stopped for a moment and was interrupted in his mind by Maxwell's words. He wanted to tell Monica the truth about their captain, and he felt a closeness to her that gave him the internal green light to tell her the truth.

A loud exhale came before he prepared to spill out what he knew. "Monica, I'm going to tell you something that I haven't shared with anybody else."

"What is it, Commander?"

Marcus could hear Maxwell's warning echoing through his mind once more as a final warning, but he couldn't have given a damn any more than he felt at that moment.

His captain wasn't there to order him around, and he felt like he had to tell somebody what Maxwell had told him, so in his mind, it only made sense to tell the woman he felt strongly for, even if they didn't exactly have the most established of relationships as of yet.

And he knew Byers, his friend since childhood, may be upset if he found out he wasn't told first.

He'll just have to get over it.

He exhaled deeply once more, a feeling coming over him that the world was finally beginning to ease off of his shoulders.

"Maxwell told me that this was going to be his last mission yesterday while I was in his quarters," he began to spew out. "He said that he was having personal problems with his family and was going to step down immediately at the conclusion of this mission."

Her jaw dropped quickly in surprise. "Wow," she responded while shock ricocheted throughout her internal organs. "I can't believe it. I don't even know what to say."

"I know, I was surprised myself. I have to admit, I was shocked, yet selfishly happy. I have to admit, at the same time, that he was going to be stepping down."

"Can I tell you something, Commander?" she asked once more before nudging closer to him as if she were going to whisper to him her own secret.

If you get that close, you can tell me anything.

"What is it?" he questioned back in a playful tone.

She took her index finger and motioned for him to get closer, a shy smirk on her face as if she were going to tell him something naughty.

"I'm really pleasantly surprised to hear that too," she whispered to him softly as if she were telling him a dirty secret. "Because that means that you'll be our captain, and I like the sound of that."

Marcus beamed upon her words. It made him feel special to hear her say that, while the warmness in his heart helped to confirm his feelings.

There was a sudden closeness to her that he had never felt before, the kind of feeling that he could only have imagined up to that point.

"I don't know about that," he humbly stated, "but I'm glad to know you feel that way, Miss Monica."

"I really do mean it. You would be a great captain, Commander."

"Thank you. But please, call me Ronnie."

She felt surprised by his request. "Are you sure that's not too informal? I mean, you are my superior, and I don't want to be disrespectful to you."

"No, I insist. I think we're past that now, Monica."

"Very well then--Ronnie," she stated slowly while shyly smiling out of embarrassment by calling him by his actual first name instead of his rank like she had been accustomed to.

A wide grin came across his face overhearing her call him by his real name. It was as if she were his actual friend and not merely an acquaintance like they were forced to be while on duty, and he suddenly felt a closeness to her that he had never felt before.

If this is a dream, I hope that I never wake up.

"So, Ronnie," started Monica, still getting over calling him by his first name while she prepared herself to inquire further about her interested male friend. "Is there anyone special in your life?"

Oh my God, she's asking me the question. She's going to beat me to the punch.

Marcus pondered over the appropriate response to not give himself too much away.

"No, not right now," he answered, ignoring his internal requests to pour out his heart immediately. "I'm still living the good old bachelor life. What about you?"

"Not at the moment," she replied before leaning closer to him and bringing secretive joy to Marcus. "I do want to know, though, because I have noticed something that I've wanted to ask you about for some time."

Marcus could feel his heart drop to his feet, his assumptions beginning to dominate that she had figured out his mysterious secret.

It looks like the gig is up.

"Well, how do I say this other than—-"

Just be honest with her.

"—-do you like Jacobs?"

What?

His jaw drooped immediately from her question, and he immediately began to fear that she had gotten the wrong idea. "Like her? Like--you mean romantically?"

"I'm so sorry to ask," she quickly replied apologetically before staring out at the top of the trees that hung below her view in shame. "I know it's none of my business, and I apologize for even bringing it up because I know I shouldn't have. Just forget that I even asked, okay?"

Marcus shook his head and felt the need to urgently counsel her. "No, it's okay. To answer your question—-no, I don't. She's nice and all, but I can tell you honestly, I feel nothing for her like that."

That's because I feel that way for you. Tell her now! Say it!

Cowardice and nerves served as the greatest enemy, and Marcus was unable to say what he had thought about at that moment. He wanted to tell her so badly, but the words simply could not escape his internal chamber.

Damn it, anyway. C'mon!

"Oh, okay," she simply stated, a feeling of embarrassment still lingering. "I'm so sorry I asked again. I know it's none of my business."

"You don't have to apologize," he told her assuredly before turning the tables on her and motioning her closer to him. "In fact, if you want to know something else, Jacobs and Dr. Jennings like each other, but they both don't know it yet."

She turned her attention back to him and smiled again, her feeling of embarrassment suddenly morphing into curiosity. "Really? That's so cute. I think that they really would look good together. How did you find that out?"

"They both have told me. They just don't know how to tell the other one yet."

"How romantic," she purred in excitement. "I just love hearing those kinds of stories. Hopefully, they can find each other soon."

"Yeah, I guess we'll see what happens with those lovebirds."

Marcus gazed once more into her eyes as a connection he had never felt before crossed his mind and his heart. He felt as if he was actually one with her, and he couldn't help but grin from ear to ear as he focused attentively into her eyes and her into his.

A sudden inclination came over him to tell her his feelings, and the fear and nervousness that had always been present suddenly seemed to be missing. A confidence and swagger that he had never experienced came over him.

The moment had finally arrived, and Marcus felt more than prepared to let her know his true feelings about her.

"Monica?"

"Yes, Ronnie?" she replied, batting her long eyelashes at him.

Marcus took a moment to compose himself, his feelings for her flowing as strong as ever. He felt ready to spill his secret of his romantic feelings towards her but wanted to find the right words to tell her.

Marcus gulped before letting his words fall out one by one of his mouth.

"There's--something I've wanted to tell you now for some time. I--just haven't found the right words--to tell you."

He paused again to battle the nerves that messed with him and tried to get in his way.

"What is it, Ronnie?" Monica asked sweetly, her eyes and smile bringing a welcoming and relaxing feeling.

Marcus hesitated again to battle back against his nervousness. He was in love with her, and he wanted this to be the moment he professed his feelings for her.

Just tell her how you feel.

He opened his mouth and began to say whatever came out, trusting that his heart would not lead him astray.

"I've wanted to tell you for a while—-that—-I--"

Unfortunately for Marcus, he had taken too long to open up his heart to her.

"Commander?" came Samia's sudden voice.

Marcus closed his eyes in frustration upon realizing that he had blown his chance.

No!

"My pardons for my interruption," Samia apologized to them both. "It is of utmost importance to inform that your navigator has returned with your friends."

Marcus felt almost ready to cry from the disappointment but did his best to carry on and not let it show. "That's--great, thank you."

A heavy bitterness swelled in his heart, but nonetheless, he was aware that he had a job to do.

"By friends, who do you mean?" Marcus asked.

"It is not of certainty," answered Samia. "Your navigator has stated it to be the 'rest of your crew' if it is to contain familiarity."

"Yes, I know who they are now," he replied, disappointment still resonating in his voice. "We will be right there."

The alien woman grinned innocently upon his words and felt that she had accomplished a good deed despite the fact that she had unknowingly ruined a moment that Marcus had waited so long for.

"That is splendid," stated Samia. "They are awaiting your company in the middle of the habitation of our beings. Join with me."

"We're right behind you," he told her before turning his attention back to Monica. "I suppose we'll have to pick up where we left off at a later time, huh?"

Monica felt dejected herself that their great conversation had ended. "I suppose. I guess it's time to get back to work."

"Looks like it. C'mon, let's get on our way."

Marcus started to make his way back into Samia's home before he was interrupted by the sweet tone of Monica's voice.

"I look forward to talking to you again soon and to hearing what you were about to tell me, Ronnie."

He stopped in his tracks and turned back towards her at the opening to the home, grinning from ear to ear. "So do I, Monica."

Marcus said nothing more before motioning with his hand for her to follow him to the village. She followed his non-verbal order and came to his side, their smiles remaining bright and beaming while they headed towards the middle of the village to meet with the others.

CHAPTER 15

Marcus and Monica walked side by side as they exited Samia's home and saw the other half of their crew standing in the middle, confused by their exact whereabouts.

"Commander!" shouted Jacobs to get his attention.

She waved her hand up in the near darkness, her motion able to be seen thanks to her fair-colored skin tone.

Marcus took a moment and took a look around himself at the town he never got to see the first time around, thanks to his near-death experience, taking in what he had missed.

The village was small, and the four other adobe-looking buildings that accompanied Samia's home fit perfectly with the concept. There was no electricity of any sort to be noticed in the town, and only the flickers of a few lit torches and their burning embers provided a poor quality of lighting in the dark village.

The profiles of other residents of the eerily quiet town occupied the other homes, but Marcus could feel their stares of wonder cut through the curtain of darkness and onto the foreigners that had now clustered together in the middle.

He couldn't help but feel that he had been transported back in time. He had never been in a town with so few people, and he never had been anywhere that lacked any sort of electricity or organized lighting system.

His attention suddenly turned to a young couple outside of one of the homes who also age-wise appeared to be as youthful, if not more so, as Samia and her father.

This is so weird.

Marcus and Monica officially joined their crew, with Marcus, however, realizing they were still down a couple of men.

"Ronnie!" shouted Byers loudly to his friend.

"What's going on?" Marcus replied as he exchanged a quick fist pump with his buddy before turning to the rest of his crew. "I'm glad you guys are alright. But where's Maxwell?"

A rude shrug of the shoulders came from the lieutenant. "I don't know. And frankly, I don't care."

"What do you mean you don't know?" questioned Marcus in annoyance at Byers' carelessness. "You haven't seen either one of them?"

Frustrated with his friend's foolish behavior, Marcus turned his focus to both Rubidoux and Jennings for some sort of legitimate answer. "How long have you guys been on your own?"

"Basically, since we broke from the ship," Jennings responded. "We were walking through the forest, and the captain insisted that he was going to take the rear. We had gone on for a while before we noticed that we hadn't heard the captain say a word for a while. That was when Lieutenant Byers turned his head and noticed that the captain was missing. And he's been gone ever since."

Nervousness began to resonate in Marcus' bones. "I see," said Marcus before turning his focus back onto Byers. "What do you suspect happened to him, Tommy?"

"I dunno," Byers answered carelessly again, his focus entirely on the surroundings around him. "By the way, the nice hokey little town you found here. It's very charming."

Marcus had had enough of his friend's stupidity. "Cut it out,

I'm being serious. He could be in trouble out there, for Christ's sake."

"Relax," said Byers, who rolled his eyes out of his own feeling of annoyance. "I'm sure the old man is fine out there. We're in the middle of alien paradise, so I'm sure the worst that could happen would be that his salty behavior can be whisked away for a moment."

Byers' words did nothing to ease the tension felt between the two friends.

"Look," started Marcus firmly, "as difficult as he can be, he's still our captain, and we need to make sure that he's okay. Oh, and by the way, I was almost killed in this so-called paradise earlier, so I have reason to worry about him."

Byers folded his arms against his chest and rolled his eyes once more, shaking his head in disbelief over what Marcus had just said. Marcus glared back angrily at his friend and frowned at his childish behavior. As much as he hated the way Maxwell could be at times, he couldn't help but worry about his well-being, especially in the foreign land they found themselves engulfed in.

Marcus's latter statement was slid by everyone except for Rubidoux, whose concern rose dramatically.

"You almost died, Commander?" asked the caring rookie, his voice cracking as if he were still going through puberty. "Are you alright?"

"I'm fine, thanks for asking," Marcus answered his young navigator, glaring at Byers, who seemed distant and uncaring. "I just had an encounter with an alien plant, but I had some good people take care of me, thankfully."

Marcus turned his head towards Monica, who smiled in response to what he had just said. Byers caught the two of them exchanging glances and raised his right eyebrow in curiosity, wondering what exactly he had missed while he had been away.

"I'm glad you are okay, Commander," Jacobs genuinely stated. "We were very worried about you."

"Thank you, Jacobs," said Marcus. "And I appreciate your help as well."

Jacobs smiled in response while he nodded his head to her in a thankful motion.

The crew circled around Marcus to await their next instruction. That was, excluding Byers, who stood outside of it behind Rubidoux, protesting non-verbally against his best friend.

Anger flowed through Marcus for Byers' rebel behavior internally, but he did his best to ignore him and focus on the remainder of his crew in need of his command.

"We must turn our attention to finding Captain Maxwell," stated Marcus. "We're missing Arraz as well, so we must keep an eye out for the both of them."

"Wait--Arraz is missing too?" Jennings asked with great concern laced in his voice. "What happened to him?"

"He disappeared, kind of like how you described Maxwell did. It's strange because it seems that they both vanished nearly the same way."

"Yes, indeed," Byers said sarcastically with another roll of the eyes. "And, may I say, how astute of you to notice something such as that, Commander? You're a freaking genius."

Marcus gave a death glare to Byers, ready to give his friend a piece of his mind for his foolish and selfish behavior.

Before he could say a word, however, Samia interrupted him from beginning.

"My pardon, but perhaps I could get assistance to find your captain?"

The entire crew turned their attention to Samia, but none more closely than Byers, who quickly turned and stared in fascination at her beauty.

"No, that's okay, we--" started Marcus before he was interrupted mid-sentence.

"We--would love your help," Byers interrupted before rushing towards her. "Hello there, my name is Byers. Thomas Byers, to be exact."

"I am named Samia," she said to introduce herself, smiling widely upon his quick approach to her.

He smirked out of satisfaction before taking her hand and holding it into his. He bent his head forward and delivered a welcoming kiss to her taken limb that made the alien woman shudder in excitement.

"Charmed," he replied passionately. "That's a beautiful name you have--Samia. It rolls right off the tongue."

Marcus shook his head in disbelief over what he was seeing. First, he witnessed the disrespectful attitude of his friend in front of the crew, and now he had seen him make the moves in front of the rest of the crew on a woman who was a stranger and an extraterrestrial, nonetheless.

Samia definitely did not seem to mind, her symbols of giddiness overriding her. "I am thankful for your kind words. It is of great nature to acquaint with a being such as your being."

"I'm not sure what you said, but whatever it was, it's my pleasure," he said to her, mesmerized by her eyes and beauty.

The commander had seen enough as he stepped in between the new lovebirds to stop their inappropriate-for-the-moment activity.

"Okay, that's enough," he told them both firmly, trying to end the awkwardness the on-looking crew had to endure by grabbing Byers' arm and dragging him away. "Come on, Tom, we've got work to do. Romance can wait."

"Hey, what in the hell do you think you're doing?" asked Byers angrily before forcing his arm away from Marcus' grasp. "Get away from me!"

"We need to talk," Marcus commanded. "Right now."

He grabbed Byers' arm and forced his friend outside Samia's home to have a one-on-one discussion.

Samia's eyes never trailed as she watched her new knight in shining armor get taken away momentarily, a look of love and lust in her eyes.

Marcus stopped in front of her home and let go of Byers, whose smile had morphed into an ugly frown.

"What's your problem?" Byers asked with hostility. "You're embarrassing me."

"No, you're embarrassing yourself," answered Marcus. "What the hell's going with you?"

Byers turned his head away from his friend and stared towards the ground like a scolded child. "Nothing."

Frustration boiled over further for Marcus. "You're acting like a damn fool. What do you think you're doing making moves on a woman, and an alien one at that, in front of everyone, anyway? You need to remember that, especially on duty, you're the first lieutenant on this crew, and you need to set an example for the others."

Byers didn't take kindly to his friend and commander's words and delivered a freezing glare to him. "Don't talk to me like that. I'm a grown man, and I can do whatever the hell I want. And if I meet a beautiful woman, you'd better believe I'm stepping up to the plate, even if I'm on duty--sir."

"But there's a time and a place for that. Right now, especially, is not the time or the place, especially when we're on duty--Lieutenant."

The lieutenant shook his head and turned his focus onto the night sky once more. "Man, whatever. Now you're beginning to sound like Maxwell."

"What in the hell does that mean?"

Byers took his index finger and poked it roughly into Marcus' chest to further punctuate his answer. "It means that you're getting bossy and controlling, just like your mentor."

Marcus swatted away his friend's extended digit. "Don't go there. We may be friends, but this is business right now. When you're off duty, you can do whatever you want and be with whoever you want. But right now, we need to focus on finding our captain and our second lieutenant because we're on the clock, and it's time for you to step up to the plate and take your job seriously."

"Blah, blah, blah," mocked Byers with a roll of the eyes. "Why do you want to save Maxwell so badly, anyway? I mean, he's a grouchy old bastard who just gives us stress and nothing else besides that. You make it seem like we're saving your father, but we're just trying to save some old, worthless geezer."

Marcus' blood pressure further rose. "You just don't get it. Your biggest problem is that you're so damn selfish. You don't understand that, no matter whether it's Maxwell or whoever, there are two missing human beings out in the middle of an alien jungle desperately in need of our help. And for all we know, they may be in grave danger."

Byers placed his hands on his hips and gritted his teeth out of frustration, doing everything he could to stop himself from assaulting his commander.

"Are we done here?" he asked Marcus.

"Yeah, I guess so. You're lucky that you're my friend, and I'm giving you the benefit of the doubt."

Byers hissed upon Marcus' statement. "Yeah, some friend you are. Pardon me for not being grateful--Commander--but as far as I'm concerned, you can go to Hell because I don't need or want your help at all--"

He began to storm away before turning his head back to hurl a gnarly insult.

"--Commander Maxwell."

Byers gave one final glare before turning his head forward and making his way back towards the meeting in the courtyard of the village, where the crew became lost in their own conversation and had paid no mind to the happenings between the two friends.

Marcus exhaled deeply, anxiety running through his gut. He wasn't an overly confrontational person, especially with those he was close with, and he did his best not to ignore the insult that his own best friend had delivered to him, although his hurt feelings suggested otherwise.

What just happened?

Byers approached the group and immediately stopped once again at Samia, engaging immediately in a conversation against Marcus' orders.

The commander shook his head, realizing what his friend was up to. "Great," he muttered to himself. "Things just keep looking up."

He took one last long exhale before beginning the seemingly long journey back to the group, who began to turn their attention back to their insubordinate commander.

What in the hell am I going to do with him?

His downtrodden mood was apparent as he rejoined the crew and prepared to give instructions.

Byers, meanwhile, was preoccupied with Samia and offered not even a glance upon the commander's return.

"I apologize, everyone," Marcus said. "But we can now begin the process of how we will divide up to find both Maxwell and Arraz."

"My pardons, Commander," Samia interrupted. "But, it is now darkened all around, and perhaps not logical for your beings to be present in the external environment. My brother and father are searching, and as are more of our people, so it is perhaps best that your beings rest in my home until it has lightened outside."

Byers nodded his head in agreement, spite towards Marcus fueling his behavior. "What a fantastic idea. That sounds perfectly logical to me."

He turned to Marcus, who glared back and realized that Byers was trying to make him look like a fool.

"Doesn't that seem logical to you, Commander?" Byers sarcastically asked him.

Marcus said nothing and folded his arms, his frustration with his lieutenant and friend now becoming overly obvious.

Nobody realized that more than Byers, who grinned at seeing Marcus' seething anger.

"My apologies," he said, ignoring Marcus before turning his

attention back onto Samia. "Our commander can be quite rude sometimes. What he means to say is that you're exactly right, and we would all love to take you up on your offer."

Samia gazed at Marcus, who didn't care if she, or anybody else for that matter, saw how annoyed he had become with Byers.

"It will be quite alright," she said to try to reassure the commander. "My brother and the others are capable and will do everything to find your fellow beings."

"That's right," Byers said annoyingly. "Everything will be just fine."

To further put the cherry on top of his outlandish behavior, Byers took the hand of his new love interest and held it high in the air to prepare for their own departure. "Now, if you excuse us, I think it's time for us all to get our rest like the lady was saying. I wish you all adieu, Good Night, adios, and all of that good stuff."

He glared one final time at Marcus and smiled wickedly before giving his full attention to Samia. He held her hand tightly and smiled with his eyes at her before scurrying off with her back into the jungle.

Marcus watched as they disappeared into the darkness and out of sight. He felt like he wanted to hit something to take out his frustration, and he could only picture his fist going right in between the eyes of Byers, his friendship with him seeming more wobbly with every ticking second. As much as he felt compelled to yell and scream obscenities, he decided to bite his tongue from saying anything that would haunt him later.

"That was disrespectful," Jacobs chimed in, which completely softened the words that crossed through Marcus' mind.

"Yep," stated Marcus simply to avoid saying anything he would regret later.

Jacobs felt compelled to apologize for her lieutenant's actions. "I'm sorry, Commander. That was totally inappropriate on his part. If I had been you, I probably would have cleaned out his clock."

My thoughts exactly, Jacobs.

"Are you okay, Ronnie?" asked Monica, forgetting momentarily that they were no longer in a private conversation as she put her hand on his right shoulder. "I mean, Commander?"

Nobody paid any mind to her slip-up except for Marcus, who appreciated the mistake. He nodded his head, glad that nobody had caught on to what had just happened.

"Yeah, I'm fine," he responded, feeling himself calm down a tad with her touch. "Everything is fine."

"That took some good self control, sir," said the jittery Rubidoux. "That was pretty intense."

As nerve-stricken as he was, Rubidoux had a way of lighting up certain moments, even though it was completely unintentional. Perhaps it was his perceived innocence and virgin-like mentality. Or, maybe it was just how naïve he could be in certain situations without realizing it himself.

Regardless, Marcus couldn't help but chuckle on the inside at what his rookie navigator had just said to him.

"Thanks, Rube," Marcus simply said to him, saving him some embarrassment that surely would have come his way had Maxwell been present. "I appreciate that."

Rubidoux smirked nervously and unsurely, although he appreciated the kindness shown to him by his commander.

"What shall we do now, Commander?" asked Jennings curiously while scratching the top of his head.

"Well, as much as I hate to admit it, it appears as though our newly MIA lieutenant could be correct," Marcus answered. "It would be pointless for us to scavenge this jungle we're surrounded in, especially with how dark it is outside. As much as we need to find them, the last thing we need to do is put ourselves in any potential danger. I guess we'll have no choice but to put our trust in the hands of these alien beings, at least until the morning."

"Do you think they can be trusted, Commander?" Jennings directly inquired, much to Jacobs' agreement, who nodded her head.

The commander exhaled deeply upon Jennings' question and shrugged his shoulders.

"I don't know," he answered. "But at this moment, we may have no other option but to trust them. Let's just pray we don't regret it later."

Chapter 16

Byers continued to tightly hold the hand of his new lady friend as they beamed at one another like school children stricken with puppy love.

They stopped at a hill that overlooked the darkened region before he looked back at Samia and smiled, his hand now gripping hers tightly.

"Would you like to sit down?" he asked her politely.

"Of great certainty," she answered, grinning ear to ear.

They sat on the grass and took in the view, the blue moonlight bringing a tint to the land, especially the glimmering river before them.

"That's our ship out there," Byers stated, pointing to his oval shaped, ugly ship, which appeared to be the size of a baseball from their vantage point. "That's what brought us here to your planet."

"It appears to be incredible," said Samia out of wonder. "I have never seen such an object. You are saying that it travels in the air?"

"Yes, it does. We live there while we're on duty also."

"Interesting. You are saying that you make your home there?"

He enjoyed her company and found great pleasure and enjoyment in her innocence, smirking before he answered. "Yeah, I guess you could say that. It becomes like my home away from home, I suppose you could say."

He continued to smile before caressing her hand with his, a flirty notion in his gaze. She sheepishly smiled back at him, nervous from uncertainty but nonetheless enjoying the attention he was giving her.

"So, have you ever left this planet?" he asked.

"I'm not sure what you mean by planet, but if you are making reference to our land, then negative. It has been my habitation since my birthing day."

"I see," he responded with great intent, even if her different use of language confused him.

No matter, he thought. She could have spoken complete nonsense to him for all he cared, and it would have sounded just as beautiful.

He felt warm internally being with her, a feeling he had never felt before with a woman. It amazed him to feel this way and to feel so strongly about someone, especially considering how quickly they had met and gotten closer.

Samia gazed into the sky, getting lost in the bright stars and large moon that shone vividly. A look of wonder etched upon her face as her hand escaped his so she could wrap her arms around her legs while she sat.

Despite not touching her for the moment, Byers could only smirk at her wonder, and he felt so unusually glad to be a part of such a moment with a woman.

"What is the feeling you experience in that outside realm?" Samia asked. "Where my home ends and another begins?"

"If you mean by what it's like in space, it's glorious. Growing up, I never imagined being a part of something like this and getting to explore the galaxy. And now, the fact that I get to see different planets and galaxies can be kind of cool sometimes. It's definitely not like anything back on Earth, that's for sure."

"It is my understanding. What is the feeling of habitation on Earth? I imagine it is quite of the blissful nature."

Byers plucked a blade of grass, which felt silky smooth as he rubbed it in between his fingers. "No, not really. I mean, it's my home, and I love it for that reason. But, especially after seeing your planet, I realize how dumpy ours really is. We've done a great job of dirtying up the air and poisoning our oceans, that's for sure. It was beautiful, I'm sure, at one point, but not really as much anymore."

"Hmm," she could only say, confused by some of his words that were foreign to her. "My pardons, but it is of great importance to inquire--what is the definition of dumpy?"

He flicked the blade to the ground and chuckled at her question, amused by her non-understanding of his slang. "It means crappy--or, maybe I should say—-unacceptable or filthy. So, for example, if I told you 'this place is dumpy,' I would be telling you that the location we were at was bad or below standard."

"Understood. Without regard, I would find pleasure in visiting your dumpy Earth."

Byers cackled loudly at her statement. He was aware that Samia did not try to make a joke, and the fact that she unintentionally said something comical made it even better.

"You're funny," he said choppily in between laughter. "I didn't realize you had such a great sense of humor."

Confusion came over her young and olive-toned face. "I am not of understanding."

"I know. That's what makes it even funnier."

She continued to feel baffled but smiled brightly nonetheless as she enjoyed her time thus far with Byers. A warm look came through both of their eyes, their desire for one another becoming stronger by the minute.

"Well, perhaps next time I can make you laugh," he stated seriously. "I'm a pretty funny guy, I promise."

Samia paused for a moment but seemed uncertain of his statement. "It is not of certainty. It is a feeling of emotion that has not been experiencing by my being."

"What? You mean that you've never laughed in your life?"

"Correct. Seeing your example of what you call 'laugh' is the first time my being has realized its existence."

Bewildered by her statement, he could only shake his head. "That's—-amazing. I guess I'll have my work cut out for me, then."

Samia shrugged her shoulders in uncertainty from his latter form of lingo but smiled once more from the chemistry she felt with him.

"By the way, I apologize for my commander being a jerk back there," he continued apologetically. "He acts a little crazy and trips on his own power sometimes."

"Commander Marcus has been most pleasant, to be of frank nature. His handsome nature complements his entire being."

Byers felt a streak of jealousy go through him, his blood boiling over her remark about Marcus, who wanted nothing to do with at the present moment.

"Is your being of friendly nature to Commander Marcus?" asked Samia in continuation.

He shrugged his shoulders upon his question before gazing himself out into the star-filled sky. "I suppose. We grew up together on Earth, but right now, we're not exactly on the best of terms, if you know what I mean."

"Oh, you are friends of childhood? What is his ability as a friend?"

"Usually, he's a great guy. But right now, he can go to hell as far as I'm concerned. It just seems like, the last day and a half or so, he's been a real jerk, and he's been acting really weird like he's hiding something, so I'm not exactly sure what to say about him right now."

Samia blinked her eyes blankly once more over his usage of words. "What is the definition of jerk?"

He chuckled once more to himself, trying to find the right words to use that she could somehow understand.

"Well--" he started to explain, taking a moment before beginning. "--a jerk is somebody who acts in a stupid manner toward others. An asshole would be a simpler and more direct term, I suppose."

"Understood. What is the definition of asshole?"

Laughter erupted from Byers, who realized he had slipped up and cursed a word that she would never be able to understand. "I'll explain that one to you later."

They both stared at the night sky and at the stars that continued to brightly glisten. It felt so peaceful and beautiful and assisted in bringing serenity to the moment as he scooted his body closer to hers. She smiled despite her oblivious nature about what his body language truly meant.

"So, tell me a little bit about your family," said Byers out of genuine intrigue.

"I reside with my youthful sibling Maren and my father."

"What about your mother?"

Samia shook her head at his question. "She expired, but my being is not certain of the events that were of occurrence. The sole item my father discussed was that she was of great beauty and that she passed shortly after the birthday of Maren. Father is refusing to discuss her expired being, which has made my being uncertain as to the exact nature of events that occurred."

Sorrow came over Byers, who held her even tighter to his side out of sympathy. "I'm sorry to hear that. That really breaks my heart that you never got to know her."

She shrugged her shoulders, mimicking the motion from one of Byers' many habits. "It is of no significance to my being. Such a relationship was of zero development before my being was of age for complete understanding, and it is my father who nourished me throughout my youthful being."

"I'm sorry again you never got to know her. At least you have your father, and from what I can see, he did a great job raising you."

Warmness exuded from her smile. "I offer appreciation for your kind words."

He gazed at her with care as her glance intertwined with his.

She bit her bottom lip and lowered her head to the ground. The attention he was offering her was beginning to make her shy.

"What is your situation with the beings of your family establishment?" she asked in an attempt to deflect some attention away from herself.

Byers picked up on her notion but continued to stare at her. "I just have my mom back home on Earth, and she's all I need because she's a saint. I've never even met my dad, so he's non-existent as far as I'm concerned. Because of that, my mom basically took on the role of mother and father since it was just the two of us, and she worked hard to make sure we had a roof over our heads and food on the table. We didn't have very much, but what we had was more than enough."

He paused for a moment and stared into the sky, his emotions beginning to run high from the love and appreciation he felt for his mother.

Samia, meanwhile, turned her stare up from the ground, her attention turning solely on him while tears welled into her eyes.

They may have had a language barrier of sorts, but at that moment, she was completely understanding of him and could relate to his feelings for the time being.

A large sigh came from Byers, who turned his head towards the ground to compose himself before picking his gaze back up at the sky.

"And now," he continued, "since I've been with SAGE, I can take care of her a bit since I get paid decently for doing this, and she can step back a bit from working so hard. Don't get me wrong, I'll never be wealthy, and honestly I hate my job most of the time. But, she is my hero and my greatest example of how much hard work pays off."

A teardrop fell from Samia's face upon his expressed feelings. "It is of my analogy that your mother is a being of utmost excellence. Your relationship with her contains incredible strength."

"Yeah, it's pretty strong. I really look up to her. Perhaps you can meet her someday."

Surprised by his latter statement and able to understand him fully, Samia felt curious about what he had just told her.

Shocked himself by what he had just said, Byers attempted to go back on his words, a feeling coming over him that he had come across too strongly to her.

"I mean--that is--if you come out to Earth sometime and meet her."

She said nothing momentarily before smiling widely towards him. "It is of possible nature. It would be of great pleasure to visit your habitation."

"It would be for me as well," he said in agreement, relief coming over him upon realizing that he had not scared her away with his boldness.

His feelings for her only continued to grow, and being in her presence alone brought him a sense of complete satisfaction that he had never felt before with any other woman. He greatly enjoyed his time with her, and nothing confirmed that more than the happiness he experienced from simply getting lost in her eyes.

The smile on Samia's face acknowledged her own feelings, her soul as intertwined into his as hers was.

"Has your being enjoyed my habitation?" she asked politely.

"It's lovely. It's almost like something out of a dream."

She beamed even more upon his glowing thought of her planet. "It brings excitement to my being that your being thinks highly of my habitation."

"I do. By the way, what is the name of your--habitation?"

"It is unnamed. While your habitation is named Earth, ours has no such entity."

"Interesting," he stated, his attention and gaze completely locked in on the beautiful alien woman before him.

Byers could feel his heart pulsating faster with each passing moment with her. He couldn't remember the last time he had felt so strongly for a woman, and he definitely couldn't think of a moment where he fell so hard for somebody so quickly.

He began to take in her beauty all around, and he felt drawn to her in so many ways. He was completely smitten with her amber eyes, which cut through the darkness and directly into his soul. He loved her long, midnight hair that draped over her back and swayed carefully in the wind.

And he couldn't help but be enamored with the contagious smile and internal beauty that she possessed.

Most importantly to him, he felt an appreciation for her company, something he had never truly experienced with a member of the opposite sex. He felt like he was falling in love with her already, almost like they had known each other for years, and he felt compelled to share his feelings with her.

"Samia," Byers began, "I don't want to come across too strongly, but I would like to know. Are you seeing anybody?"

"I see our beings," she answered unknowingly.

He chuckled at her innocent and naïve answer. "No, no. I mean, are you married, or do you have a boyfriend?"

"Negative. I do not have a spouse attached to me, nor does my being contain an attachment with an opposite being."

Byers beamed brighter upon her answer, and his hopes raised further by her confirmation that he was clear to make a move.

"What is the purpose of your question, Thomas?" inquired Samia.

A warm feeling passed through him upon her calling him by his formal first name. Only his mom called him that whenever he got in trouble in his younger days, but hearing Samia say it made him enjoy being called by his real first name.

"Well," he began, pausing momentarily to say the right thing as he took her right hand and picked it up, holding it with great care in between his palms. "I know I just met you, but I feel so close to you. I've never felt this way about any woman, and I know deep down how special and unique you really are."

Byers' heart began to thump in his chest. He had never felt so nervous about asking a woman out. The fact that he never had even asked a woman before, however, definitely didn't help.

He had been used to night-night stands and brief flings with women and knew exactly the right words to get them to sleep with him.

When it came to actually romancing a woman, however, he was an inexperienced virgin who was without a clue.

"Samia," he continued, "what I'm trying to say is that I like you, and I would love to get to know you more and see where this takes us."

She felt extremely intrigued by his expression of feelings. "Does your being speak of romantic feelings to my being?"

"Well—-if I understand you right, then yes," he answered, worried about her response. "That is, of course, if you feel the same way."

"It is of great assumption that my being does agree. It is of great warning that I present to your being as my being is not certain of these feelings of love. It is a unique and different feeling for my being."

He nodded his head as he could feel his palms begin to precipitate a bit from his nervousness. "Don't worry, and I have never felt these feelings before either, so we can work through them together."

Samia appeared satisfied with his response but still needed assurance as she herself felt unsure of what exactly to do next. "Assume the feelings of your being are not of a factual nature?" she inquired.

"Trust me, they are," he said.

Much to both of their surprises, Byers leaned towards her and kissed her out of impulse to answer her question further.

Their lips remained locked, their hearts beating as one and their souls intertwined together under the twinkling stars that seemed to shine brighter upon the beginning of their intergalactic love.

Chapter 17

Marcus stood in the entry room in Samia's home and watched on while his crew took advantage of their downtime to catch up on rest.

He glanced primarily at Rubidoux, who lay against the wall, his head hanging down while drool hung from his bottom lip as he snored loudly.

The commander shook his head but was glad to at least see that the usually tense Rubidoux was finally at ease. Based on how quickly the rookie fell asleep, it was Marcus' best guess that he probably hadn't slept much since beginning his service with SAGE, and he could not help but reminisce back to his first mission and the many sleepless nights he experienced as well.

He turned his attention from his rookie navigator and onto his veteran navigator, Jacobs, who had followed suit with Rubidoux and completely crashed. The long hours they both endured before landing appeared as if they had caught up to them both. She lay flat on the floor and her hand resting atop her stomach as her mouth hung wide open, occasional mild groans suggesting that she was either having a great dream or a horrible nightmare.

To her left lay Jennings, who belted out the loudest snores

thanks in large part to the awkward position his head had turned while he slept.

The sight alone of Jennings sleeping put a cramp in Marcus' neck as he grimaced upon the sight and rubbed the imaginary pain that began to pulsate.

Perhaps by coincidence, or not so, Jacobs and Jennings slept close to one another, a sight that made Marcus chuckle to himself out of irony.

When are they going to figure it out? But then again, when am I going to figure it all out with Monica?

Right on cue, he turned his attention to Monica, who lied in a fetal position as if she were cold.

Marcus smiled and leaned down to open his bag. He pulled out a neatly wrapped up cashmere blanket, which had been folded into a small square, and began to unfold it, flinging it twice in the air in an attempt to get some of the wrinkles out.

Marcus took the blanket and placed it over her, a slight groan coming as it made contact with her body.

She looked so sweet, so innocent, and extremely beautiful as she grabbed the blanket that covered her from her shoulders to her knees and held it tighter to herself.

Hopefully, you're having the sweetest dreams of all.

He smiled once more and resisted the urge to kiss her on the cheek, hoping to save his first kiss with her for a more memorable moment.

Marcus felt exhausted and wanted to join his crew in catching up on rest, but he had volunteered to be the lookout and take one for his team for the benefit of his tired and worn out crew.

He also wanted to be ready in case there was a sighting of Maxwell or Arraz, who both still were mysteriously missing and he worried greatly about.

Marcus also wondered about Byers' wellbeing despite his recent foolish behavior. Although the past day and a half had been strenuous at best, his brotherhood type of love for him conquered all.

I'm still going to give him a piece of my mind when I see him.

He sighed deeply to himself and began to step outside of Samia's home when he suddenly collided with somebody accidentally in the dark.

"What in the--?" asked Marcus out of surprise.

"My pardons, Commander," Samia apologized to him quickly b**efore** hurrying past him and into her quarters.

Marcus watched her enter her room and knew that surely Byers was not too far behind. He marched out through the doorway and saw Byers at the center of the village, skipping along joyfully.

"Hola!" he shouted towards Marcus, uncaring of slumbering residents.

"Shhh," instructed Marcus back to him in a loud whisper. "Keep your voice down."

Marcus rushed towards his friend before they met in the middle, the bright moonlight helping them to see in the dark.

"Where in the hell have you been?" Marcus asked angrily.

"Just out for a little fresh air with the lady," sarcastically answered Byers.

"Fresh air, my ass. What were you doing, and what do you think gave you the right to defy my orders?"

Byers smirked out of amusement and frustration. "I told you-- I was out getting fresh air with the lady. And what we did is none of your business."

Sickness came over Marcus, who feared that Byers had done a dirty deed with Samia. "You didn't—-please tell me that you didn't take advantage of that poor alien woman."

A heavy sigh came from Byers, who shook his head upon his friend's assumption. "Relax, I didn't do anything inappropriate. And she's no alien, and she's a lady. So get your facts right next time."

"She's not a lady. She may look like us, but she's still an extraterrestrial being we know close to nothing about. And knowing the way you are, you, of all people, especially need to stop before someone gets hurt here."

The ,simmered-down anger between the two friends began to boil once more.

"Don't tell me what to do, Ronnie," Byers told him, his voice spiking greatly in volume as he wagged his finger at Marcus. "You may be my so-called superior officer, but don't take that as a reason to boss me around and tell me how to run my life. And by the way, Samia is a wonderful person, and if I want to talk with her, then that's my business, not yours. So, butt out and leave me alone about it."

Marcus slapped Byers' finger away before miming the gesture on his own end. "You need to remember something here, Tommy. We're on duty and not on a quest for love or sex. One of your biggest problems is that you can't differentiate between business and pleasure, and I feel like I've got to babysit you half the damn time."

"Get that goddamn finger out of my face," Byers commanded.

Marcus did as requested and put it down before continuing on his rant.

"The bottom line is, you turned your back on the crew and disobeyed me when I told you not to go with her. You might be my friend, but that does not mean you have the right to disrespect me like that."

Byers had had enough, and he no longer cared about sparing Marcus' feelings.

"Whatever, Maxwell," he shot back in insult, firing an intentional shot to get Marcus' goose.

The hard feelings between the two reached war-like conditions upon Byers' insult.

Marcus gritted his teeth and was prepared to do battle with his friend. "Don't even go there with me again. You need to seriously grow up and show me some respect."

"Right back at you," Byers stated, deflecting his friend's statement.

"I've had enough of this for one night," Marcus declared. "I'm not doing this anymore with you. So, I'm making an executive decision on how you are going to pay back your dues. I'm going to get some rest, and as your punishment for disobeying your superior, I will expect you to be on the lookout until daybreak. So, you'd better make yourself nice and comfortable because you're going to be here for a while."

Byers cocked his head and delivered a death glare to Marcus, his anger creating fire in his light-brown eyes.

"I refuse--Commander," growled the incensed lieutenant. "You can't make me do that, and above all, I refuse to do that."

"I can, and I will," Marcus commanded as he thrust his face into Byers' like a drill sergeant with his cadet. "Maybe this will teach you some self-responsibility and respect for others for once in your life, you prick."

Byers said nothing but glared wickedly at his superior officer and friend as a means of defiance.

Marcus felt bent on having the last word and was satisfied that it had appeared that he had shut down his lieutenant's rapidly moving mouth, at least for the moment.

"Good Night, Lieutenant," Marcus strongly told him before turning to head back to Samia's home.

Byers stood like a statue; his hands balled into fists by his side before he delivered a verbal low blow.

"Don't be mad at me because I'm a bigger man than you. At least I can take care of my business."

Marcus stopped in his tracks upon Byers' words, tightened his jaw and turned around to deliver a frightening look of hostility.

"What did you say to me?" he angrily asked.

"You heard me," Byers said, his face turning spiteful. "You're just upset because I made the moves on Samia, and you still don't have the balls to ask Monica out. You can say all you want about Samia not being human, but at least as a man, I pursued the woman I wanted. You, on the other hand, are too pathetic to even do anything about it. Hell, you can't even admit to me, the guy you've known almost your entire life, how you feel about her. Admit it--you're nothing but a goddamn coward."

Marcus could feel himself about to erupt out of his own skin from Byers' hurtful words. "You'd better take that back, asshole."

"Make me," challenged Byers. "That is if you're man enough."

Marcus' anger reached its tipping point as he exploded towards Byers like a cannonball and tackled him to the dirty, sandy ground, a cloud of dust exploding in the sky to symbolize the start of their brawl.

Byers threw a haymaker punch at Marcus that ricocheted off of his cheek and sent the commander backward.

Marcus recovered quickly and landed his own uppercut under Byers' chin before putting his hands around Byers' neck in a choking manner.

Byers gasped for air and connected on another punch that hit Marcus dead in the middle of his face but did little to faze the commander, who further tightened his grip before throwing the lieutenant roughly like a rag doll onto the ground.

The loud noises and insults they screamed at one another awoke the village, including the sleeping crew at Samia's home, who rubbed their tired eyes and tried to regain their equilibriums from deep sleep as they scurried outside to make sense of the happenings that were occurring before them.

Monica and Jacobs stumbled their way toward their commander and lieutenant, whose brawl had begun to escalate with expletive insults and threats.

Byers was able to free himself from the vice grip hands of Marcus and thanked his friend by delivering a kidney shot that sent Marcus kneeling to the ground to gasp for air.

Pity was of no interest to Byers, who delivered a body slam to the fallen Marcus and wrapped his arms tightly around his neck, a menacing scowl on his face of a man ready to make the kill.

Monica and Jacobs begged and screamed for the two men to stop, but their cries were to no avail.

Marcus had one more trick up his sleeve and elbowed Byers right in the middle of his chest cavity.

Byers coughed and tried to get back the air that had been forcefully taken from his lungs but was stopped from getting a nice breath of air thanks to Marcus, who wrestled him to the ground.

Both men began to tire but refused to raise their personal white flags out of pride.

They continued to wrestle and roll on the ground, filling the air with more expletives and insults until they stumbled onto a pair of familiar leather boots that stopped them both in their tracks.

"Enough!"

A loud gasp came from the crew and village upon the sight of the older figure, who appeared ready to take on the role of disciplinarian.

Marcus' dirtied and bloodied jaw dropped in agony as he realized he had seriously messed up.

"Captain--," he stuttered, "I—-can explain."

"You will explain nothing," Maxwell fired back. "Get your sorry asses up before I pick them up for you."

Marcus and Byers did as they were sternly requested and properly dusted off their dirty uniforms.

The villagers stood in stunned silence upon the imposing figure that Maxwell presented.

"Captain, thank goodness you are safe," Jacobs said. "We were worried sick about you."

"Yes, thankfully, that is the case," replied Maxwell in agreement, his stare still fixated upon Marcus and Byers. "It is unfortunate, however, to come back to this."

The crew quickly gathered into formation and nervously saluted their captain.

Byers and Marcus lagged behind, still trying to reorganize themselves, much to Maxwell's dismay.

"So, I leave you in charge for not even a day, and this is what happens?" he asked angrily, storming towards his commander. "How in the hell do you expect me to believe you can manage this crew once I am gone?"

Marcus felt his six-foot frame reduce to a pint-size in shame. "I'm--I'm sorry--sir. I--suppose things got out hand."

"That's putting it very kindly, Commander,"

The captain's glare turned rapidly onto Byers, who gulped upon the imaginary spotlight that now shone brightly upon himself.

"And as for you, Lieutenant," continued Maxwell, "how do you explain the embarrassing debacle that I just witnessed?"

The lieutenant's jaw drooped ajar in a weak attempt to find some sort of viable excuse. "I--lost my cool, sir. I apologize for my actions."

A violent shake of the head came from Maxwell, unsatisfied by the reasoning given by Byers. "You know, it's really too bad. It's unfortunate, more than anything, because you just may be a reason why your friend doesn't get my position when I retire after this mission."

The crew gasped in unison upon the verbal bomb that Maxwell had dropped on them.

Maxwell picked up on the surprised expressions on the faces of his crew. "Am I to really believe that Marcus did not inform any of you that I was retiring after this mission?"

Byers turned his attention back to Marcus and delivered a disgusted glare that he had not been informed of Maxwell's secret.

"No, sir," answered Byers angrily. "He certainly did not tell me."

"I'm surprised," stated Maxwell as he made his way directly in front of Marcus, who gazed out into the unknown, trying his best to suppress his frustration and embarrassment. "I guess that I can at least give you credit for keeping my secret as you swore. At least you got that part right."

Maxwell glared at Marcus and smirked, loving the misery on the face of his commander. He definitely relished the moment to show up, Marcus, and it was more than apparent to every member of his crew.

An evil grin came across the captain's face before he leaned closer to his commander to grill him further. "That is--unless you have told somebody else my secret. Surely you weren't that foolish to defy my orders."

Marcus stood stone-faced, his heart racing internally although he attempted to hide that he had indeed shared the secret. He was stuck in between a rock and a hard place and could feel Maxwell putting more of a squeeze on him to get him to talk.

"Or—-did you indeed defy my orders?" inquired Maxwell, curious by Marcus' non-response.

Silence remained for the commander, who offered nothing again as the truth began to eat him up inside.

"Your non-response is concerning," Maxwell stated in observation before leaning inwards closely to Marcus' ear. "I will ask you once again--and please be honest because you know that I will find out. Did you spill my secret?"

The commander cracked under the extreme pressure, sensing that he had been caught red-handed.

"Yes, sir," he answered quietly. "I did."

The captain appeared annoyed yet amused by his response. "And who did you tell, Commander? "

Marcus closed his eyes for a moment, fearing the repercussions that would be coming for Monica. He knew Maxwell had him trapped, and the last thing he wanted was to see her feel the captain's full wrath as well, even though he was more than certain that Maxwell was aware of who he had told.

Maxwell leaned in even closer, his vile breath making Marcus feel even sicker than he already did. "This is no time for bashfulness, lad. Either you tell me right now or I report each and every one of you for termination."

A large lump gathered in Marcus' throat, obstructing him from saying anything momentarily.

Maxwell applied even more pressure to get his commander to

talk. "Tell me now, Commander, or they all pay the price for your sin."

He gulped before quietly forcing out the answer that his captain had so eagerly been waiting for.

"Monica."

Maxwell smirked wickedly out of enjoyment from seeing Marcus squirm before making his way toward Monica, whose face began to flush with anguish from his incoming presence.

"Miss Brackenridge," he said while stopping in front of her, the glow from his face only radiating brighter from the mental torture he was inducing. "Ah, my dear--it looks like, unfortunately, you're now stuck in the mud with both of these two, doesn't it? It is unfortunate, but alas, you must also be punished for your own actions. Is that understood?"

She closed her eyes to hold back from crying in front of him.

"Yes, sir," she whispered.

Maxwell smirked and gazed up at Samia, who stood frightened from the berating she had witnessed.

"What in the hell are you looking at?" he rudely asked her, his smirk flipping quickly to a scowl.

"My pardons," she began to explain, "but our beings have never encountered an aged being."

He appeared confused and stared at the baker's dozen youthful beings that occupied the village, their faces frozen like stone.

"I'll be damned," he said to himself. "Looks like I'm stuck with a bunch of kids."

She took one step towards him in an effort to show her friendly intent. "It is a spectacle and wonder that we see an aged being such as your being. It is of great difficulty to act of normal status."

He took his eyes off of the rest of the village and glared with great annoyance at her. "Well, I suggest you get over it, you stupid girl. It's no secret that I'm old, so don't patronize me. Have some respect for your elders and mind your own fucking business, you dumb little bitch."

Byers felt as if he wanted to crawl out of his skin and pummel Maxwell for his harsh treatment of Samia. If not for his active duty status, it would have been a different story for the angry, clench-jawed lieutenant.

Although she did not understand some of the captain's references, the tone in his voice alone made her eyes well with tears. "My pardons."

"My pardons?" Maxwell replied in mockery. "What kind of shitty use of the English language is that? You don't dare speak to me if you can't speak correctly."

Sadness went through Samia's heart from the verbal berating she was enduring. She had never been talked to by anybody like that, and she offered nothing other than a hanging of her head to express her sadness.

Maxwell did not let his foot off of his personal brashness pedal. "Pitiful," he told himself while shaking his head. "Absolutely pitiful."

Anger pulsated through Byers, who clenched his fists to stop himself from doing something he would regret.

"I'll show you pitiful," he growled to himself, a mental image coming to his mind of going physically haywire on Maxwell as payback for attacking the woman he loved.

Not hearing what Byers had said, Maxwell continued his tirade and stared at a young couple who fearfully gazed at him from the outside of their home.

"What in the hell are you staring at?" Maxwell rudely asked them.

The wide-eyed couple made their way back inside their home, afraid of any potential confrontation with the abusive captain.

Maxwell grinned once more from sick satisfaction before making his way back to his in-formation crew to continue his power trip.

"Now that all of that is out of the way, is there any other important things you forgot to tell me, Commander?"

Marcus bit his bottom lip, afraid to tell his captain the last bit of bad news.

"Unfortunately yes, sir. We are missing Arraz, and we have been unable to find him. We've looked everywhere, and some of the locals here are trying to help us find him, but to no success so far."

Much to Marcus and the crew's surprise, Maxwell did not seem to pay much mind to the news. "Oh, right, he's missing, isn't he? Well, all I can say is that you can tell the locals to stop searching, because if they find him, they're not going to like what they find."

The crew stared at their captain in disbelief over his nonchalance.

Marcus, baffled by his captain's lack of care, attempted to inquire further. "What do you mean by that, sir?"

"I mean that he's dead, Commander," Maxwell told him coldly.

The crew gasped in unison from the captain's statement.

An icy chill ran down Marcus' spine before he attempted to inquire further. "He's--dead? How—-how do you know that, sir?"

"Because I killed him myself," Maxwell responded.

Chapter 18

The crew stood in stunned silence before Maxwell, his chest puffed out like a proud man.

"Wha--what do you mean you killed him--Captain?" asked Rubidoux, his voice cracking and his face flush with fear.

"Well, I shot him right through the heart and put an end to his shitty little life," callously explained Maxwell. "That asshole had it coming to him, so I put him out of his misery."

Marcus could feel his heart break as Arraz's death began to hit him. "What do you mean he had it coming, sir?"

"He tried to kill me, Commander. I was walking along through the forest when I heard something coming from the bushes. I took my gun out and asked who it was. The next thing I knew, Arraz bolted out, pointed his gun right at me and told me he would blow my head off if I got any closer. I told him it would be wise for him to put down his weapon, and I would forget the whole thing, but he told me that he wanted me dead, and he demanded I put down my gun."

The village was as quiet as could be while the crew intently listened to Maxwell's story.

Marcus felt short of breath, his heart beginning to ache from the loss of his fallen lieutenant.

Maxwell focused his glare individually at each broken-hearted member of his crew before settling his stare intently on Marcus to finish his tale.

"So, I made it seem like I was listening to his orders, and I began to put down my gun, but little did he know that I had my secondary laser pistol in my pocket, and as I prepared to lay the gun on the ground, I took out the pistol and shot him twice right in the chest. He grabbed his chest and crashed onto his back, and I watched him take his last breath as all of the blood from his body oozed out completely."

Depression and melancholy dominated the feelings immediately of the shell-shocked crew.

Maxwell, meanwhile, appeared more than satisfied by the means of his fatal act. "Oh well, he was nothing but a traitor when it came down to it, so there's no need for sympathy for that dead bastard."

Shock and disbelief filled the air upon Maxwell's bold comment, and it was surprisingly Jennings who was the first to voice his concerns.

"Captain, I suppose this may not exactly be my place to intervene, but I feel at the same time I must say that I'm not sure how I feel about you telling us not to have sympathy for Arraz. Even if he was a traitor, he was still a person and a young man who seemed like he had a great deal of ambition in his life."

Maxwell's face flushed with anger from Jennings' statement. "You are correct to say it is not your place to intervene, Doctor. And, perhaps, you need to remember that you are here to be our physician and nothing more. Do I make myself clear?"

The threat did little to simmer down Jennings, who suddenly had risen with confidence from his quiet ways. "I understand my position, sir. But with all due respect, we are still talking about a human being who has a mother and father and other family and friends back home who love and care about him. So, to say it is of no matter to us is, quite frankly, astounding and unrealistic."

Maxwell's anger had reached its official impasse. "That is

enough, Doctor. It would be wise for you to stop while you are ahead. That is unless you support a traitor."

Jennings felt his inner monologue tell him to back off, sensing the danger that awaited him if he rebelled further in the no-win battle he found himself embroiled in. "No, I do not, sir."

"Good answer," the captain told him before delivering a death stare to Marcus and Byers. "I'm sure that you do not want to end up paying the price that these two numbskulls will end up paying."

Concern adorned both of their faces as they continued to feel trapped in the pressure cooker of their captain.

Samia continued to stand in curiosity, wonder filling her eyes as she still was unable to get over the spectacle of age she saw before her.

"Why in the hell do you keep staring at me?" Maxwell asked rudely. "I told you to mind your own damn business, you stupid girl."

"My pardons once more, but I had a question of importance to your being.

The mean streak inside of the captain rose back from within. "What is wrong with your use of language? For God's sake, you speak like a confused dictionary."

Samia, unable to fully understand what he had told her, simply gave sad eyes to express her feelings about the condescending tone directed at her.

A loud sigh of annoyance came from Maxwell, who agreed to momentarily give up his personal fight. "What is it you want, creature?"

Samia paused before she spoke, trying not to let her emotions get the best of her. "I only wanted to inquire if your being had sight of my brother or our beings?"

"What kind of question is that? I do not know who your brother or your people are, so don't even ask me something like that, you stupid little--"

"Enough!" Taark's angry voice commanded aloud as he

stepped out of the shadows his home. "The behavior of your being has reached the point of ending."

Maxwell gave a sour expression of anger and squinted his eyes in an attempt to identify in the dark who was the owner of the command. "Who in the hell are you to speak to me that way--boy?"

Taark paid no mind to Maxwell's question before approaching his daughter and holding her tightly in his arms, a loud sob coming immediately from the emotionally damaged Samia.

"Is your being stable?" he asked in a comforting tone.

The captain stood befuddled from being ignored by Taark.

"Excuse me, but I asked you a question," Maxwell rudely interrupted, his anger now overpowering in his voice. "And I will not be ignored, son."

"Silence your being," commanded Taark, still holding Samia tightly. "The other beings may have a fear of your being, but my being does not possess such nature, even if your being is aged and superior. Phrases of ignorance may harm the being of my daughter but will not pierce the heart of my being."

Maxwell's jaw dropped from the latter statement. "Your--daughter? You mean to tell me that you are this woman's father?"

"Your statement is exact."

Maxwell's eyes grew large from disbelief, his focus switching back and forth from Samia and Taark. "Surely you are joking. For God's sake, you look only old enough to be her brother."

"Her brother, my being is not. My being was born many moons before my daughter."

The captain growled in anger before picking up where he left off. "Well, your daughter needs to learn to mind her own business. It is not polite to stare, after all."

"Do not threaten," Taark fired back. "Your being may be superior now, but my being was ruler long before your arrival."

Irritation further boiled Maxwell's blood. "What kind of nonsense are you talking about?"

"It is an ignorant act of your being. Your being may now be of ruler stature, but my being will not agree with such harmful behavior to my daughter of such a ruler."

Maxwell was taken aback by the last word that had left Taark's mouth. "Ruler? What do you mean by—-ruler?"

Samia sniffed loudly while she rose her head from the comfortable chest of her father, her eyes reddened by the tears that had streaked her face.

"Take care, my child," Taark whispered to her. "It is important to not allow fear the opportunity to cloud the heart of your being."

"Not to interrupt this tender moment," Maxwell rudely stated, "but you once again did not answer my question, and I demand an answer."

The gruff alien man had finally had enough of Maxwell's bad attitude. "Your being has already heard my being, and it is requested that your being do not behave with ignorant intents."

A half smile came across Marcus, who savored the moment of seeing somebody not fear the sharp tongue of his captain.

Not so much of a badass right now, huh? Maybe I should take a page from Taark's book.

The veins began to further pulsate in the captain's temple from the alien's response. "Ignorance? The only ignorant thing I see is an idiotic creature unwilling to answer my question. Now, I will ask for the last time: what do you mean by ruler?"

"It is of the exact nature that has spewed from the oral portal of your being. It appears the mind of your being needs rehabilitation."

Maxwell's face went blank as the light went on in his head. He blinked his eyes violently in an attempt to wrap his head around what he had just heard.

Silence filled the air of the village as the crew and villagers alike could do nothing else but to stare at the old man who stood frozen in motion.

Marcus' heart especially dropped to his knees from the significance of Taark's words.

"Are you saying—-that I am now your ruler?" asked Maxwell, who chuckled in disbelief. "How—-how can that be?"

Samia's sobbing discontinued momentarily, an appearance of fright now covering her face.

"The reasoning is that your being is the elder resident of the Earth star that our beings have awaited," she answered, softly sniffling. "The ancestry of our beings has suggested this event to occur. It is of a realistic nature upon the arrival of your being."

An evil grin came across Maxwell's face, his crooked smile giving away the notion of sinister thoughts that ran through his mind.

He chortled softly at first until his laughter began to bellow and shake the crisp night air violently with great discomfort.

Marcus held his head low, sensing the hell they were all, human or not, about to endure from their newly minted dictator.

CHAPTER 19

The early morning sunlight did little to cut the cold chill that ran through Marcus and gave him a shiver unlike any other as he walked through the forest with Byers and Monica trailing closely behind.

They had been sent on an assignment by Maxwell, the newly appointed ruler of the land, to cut down trees and gather up wood to make a fortress for him as punishment for their actions.

Marcus thought about the dislike he began to feel for his captain and how he especially didn't appreciate the power trip he felt that Maxwell was on thanks to his recently christened position of an almighty figure.

Nevertheless, he knew he truly had no present choice but to do as his superior commanded, although he began to no longer feel even a slither of respect for his captain.

He couldn't help but wonder about the legitimacy of Maxwell's story and couldn't help but wonder what truly happened between him and Arraz. As naïve as Arraz could be, especially with a weapon in his hand, he also wasn't crazy enough to kill.

At least, he didn't think he was.

A crisp feeling filled the air, and Marcus could feel the cleanliness of the air in every breath he took, although it felt extra chilly at this moment.

The sky had morphed back from darkness to a crystal blue. Happy chirping filled the air once more of the exotic bird-like creatures as they made themselves at home randomly on the open branches of their choice, unknowing of the bad times that had come over the villagers and the visiting crew.

I wish I could be a bird and sing a happy tune, too, right about now.

He turned his head and stared at Byers, who delivered an angry glare that informed him loud and clear that he was still furious about their altercation.

Deciding to avoid any possibility of another nasty fight, he turned his head and stopped at a large tree, throwing down the bag that hung over his right shoulder as a loud thud accompanied it. Marcus began to dig in his bag. As he took out a small rectangular box and pushed the button on its side, which transformed it into a large saw.

Marcus glared upwards and saw a couple of the bird creatures in the branches who curiously looked at him, pondering what was about to happen.

"Sorry, fellas," he said apologetically, as if they could understand what he was saying. "It looks like you're going to need to find a new home."

Marcus picked up the saw and turned his focus onto Byers, who folded his arms in an act of protest.

"Well, are you going to help me, or what?" asked Marcus, the tension between the two remaining as the elephant in the room.

A murmur came from Byers, who was prepared to curse out his superior and friend. He reluctantly grabbed one side of the saw and Marcus the other as they picked it up and placed the sharp edge against the trunk of the tree in preparation for cutting it down.

Monica watched from a distance while the two men silently

prepared themselves and began to see to and fro away and towards one another.

"Is there anything I can do to help?" she kindly inquired.

"Just sit there and be quiet," Byers told her sharply.

Marcus stopped sawing and gritted his teeth at his friend over his rude answer to Monica. "Don't talk to her that way, asshole."

"Don't tell me what to do," Byers fired back before stopping his own motion. "You might be my commander, but you're definitely not my 'ruler' like your retiring captain is."

Marcus only shook his head, deciding to bite his tongue and not say anything else he would regret later.

Byers, on the other hand, was not as considerate. "Oh, that's right, you didn't tell me that part about Maxwell retiring," he sarcastically added. "Silly me--how quickly I forgot that my own friend didn't tell me something important like that."

Frustration began to boil over for Marcus, who quickly dropped his act of coolness. "Man, you are so petty. We wouldn't have even been in this mess if it hadn't been for you."

"Is that so?"

"Yeah, that's so, pal."

Marcus dropped the end of his saw to stage his own protest against Byers.

Byers mimicked his friend's motion and threw down his end, the animosity towards one another beginning to grow to an all-time uncomfortable high.

Monica's face became flustered with fear as she could see things beginning to get hairy once more between the two friends, who behaved a lot like enemies at the moment.

Byers' right hand balled into a fist and shook it towards Marcus. "You've got some nerve, you dick. Now you're keeping secrets from your own friends. I can't believe you would tell her the truth before you told me."

"Grow up, man," Marcus growled back. "It was nothing personal. But now that I see this, maybe I really did make the right choice in not telling you shit."

"I'm sure you feel that way, especially telling your girlfriend. I bet now that she knows how you feel, you'll always go to her first for everything, won't you?"

An awkward silence filled the air from Byers' last remark, who was confused by the lack of a response.

Marcus' jaw hung low in disbelief over Byers blowing his cover in front of Monica.

Monica stunned over what she had just heard, rapidly turned her head to Marcus and stared blankly at him.

"Wait, you did tell her, didn't you?" asked Byers, who worried that he had screwed up royally.

"No," Marcus answered through his teeth, "I didn't."

Byers' mouth puckered up almost as if he had sucked on a lemon, a sudden realization coming over him that he had over-stepped his own boundaries. "Oh--shit."

Marcus turned his attention to Monica, whose gaze had already been on him, her doe brown eyes looking soft but unreadable to him for the moment as her smile faded.

His heart raced as he knew the secret he had long hung onto had been released into the open.

He wanted to speak but was unsure what exactly to say. He tried to open his mouth, but nothing came out. He felt nervous, afraid and uncertain over what possibly could happen next with her, and the poker face she exhibited did little to ease his worries.

Byers remained frozen in complete silence, wondering what he had just done. He felt compelled to say something as well but couldn't quite come up with the right words to offer up some form of apology.

The worries intensified inside of Marcus, who eagerly awaited Monica to say anything, even if it was negative, to give him an idea of where she stood.

What is going through her mind right now? Should I say something?

He finally felt ready to speak up and say something until Monica beat him to the punch.

"Ron—-nie?"

"Yeah?" he asked, his heart beating a million miles a minute.

"Is--that true?"

"Well--I've wanted to tell you--"

The world around Marcus felt as if it had completely stopped. There was an unusual silence in the air, and everything around him felt as if it had been frozen in time in waiting for his answer.

He took a deep breath and closed his eyes for a moment in preparation for perhaps the biggest moment of his adult life.

Here goes nothing.

"--yeah, it's true. I--really like you, Monica, and I want to see if you would like to--go out with you sometime. That is--assuming we get out of here."

How cleverly romantic and original you are.

Monica said nothing and stood in frozen silence, her face continuing to give absolutely no indication to Marcus, who eagerly awaited to hear what she had to say.

C'mon, say something. Anything.

She blinked her eyes and licked her lips, an answer finally preparing to leave her luscious lips.

"Wow," she stated. "I mean, I had a feeling, but I didn't know for sure."

"I'm--sorry that I didn't get to tell you earlier," Marcus apologetically said to her. "I've been trying to tell you for some time, but I just haven't been able to up to this point."

A smile finally came over Monica, a sign that gave Marcus encouragement even though she hadn't quite told him herself how she felt.

Relief came over him that he was finally able to tell her the truth, even if it hadn't happened quite like he had envisioned.

Still, he couldn't help but wonder what the future held for them both.

They stared at one another as if they were in a trance, a smile of enamor coming across them upon the breaking of the ice in the form of Marcus' true feelings being revealed.

"Um, I hate to interrupt you two," interrupted Byers, "but we've got an evil dictator back at the village who is eagerly awaiting the lumber he's requesting us to gather for his new home. So, we'd better get our ass in gear and get the king what he wants, Commander."

Marcus knew that Byers was right and turned his focus to his friend, even though he felt as if he were in no rush to return to the hell that awaited him. "You're right. And we're in enough trouble as it is, so I guess that we'd better get to it."

He gazed back towards Monica's way once more and smiled brightly at her.

The beaming smile from her end acknowledged him back and gave him that warm and fuzzy feeling that she always seemed to garner from him.

"Well, I guess we'll talk more later on," Marcus told her simply and sweetly.

She nodded at him in acknowledgment. "Yeah, I guess so."

Byers once again interrupted their moment, the urgency inside of him beginning to fester further. "Enough already, you lovebirds. Let's get this shit over with."

"Hey, relax," Marcus instructed, his fury beginning to rise once more. "Give us a moment, pal."

"I'll give you a moment--" responded Byers, who stepped towards Marcus and prepared to attack him once more.

Their altercation was interrupted by a surprise referee; however, Monica stepped in between them and felt the need to defuse their differences.

"Enough, you two," she ordered with surprising strength. "For God's sake, this is really the last thing we need right now, so I'm going to ask you as nicely as I can to drop whatever issues you both have with one another immediately, please. You guys are friends, and you can't forget that."

Marcus and Byers stared at one another and nodded out of agreement at how right she was.

"You're absolutely right, Monica," Marcus sheepishly said.

"I'm sorry, Tommy. I know that I haven't been a great friend to you lately. There's been a lot going on, but that's no excuse for my actions. I apologize that I didn't keep you more in the loop, and I'm sorry it all came down to this."

"Me too," Byers agreed. "I'm sorry I've acted the way I have towards you. I shouldn't have been as disrespectful as I was to you in front of everyone, and I should have treated you with more respect."

Marcus held his right hand out and balled it into a fist. "Are you still my brother from another mother?"

Byers glared quickly at Monica, who nodded her head to give an extra push before turning his attention back onto Marcus.

"Always," he stated, smiling as he extended his right fist and pumped fists with Marcus.

The tension immediately lifted from the area as Marcus and Byers' feud had officially come to an end.

Marcus stood with his hands at his side, another smile coming across his face from satisfaction. "Glad we're back on the same page with each other again, Tommy. But, as you said, we'd better get back onto taking this tree down before Maxwell comes looking for us to knock our skulls around."

Byers groaned in agreement. "Yeah, I guess. Well, let's go ahead and get this out of the way."

"Pardon me, guys," Monica interrupted them sweetly as she pointed towards the tree before her before they prepared to pick up their saw to get back to work. "But, didn't you guys begin cutting down that exact tree in front of you?"

Marcus and Byers knelt on the ground with a saw in hand and stared at Monica in confusion by the nature of her question.

"Yeah, that's right," answered Byers. "Why?"

She paused for a moment to gather the right words for what she was about to say.

"Well, I don't know how to explain this," she started. "But that tree looks like it hasn't even been touched. It looks immaculate."

They dropped their saw once again and hurried to the tree to see what she was talking about.

"Ronnie, am I going crazy, or did we start cutting into this tree?" Byers inquired, his hands pointing towards the trunk where they had begun to carve.

"Yeah," answered Marcus. "I mean, at least I think we did. Didn't we?"

He stared at confusion towards both Monica and Byers, who themselves remained mystified by the uncut nature of the tree they had begun to carve.

"So, if we really did saw into this tree, then where is the cut?" inquired Byers.

Marcus' face froze solid, his mouth open but muted as he was unable to get any sort of explanation out that made sense. He stood up and carefully approached it, a feeling of uncertainty embedded in his gut as he took his right hand and began to scale down the trunk in an attempt to see if he could feel any sort of proof that the sawing they had begun actually existed.

He caressed its trunk but felt nothing, confusion beginning to toy with his mind.

"I--don't know," was all he could offer Byers.

Marcus stared at Monica, who could only shrug her shoulders as he once again looked down at the trunk, lost in confusion.

"It can't be," Marcus said to himself, his hand still caressing the area he was certain they had begun to slice into from their amateur lumberjack work.

A groan suddenly came from a large bush closest to Marcus, who crouched to the ground and tried to grab his gun, preparing for whatever may be coming their way.

Unfortunately, he had forgotten that their guns had been taken from them by the new ruler of the land, who wanted to ensure that they would not try to be heroes and plan a revolt against him.

Marcus motioned with his left hand to Byers and Monica to hold their spots as they huddled together, ready for a potential fistfight for whoever, or whatever, waited for them in the shrubbery.

Another groan came, louder this time than the previous one, that let them know it, or he was closer than before.

Whoever it was, or whatever it was, they were close, and it was only a matter of time before they were ready to burst from the shrubbery.

Marcus' hand remained raised, although his internal instincts were prepared to beat his unknown opponent to the punch and draw the first contact.

The source of the sound finally staggered its way towards them from the shrubbery.

Their jaws dropped in unison from who they discovered was behind the bush.

"Please--help me."

"Arraz!" Marcus screamed in delight.

"Kill him!" shouted Byers. "He's a traitor!"

"No! Don't touch him!"

Arraz stumbled towards them in an altered state, a confused appearance glimmering in his foggy eyes.

"Arraz!" yelled Monica in joy. "You're alive!"

"Help--me," Arraz said in a muffled plea. "Please."

His eyes rolled in the back of his head before his body suddenly gave out and crashed onto the grassy substance underneath him.

"Dear God," said Marcus before stumbling to his feet and towards Arraz's temporarily out-of-order body.

Byers and Monica rushed to his side as well, and Marcus took his finger and put it on Arraz's neck to check his pulse.

"Is he a goner?" Byers asked half-sarcastically.

Marcus shook his head, somewhat annoyed by the callousness of Byers' question. "No, he's still alive. But I'd guess he won't be much longer if we don't do something quickly."

"What should we do, Commander?" Monica asked, her voice trembling.

Byers couldn't resist the moment to jest. "Maybe we should take him back to the village so Maxwell can finish him off. I never liked the guy anyway."

Marcus turned his head and glared at Byers to give him a non-verbal message to tone it down with the wisecracks.

Almost as if she had read Marcus' mind, Monica stepped in and did the talking for him, albeit a lot more politely than he would have.

"Please don't say things like that. It's inappropriate."

Much to Marcus' surprise, Byers appeared embarrassed by the kind reprimand he had been given, a slight shade of blush beginning to flush through his caramel-colored skin.

"Sorry," he mustered out of embarrassment. "That was wrong of me to say."

Impressed by the effectiveness of her tactic, Marcus gave a quick stare of approval to Monica and smiled before turning his head down at the body of his fallen lieutenant.

"What should we do with him?" asked Byers.

Marcus could only think of one idea to possibly help Arraz. "We need to get him back to the ship. Tommy, help me pick him up, will you?"

"Shouldn't we at least cuff him?" Byers asked. "I mean, as much as I hate Maxwell, who knows? Maybe it really is true that he tried to kill Maxwell."

Marcus shook his head at the suggestion but then again could understand where Byers was coming from. "Alright, go ahead and place the electro cuffs on him. But hurry, we've got to get him out of here before Maxwell sees us with him."

Byers scurried through his bag and quickly locked the mechanical cuffs onto both of Arraz's wrists.

The two men picked up Arraz and hurried towards the ship, with Monica scurrying behind in an attempt to secretly get the suspected assassin safely on board.

Chapter 20

Arraz lay on the metal table in Jennings' examination room, unconscious as Marcus, Byers and Monica hovered over him. His arms, still locked in the electro cuffs, hung above his head and over the edge of the table.

"Who'd have thought it, huh?" Byers asked, shaking his head.

"What do you mean?" questioned Marcus to him.

"That he really was crazy enough to try to kill somebody," Byers answered. "I always knew there was something off about him."

Marcus shook his head in disagreement. "We don't know that for sure. So let's just hold up on that theory for the moment, okay?"

Byers rolled his eyes upon his friend's statement, his mind already made up over what he thought about the accused lieutenant.

"Do you think he'll be alright, Commander?" Monica asked with great concern.

"I hope so," responded Marcus. "He looks like he's been through the wringer, though."

"I wonder what happened to him. Captain Maxwell said that he killed him, but if that's the case, how is he still alive?"

Marcus scratched the back of his head in bewilderment. "I don't know. I see these holes in his shirt, and there's some blood around them, but his skin doesn't possess any sort of proof of wounds in that area. Unless he was shot somewhere else, perhaps."

Marcus lifted up his tattered shirt and examined Arraz's chest, which appeared immaculate and unharmed. He shook his head and exhaled in confusion.

"Or maybe Maxwell just made the whole thing up about killing him?"

The quietness in the room was interrupted suddenly by Arraz, who had awoken in an angry and confused state and began to violently rock his body, his dead-weighted arms anchoring him down to the table.

Monica stepped back out of fright before covering her mouth with her hand.

Byers' eyes grew large upon the sight of his fellow lieutenant's abnormal behavior as he, too, joined Monica in stepping away from Arraz.

Marcus, however, stood his ground, doing his best to maintain his composure despite the fact his heart was beating inside of him like a drum.

Arraz growled loudly, a lost look glowing through his eyes that stared upwardly at the ceiling of the examination room.

It took a moment before he finally calmed down, and his body ceased with any more movement, his rapid breathing still remaining, however.

Marcus tiptoed slowly towards him and stood above him carefully, a soft look coming over him to try to further settle down the shell-shocked lieutenant.

Arraz blinked his eyes and stared at the commander, confusion still dominating his sight.

"Arraz?" Marcus asked cautiously. "Are you alright?"

Blinking of the eyes and a gulp was the only response Marcus received as Arraz was still recovering from the shock he had just experienced.

Monica took a step forward, her mouth still completely covered by her hands from fear.

Marcus gazed quickly at her before turning his attention back to Arraz.

"Arraz, it's Marcus," he carefully told him. "Commander Marcus."

Arraz nodded his head and closed his eyes. "Yes--Commander. Where—-am I?"

"You're on the ship in Jennings' examination room," answered Monica, uncovering her mouth before taking another step forward towards Arraz. "You passed out asking for our help out in the forest."

Another nod of the head came from Arraz. "Yes--I remember," he said before opening his eyes and staring at his cuffed hands. "What--is this?"

Marcus bit his bottom lip and tried to think of how he should start what was guaranteed to be an awkward conversation.

Arraz gazed up at Marcus as he still awaited a response. "Why--am I cuffed?"

The commander allowed himself another long moment before deciding to be upfront with his response. "Listen, Arraz--we're really glad to see that you're alive, but there's something important we've got to talk to you about."

"What is it?"

Marcus tried his best to think of the right wording to use.

Where do I even start?

"I'm not sure how to begin this, but here goes--" continued Marcus before he was interrupted midsentence.

"Why did you try to kill Maxwell?" Byers rudely asked.

Marcus stared back at Byers angrily. "What in the hell do you think you're doing?"

"What?" asked Byers, unaware of any wrongdoing that he had just done.

Arraz's mouth dropped upon Byers' bold accusation. "Kill--Maxwell?"

Marcus could sense his friend was about ready to say something else stupid and held his right hand up towards Byers in an effort to summon him to be quiet.

Byers crossed his arms, rolled his eyes towards the ceiling and reluctantly followed the instructions he was given.

Marcus turned his back towards Byers and turned his attention solely back on Arraz, whose confusion was apparent in his lost eyes.

He took another moment and cleared his throat before beginning his explanation to Arraz.

"Well--Captain Maxwell informed us all that you attempted to assassinate him in the forest. He said that you had lost your mind and that he had no choice but to kill you out of self-defense."

"What? No!" yelled Arraz.

He attempted to pick himself up from the table but unsuccessfully crashed back onto the unforgiving metal surface.

Byers rushed towards Arraz in an attempt to hold him down but got held back by Marcus' authoritative arm.

Monica took another couple of steps back out of fright, her nerves on full edge.

Arraz hysterically moved himself as best he could on the table to try and escape but was unable to lift his weakened body. He hissed loudly in between his teeth, his breathing erratic and irregular.

"Relax," Marcus commanded in a calm tone. "Calm down."

Realizing that his efforts were futile, Arraz did as his commander instructed and ceased with his attempts.

Marcus peered down at Arraz, who opened his eyes and remained still on the table.

"Good," the commander said as he walked towards the other end of the table towards Arraz's head. "Now, are you ready to tell the truth?"

"I--told you the truth," answered Arraz, who eyes followed that of the location of Marcus' body. "I--didn't try to kill Maxwell."

Marcus shook his head and scratched his forehead. "I would love to believe you, Arraz. Unfortunately, it's also your word against Captain Maxwell's, so you're facing an uphill battle on that one alone."

Arraz rolled his eyes back in his head and nodded his head. "I'm--aware, sir. But--with all due respect--there is something--you need to know."

Curiosity came over Marcus upon Arraz's words, who took a moment to compose himself before slowly continuing his point.

"Captain--Maxwell is not--as trustworthy as--he portrays himself to be. I--have witnessed that--as I'm sure--you have. He--possesses a twisted dark side--and--I saw it myself when--when—"

Arraz took a deep breath and closed his eyes but failed to finish the sentence, his tired body doing its best to take a rest.

"When he what, Arraz?" asked Marcus anxiously.

The lieutenant fought through his body's demands and smacked his lips before finishing what he wanted to say.

"--he murdered me--sir."

Marcus' eyes widened as suddenly Arraz's words began to click in his mind. It was not Arraz who was the murderer.

Rather, it was Captain Maxwell and the genuineness in Arraz's eyes told him the truth that he needed to know.

Byers scratched the back of his head and proceeded on his own investigation. "So, if you really were killed yesterday by Maxwell, how in the hell are you still alive?"

Arraz shook his head. "I--honestly don't know. I wish--I could answer that question for you--but I can't."

"Why not?"

"Because--I really don't know how I'm still alive. The only thing I remember--is that Maxwell approached me—-along with--some other man. He--ordered me to put down my gun, and--

because he was my captain--I obeyed. I mean--who would have thought he had--malice in his heart? Especially--for us?"

Marcus' face fell blank upon the beginning of Arraz's story, a cold chill running down his spine from his latter statement, although his eyes remained fixated on the recovering lieutenant.

"The next thing I knew--they began to pulverize me with laser shots to my chest," continued Arraz while tears welled in his tired eyes. "I--fell to the ground in a pool of my own blood, and--the last thing I remembered before I blacked out was seeing Maxwell's face. His face--was so cold--and his smile--was as if he relished what he had done. I'll never forget that."

A vivid picture ran through Marcus' mind, almost able to see the action occur while Arraz told his story.

He gazed up at Monica, who was shivering, surely in fright from the horror she had heard.

Byers stood poker-faced throughout, an oddity for the comic-lucid lieutenant who was not taking this matter lightly.

Marcus' mouth hung up, a sick feeling coming over his stomach from the gruesome act that had been described to him. "What do you remember happening after that?"

"Well--the next thing I knew, I--woke up and it was early morning," replied Arraz. "I--thought at first that maybe I had been sent--to Heaven, but--when I got up, I peered down and saw my dried blood on the ground and--remembered. When I--looked at my chest--though, there was--nothing there. Almost as if--I--had never been shot. What happened--you may ask? I don't--know."

The silence continued to fill the air of the laboratory as the three crew members offered their continuous full attention to Arraz, who smacked his dry lips before adding to his story.

"It was shortly after--that I ran into you all. It's funny--because I really do feel better than ever. Except--I feel so tired--and hungry. Do you--have a food pill I can consume?"

"Yeah, sure," answered Marcus before turning his head

towards Byers. "Tom, can you get a food capsule from the bag, please?"

Byers knelt down and reached into his green bag and began to mutter to himself in a high-pitched, mocking voice. "Get me this, and get me that. What's next, you're going to put a leash around my neck?"

"What's that?" asked Marcus.

"Nothing," was his curt reply before handing over the requested item. "Here you go."

"Thanks," he said to Byers, giving a look of confusion at his behavior before turning towards Arraz. "It looks like we've got country chicken and biscuits here. Does that sound good?"

"Delicious," replied Arraz simply, smacking his lips in anticipation of the flavor explosion that was about to erupt inside of his mouth.

Marcus dropped the capsule down the open cavity while Arraz closed his eyes and began to suck on the pill to enjoy its full benefits of flavor and hunger satisfaction.

He could taste the creamy, peppery country gravy that had been splashed over the fried chicken breast and could feel the buttery flakiness of the biscuits that perfectly complemented his dish.

A warm feeling came over Arraz, who felt for a moment as if he were back home before swallowing the pill so it could begin its next phase of canceling out his hunger.

"Mmmmm," hummed the ravenous lieutenant in approval from the goodness of the quick meal he had gotten. "Thank you-- I needed that."

As bad as he felt to interrupt Arraz's blissful moment, Marcus felt compelled to further dabble into the entire issue of the lieutenant's phoenix-like rise from the dead, his curiosity reaching an all-time high.

"I know this may not exactly be the most appropriate time to ask, but I feel compelled to. Arraz--are you sure that you actually died? And, more importantly--are you certain about your story and that you yourself did not attempt to assassinate Captain Maxwell?"

Arraz froze in confusion upon Marcus' questions, the tasty flavors still resonating in his mouth as his speech began to speed up to a brisk walk.

"Well--to answer your first question, Commander, I've--never died before, but--my hunch is--yes, since I remember taking my last breath. And, secondly--I've never been so certain of anything in my life, Marcus. I--would never have tried to do anything like that, but--now that I know how--evil Maxwell really is, I--can't say I wouldn't think twice about it now."

Marcus, Monica and Byers offered nothing but silence while they took in everything that Arraz had told them.

"You--have to believe me," begged Arraz in addition. "Please."

Marcus peered over Arraz and directly into his glazed eyes of weariness and concern.

"I believe you, Arraz," he stated before reaching down to unlock the electro cuffs. "I'm sorry we had to put you through this, but hopefully, you can understand that we had to be safe rather than sorry."

Not everyone felt the same, however, as Byers vented his immediate frustration.

"Wait a minute. Do you mean to tell me that you're just letting him go like that?"

"Yep," Marcus answered definitively, offering no wiggle room with his response.

Byers threw his arms in the air out of disgust and disagreement. "Whatever. What the hell do I know, anyway? I mean, I'm only the first lieutenant on this ship. It's not like my opinion matters, right?"

Monica was not amused by Byers' unnecessary rant and wanted to let that be known, unafraid of what her superior would say.

"Byers, be quiet," commanded the usually polite woman to him.

Marcus smiled out of amusement at seeing his long-time buddy be put in his place by somebody other than himself or Maxwell, and by Monica, no less, who he would have never imagined to have been capable of such a deed.

Byers, meanwhile, seemed embarrassed by the unexpected reprimand, realizing instantly that he was indeed wrong.

"Sorry," was all he could muster sheepishly before tilting his head downward as if he had just been sent to a timeout.

Monica turned her attention back to Arraz, who was massaging his wrists, which had just been set free, and began to lift his body slowly from the examination table.

"Arraz, do you know who that man was who you said was with Maxwell?" she asked.

Arraz blinked his eyes in an attempt to reboot the memory in his mind that was still fuzzy from his rejuvenation.

"I--had never seen him before that moment," he answered, his speech beginning to regulate. "I'm sure that none of us have, though. He was a young guy, maybe in his early 20's or so. He-- had dark hair, dark eyes and olive-colored skin, and his face was absolutely emotionless like Maxwell's."

"Well, whoever he is, I'm pretty sure he didn't come back to the town with Maxwell," stated Marcus.

"Do you think that maybe he's one of the aliens on this planet?" Monica asked.

Marcus shrugged his shoulders. "I don't know. But whoever he is, it's best that we keep our eyes open for him, because he could be anywhere."

"The assumption of your beings is precise," a deep voice answered as a long-haired, well built young man stepped from the door, a laser gun pointed ahead toward the four of them. "It is of unfortunate nature that the eyes of your beings are not of an ultimate state of clarity."

Marcus and Byers stood in front of Monica to screen her from harm while Arraz stumbled to the floor and tried to find some sort of viable weapon in his bag.

The man fired a shot at the ceiling as a warning. "Halt and disengage from the behavior of foolish proportions."

"Not on your life, pal," Marcus said in rebellion before attempting to charge at the alien man.

Unamused yet unfazed by the courageous act, the alien man fired another shot that forced the commander to dive to the floor to avoid a fatal blow to his head.

Realizing that he was nothing more than a sitting duck, Marcus refrained from any other attempt and threw his hands up in the air to admit surrender, the pointed barrel of the gun from the man assisting in his decision.

"It is of secondary recommendation of my being to cease behavior of foolish proportions," the man said to Marcus. "Expiration of your being will proceed with repetition of rebellion."

Byers, Monica and Arraz followed their commander's lead and raised their arms in surrender to ensure they did not give the alien being any more motivation to shoot.

The male alien's eyes largely grew upon the sight of Arraz. "Your return has occurred."

The internal light bulb went off inside of Marcus, who realized who they were dealing with.

"I'm guessing this is the guy, Arraz?" he asked.

"Aye, sir," answered Arraz softly while nodding his head.

"Your being is of living stature," the man continued to Arraz. "It is of great certainty that your being is of full awareness."

The crew stood in confusion over the man's statement, whose abnormal language did little to assist them.

"What are you talking about?" Marcus inquired. "Who are you, and how in the hell did you get in here?"

The man pointed his gun directly in between Marcus' head and sent a target beam in between his eyes to silence him. "The questions of your being will contain such answers in time. It is my recommendation that your beings proceed along to the location of our master."

The crew followed the orders of the armed villain against their will and proceeded to move along as hostages out of their own ship.

Marcus took the lead, with Arraz taking the rear, as their nightmarish adventure took yet another turn for the worst.

Chapter 21

The four crewmembers marched in a single file line as they began to approach the town under the pressure of the mysterious alien man who trailed closely behind, ready to fire at the slightest act of anarchy.

Marcus, at the very head of the line, turned his head back and smiled at Monica, who was right behind him, in an effort to reassure her that everything was going to be alright.

She smiled back at him even though her nervousness was at an all-time high over what awaited them all next.

"Look forward, creature," instructed the man before pointing his gun towards Marcus' head to further threaten. "Cease with the actions of your being."

Marcus glared at the man with disgust while Byers shook his head at how he saw his friend get treated by the complete stranger who held all four of their lives in his hand with a single flick of the finger.

The commander followed the orders of the villain and looked forward at the view of the town which now began to engulf the full range of his vision. His thoughts began to rush through his mind as he couldn't help but to wonder what surprises were awaiting them.

The only hope he had was that the rest of his crew was unharmed, considering what Maxwell had already attempted to do to Arraz.

God save us all.

The sun shone brightly and warmly and hung in the sky like an ornament, the heat seemingly intensifying further the closer they got to the town.

The alien took the barrel of his gun and pushed it roughly into Arraz's back.

"Hey!" he growled at the assailant. "What's the big idea?"

The alien man scowled back and lifted the barrel against Arraz's left temple. "Silence to your being. Further actions of tomfoolery will result in expiration."

Anger pulsated through Arraz's body, although he resisted all temptation to boldly intercept the man's gun and slaughter him at that moment due to the gargantuan size advantage he faced from the alien.

Marcus turned back once more and could feel his compulsion to stick up for his crew member rise inside of him. "Leave him alone, you asshole."

The man glared at Marcus and caught up to him at the front of the line. He took the barrel of his gun and wedged it into Marcus' stomach, causing the commander to exhale in agonizing pain before falling to one knee.

The villain offered no sympathy as he hovered above him, the other three members of the crew having no other choice but to watch their commanding officer suffer.

"Arise," the alien man coldly told him while aiming for Marcus' jugular to ensure heroics would not follow.

The usual mild-mannered Monica had seen enough and could no longer bite her tongue.

"Leave him alone!"

The man's gaze left Marcus and focused onto Monica as he sidestepped towards the lovely young woman, fury raging in his eyes from her bravery. "It is suggested that your being maintain compliance or suffer consequences of similar proportions."

Monica felt the boldness running through her veins. "Or, what? Are you saying that you would assault a woman?"

"Your being is of precise nature," answered the man, who stuffed the barrel of his gun into her chest and prepared to fire to show that he meant business.

Marcus rose to his feet and quickly grabbed the gun to protect the woman he loved and prevent further violence. "I wouldn't do that if I were you. Leave the lady alone."

"If it is the request of your being," the man responded before clocking Marcus across left side of his face with the butt end of his weapon.

The commander crashed to the ground and groaned in agonizing pain from the cheap shot he had taken.

Byers stomped over towards the villain who just assaulted his friend, anger erupting inside of him like a volcano. "You son of a bitch."

The man stopped Byers in his tracks by firing a shot that nearly took off his ear and stopped him in his tracks. "The expiration of your being will follow with such an act of tomfoolery."

"Tommy," Marcus said to Byers while staring at the ground in agonizing pain. "Don't. Please."

The man maneuvered his gun around the skulls of all four of the crew members as a way to remind them of who held the upper hand.

Byers, following the order again of his friend and superior, raised his palms upward in surrender to avoid any further conflict.

Monica and Arraz followed the lieutenant's lead against their wills and ceased with their brief moments of anarchy to spare their lives for the moment.

Marcus slowly rose to his feet and nearly tumbled again onto the ground before catching his balance and standing straight up, a glare of dislike and hate glowing in his eyes towards the enemy in front of him as he reluctantly followed his violent and forceful tactic.

Paying no mind to the hateful stares he received, the alien man waved his weapon towards the direction of the village as a non-verbal command.

Marcus reluctantly followed orders and spearheaded the movement, the town now directly in his sight. He hated the fact that he was being bossed around, and he hated even more feeling like he had no control over the situation. He couldn't help but to wonder how they got into the mess they found themselves in, and how they were going to get out of the living hell that was indeed reality.

How did this man gain control of us? And who in the hell is he?

They officially entered the town, which had become even more eerily silent than it already had been, and found Maxwell in the middle of the village, towering over his own captives who knelt before him like brainwashed slaves.

An evil smirk came across the face of Maxwell upon the turning of his head to the newest captives.

"Well, well," he stated. "Look who decided to join us."

His eyes focused down the line and directly at Arraz, which only intensified the wickedness in his grin. "Lieutenant Arraz, you are still alive, I see. It looks like we didn't quite finish the job, huh?"

Samia's eyes grew large upon the sight of the alien man, whose gaze also fixated upon her simultaneously. Tears welled in her eyes while her lip quivered in fear.

"Brother?"

Taark quickly rose his head from the ground to catch a glimpse of what his daughter had just said. "Maren? What is the reasoning of your being?"

"Silence, Father," demanded Maren coldly. "Your being is undeserving of explanation."

Taark attempted to get up to approach his son but was met with great and immediate resistance.

"Sit down," commanded Maxwell before pointing his gun at Taark's head. "You take one more step, and I'll blow your goddamn brains out."

Maren, taking no account for the fact it was his own father, drew his own weapon and appeared eager to pull the trigger.

Taark followed Maxwell's orders but gazed into Maren's eyes with confusion. "You are the son of my being. What is the reasoning?"

"Quiet," Maren commanded, his voice extra-sharp with firmness.

"Maren?" Samia asked tearfully. "It is of begging nature of my being, Brother."

With surprising hostility, Maren pointed the barrel against his sister's temple and cared not for her pleas. "Is your being of deaf nature? Or does your being desire to be expired?"

Tears rolled down Samia's cheek, her feelings hurt greatly by her own brother's coldness. She could not understand what she was witnessing and could not understand what had happened to the only brother who once loved her so greatly yet suddenly treated her so terribly.

Maxwell reveled in the sight and chuckled madly. "Well done, my boy," he said before placing his palm on top of Maren's gun. "We have much bigger fish to fry than this, though, so save your energy."

Maren nodded towards his new superior and lifted his gun away from the head of his sister before holding it close to his chest like a young boy with his toy.

Marcus shook his head at the sight of Maren behaving like a trained pet. He couldn't help but wonder why Samia's brother had betrayed his own people, and how he and the power-driven captain had even conversed so quickly together as they had.

However they got together, he's going to find out how evil his 'master' really is.

The sun radiated off the pasty-skinned Maxwell, who marched towards Marcus' line with great intent.

He glared at his captured commander, a wicked grin etched over his face as he appeared to be amused upon seeing his former student and right-hand man powerless.

Marcus could feel the joy in Maxwell's decayed heart, thoughts revolving instantly in his mind about any possible ways to break free from the wretched command of the insanity-driven captain.

The captain passed by Marcus and grunted in disgust, his evil smirk never fading before he stepped by Monica and Byers and halted his pace upon reaching Arraz, who delivered an icy death stare to his superior.

Maxwell picked up on the glare and deflected it back at his young lieutenant. "Arraz, you foolish boy. How you are even alive is beyond me."

"It is of the belief of my being that his being is aware of the secret, sire," Maren interjected. "My being contains certainty of this nature."

Maxwell raised his eyebrows at his alien apprentice quizzically. "What is this secret that you are blathering about?"

Maren appeared confused by his response. "Your being has not been made aware, Master?"

The blank response on Maxwell's face was the only response he offered to his pupil.

The alien man smiled wickedly. "Allow an explanation of my being."

He bolted past Maxwell and behind Arraz, driving the barrel of his gun into the back of the lieutenant's skull. "Answer the inquiry of my being. Did you participate in consumption of liquid?"

Arraz raised his eyebrow in confusion from the question. "You mean, did I drink water?"

"It is an exact question. Answer with truthful nature."

Arraz's face turned sour by the demanding nature of Maren, whose ill-tempered ways reminded him closely of Maxwell's. "Yeah, I did. Why?"

"Leave him alone," Marcus interrupted angrily. "He's been through enough."

"Silence, creature," demanded Maren. "The continuance of your being will permit my being to provide expiration."

Maxwell raised his palm towards Maren to try to settle him down. "What are you getting at with your question?" he asked his extraterrestrial comrade.

"The answer of his being is confirmation, sire. It further clarifies the state of being and the hypothesis of my being. His being consumed the liquid of sacred nature. It is of legend that a being of Earth quality that consumes the matter is of everlasting and youthful characteristics of eternal nature."

Despite the confusing wordage used, the crew immediately picked up in unison what the alien man was getting at.

Marcus could feel his heart drop to his stomach before he stared at Arraz, realization setting in that he was now dealing with an immortal being.

Arraz blinked his eyes blankly, his own realization setting in that his defiance of his commander's orders a day earlier ended up saving his life from malice and gave him eternal life that instantly changed the course of his life cycle.

Maxwell's face glowed before he turned his gaze to Arraz out of fascination.

"Did I just hear what I thought I did?" he asked as he turned back towards Maren to await an answer. "Did I really just hear that he will live with eternal youth?"

Maren nodded his head, and smirked back at Maxwell, feeling the pleasure the captain was about to feel with his response.

"It is of correct nature, sire."

Euphoria and wonder filled Maxwell's heart upon his answer, a smile of great wickedness cutting through his bearded face. "So, what if I shoot Mr. Arraz once again in the heart? Will he die?"

"Negative," answered Maren directly. "The death of his being will be temporary before his being is of restored status."

Maxwell pointed the gun towards Arraz's head. "How about his brain, then?"

Maren shook his head. "The brain matter will heal completely as the liquid has filtered through the body of his being."

Disbelief draped the face of Maxwell, who put down the gun and gave Arraz as if he were unsure of what to do next.

Quietness exploded through the air while everyone waited for the captain's next move.

Thoughts filtered quickly through Marcus' mind. He knew, much like he was certain that Maxwell especially did, that Arraz was protected from death at the hands of their captain-turned-assassin, which he was certain drove Maxwell to a point of insanity and curiosity simultaneously.

The commander's head turned to that of the beings of the planet. He now began to fully understand why they all had the youthful look they exhibited, as well as the secret that Maren had briefly stated earlier. It was incredible in his mind that an innocent substance was the reason for the youthful states of every inhabitant of the planet and it was even more amazing that his own lieutenant was saved thanks to disobeying his orders.

Marcus' head turned back towards the direction of Maxwell, who remained silent as his blank stare turned towards Maren.

For one of the few moments, Maxwell was speechless, an oddity in itself considering his iron-strong, alpha-dog personality

Maxwell closed his mouth and gave himself a moment before he once more tried to get the right word out. "So," he started slowly. "You're saying--that he'll live--forever?"

Maren nodded his head. "Your inquiry is positive."

"And--he's going to look like that--for eternity?"

Maren simply nodded his head, a half smile assisting his non-verbal answer.

The gears in Maxwell's head began to spin violently while evil thoughts began to filter through his polluted mind. He was a frightening enough man to deal with on a regular basis, but he was downright terrifying now that his true evil nature had begun to dominate.

"So, if that's the case--what will this liquid you speak of do for me?" Maxwell asked.

"Is your being asking aside from eternal living?" inquired Maren.

"Yes," replied Maxwell. "Will it--make me youthful once more?"

Maren scratched the back of his head. "It is not of certain answer. It is assumed it would reverse the aging process, but is of unknown status."

The corners of Maxwell's mouth began to curl once more into a wicked grin. "So, it is possible, then?"

Maren's grin agreed with the captain's. "The assumption appears logical. It is suggested that we test such a hypothesis, sire."

Maxwell's evil grin only intensified upon the thoughts of possibly regaining his youth.

"Yes, I think you are correct," he said, laughing aloud as the captured village and crew could only be witnesses in the captain's diabolical new scheme. "We must head to the source of this liquid immediately."

"Positive," said Maren, who pointed northwest towards a giant hill that sharply steered upwards towards the sky. "It is vital our beings travel to the source for an event of potential significance."

Maxwell nodded his head upon the suggestion of his new right-hand man. "Very well, then. Round up the kiddies because we're going on a field trip."

Maxwell and Maren chortled together, even though Maren was not exactly certain of the meaning of Maxwell's latter statement.

Marcus and Byers shook their heads at one another, an invisible vice of despair further tightening upon their respective necks.

"God help us," Byers quietly stated as Maxwell's evil and hysterical laughter violently shook the core of the quiet village.

CHAPTER 22

The mood and situation were dark for the hostages, who found themselves sandwiched uncomfortably between their two perpetrators.

Maxwell led the way up the hill, the warm sun beginning to make its course downward to the east.

Marcus stared in confusion, his mind still struggling to grasp the fact that the sun did not set in the west like he was accustomed to back home.

He sensed a hostile look from Maren, who stood three deep behind him as their single-file and uniformed line. He couldn't help but feel as if he was being watched by an overly strict boot camp drill sergeant who was hell-bent on making life miserable for his cadet.

Get a grip, I'm just staring at the sun.

Marcus wondered what had driven Maren to the point of insanity he had reached, and he wondered how the extraterrestrial man had even teamed up with Maxwell in the first place.

He looked back momentarily at Byers, who marched directly behind him. "You alright?" he asked him.

Byers hunched his shoulders to answer his question non-verbally, unsure of how to answer precisely.

"Don't worry, we're going to get out of this somehow," whispered Marcus to him before he gazed behind Byers and slightly smiled at Monica to help quell her fears with quiet reassurance.

Marcus' actions did not go unnoticed by Maren. "Silence!" he yelled with hostility.

The commander turned his head back towards the front and focused on the salty hair of Maxwell that shone brightly in the luminous sun.

A sick feeling came over Marcus, who felt awful for the rest of the crew.

He wondered if he had missed some visible clues along the way that could have helped them all from being in the perilous situation they all found themselves in, and he couldn't help but wish that he would be able to save each and every one of them from the dangers their own captain had immersed them into.

Marcus reminisced about the heart-pouring session he had with his captain, which seemed phony and like a distant memory at this point. He wondered about the story Maxwell told him of his disconnected relationship with his family and was curious if it had factored into his lunacy.

He couldn't help but also question, however, whether or not his captain had been insane the entire time and that perhaps he had just simply missed seeing all of the signs.

Maybe we really never knew him all along.

Marcus' focus shifted to Samia, who marched directly in front of him and behind her father as they both listlessly followed Maxwell's lead.

It was obvious to Marcus that both members of the alien family were in a state of shock, not only in regard to their current situation as hostages but especially regarding the fact that their own blood shared responsibility in their captivity.

"Pssst," Marcus whispered to Samia in an attempt to grab her attention.

The try was unsuccessful as she continued to follow without an acknowledgment.

"Samia," he whispered in a second attempt, hoping her brother would not hear.

The second time turned out to be the charm as she slightly cocked her head to give a profile of the right side of her face. "Commander?"

He turned his head quickly to make sure Maren was not looking before responding. Much to Marcus' surprise, the stares of the alien man were occupied by something other than him.

"If you don't mind me asking," he began to ask her softly, "why don't you and your father attempt to do something since you both cannot die?"

"Our beings are capable of perishing nature. "The weaponry of your beings would be a cause of casualty."

Marcus was confused by her answer, and his face did little to mask his feelings. "I thought you people lived forever."

She closed her eyes momentarily and shook her head. "The youthful state of our beings is for eternity, but our beings as well share a common vulnerability to that of your beings."

He was ready to ask his next question but paused for a moment to ensure the coast was still clear. Maren still appeared focused on other items except for them, much to his surprise.

"How can that be if you people drink that liquid, too?"

"Consumption of the liquid has fatal results for our beings. It can consume and eradicate vital organs, causing the cessation of the bodies of our beings."

Marcus drooped his jaw in agony upon her response. "I wish Arraz had done something, then."

She shook her head upon his response. "Negative. The wisdom of his being contained a decision of correct nature."

"How so?"

"Silence!" Maren interrupted, his attention focused back onto Marcus upon hearing the quiet chatter between Marcus and his sister.

Samia gazed upon her own brother, who coldly rejected her, wanting to look with hostility and rage. She turned her head back forward for personal assurance, fearing what her own flesh and blood would potentially attempt to try with herself or their own father.

"An explanation is to wait with the requirement," she whispered in an attempt to squirm away from the unwanted attention she was receiving from her own brother.

Her wish was finally granted upon Maren's stare leaving her and instead towards the hapless Rubidoux, who himself turned squeamish upon the alien's glare.

Marcus shook his head in frustration from the hostile treatment they were forced to endure.

If I get free, as God is my witness, I'll kill them both.

Questions still filled Marcus's mind, and he ignored his own intuitions to attempt to get more answers. "Where are we going?" he quietly inquired to the extraterrestrial woman ahead of him.

Samia's eye caught her brother, whose focus remained away from herself and Marcus. "It is named Barel."

"What in the hell--" he asked before catching himself getting louder. He took a moment before continuing his question in a lower tone to avoid the wrath of Maren. "--is Barel?"

"In the legend of our beings, it is the location of original origin," she explained, once more keeping an eye on her brother, who still hadn't noticed their conversation. "Our beings are of the belief it is from the pureness of the liquid that created the form of our beings many moons ago."

She stopped her explanation momentarily to once again catch a glimpse of Maren, who, gun cradled to his chest, was preoccupied still with intimidating the rookie navigator Rubidoux. "Your superior will partake in the foundation of the liquid. His being will attempt age reversal."

"Will it work?"

Her answer was interrupted before she could even get the words out of her mouth.

"Silence!" Maren demanded before steaming ahead to catch

up to them both. He slowed down his stride and immediately hovered over Marcus' side.

"What is the meaning of these interruptions?" he asked, poking Marcus' ribs with the barrel of his gun.

A sarcastic smile came across Marcus, who contained no respect for the armed, alien man. "Ah, I'm so glad to see you. We were just discussing how nice of a guy you were and how happy we are to be hostages for you two gentlemen."

Maren was far from amused by Marcus' statement and let it show immediately by pointing his weapon at the commander's temple. "The rebellious behavior of your being is of a dangerous nature. It would be wise for you to discontinue."

Loud snickering came from Byers, who enjoyed hearing the snarky response from Marcus and did little to hide his joy.

Maren's annoyance raised further upon the laughter as he zipped the tip of his gun from Marcus' temple and instead thrust it roughly against the one belonging to the delirious lieutenant, whose jolly chortling quickly ended with an abrupt snort.

"The warning is equal for your being," stated Maren sternly, his finger violently rubbing the trigger out of great anticipation.

Byers stared down Maren, refusing to fully compensate for his pride and manhood. "No need to get pushy here, pal."

An angry stare came from Maren, who offered only a non-verbal response of tapping the barrel of his weapon against the lieutenant's temple.

Byers, unwilling to offer a shred of fear, turned his head forward and pretended to ignore the threat that coldly scraped against his skull.

Maxwell, overhearing the exchange between the two, stopped on a dime and created a momentary domino effect of stoppage. He glared at Maren and held up his right hand to gently scold his apprentice. "Maren--now is not the time, my young friend. You will have your opportunity, I promise."

Maxwell waved his hand in an effort to motion Maren to put down his weapon.

Maren complied with the captain's orders and peeled the barrel of the gun off of Byers' temple reluctantly, a loud groan of frustration leaving his throat.

"Now, now, there will be plenty of time soon to begin shedding blood, I promise," Maxwell informed the disappointed Maren in an effort to appease his apprentice.

Maren smiled wickedly before placing the gun once more closely to his chest and nodding with approval as his master.

Rubidoux, his nerves at an all-time high, gulped at the thought of what could be coming next while a sour appearance on his face further backed it up.

"As you were," Maxwell commanded to Maren, who followed the order and marched back behind Jennings, who so happened to be the unfortunate one to be in front of the crazed alien.

The captain stared directly behind him at Jacobs and delivered an icy stare toward her that was overflowing with the purest of evil and hatred. "Move, woman," he rudely commanded to her.

She offered nothing except an angry glare before reluctantly following his command against her will to avoid any further possible conflicts or threats.

It was a matter of moments later that the end of the incline approached in the distance, much to the relief of the tiring captives.

Marcus, his uniformed shirt soaked with sweat, sighed heavily, his legs aching from the marching and hiking they had done since the early morning hours.

He could feel the exhaustion not only in his own body but as well as the remaining captives who endured the punishment with him. He wanted to get everyone out of the horrendous situation they found themselves in but he also realized that they were helplessly dealing with two armed maniacs who could go on a killing spree at any moment.

Marcus could sense the despair in everyone, including Monica, who he especially felt great conviction in protecting.

As God is my witness, if we get out of here alive somehow, I'm never going to let anything or anybody harm her.

Two questions instantly came across his brain: how were they going to get out of this mess, and what was going to happen to them all, assuming that Maxwell got his wish and regained his youth?

Only time would tell as Maxwell officially set foot on the top of the grassy incline and began to make his way through Barel's dark and cavernous opening.

Mysterious stuffiness filled the air as the rest of the captives engulfed themselves one by one into the dark opening.

Chapter 23

A trailing Maren was the last to enter the pitch-black cave as he took an unlit torch that hung from the wall. He rushed outside and returned in the blink of an eye, his torch now fully lit.

Instant lamination came from the fiery torch and raised Marcus' curiosity about Maren's lighting technique. "How did he get that lit so quickly?" he whispered to Samia, his voice echoed by the cavernous environment around them.

Samia turned her head coyly, fearing the potential wrath of her brother. "It is lit by the exterior light," she responded as if she were answering a silly question. "Your being does not contain awareness of this nature?"

He was taken aback by her sharp question, which he felt, questioned his intelligence. He only shook his head to avoid being caught, his own realization sinking in that Maxwell and Maren easily heard his whispers in the hollow environment.

Maren held up the torch with one hand while holding his gun with the other and pointed his weapon directly into Jennings' back to keep the mild-mannered doctor in line.

"The liquid is upcoming, sire," he yelled to Maxwell, his voice vibrating rapidly against the wall.

The statement by Maren, much to his own surprise, was

unnecessary, as Maxwell stopped and stood in awe upon their arrival at the cave's sanctuary.

A gigantic statue of a muscular, long haired man stood above the large round pool of liquid that reached out to them. Smaller statues of muscular men circled the holy area of liquid, almost as if they were protecting the precious substance that flowed internally. Two gigantic busts of women's heads, meanwhile, served as the source of the substance, which flowed from their open mouths and downward into the pool.

Marcus had an instant moment of déjà vu, although he could not quite put his finger nor identify why.

Maxwell's jaw dropped in splendor upon the sight before him. "It's--beautiful. It's almost like a dream."

His captain's statement gave Marcus the sudden reminder he needed.

My God, these are the same statues I saw in my dream after I was poisoned.

It hit him like a quick strike of lightning. He realized then that he had been served warning of this subconsciously within his own mind.

Somehow, someway, he had known all along in the back of his mind that Maxwell would turn on them, and the dream that he had experienced was in fact, a vision that he was given that they were all in grave danger with the man he thought was in complete charge and control of the wellbeing of them all.

Marcus felt even worse that his own brain had tried to warn him in advance. If only he had heeded the warning he received in his dream, then perhaps, he felt, he could have avoided the sticky situation that he and the rest of his fellow captives found themselves involuntarily engulfed in.

Why didn't I pay more attention beforehand? Was the answer in front of my face the entire time?

The line began to break up slightly, although it was still controlled by Maren, who clustered everybody together tightly and began to threaten once more as he pointed his gun at the captives he controlled. "It would be wise to obey the orders of the being of our master and not act upon foolish intention."

Maren took his torch and set two more on fire that were stationed onto the wall to give the questionable lighting to the dreary cave, although mysteriously, there seemed to be a somewhat sufficient amount of light in the water sanctuary.

He floated to his father and smiled with evil intent before passing the torch to him, a sense of great enjoyment coming from him out of getting to order his old man around.

"Corral this," he coldly ordered with an antsy trigger finger waiting on his other armed hand. "Any foolish behavior and suffering will await your being."

Taark followed his son's orders begrudgingly and took the torch from him without resistance.

A feeling of melancholy consumed the father's heart over his only son's erratic and evil behavior. He could not understand what had come over Maren yet still felt the need to extend an olive branch of peace.

"Maren," Taark began in an effort to reach the heart of his son, who refused to look up at him, "it is of begging nature of my being that--"

"Silence!" responded Maren to interrupt his father's attempt before firing a shot that buzzed by and nearly blew off one of his father's ears. "Discussion is not an option of viable nature--Taark. Such future behavior will result in the termination of your being."

Samia rushed to the side of her father, who grabbed his ringing ear and glared with sadness at the monster who had consumed the body that once contained his son.

Marcus felt a sense of rage at seeing Maren's disregard of respect for his own father. "That's enough already. That's your father, for God's sake. Show some respect, you asshole."

Maren scowled at Marcus and aimed in between the commander's eyes. "My being has informed yours several times for silence, creature. It will be of noble advice to your being for silence."

Marcus paid no mind to the threat of Maren and felt the need to inquire further with Samia's father. "Sir, with all due respect, why don't you step up to him and challenge him?"

Taark looked at Marcus and shook his head. "It is not of logical choice."

"Not of logical choice? You've got to be fucking kidding me. I know he's your son, but you're his father, so why don't you approach him?"

Samia stepped in front of her father and began to speak for him. "The nature is complex," she told Marcus.

"Complex, my ass," said Marcus, who was rudely interrupted from what else he had to spew upon being picked up like a rag doll by Maren.

The alien assassin drove him against the wall with earth-shattering force, giving Marcus' bones an unwelcoming tremor.

The rest of the captives could do nothing more than stare in fright while their commander was being tortured for his insubordination.

An evil grin crossed Maxwell's face, and he chuckled wickedly upon the enjoyable sight that he took great delight in watching through his aging eyes.

"If you are to speak once more, ashes will remain of the body of your being," Maren told Marcus with the sharpest of intentions.

Maxwell, now in full-blown laughter, clapped his hands together out of satisfactory applause. "Very good, my young friend. I applaud you for your efforts, but please, I'll need you to wait a little longer to finish him off. First, we try this little experiment. Assuming it works, the real fun can then begin."

Maren groaned once more out of frustration, his thoughts roaming towards extreme violence and homicide. He wanted nothing more than to eradicate Marcus, and nobody knew that more than the commander, despite the tight grip that was removed from his neck.

The secretly merciful Marcus gasped for air and slouched on one knee to the ground to further catch his breath.

Maren, witnessing the commander's cardiac distress, laughed upon the sight. "Pathetic creature," he said before pulling out his gun and aiming it between Marcus' eyes. "Come, creature. Defiance is not logical for your being unless there is a wishful nature your being contains for expiration."

Marcus gave Maren a death glare but followed his command to avoid any further issues, stopping by the side of the alien man.

"Negative," said Maren to him. "Your being is to be placed in the front of mine."

Marcus rolled his eyes and followed through on the second command against his will, stopping in front of Maren.

Maren acknowledged the commander's perfect execution of the order he had been given by placing the barrel end of the gun against the back of his skull.

Embarrassment ran through Marcus' veins. He felt like a prisoner, and as much as he wanted to cause chaos, he knew that one wrong move would prematurely end his life, much to his own disadvantage.

I swear, when I get my chance, it's going to get really ugly for him.

He glanced to his right and directly at Monica, whose worrisome eyes met his out of disdain from the treatment he was receiving from Maren.

Byers, standing right next to her, shook his head out of helplessness as he could do nothing more than watch his friend be the focal point for abuse.

"Forward, creature," demanded Maren to Marcus.

Marcus, who was aware that he had no other choice but to follow orders, glared ahead at Maxwell, who relished in seeing his commander suffer greatly at the hands of his new right hand man.

The captain's grin didn't fade as he turned back towards the pool of liquid momentarily and then back at the captives, who stood frozen in mystery.

"Ladies and gentlemen," he addressed the crowd unpleasantly, taking umbrage upon himself at the importance of the moment. "This is a unique opportunity that we, or rather I, am about to embark on. If these aliens' myths are true, I will come back a much different man."

Maxwell began to unbutton his red long-sleeved shirt and took it off, throwing it to the ground emphatically, an unwelcome sight for all, considering the body fat and wrinkles he exhibited.

"Somebody please kill me," Byers mused aloud. "Do we really have to watch this?"

"Silence!" shouted Maren in response.

Byers cleared his throat but remained visually disgusted upon realizing that he would be required to see his wrinkly captain nude.

Maxwell, unfazed by the lieutenant's remark, took off his black, sleek pants and quickly removed his briefs to expose himself in all of his non-glory.

The captives cringed in disgust upon the sight, which again did little to dissuade Maxwell, who proceeded to walk towards the pool.

Maxwell gazed at his own reflection at the top of the liquid, hoping it would be the last time he saw the badly aged self that he had transformed into.

Gone, he was hoping it would be the stretch marks, the salt-colored hair, the wrinkles and age spots, and his mind could not help but wonder what would be awaiting him on the other side once the immersing of his body was complete.

A deep exhale came from Maxwell, who dove headfirst into the pool of the mysterious liquid.

The watery liquid splashed loudly upon impact with his body and rained upon the edges of the grainy floor that surrounded the pool.

Marcus, watching in curiosity, could sense dark hopes begin to enter through his beaten heart.

Maybe, with any luck, the old geezer will drown in that stuff.

A moment of feeling bad crossed Marcus' heart for thinking such thoughts, but at the same time, he also knew that Maxwell wouldn't have given a rip if the shoe had been on the other foot. He had already attempted to kill Arraz, so that was all Marcus had to keep in mind to change his mind about feeling awful about his desire.

And he was almost positive that everybody, with the exception of Maren, wished for something awful to happen to Maxwell at that moment.

Any such negative hope vanished upon the sight of Maxwell rising himself from the pool like a phoenix. He barreled out of the pool of liquid and stood freely on the partially dampened floor, dripping wet while trying to recapture steady breathing.

He gazed directly at Maren, who gave no verbal clue regarding the end result and said nothing.

The captain's eyebrows rose in anticipation of hearing something.

"Well?" he asked Maren, waiting for word on his results while brushing the excess liquid from his beard.

A stone-faced Maren shook his head. "Apologies, sire," he stated. "The attempt has deemed unsuccessful."

A clearly crestfallen Maxwell rushed back to the liquid source and stared at his reflection once more, only to see the same old face he had gotten so used to seeing.

"Damn it!" he screamed in a rare moment of vulnerability before clocking the water out of frustration with a closed fist.

Maren quickly came to Maxwell's side to attempt to console his leader. "A positive is the everlasting life inserted in your being. It is at this moment that eternity is the possession of your being."

Maxwell angrily glared at Maren, unmoved by his words. "What is the point of everlasting life if I look like this, you idiot? I'd rather just die."

A smirk came over Marcus from not seeing his captain get his way, and he couldn't help himself but to feel rather amused by his latter statement.

Trust me, we all agree with you on the last part, pal.

Suddenly, Maxwell gasped loudly and grabbed his chest as he had suddenly been stricken with cardiac arrest.

His face became flush with panic as the air in his lungs escaped him, and his internal operations called for a state of emergency. The captain fell onto his knees, his breathing becoming more rapid by the second in a feeble attempt to breathe.

Every eyeball in the cave watched in wonder while the captain continued to struggle.

Marcus, somewhat enjoying the sight before him, suddenly noticed something different as he looked at the beard wrapped around Maxwell's face.

Why does his beard suddenly appear to be less gray?

A loud groan echoed through the cave as Maxwell's face began to rapidly change. His silver eyebrows and hair followed the direction of his beard and suddenly turned to a darker brown. His once dull eyes regained a glossiness that had long been missing while the color in his eyes transformed from a tired to an electric blue. The hair on his chest bristled and darkened while muscles in his core area and arms conquered the flabby appearance that had once been in charge.

The women especially gazed in fascination as they witnessed the end of their old and wrinkled captain and instead were presented with an invigorated and rather handsome younger man who now knelt before them.

After a few moments of silence, Maxwell opened his eyes and cocked his head upward to reveal a fresh young face draped with a dark beard.

He appeared beyond unrecognizable and began to blink his eyes in an effort to adjust himself to his newfound perfect vision.

Jacobs gasped loudly and covered her mouth with her hand out of surprise.

A pale color came over Rubidoux, who appeared as if he were ready to faint over what he had just witnessed.

The rest of the captives and Maren, meanwhile, hung their

jaws in shock over the sight of the young man who had replaced the previous one.

Maxwell slowly began to rise to his feet, his stare remaining on his right hand, waiting for an update.

He stood tall upon rising completely and turned his head at Maren, who still was yet to offer a word.

"Well?" asked the rejuvenated captain, his voice sounding even sharper and more demanding in its youthful nature than it ever had before.

Maren attempted to move his mouth, which operated as if it had been stuck in cement. He wiggled his jaw to loosen it up before finally attempting to answer.

"Sire--your being--has achieved youthful stature."

Maxwell picked up his arms and observed his hands and bulging biceps that rippled upon his command.

A defining fear slithered through the hearts of the captives as they watched the newly minted, youthful madman laugh hysterically as he raised his palms to the sky.

There was no telling what Maxwell was capable of now, and nobody understood and feared that more than Marcus, who realized that his lunatic former captain had gained even more of an advantage over them all.

Chapter 24

The hard sound of the steel prison door closing did little to soften the devastating blow dealt to the captives, who were securely locked into the jail cell on board the ship.

Maren cruelly stood on the outside, grinning wickedly as he stared at the helpless beings on the other side for a brief moment before marching away.

Byers hung his head while sitting on the grimy floor and rested his back against the dirtied wall. "Man, how in the hell did we end up here?"

Marcus sat on the other side of the wall and tapped the floor, searching internally for answers.

He glared up at Byers, whose eyes crossed his with great desperation as if he were waiting for his friend and commanding officer to come up with some sort of instantaneous solution.

A tilt of the head came from Marcus, who scanned the room to quickly check on his fellow captured mates. The lost expressions on their faces, crammed into the depressing cell with him, said everything he needed to know, and he couldn't help but feel as if he had let everybody down when they needed his leadership most.

Tommy was right. How in the hell did this all happen?

Marcus gazed quickly to his left and directly at the lovely Monica, whose head drooped towards the ground, her spirits clearly wrecked from their dubiously dire situation.

It hurt him so greatly to see her so broken, and he wanted nothing more than to be the valiant hero and save the day, much like the superheroes he idolized growing up.

The coldness of the prison cell, however, reminded him harshly of the grave mortality that laughed in his face and sent him immediately back to reality.

I sure could use some of those superhuman powers right about now.

Monica gazed up and matched her look with Marcus, who could still see life's resonation through her eyes. He smiled slightly towards her to give assurance that they were going to survive their perilous situation and live to tell the tale.

The only trouble was he wasn't exactly sure at that moment what to do or what exactly would be the smartest thing to tell her to soften the situation.

Jacobs sat to the right of Monica and stared through the bars of the cells, trying to see if she saw Maren or Maxwell hanging around closely. "I just can't believe that our own captain has done this to us. We trusted him with our lives. How could he possibly live with himself after something like this?"

"Yeah, like he honestly cares," answered Byers sarcastically. "We're all stuck in a cell, so what does that tell you, huh?"

Jacobs' face soured upon his response. "No need to be a jerk, Lieutenant. I was just wondering aloud."

Byers was not about to be without the last retort. "Well, wonder aloud to yourself because I don't have time for stupid inquiries such as yours."

Jacob's rage finally boiled over from his negative attitude. "Don't you dare talk to me like that, you asshole? You don't have the right to speak to me that way."

The two's verbal barbs continued and became even thornier as

Jennings tried unsuccessfully to intervene and interrupt the heated argument for the sake of both of them.

"Knock it off, please," he calmly commanded, even though deep down inside, he felt the unusual need for himself to pulverize Byers for speaking the way he did to the woman he cared for.

Samia coolly tried to hold back Byers, who had risen to his feet to meet Jacobs in the middle of the cell. They bumped chests and breathed hot, putrid air towards one another while sour words oozing with resentment flew from their mouths towards one another.

Taark appeared disgusted at the sight, although it was rather amusing for the others to see the much shorter Jacobs hold her own against the bigger and brawnier Byers.

Something suddenly snapped in Marcus, who awoke from his short bout of depression and quickly sprang upward to referee the two of them.

"That's enough!" he solidly commanded, although their confrontation still continued.

Realizing his initial request had been ignored, the commander grabbed Byers by the collar of his shirt in an attempt to shut him up.

Byers got in one more verbal jab as he growled at her like an animal. "You stupid little--"

"Shut up!" Marcus interrupted, screaming at them both even though he directed his attention to Byers mostly.

Byers was stunned by his friend's actions against him. "What's up with you?" he asked with feign ignorance, as if he had done nothing wrong.

"What's up with me?" Marcus replied with annoyance. "I was going to ask both of you the same, and especially you, Tommy. You're the first lieutenant on this crew, for God's sake, which means you're a leader of these people, and you're responsible for them all. You, of all people, should already know that. You're a leader of this crew as well, for Christ's sake."

The usually mouthy Byers could offer no rebuttal for his actions and simply nodded his head in agreement.

"You're right. I'm sorry," he softly stated to Marcus.

Personal accountability dominated throughout Byers, who felt the inner need to own up for his wrongs.

He turned his attention to Jacobs, who herself appeared embarrassed by her behavior.

"I'm sorry, Jacobs," he apologized sincerely to her. "I was wrong to treat you the way that I did."

Jacobs nodded her head to him softly and felt her own need to take responsibility also. "I'm sorry as well, Byers. I shouldn't have let my anger take over."

Byers nodded in acknowledgment and turned to face the rest of his fellow captives humbly. "I'm sorry to each and every one of you, as well. My actions were uncalled for and unprofessional."

Jennings and Rubidoux nodded in appreciation, and Arraz was at their side.

Samia came behind Byers and placed her hand on his shoulder as a sign of support before offering a gentle massage to support his apology.

Only Taark offered no sort of acknowledgment over Byers' apology as he sat listlessly staring at the lieutenant, who gazed right back at him in an attempt to read his reaction. "Your beings are abnormal with interactions," he dully stated, completely out of tune with what had transpired.

The alien father turned his attention to the situation and felt further confusion about his daughter's behavior. He felt uneasy over seeing her interactions with Byersand could not understand for his life how she could possibly be deeply enamored with an Earthly man such as him.

Marcus, meanwhile, felt satisfied by Byers' response and turned his attention to the downtrodden Jacobs, who was visibly upset at herself for her own actions.

Sensing she needed a pick-me-up, the commander draped his

arm across her shoulders to help soothe her ill feelings. "Are you okay?"

She nodded uneasily as she attempted to appear valiant in front of her commanding officer, even though Marcus was not fooled in the slightest.

Jennings especially kept a close eye as he was prepared to come in if needed for added support.

She maintained her composure and resisted the urge to weep from shame before heading towards the empty space between Rubidoux and Jennings, who visually appeared as happy as could be that she was preparing to sit next to him.

Marcus now stood alone as Samia and Byers followed Jacobs' lead and sat in between Taark and Monica. He peered at his mixed bag of fellow captives, who he could feel were now counting on him more than ever for guidance and leadership.

Only the stoic loner Taark appeared to be in no need of encouragement, disconnect more than apparent from the lost gaze in his eyes as he stared blankly away from them.

Despite the mental absence of one of his fellow captives, it was more than apparent to Marcus that it was a vital time for him to shine and to show the others what type of leader he truly was.

His galvanizing moment had arrived, and he felt more than prepared to face it head on as he took a quick look around at the longing faces that waited for his words.

"My friends--as you are well aware, we have been duped and deceived by those we have trusted. They have lied to us, kicked us to the proverbial ground and have tried to spit on us."

Taking a moment to let his words further settle in, he stared at each and every one of them and was met with complete attention from everyone not named Taark.

"Yet, here we are, and we are still alive and kicking," he continued. "They may have us locked up in this cell, but this is not how it ends for us. We must maintain our hope and our composure and be ready for the opportunity when it arises. And when it does, we must fight like hell to get back the freedom that is rightfully ours."

He turned his head towards Monica, who beamed in approval of his words of leadership and appeared to be proud of him, as if she had witnessed a coming-of-age moment that had just blossomed before her eyes.

Marcus kept his composure and refused to crack a smile, although his heart gleamed with an unwavering determination that he never had felt before in his full career with SAGE. He felt a sense of hope finally, even though the odds still remained strongly opposed against them all, and could feel the leadership strength inside of him begin to explode.

He peeled his eyesight from her reluctantly and regained his full focus the others to finish his monologue.

"No matter the end result, I want you all to know that I believe in each one of you and that I consider myself fortunate to be leading you all. We will not allow ourselves to be victims any longer, and we will rise from this hell we have been mired in together and bring justice against those who have wronged us."

The focus on his comrades' faces said it all to Marcus, who felt the warm glow of their attention in full force.

He turned his attention to Byers, who nodded and smiled at him in acknowledgment, with Samia grinning out of the corner of his eye by his friend's side.

His attention then shifted to the approving faces of Jennings and Jacobs, the two clueless lovebirds who had unknowingly found their ways to sit next to each other.

A rare confident smile then came across Rubidoux, who for once appeared at ease and comfortable with the group.

Arraz also grinned in agreement as Marcus' stare passed him by, which completed those who had paid complete attention to his speech, at least that he was aware of.

Much to Marcus' surprise, however, and out of the corner of his eye, as his sight passed Arraz, he was able to see a nod of the head from Taark, who, although stone-faced, appeared in connection with what the commander had just finished preaching.

Wow, maybe I even got HIS attention. Not bad, Ronnie, not bad.

Despite the good feelings that brewed internally, Marcus still denied himself the opportunity to smile, opting instead to continue with the stern look that he had donned throughout.

"No matter what happens, we fight to the end," he concluded as his inner strength pulsated strongly throughout his body. "And even if Death comes to our doorstep, we go down swinging without giving them any further satisfaction."

He felt completely in charge, and in his mind it was official that he had become the de facto captain that was badly needed by his emotionally damaged crew members, who soaked up his passion in complete awe.

Pride had officially been restored to them all, even if their situation still appeared to be dire and unhopeful at best.

Marcus' eyes fixated upon Monica, whose eyes danced in pleasure towards him in approval.

Feeling a tad more at ease, especially thanks to her presence, he finally allowed himself a smile as the corners of his mouth curled upwards smoothly.

Even if we don't make it out of here alive, at least she saw me at my glorious best.

Cautious optimism suddenly filled the air of the dead cell that suddenly had been brought back to life. They no longer felt like victims of circumstance, and nor were they the same prisoners they were even moments earlier. Freedom rang through their hearts for the first time in a while, even if the metal bars they found themselves behind attempted to suggest otherwise.

A confused Maren evolved from the opening on the other side of the bars and stood in front of the locked door, his gun pressed against his chest as he did not know what to make of the brightness that seemed to radiate from inside the cell.

"What is the meaning of these happenings?" he inquired

harshly, his stare turned directly towards the newly brandished leader of the pack in an effort to get the answer he felt he deserved.

Marcus waltzed slowly towards Maren and stood confidently in front of him, the bars serving as his crutch to be cavalier. "That's none of your damn business."

Maren, blown away by Marcus' bold response, gritted his teeth and seethed in anger.

It was obvious in his eyes that the extraterrestrial man would have liked none other than to blow his brains out from his casual behavior, and nobody could sense that more than Marcus, who almost seemed to relish in seeing the fiery anger burn inside of Maren.

C'mon, shoot me. You know you want to. What's stopping you, anyways, you alien bastard?

Maren resisted the temptation and did his best to ease the anger inside him.

"Our noble leader requires your attention," he stated with a sulking tone before taking his key card and placing it in front of the security device, which beeped in acknowledgment and slid the iron bars to his right as the gate opened up. "Come."

Marcus stood momentarily and turned his head to Byers, who stood directly to his left and simply nodded his head in a mode of charade.

Another nod of the head was returned in acknowledgement before turning his head to his right and into the eyes of Monica, who stared longingly back at him.

"Be careful, Ronnie," Monica warmly advised.

Marcus smiled at her care-filled words, amazed once more by the kind of woman she was. "Don't worry. I'll be alright."

An upset Maren growled at them, unhappy with the pleasantries that had been exchanged. "Cease, creatures. Your beings' compliance is immediately demanded."

Marcus gazed one last time at Monica before reluctantly turning away from her beauty to avoid any further and unnecessary lambasting.

That damn pushy alien bastard, anyways.

Anger resonated through Marcus, who glared with hatred towards Maren while stepping out of the cell and momentarily back onto the side of freedom.

"Pause," ordered Maren to Marcus, who complied and halted on a dime.

Grabbing the bars quickly, Maren slammed the cell door with power, the deafening clanking of the iron serving as confirmation of its locked status.

He picked up his gun from his chest and pointed it between Marcus' shoulder blades. "Move," he commanded forcefully before roughly poking Marcus to further force the action.

Smirking despite his hatred for the armed alien man, Marcus glared back at the closed cell towards his equals before following the verbal and physical order given him to march out of the brig area.

Marcus didn't know where he was going and what was going to happen next. The only thing he knew was that he was not going to go down without a fight, even if death awaited him on the other side.

Chapter 25

Over the mountain and through the woods, to Maxwell's quarters, we go...

Marcus' sarcasm, even internally, had reached an all-time high even though a monumental moment of despair such as the one he faced head-on as the rickety doors to the elevator opened and invited him unwelcomingly to him and his captain's personal floor.

Maren was in no mood to mess around like usual, commanding his prisoner to move once more by poking him in the back again with his gun.

Marcus rolled his eyes upwards as he had tired of the abuse and belittling the alien had continuously exhibited towards him.

I swear to God, this guy's going to get it from me sooner or later. And when he gets what he deserves, I'm going to poke the hell out of his dead body.

They passed Marcus' room first, and the commander gazed momentarily towards the shut door of his quarters and couldn't help but wish that he could have grabbed the extra gun he kept underneath his bed.

Boy, that sure would come in handy right now.

Maren noticed the turn of his head and roughly stuck him once more in the back of the neck. "Cease. Regain focus."

Marcus' tolerance continued to be tested, although he resisted turning around and creating mayhem before his meeting with Maxwell even occurred.

He knew, however, that his new-found motivation and drive would be all for nothing if he snapped at the wrong moment and was shot down and killed for his heroic attempts.

Just keep your cool. Be patient, and just play along for now. Your chance will come.

The suspense of what was coming next was about to end as they stopped outside of the closed, cold door to Maxwell's quarters. Maren proceeded to push the orange button to summon his master, his finger caressing against the trigger and the barrel of his gun pointed upward and against the back of Marcus' skull.

Maxwell immediately responded to Maren's push of the button. "Is Marcus with you?"

"Affirmative," confirmed Maren. "The creature is in my possession."

"Come in, then."

The door swiftly slid open quickly to reveal darkness on the other side.

Maren, true to his own fashion, poked Marcus in the rear end of his cranium to get him to go.

Marcus growled upon the further abuse but decided to continue to play along, marching into the dark atmosphere that awaited him.

An eerie chill came down Marcus' spine over the uncertainty that awaited him, the room void of the entirety of noise.

He arrived in the heart of the quarters of his now insanity-driven former captain, who stood behind his cherry-wood table, his back turned towards Marcus and Maren. A dimmed light hung directly above him and made his newly darkened hair glisten.

"Leave us, Maren," commanded Maxwell.

"Sire?"

Maxwell's tone sharpened harshly towards him. "I said to leave us. Do as I say."

"Aye, sire. My being shall await further instruction externally."

Maren turned and hurried out of the room while Maxwell waited for the door to open and close as confirmation that he was alone with Marcus.

The captain turned around and sat at his desk, his face draped entirely in the dark matter around him.

"Sit down, Marcus," he ordered, his tone softening slightly.

A defiant touch penetrated through Marcus' bones. "You're not my captain anymore. So, I guess I don't really have to listen to you anymore, now do I--John?"

Against his own nature, Maxwell declined to get angry and instead only exhaled deeply. "You always have been a mouthy one, Marcus, but that's one of the things I've always kind of liked about you, I admit."

Marcus was unimpressed by the rare compliment given by Maxwell, his focus remaining on the business at hand. "Care to shed a little light in here?"

"I will if you sit down," bargained Maxwell.

"Fine," replied a nodding Marcus, who sat down in the chair and stared at the darkened face of Maxwell. "Now it's time for you to hold up your end of the bargain."

Maxwell nodded his profiled head in acknowledgment. "Very well. Lights, three-quarters!"

The lights intensified at seventy-five percent of its capacity on command, and much to Marcus' surprise, he stared into the fresh young face of Maxwell that now adorned a new surprise.

"You shaved," the commander noticed immediately on the now baby-faced Maxwell.

A sly, evil grin crossed Maxwell's face, which contained a few bloody nicks around his jawline while he folded his hands on top of his desk. "I figured I should fully complete my new look."

Marcus couldn't believe his eyes over the incredible transformation Maxwell had undergone in the past several hours. He looked youthful, full of energy and vigor, and most importantly, extremely dangerous, and the villainous venom that floated in his eyes further suggested that to be true.

It's too bad that I'm going to rob him of his youth.

Marcus leaned back in the leather chair and folded his arms. "So, what do you want?" he asked, getting straight to the point.

Maxwell seemed somewhat taken aback by Marcus' no nonsense approach. "My, how business-like we've become, I see. There's no bullshitting with you, is there?"

Marcus sat silently like a statue, refusing to immediately respond.

The captain stared at him and realized there was no extracurricular talk that would be involved.

"Very well. If that's how you want it, then so be it," Maxwell continued with a raise of his eyebrows. "The reason for me bringing you here is because I want to give you an opportunity that may intrigue you."

"I don't want anything from you," Marcus snapped back, refusing to give a moment to even stew it over.

Maxwell shook his head at the commander's rapid reaction. "How would you know if you don't even give me an opportunity to present my proposal to you? You might just like what you hear."

Marcus' glare intensified, and for the first time ever, he could picture himself murdering his captain. It was a strong indication, especially in his heart, how much his feelings for his former commanding officer had completely changed.

"No, I won't because you are a murderer and a betrayer," was the straight-edged statement that left his lips. "And my respect for you is non-existent, John."

Maxwell, surprised yet somewhat amused by what he was hearing, chuckled to himself. "My, how bold we've become. I suppose I must say that I do agree about the first part, and I have no regrets about admitting that."

The youthful captain arose from behind his desk and towards his fish-filled aquarium, his pace the speed of molasses as he began observing his beloved pets.

"With that being said, I do also have to confess that I've always admired your mentality, but I especially like this side of you," he continued. "One thing that I know for certain is that you don't take shit from anybody, and I suppose I've always somewhat appreciated that about you from a distance. But, for this particular moment, I ask for your complete silence so that I may tell you something that could very well change your mind."

Marcus' eyes shifted directly from Maxwell's back to that of the desk. He realized, suddenly, that his captain may have unknowingly let down his guard as he fixated his gaze on the feather pen embedded into its crystal ink jar, which called out to him as a means to his and the captives' escape and survival.

The pen is mightier than the sword.

He gazed up quickly at Maxwell, who was still lollygagging his way towards the fish tank that his attention had been turned to entirely.

Knowing that he would have to be quick about it, he turned his stare back onto the pen and swayed his eyesight upward and downward like a pendulum to ensure he was not going to be caught before he was able to make his attempt.

This could be the ticket for us all to freedom.

Maxwell, surprisingly unaware of his surroundings, reached the aquarium and leaned towards it, gazing at the multitude of colored fish that swam freely through the lit water. He had no idea of what was going on behind his back and still did not bother to look back to check on his former commander.

"That's better," stated Maxwell, who had mistakenly assumed that Marcus was willing to cooperate.

Taking his index finger, the captain began to slide it against the glass and followed the bright yellow flounder that floated its way through the water, his thoughts making him further believe that he had Marcus wrapped around his controlling finger.

"I am presenting you with the opportunity to cease your pitiful rebellious actions while you are still relatively unscathed and, most importantly, alive, to join us instead," he continued, his back still facing Marcus. "You would be a valuable asset for us, and you may just be exactly what we need to fully execute the remainder of our mission."

Marcus gazed at the pen once more, realizing that his time was quickly running short.

Quietly putting out his hand, he began to reach for it, his gaze fixated on Maxwell, who remained preoccupied with his fish, to ensure that he was not going to be caught.

The softness of the feather never felt better as it brushed against his palm. He quietly closed his palm around the pen and lifted it gently from the jar of ink, being overly cautious not to let the tip of the pen clink against the side of the crystal.

"But, regardless, it's time for you to face facts, Marcus," continued Maxwell, unaware of the happenings that had occurred behind him. "You and your friends are in a hopeless situation. The residents of the town here are useless and worship the ground I walk on, so you can forget about extra reinforcements. It is with that being said that I extend an olive branch to you as a sign of generosity on my part to spare you the agonizing death that is sure to come your way shortly should you refuse. That is unless you accept my offer and join us."

Maxwell rose back up from his crouch and turned back towards him, delivering a menacing look in the process as an attempt to intimidation and to further assist Marcus in his decision-making.

Little did the captain realize, however, that Marcus had just hidden his office supply-turned-weapon onto his lap and under the desk.

Offering no hint of wrongdoing, Marcus defiantly stared at the young face of his captain and continued as if it was business as usual to offer no such hint into what his thoughts were.

"So, what do you say, Marcus?" asked the captain in a

demanding fashion, stopping at the right side of the desk and lurching downwards to hover over Marcus' head. "Are you ready to escape this living hell you've been mired in and do something about it?"

Marcus smirked at his captain, ready to give his answer.

"Yeah," he answered, gripping the pen tighter in his hand. "I am."

In the blink of an eye and with all of the might he consumed, Marcus swung the pen in a roundhouse move and made the impact he was hoping for. The sharp tip pierced through Maxwell's neck and instantly penetrated deeply into his throat cavity.

Maxwell's screams of hysteria bounced off the walls, his face flushed with agonizing pain.

Grabbing his wounded neck, he crashed to his knees while blood streamed down rapidly from the point of contact and blended into his red uniformed shirt.

Marcus rushed to his feet and further forced the pen deeper into Maxwell's neck, whose teeth gritted in anguish from the pain that had overtaken him.

A sense of redemption rang through Marcus, who enjoyed watching his mad with, powerful, commanding officer be on the other end of punishment and pain for once. He continued to apply maximum pressure as the pen embedded itself further into the neck.

Engulfed with despair, Maxwell choked violently in a futile effort to catch the oxygen he needed to survive.

"Goodbye, Captain," stated Marcus ruthlessly while watching Maxwell's eyes roll into the back of his head before taking his last breath.

Maxwell had died, but Marcus knew that it was only temporary, thanks to the liquid that had permanently altered him.

Acting quickly, Marcus knelt to one knee and pushed Maxwell to the other side to grab the handgun that was nestled into his belt.

He held the gun in his hand and turned his head back at Maxwell's body, which was still void of life. He aimed the gun at Maxwell's heart and fired a shot that punctured through his chest, hoping faintly that it would be the shot that officially put an end to Maxwell's reign of terror.

Marcus felt conflicted about what he had done, primarily as if he himself had become a murderer and done the wrong thing.

At the same time, however, he felt satisfaction over killing Maxwell, peering down somewhat proudly at the act he had committed as Maxwell's dead body lay frozen on the ground and despair remained plastered through his motionless face.

The door opened swiftly .Marcus immediately reacted and hid behind the wall next to a hallway that led to it.

Maren, unusually unarmed with his gun hung on his belt, stopped at the mouth of the entrance and stood in alarm upon seeing his deceased leader lying on the floor, a pool of blood now expanding beneath him.

Rushing to Maxwell, he knelt down upon reaching the captain's deceased body and touched his neck, feeling only a non-existent pulse.

Maren, shocked by the sudden turn of events, blinked his eyes out, unsure of what to do next.

Hiding in the curtain of darkness behind his enemies, Marcus rested his back against the wall while fascination rushed his brain upon the sight. It seemed cruel, but he enjoyed what he was seeing as the shoe had officially fit on the other foot.

He was a killer for the first time in his life, and the adrenaline that rushed through him gave him a high he had never experienced before. He was frightened somewhat by his enjoyment but justified his actions to himself by remembering what both Maxwell and Maren had done to them all.

Now, it's time to make my next move.

Marcus tiptoed quickly and crept up on Maren, whose focus remained solely on the deceased Maxwell.

Payback's going to be a bitch for you.

Aiming his gun at the back of Maren's head, a grin scaled his mouth, revenge feeling oh so sweet and within his immediate grasp.

He enjoyed being on the other side of the fence and could already picture himself sending a laser shot right through the back of Maren's skull.

"Freeze, asshole," he solidly commanded to Maren.

Maren gritted his teeth and reluctantly followed the commander's orders.

"Give me your gun," instructed Marcus.

Once again, doing as instructed, Maren passed the weapon softly and without delay.

Marcus took the gun and placed it in his open hand to double barrel himself. "Now, put your hands behind your head."

Maren did once more as ordered and placed his hands behind his head to avoid any sort of conflict.

Marcus felt completely in charge now, and he began to see the light at the end of the tunnel for the first time.

"Is it the intention of your being to kill cowardly?" asked Maren in an attempt to guilt Marcus of killing him as well. "Is my being to suffer expiration by the hand of your being without a fair opportunity like that of our master?"

Marcus could feel the need for homicide flowing through him once more, a yearning rushing through him to further sweeten his revenge.

With both of his index fingers on the two triggers, he was prepared to fire and complete the payback he desired to have.

His mind, however, suddenly decided to change the script as he resisted the strong urge that pulled him towards changing his decision once more.

"No," answered Marcus, who felt a change of heart dictate a change in plans. "I've got something better in store for you."

CHAPTER 26

Marcus could immediately feel the difference once he stepped outside of Maxwell's chambers. The air, while somewhat stuffy, felt fresher and easier to breathe, thanks to the freedom he had taken back.

"Freeze," commanded Marcus to Maren before turning back and firing three shots towards the creases of Maxwell's door for a bit of extra insurance in case his captain was to have regained consciousness shortly.

A strange, cold feeling engulfed Marcus' heart. Perhaps it was the fact that he had never committed homicide on a man before, let alone the fact that it was his commanding officer who was his victim.

Whatever the reason, he began to second guess if he had indeed done the right thing.

I don't want to be like him. I don't want to turn into him.

Marcus shook his head quickly to turn away the internal mind games that he began to play with himself. "Move to the elevator," he commanded to Maren, who followed orders and marched accordingly.

Marcus gazed back at the closed door to Maxwell's quarters, his own mind once more playing tricks on him. The hallway seemed darker than usual, especially around the area of Maxwell's quarters, and he could feel his own guilt try to keep him from feeling justified in his actions.

Goosebumps splurged onto his arms while a cold chill cracked down his back. Guilt and regret pumped through his heart now as he began to heavily question what he had done.

I did the right thing, didn't I? After all, he did kill Arraz. And he probably would have killed me if I hadn't beaten him to the punch--right?

His insecurity began to frighten him more than he could have possibly imagined. He felt dirty for the deed he had committed, vileness pumping through his heart as he suddenly felt no better than the wicked captain he had disposed of by his own hand.

Suddenly, however, as if another side of him attempted to play devil's advocate, he began to wonder why it felt somewhat satisfying to have killed his superior officer in the manner in which he had. He couldn't help but grin momentarily as he thought about it, and admittedly, it was somewhat pleasing to him that he watched Maxwell suffer for all of the evil things he had done to him and his crew.

The conflict that generated furiously inside of him was confusing, and he wasn't quite sure what to make of it. Was it wrong for him to feel proud of himself for killing Maxwell, or was he justified in feeling so?

His heart felt torn as they reached the elevator door that had remained ajar as if it had been waiting for them both the entire time.

Marcus pointed the gun at the right temple of Maren while taking his index finger from his free hand and pushing the button to take them back to the basement of the ship where the others were still incarcerated.

"Don't try anything funny, or I'll blow your brains out," he ordered Maren, who responded with a cold, hard stare that cut through him.

You can glare me down all you want. I'm in control now.

The script had officially been flipped in Marcus' mind as the elevator skidded its way down the chute before screeching to a stop on the second floor.

Marcus began to feel slightly antsy in anticipation of releasing his comrades from the prison and carrying out his plan for the martyr who stood next to him.

He thought about the cruel treatment he had already endured from Maren especially, who almost seemed as if he had earlier gone out of his way to make the commander's life a living hell. He wondered if there was a chief reason behind the torture and if perhaps Maxwell had told him something to further motivate the extraterrestrial to carry out such dastardly deeds.

Or maybe he's just jealous.

Marcus chuckled to himself, careless as could be that Maren could see the joy that began to rush through him.

"What does your finding to be of humorous value?" Maren asked out of annoyance.

Marcus chuckled a moment before answering. "I was just thinking about how nice it is to be in control now," answered the commander, "and how glorious it will be when I kill you myself."

Maren did not take kindly to Marcus' response, as the murderous glare in his eyes further suggested.

Unafraid of the alien man's increasing anger, Marcus smirked back at Maren with great enjoyment.

I love it. Just keep fueling my fire, why don't you?

The elevator door slid open to the basement upon the bumpy stop. Marcus took the barrel of his gun and decided to give Maren another taste of his own medicine by poking him in between the shoulder blades, ensuring to put a little extra oomph into it.

"Move, creature," he ordered with a wide grin that detailed the kick he got out of his opportunity for payback. "Put your hands behind your head."

Maren growled out of disapproval yet obliged with the orders he had been given. Marcus, meanwhile, peered back to make sure there were no other unwanted visitors around, his paranoia beginning to get the best of him. He knew there was a strong possibility that Maxwell could have come back alive, but he at least felt more secure knowing what he had done to prevent the captain from escaping so easily.

After a right turn that led to them to the prison area, Marcus could see Byers leaning against the bars at the front of the cell, and his head rested against the hard metal restrictors. He had fallen asleep while standing, a sight that amused Marcus.

Poor tired bastard.

Ignoring the exhaustion that tried to sneak into his bodily system, Marcus trailed behind the leading Maren into the cell full of slumbered individuals.

Exhaust even got the best of Samia and Taark, who were both passed out asleep sitting on the hard floor, their backs resting against the tough walls. Samia looked particularly cozy, with her head resting on her father's left shoulder.

I bet that Tommy would be sleeping even better if he were in her father's place right about now.

Each one appeared comfortable, and Marcus felt terrible about having to end their states of being. After everything they had all been through, it was hard to blame them all for catching some shut eye and recharging their internal batteries.

Maren stood stone-faced and lacked expression while staring out into nowhere. Marcus continued to point the gun at the back of Maren's head, not allowing any sort of leeway for the renegade alien in case he attempted any sort of rebellious action.

A loud snore that came from Rubidoux did little to affect the sleeping crew as the rookie lay in an awkward position that contributed to his snoring. It amused Marcus that the quietest and most timid of his crew was also the one making the most noise right now, and he couldn't help but grin over the irony of it.

His eyesight slid to the right to capture a glimpse of Jacobs and Jennings, who slept close to one another and appeared cozy with one another. He couldn't help but wonder, perhaps because of his knowledge of their feelings towards one another, if they had somewhat tailored that, even unintentionally, by design.

And, of course, he had to gaze at Monica, who appeared angelic in her sleep while she lay on her arm on the hard floor, making it appear more comfortable than it actually was. She groaned slightly as if she were deep in a dream but appeared to be at great peace for the most part.

Whatever you're dreaming, hopefully, it's sweet, my dear.

As much as Marcus didn't want to be on the other side of those bars again, he sure wouldn't have minded being there right now, especially if he had been so lucky to have lied next to her.

Soon enough, I'm hoping, that will be a reality and no longer a dream.

Realizing the need to get the process going, despite resisting the urge to leave his friends alone, Marcus tapped on Byers' shoulder to wake his friend first.

Byers only groaned as he turned his head the other way and tried to ignore the culprit responsible for interrupting his sleep.

"Wake up, Tommy," ordered Marcus while continuously poking his friend with the tip of his finger. "Wake your sorry ass up."

Byers groaned once more but began to slowly open his eyes while battling deep sleep. "Wha--what?"

He batted and rubbed his eyes in a feeble attempt to regain his sight. Through blurred vision, he could see the profile of Marcus pointing the gun at Maren, who continued to look into the yonder.

Thinking that he was still dreaming, Byers rubbed his eyes once more to make sure that he was actually seeing what was before him, smiling broadly upon the confirmation his own eyes had given him before rushing to his feet.

"Ronnie, you're alive! I can't believe it!"

"My, how little faith ye have, young grasshopper," Marcus stated jokingly while shaking his head at his friend. "Didn't I tell you that I'd get us out of here?"

Byers laughed off his friend's teasing. "Yeah, but the trouble is, the rest of us besides you are still locked in here. So, your job is not quite complete yet."

"Alright," said a chuckling Marcus. "Well, maybe I'll let everyone out except for you."

The two friends laughed at one another joyously for a moment before Marcus turned his head towards Maren and instantly became more serious. "Open the cell."

Maren slowly reached for the key card on his belt and began to struggle to get it off.

"Hurry up," demanded Marcus to further give Maren a taste of his own pushy medicine. "We don't have all day here."

The extraterrestrial man stared angrily at the commander before taking the card and slowly placing it against the scanner.

A loud beep confirmed that the cell had indeed unlocked, but that did little to ease Marcus from increasing his pushiness.

"Open the cell," he demanded to Maren. "Open it now."

Maren once more unwillingly obliged and opened the cell, the loud creek that came from the sound of the sliding bars awakening the rest of the captives, who yawned and rubbed their eyes while attempting to regain consciousness.

Byers, the first to step out of the cell, clustered closely to his pal. "What happened to Maxwell?"

"Let's just say I put him out of his misery," answered Marcus quietly. "I'll explain later."

Byers smirked and leaned towards Marcus' ear to exchange something privately. "Monica was really worried about you, just to let you know."

Marcus stared at his friend, who nodded his head as reassurance. He smiled at the thought and turned his attention to Monica, who gazed back at him and beamed her luminous smile to give him a warm, non-verbal hello.

Warmly smiling back, he resisted the urge to go up and embrace her, his own internal instincts held him back to inform him that the hugs, and he hoped kisses, would have to wait for later.

Meanwhile, Jacobs and Jennings simultaneously rose to their feet, not taking a moment as they quickly bailed out of the cell and into the aura of freedom.

Arraz and Rubidoux sluggishly got up and were the last to leave the cell, thanks to Samia and Taark beating them both to the punch as the last to be incarcerated.

Rubidoux yawned loudly and tried to rub the sleep out of his eyes.

Marcus, feeling somewhat playful, jokingly hazed the young navigator. "C'mon, rookie, we don't have all day."

"S--sorry, Commander," Rubidoux apologized, not picking up on the joke as he stumbled out of his cell.

Samia and Byers united and embraced as they kissed one another out of joy. Taark, not seeming amused by the gesture between the two, glared at Byers with disapproval.

Taark's attention, along with Samia's, rapidly shifted to that of their vilified loved one, Maren, who continued to look away unemotionally and refused to meet his eyes with that of his father or sister.

Marcus, seeing the growing tension between the family members, proceeded with his plans by turning his attention back to that of his captive.

"Get into the cell," he commanded to Maren, who offered no hesitation as he followed suit on the order and shuffled into the now-empty cell that anxiously awaited his presence.

A satisfactory smirk came over Marcus, who closed and shut the cell door swiftly, the iron bars clanging upon closure, sounding as sweet as possible to the commander.

Byers felt the urge to say something to Maxwell's apprentice and decided to capitalize on the opportunity.

"It doesn't feel so good to be on the other side, does it?"

"Tommy, don't," instructed Marcus to tame down his friend's spiteful motives.

Byers, fighting the urge to continue, nodded his head and decided to listen to the orders of his commander and friend, much to his own chagrin. He backed away from the cell and conjoined himself to the side of Samia, who seemed somewhat satisfied by his behavior a moment earlier.

Taark stepped towards Marcus cautiously as the commander could feel the hulking man in need of his attention.

"It is an inquiry of my being to yours that my being is allowed to speak directly to my offspring."

Understanding the oddly phrased request, Marcus nodded his head, stepped back and slid his way between Monica and Arraz to get fully out of the way.

Taark slowly approached the cell where his son was occupied and stood there silently, and his gaze fixated directly into the eyes of Maren while he prepared himself to speak.

Samia left the embrace of her love, Byers and joined the side of her father, her eyes locked in towards her emotionally lost brother, who turned his back from the attention his family was giving him.

"Seed of my being," the father began towards his son, his voice uneven with emotion. "What is the vital explanation for the recent happenings?"

"My being offers no explanations," answered Maren, his voice monotone and void of care. "Nor is my being of willing nature to concede one to your being or that of my sister."

Samia's eyes began to water upon her brother's nonchalance. "Brother, I beg upon your being. Concede if it is a matter we have bestowed upon your being."

Maren's face remained unchanged despite his sister's emotional output. "Nay, for my being has nothing to concede. Following the noble leader that has been sent to us is of utmost priority. Our Excellency is wise and noble above our beings, including that of the beings of the creatures of Earth."

Taark visibly cracked with emotion, and his softer side began to filter through upon his gruff yet youthful face. "Our Excellency is not of that elderly creature, for the heart of his being contains wickedness and fatal consequences. His being will conquer and be the destruction for the lifecycle of our beings, as well as the beings of Earth."

Tears welled in Taark's dark eyes and trickled down his bearded face, his emotions now on full display as a last gasp effort to attempt to save his son.

Maren, however, was unimpressed by the display, continuing to show zero remorse towards that of his own family.

"Maren," continued Taark, his voice now trembling in desperation, "what are the explanations for the happenings of your being? The hearts of my being and that of your sister contain adoration for your being despite the recent occurrences that have been exhibited. It is on begging nature that my being implores yours to remove the erroneous feelings of hatred and return to the natural state that is of what our beings have knowledge of."

Maren turned his head to face his father directly and crunched his face into a frightening glare radiating with anger. "The feelings of hatred of my being are true. My being contains no allegiance to your being or that of my sister, for the devotion of my being is solely to that of our Excellency, who will rise from the dead and exact his revenge triumphantly. The perishing of your beings will be the trademark of a new era for our home and beyond, and your beings will have no resource for survival."

Heartbreak engulfed both Samia and Taark, who together realized that they had officially lost their brother and son, respectively, through their tears of sadness.

Annoyed by their weeping, Maren coldly glared at Taark and Samia and seethed upon the sight.

"The nature your beings exhibit contains pathetic qualities. It is of great misfortune that my being is associated with such pitiful behavior."

The rest of the crew, meanwhile, could only stare on in sadness for watching their two alien comrades have their hearts ripped out by that of their own blood.

"Tragic," Jennings simply stated while shaking his head.

"That has to be one of the saddest things I've ever seen," said Jacobs, who herself shared in Taark and Samia's heartbreak with her own tears. "How could he treat them so badly?"

Keeping cool and collected, yet doing so unconsciously, Jennings got closer to Jacobs and swung his right arm over her shoulder in an effort to soothe her own pain.

"I haven't felt this sad since my Nana died," the young Rubidoux pronounced to his fellow crewmembers without shame.

"I've never had a Nana, and I'm not sure who that is, but I'm sure losing one is a terrible thing," Arraz responded to the rookie's statement, not even sure of who exactly Rubidoux was referring to.

"It is," answered Monica sadly, fully understanding what the rookie was referring to while reliving the death of her own.

Her eyes were busy, and her heart was occupied as well, she glared over at Byers to push him into doing the right thing for Samia.

"Go over there and say something to her, please. She needs you, especially right now."

Byers nodded in agreement and slid quietly towards Samia before taking a page from Jennings' book and draping his arm over her petite frame.

Marcus felt his own melancholy going through him. His heart, while breaking for the father and his daughter, instantly became enraged towards his alien rival.

Surely, he wasn't always this way. What made him become such a heartless bastard? And what did Maxwell do to him to make him into the monster he is now?

At a loss for external words to express his own grief, he turned towards Monica, who struggled on her own behalf to keep her composure together emotionally.

"Are you okay?" was all he could muster towards his secret sweetheart.

She nodded her head and closed her eyes for a moment to keep the tears from flowing. "I just feel so awful for them both. He's their family, and he's treating them like they're nothing to him. The worst part is that you can tell how much they love and miss him. It's just so tragic."

"Yeah," agreed Marcus sullenly. "You can really tell."

Monica turned towards Marcus and rested her head on his chest, her emotions beginning to spill over. "I miss home," she whispered to him. "Seeing this makes me miss my family so much. I just want to see them again and tell them how much I love them."

"Me too," he replied in agreement, resisting the urge to follow the lead of Jennings and Byers in favor of keeping professional.

She raised her head and sweetly gazed up at him, her presence feeling ever so safe with him nearby. "I was happy to see you made it back alive after your encounter with Maxwell. I don't know what I'd do without you."

Marcus grinned from ear to ear internally over her latter statement, his heart feeling as if it had suddenly been draped in velvet.

She cares about me. If I die now, at least I can do so as a happy man.

Disciplining himself further, however, he gazed down for a moment at her before staring back ahead toward Maren to not allow his feelings to become too transparent.

Keep it professional. Just keep it professional.

Thankfully, and right on time for Marcus' behalf to keep him from unlocking his vault of feelings, Monica continued on with another question.

"What happened when you met with him, and how did you escape?"

"Oh, it's a long story," he replied, happy that he got to keep his personal vault locked for a better moment. "I'll tell you everything once we start heading home. But first, let's see what we're going to do with Maxwell's little alien imp."

Monica nodded her head and happily buried her face into his

chest, the reality of the mission ending and their return home suddenly seeming imminent and no longer doubtful.

Just before her positive feelings could filter through, she lifted her head from Marcus' chest and gazed up at him.

"Do you hear something?" she asked Marcus out of confusion.

Searching around, he, too, could hear what she could in the form of a muffled voice.

Realizing that he had turned the volume on his intercom to the lowest setting, he immediately tapped on it to increase the volume.

A struggling, gravelly voice suddenly cascaded through the dingy cell.

"Mar--cus. Mar--cus."

Immediately identifying the tone, Marcus' blood instantly froze to ice cold.

"Max--Maxwell?"

"Yes. Your doom--is near."

Marcus turned his attention to Maren, who met his glare with an evil grin that sent a creepy chill down the commander's spine.

CHAPTER 27

———————

Laughing hysterically through hollow coughing on the other end of the intercom, Maxwell reveled in the glory of his eternal life blessing that had saved him from the depths of hell that surely should have awaited him.

Disappointed but unfortunately not surprised by the sudden turn of events, Marcus continued with his brave front with Monica steadfast by his side, even though his heart felt as if it were prepared to sink into a bottomless pit of depression.

I've got to stay strong for her and everybody else.

"Very--well done," Maxwell continued slowly. "I honestly--didn't think you--had it in you to--try and murder me. It must--however--be unfortunate--for you to know--that--you cannot kill--an almighty being--such as--me."

Marcus shook his head at his former captain's boldness. "The only almighty being is God, and you will never be mistaken for Him."

"That--will be up for debate--soon enough," Maxwell proclaimed with a careless chuckle. "Nothing--can stop me now. It was--a noble attempt on--your part--to--stab me, but—-not good enough."

Surprised by the comments of Maxwell being stabbed,

Monica stared at Marcus, beginning to get somewhat of an idea regarding how things went in Maxwell's quarters. She felt curious upon hearing Maxwell's words and couldn't help but wonder where that side of Marcus indeed came from.

"You're more--clever than--I gave you credit for, especially--melding my door shut," continued the captain. "But--you have done little more than--to poke--the hibernating bear. And now—he's ravenous and ready--to hunt his prey--for dinner."

Byers, overhearing the conversation between Marcus and Maxwell, felt the compulsion to get involved. He kissed Samia's forehead before leaving her side to join his friend in order to listen in closer.

Marcus paid no mind to his friend, however, as he attempted to focus on the analogy made by Maxwell. "What in the world are you talking about?" he asked the captain.

An evil snicker came through the intercom and erupted into hollow laughter from Maxwell. "You have made some--critical errors--boy. First, you--failed to realize that--I am now--immortal. You can--murder me all you want and--be as creative as you choose, but--I will always rise from the dead. It's a feeling--like no other. And secondly, you failed--in trapping me--in my own quarters."

"What does that have to do with anything?"

Maxwell evilly chuckled once more. "You failed--to remember that--I have a secret escape door. And now--it is of your--utmost misfortune that--I am--officially on the prowl and--ready to shed the blood of each--and every one of you."

Marcus felt ill upon Maxwell's slow moving, lingering ladder statement, his mind instantly turning up the dial on his internal panic.

Unfazed by the captain's threat, unlike his commander, Byers decided to finally get in on the verbal jousting. "We'll see about that, asshole."

The manic captain chortled upon his lieutenant's boldness. "Indeed--we will. Consider this--a final warning for you all that--

the king has returned--to reclaim his throne. And nothing--and nobody--can stop me now."

Marcus handcuffed emotionally with worry, could offer no other strong statements toward his captain.

Byers, usually strong-tongued and ready to fire back verbally, could also offer nothing more than to peer aimlessly toward his friend.

A final triumphant chuckle came from Maxwell, who realized the power of his threatening words. "You--are all doomed. May God--or rather myself, have mercy--on each one of your--pitiful souls."

A deathly silence came through the intercom upon Maxwell's final warning, sending a worried chill throughout the body of the shaken Marcus. The temporary feeling of control he felt had suddenly been robbed from his grasp, and he could feel momentum beginning to shift back to that of his captain.

"What are we going to do?" Monica asked aloud.

Another heroic moment came over Byers, who felt the need once more to interject. "I'll tell you what we're going to do. We're going to go in there and show the good old captain how things are done around here now. Isn't that right, Ronnie?"

Marcus ignored the cavalier statement from his friend and hurried towards Samia and Taark, who were still attempting to get over their grieving.

"I'm sorry to interrupt your moment," he softly began to the alien father and daughter, "I understand this is a sensitive time for you both, but please, I must ask since we are running out of time. Is there anything we can do to destroy the captain permanently?"

Taark shook his head upon his question, his dark eyes blood-shot from weeping. "Negative. The existence of such a thing for the being of our superior has never been subjected to knowledge. It is of the belief that once our ruler has arrived, his being will lead our beings throughout eternity."

Samia sniffled but felt the need to add further to her father's explanation. "Your leader has consumed the liquid of which our beings cannot. It is for that reason that his being is incapable of death according to the knowledge consumed through the beings of our ancestry. It is of true misfortune that our leader possesses evil as his being does, but our beings contain no knowledge to assist in the inquiry of your being."

Their answers only further dejected Marcus, who sighed heavily with great angst. "So, in other words, we're nothing but sitting ducks?"

Taark and Samia appeared confused by his Earthly statement.

"What are these ducks you speak of?" Samia asked at the wrong possible moment.

"Never mind," mused Marcus, who began to openly think about what could possibly be their next eventful move.

"So, what do we do now, Commander?" Jacobs asked inquisitively.

Marcus paused as he quickly peered over his bewildered crew and their two alien comrades, who all met eyes with him out of desperation.

Maren laughed wickedly upon the openness of despair in the room. "Foolish behavior exhibits your beings. Nil is to be done, for our ruler has risen and will live forever after. Doom is pending for your beings, including the one they call Arraz, whose being has also consumed our sacred liquid."

He turned towards Arraz and pointed his finger, his smile beaming brighter as if he found himself suddenly on the other side of the cell. "Shortly, it will be your being to be locked up once more as a slave and source of torture. Your being will witness the destruction of your people and the enslavement of mine to mark a new era. It is like what has been spoken by our Excellency--the doom of your beings is near."

Arraz held back the urge to open the cell and kept his composure, using a cold stare as his only means of weaponry.

Maren put away his pointed finger and continued his menacing grin, and his glance fixated on that of the young lieutenant.

"The moment of perishing for your being is soon to come," he warned boldly. "And my being will find enjoyment to spit on the deceased bodies of your beings once victory has been accomplished."

Unexpectedly and suddenly, the young and green Rubidoux, stone-faced and equipped with a deadly glare, marched slowly towards the imprisoned alien with great conviction.

"The only deceased carcass here is going to be yours," he stated matter-of-factly. "And soon, your ruler will join you."

Surprise bounced throughout the room for the crew, shocked by the usually unsure Rubidoux's boldness.

Byers cracked a smile upon the disappearance of Maren's smirk, who himself seemed surprised by the rookie's sudden turn of confidence.

Marcus' jaw dropped and remained in form while Rubidoux turned back towards him, his new spirit remaining bright as ever.

"Commander, I am ready to take on our captain and bring an end to his reign of terror once and for all," he announced proudly and with great strength.

The commander could only smile like a proud father who watched his son grow before his eyes instantly into a man.

"As am I, Commander," stated Jennings with inspiration. "I may not have much ability with a weapon, but I sure as--hell will try."

The surprises only continued with the clean-mouthed Jennings dropping an unusually bad word, especially by the spotless doctor's standards.

Marcus' own confidence began to grow, his senses picking up on the increasing momentum that began to swing back their way.

"So, are we in on this together?" he asked to his crew.

"Aye, sir," Jacobs said while smiling towards Jennings for his brave display.

"You know it," answered Byers while patting Marcus' shoulders to assist in his response.

"Absolutely," Arraz replied with a fist in the air in approval.

"Yes," Monica simply answered with an approving grin towards the commander.

Receiving the answers from his crew he had hoped for, Marcus could only hope that Taark and Samia included themselves in the plan.

"Can we count on your help as well?" he asked them cautiously.

Taark gave no indication by his facial expressions but slowly extended his hand towards Marcus approvingly.

"Our beings concur to your request," acknowledged Taark to answer Marcus' question.

An appreciative smile came over Marcus towards Taark, who finally broke his unemotional state and beamed right back at him to further prove that he was placing his trust in the commander's hands.

"Very well," said Marcus simply. "We're all in this together, then."

Rubbing the end of his chin with his palm, Marcus began to ponder on the fly of their plan.

"So, I have an idea, and here's what I'm thinking," he stated, thinking as he spoke. "We only have two guns, so therefore, we need to be creative and split into groups. But, first and foremost, I need a volunteer to watch over our prisoner."

Without hesitation, the suddenly brave Rubidoux extended his hand upward.

"Rube--are you sure you'll be okay to watch over him? The one thing you need to remember is that you won't be armed at all, so keep that in mind."

The rookie smirked and peered over at Maren. "No problem, I can handle him just fine."

Marcus nodded his head in approval. "Very well," said the commander to him before turning his attention to the rest of the crew. "As for us, we're going to split up accordingly--"

He paused in the middle of his sentence and gazed towards Arraz, surveying him head to toe.

Confused by his commander's actions, Maren gave a baffled expression in return. "What are you doing, Commander?"

Marcus scratched the bottom of his chin while consummating his thoughts.

"What size uniform do you wear?" he asked Arraz.

The odd question further perplexed the lieutenant. "Eighteen. Why?"

Marcus placed his answer to Arraz on hold for a moment while turning his attention toward Samia. "Will Arraz be revived should Maxwell murder him once more?"

"Positive to the knowledge of my being," she answered. "What is the reasoning for the question?"

Marcus turned away from her and stared back at Arraz, preparing to answer both of their questions simultaneously.

"Because we're going to need a decoy, and he's the best candidate we've got."

CHAPTER 28

Arraz quickly zipped up Marcus' uniform, which fit him a little large.

Marcus, meanwhile, had already dressed himself in Arraz's outfit that fit him extra snugly.

"This feels a little tight in the crouch, especially," he told Arraz jokingly.

Arraz shook his head upon his commander's ribbing. "At least I'm not getting a bigger uniform to hide that fat ass of yours."

Jacobs intervened to serve as the mediator for both men and get them back on the serious path. "Please, guys, we need to hurry."

Arraz felt odd while gazing down at Marcus' royal blue uniform, realization suddenly hitting him that he was indeed wearing another man's uniform.

"So, what's the purpose of doing this, anyways?" he asked his commander curiously.

"Well, I'm going to have you lead us, but we're going to be following you from a distance," explained Marcus. "My thinking is that because you're wearing my uniform, Maxwell will think you're me. And, if my guess is correct, he'll definitely be going for my head this time. So, if I'm right and he happens to go for the kill, he'll think he murdered me when it will actually be you instead. I know it sounds bad, but since you live eternally now, it's really the only option for us. The bottom line is, once he makes his move, we'll know where he is, and that's when we'll make ours."

Arraz was more than annoyed by the idea. "I know about my new condition and all, but I should let you know that it still hurts like hell to die. I just want to pass that along since I know that you wouldn't possibly know or care."

Marcus smiled upon Arraz's half smart-ass remark. "Look, I'm sure it's not easy, and I'm sorry" he said, not paying much mind to his concern. "With that being said, just make sure you keep your intercom on and don't mess with the volume because we're going to need to hear what he's saying."

"What if he begins to ask me questions? I don't sound like you, so he would know it's me if I answered."

"Just don't say anything. Remember, we can't afford for you to blow our cover."

Arraz nodded his head upon Marcus' latter statement. "Alright, but I only have one request. May I please have one of the guns?"

Marcus smirked at his gun-addicted crew member's question, who, even in the most urgent of situations, could not help himself.

"Sure," he answered simply before handing one to him. "You better not do like you did last time, though."

A smile etched across Arraz's face. "Don't worry, I think I learned my lesson."

Marcus simply nodded his head. "Alright, if that's the case, then let's get this going."

Turning quietly, Arraz lead the way out of the cell area, his gun armed and ready while he rested it against his chest.

Marcus held his hand out to halt the rest of his crew, waiting purposely for a couple of moments before signaling them to follow.

Passing through the door opening, he quickly turned his head back and quietly gave orders to the young Rubidoux. "Lock the door right now, and be on the lookout for Maxwell."

"You got it," the rookie replied.

Marcus gave a thumbs-up to Rubidoux and began to follow Arraz along with the others.

Immediately following the orders he had been given, Rubidoux hurried to the door and locked it for further protection.

The commander led his crew as they kept a distance of a few yards from Arraz, who carefully led the charge as the decoyed leader.

Internally nervous despite his everlasting status, Arraz made his way down the hallway in the basement, his steps cautious while he consistently checked the environment around him in case a surprise by Maxwell was around the corner.

He could sense that his captain could be anywhere near, which made a shiver penetrate down his body upon the thought of his former captain watching him closely in secret.

He could feel his presence, and the danger of his captain lurked around every corner of the eerily quiet ship that suddenly reeked of evil.

Arraz reached the elevator unscathed and stepped inside rapidly, waving his hand to summon the others that the coast was clear.

The group quietly proceeded onto the elevator, the doors sliding to a close quickly upon the entry of the final crew member. Arraz peered over at Marcus and held up his arms as a verbal method of asking which floor to proceed to.

Marcus held up four fingers in a charade to remain quiet in an effort to avoid the possibility of Maxwell hearing their plan before having an ample opportunity to execute it.

The elevator skidded its way toward the fourth floor, bumping twice along the way against the shaft before jerking its way and stopping at its destination, which revealed total darkness on the other end once the doors opened.

"Lights!" Marcus commanded quietly into Arraz's intercom to summon the ship's computer system but to no avail.

Byers shook his head and groveled. "Great, now the lights aren't working."

"Ssssh," instructed Marcus in a whispered tone. "Keep your voice down."

A chill came down Marcus' spine, his senses telling him that his captain was near. The non-operational state of the lights only helped to confirm his theory.

Surely, Maxwell has to be hiding somewhere on this floor.

Marcus tapped Arraz on the shoulder to help summon him to move.

"I can't see anything," Arraz whispered to Marcus.

"Just go," commanded Marcus quietly. "We have no choice."

Arraz reluctantly engulfed himself blindly into the sea of black before him, his nerves shot and fearing what may be awaiting him in the darkness.

Marcus waited momentarily while Arraz entered the curtain of black to allow the buffer zone he was estimating.

"Now," he whispered behind him once his internal instincts approved of the decision.

The blinded crew proceeded unknowingly down the hallway without any sense of where they were truly going.

Suddenly, a loud voice came from the intercom, startling the entire crew half to death.

"Are you there, Marcus?" asked Maxwell through the intercom suddenly.

Arraz, startled by the captain's voice, paused in his tracks, unsure of what to do next.

Marcus, sensing that his decoy had stopped moving, whispered a halt back to his group to try and pick up any trace of their captain being close by.

A wicked chuckle came from the intercom that sent chills throughout his former captives.

"I was just thinking--we've never played Night Watch together, Marcus, so why not try now?" explained Maxwell. "Only, we'll be playing my edited version. As you can clearly see, I have shut down the lights to see how well you can survive in the dark without any sort of assistance from your mask. Luckily for me, I have my own, so I won't be burdened with the same handicap. So, think of me like the ravenous lion in the night jungle, hunting his helplessly blinded prey that has no choice but to hope they're not his next meal. I'll be able to see you, but the question is, will you be able to see me in time before you become my prey?"

Marcus gritted his teeth upon realizing that his plan already could have gone awry.

If he can't see the color of the uniform, how are we possibly going to trick him?

Maxwell chuckled once more before delivering a warning to his decoyed target. "By the way, I've set up a nice little booby trap somewhere near you. Let's see if you can find it before it finds you."

Right on cue, Arraz felt the floor beneath him suddenly disappear. He let out a scream of horror as his body began to freefall downward.

Marcus cautiously approached the area where he had heard Arraz fall and heard a loud thud as the decoy slammed against the floor. He began to worry about Arraz, even though he knew that eternal life was the lieutenant's best companion at that moment but withheld inquiring on his wellbeing out of caution that Maxwell may be near.

Monica and Jacobs collectively gasped overhearing Arraz's scream but quickly covered their mouths, forgetting momentarily that their sounds could potentially backfire on them.

Arraz screamed in agonizing pain and grabbed his leg, which shattered from the long fall he had just taken.

Suddenly, Maxwell's whereabouts had finally been revealed,

and the captain let out grotesque laughter due to the success of his trap.

With great anticipation, Maxwell stepped through the pitch-black nature and peered down at the curled-up body of who he believed to be Marcus, a grin of splendor hidden behind his fitted mask.

"Well, well, Marcus," he stated with great satisfaction in his voice. "I suppose that I must applaud you for your valiancy over-all. Unfortunately, much like the rest of your weak friends will soon discover, your efforts will be all for nothing. I will conquer and destroy any futile being who attempts to disrupt my plan for domination, and that especially includes you."

He pointed his gun toward Arraz's head and aimed for the back of his skull, his breathing heavy, accompanied by choking laughter underneath the stuffy mask that plastered his face.

Unbeknownst to the captain, the real Marcus stood over the dark hole that had sent Arraz to his demise, waiting patiently to see if his captain could send him a clue to his location.

Carefully aiming his gun, Marcus waited in anticipation for Maxwell to fire and light his location momentarily with a laser shot that appeared to be only a matter of moments.

"Goodbye, Marcus," Maxwell concluded to his decoy coldly. "May your pathetic soul burn for all eternity."

Maxwell finally fired a shot that sliced through the back of Arraz's skull and, unknowingly to himself, followed his hidden commander's own trap to a tee.

Using the flicker of green light to his advantage, Marcus capitalized on the momentary source he had been given and fired directly at Maxwell, hitting his captain in between the shoulder blades and instantly soiling his uniform top with blood.

Groaning in pain from the surprise shot he had taken, Maxwell lifted his gun immediately and fired upward through the booby-trapped hole he had created.

"What the hell?" the stunned Maxwell asked aloud while trying to decipher where the hit had come from.

Marcus fell to the ground and crawled back towards the elevator as quickly as possible.

"Everybody, run!" ordered the commander to his fleet, who followed his orders without hesitation.

Maxwell rubbed in between his shoulders to feel exactly where he had been hit.

Confused by the familiar command he had just hear, Maxwell gingerly rushed to the deceased body before him and turned it around to reveal the blood-painted face of the phony-clothed decoy Arraz.

"Shit," stated Maxwell to himself, out of the realization that he had been tricked into killing the wrong man.

Feeling feeble and uneven due to the amount of blood he had lost, the captain managed to pick up his gun and fire back through the hole towards Marcus, hoping to land some sort of shot on his former commander.

As the lasers harmlessly rocketed through the hole and came nowhere near him, Marcus rose to his feet and began to hurry along with the others toward the elevator.

Monica stood by the elevator door as she held it up, waiting for Marcus to join them.

"Ronnie, hurry!" she screamed.

"Get to the deck!" he ordered. "And get us out of here. I'll take care of Maxwell."

"But, Ronnie--" said Byers, attempting to intervene.

"Tommy, for once in your life, do as I say," Marcus strongly commanded while interrupting his friend. "Get them the hell out of here."

Byers offered no retort back before hitting the button on the elevator and following his commander's orders.

Marcus could sense Monica's concerned stare through the darkness while the doors closed and officially separated them both.

He smiled internally for a moment before firing round after round of lasers that pierced the unstable and weakened area of the floor. He began to step back as he continued to fire, putting faith in the fact that he connected in hitting his lunacy-fueled captain.

"Had enough?" he boldly asked his captain.

His question was met with a muted response, which instantly raised his curiosity level.

Wondering if perhaps he had committed homicide on his captain for a second time, he knew he was in no position to visually verify it due to the blanket of darkness that engulfed his vision.

What should I do?

Going purely with his gut instinct, Marcus backpedaled towards the elevator and hit the button to summon it, praying internally that he was making the right choice.

Little did Marcus realize that the elevator he had summoned, however, still contained his crew members, whose escape plan had been foiled.

"Dear God," stated Byers, who realized that the elevator had made a most unwelcoming stop.

A gasp came throughout the helpless and unarmed crew, who could do nothing more than watch as the door opened to Maxwell's armed silhouette.

"Oh, so close for you all," he commented while placing his foot between the elevator door to ensure they would all not be going anywhere. "This is why I'm glad they never built stairs on this ship."

He turned his night-vision stare towards Monica, who could sense the captain peering directly at her.

"You and I have some business to attend to, my dear," he stated to her before grabbing her arm. "Come with me."

A surprising and heroic surge came out of nowhere from the mild-mannered Jennings, who attempted to stand in Maxwell's way by grabbing the captain's arm. "Get your hands off of her, you bastard."

Maxwell swept Jennings' grasp away and decided to swiftly reward Jennings for his bravery by shooting him in the right knee.

Screaming in agonizing pain, Jennings spilled to the floor and grabbed at his freshly wounded limb.

"Desmond!" Jacobs screamed before immediately coming to his aid, unafraid that her feelings for him had officially been exposed.

Smirking at the damage he had caused, Maxwell felt negative remorse for what he had just done.

"Next time, it'll be your heart that I pierce instead," he said in a scolding manner to the injured Jennings before turning his attention to the others. "Do any of the rest of you have anything else to tell me?"

Muted silence met his question as the crew realized they were stuck between a rock and a hard place and had no choice but to do as the captain said.

"That's what I thought," stated Maxwell coldly. "Pick the doctor's disabled ass up and take him with you. That is unless you want your dead bodies to come along."

Offering no resistance, the crew blindly made their way out of the elevator, with Jacobs assisting her internal crush onto his feet and out.

Maxwell prepared to step onto the elevator that now only contained Monica but stopped momentarily and shot at the button display on the wall to disable access for the others.

"Time to put the kids in timeout," Maxwell said, grabbing Monica's arm tightly while the door slid closed. "You and me have business to attend to, my dear."

Byers slapped the sealed door and stared into the pitch black before him, a realization coming over him that the momentum they had worked so hard to gain had suddenly evaporated from their collective grasp.

Chapter 29

Maxwell removed his mask from his face and threw it to the ground before taking a deep breath of fresh air, his grasp remaining glued onto the captured Monica.

"Where are you taking me?" she asked him.

He chuckled upon her inquiry. "That is of no concern to you, my dear. Let's just say that you're my new bargaining chip for your boyfriend."

"What do you plan on doing?"

Maxwell wickedly smirked, realizing the ball of power had officially gone back onto his court. He enjoyed being in control, and he felt not even a shred of guilt for turning his back on his own crew.

The elevator skidded to a halt upon reaching the basement, and Maxwell wasted not even a millisecond of time dragging Monica along once the door slid open.

He took his gun and fired once more at the panel on the left of the elevator to disable it from any further activity before stopping outside of the sealed elevator door and gazing at his captive.

"This should buy us a little more alone time," he creepily said before stroking the ponytail in the back of her head with his available hand. "My, you are quite the pretty one, aren't you?"

Having no concern for her own well-being and refusing to be sexually harassed, Monica slapped away his hand.

"And feisty too, I see," he added with a slime-filled smile. "I can see why Marcus likes you so much. It's too bad when I'm done with him, and you'll be mine instead."

Monica ditched her nice girl routine, and her inner strength from within began to ooze out of her. "Over my dead body."

Maxwell chuckled at her defiance. "Let's not get too carried away here, my darling. We have a bit of extra time now, so I'm sure I'll be able to show you what kind of man I really am. But first, go to the cell. We have to pay a quick visit to a friend."

He took his gun and pointed it towards her right temple as a little extra incentive to follow his command.

An uncomfortable and nauseating feeling came over Monica, who cringed externally from his unwelcoming comments but went along with his latter order as a method of survival.

Time had come to a standstill, meanwhile, for Marcus, who stood at the elevator door on the fourth floor and waited for his summon to be answered, not knowing that it had actually been put out of order by his homicide-obsessed commanding officer.

Why is this elevator taking so long?

It was strange, even for the rickety elevator they contained, for it to take the amount of time it did, and he couldn't help but wonder if it had broken down at the wrong moment.

That would be fitting, now, wouldn't it?

A faint voice suddenly crept into his hearing.

"--nie?"

It sounded like Byers, but he wanted to be cautious out of fear that Maxwell was somewhere near.

He remained silent as he stepped deeper into the darkness once more carefully.

"Ronnie?" the voice came in more clearly and loudly, which he now confirmed as belonging to Byers. "Can you hear me?"

Marcus blindly stumbled his way forward a bit and took caution with each step he took on the creaky and shot-up floor.

"Tommy?" he responded. "Yeah, I can hear you. Are you below on the third floor?"

"Afraid so," answered Byers, who made his way through the dark and nearly fell over the still-deceased body of Arraz before tilting his head upward to speak through the gigantic hole above his head. "I have bad news: we didn't quite make it to the deck because Maxwell stopped us in the elevator on our way down. He must have known or overheard our plans. He hijacked us out of the elevator and took Monica with him."

The blood running through Marcus' veins chilled to an icy cold upon hearing Byers' ladder sentence. It was the greatest fear that he had possessed since Maxwell had gone berserk, and it killed him internally, with a feeling coming over him as if he had failed the woman he cared so passionately about.

Marcus placed his head in his hands and knelt on the floor as Byers stood underneath the floor cavity, awaiting any sort of response from his childhood friend.

"Ronnie? Are you okay?"

Marcus raised his face from his hands and drummed up some fake external strength to give an answer. "Yeah--I'm okay."

Byers was not fooled by Marcus' phony strength. He could sense his friend hurting deeply while his thoughts attempted to scrap together a perfect response for the difficult situation.

"I'm sorry, Ronnie. I'm sure she's going to be okay, though. "We're all going to be okay, though, right?"

Marcus could now sense that his friend was aware of his insecure feelings oozing out and was not fooling him with his false demeanor.

"Yeah, we're going to all make it out of here," he said in a reassuring manner to deflect attention away from himself. "Are you guys all okay?"

"Yeah, for the most part. Maxwell shot Dr. Jennings in the leg, so I think his knee's all busted up. But overall, I guess we're all doing as dandy as possible."

A loud groan echoed through the third and fourth-floor hallways, which prompted Marcus to draw his gun and stumble through the dark to prepare himself blindly for the unknown visitor that had joined them.

Byers, helpless without the assistance of vision or a weapon, proceeded anyway to get to the bottom of their new problem. "Who's there?"

Grumbling evolved from the question as a voice answered his question.

"It's--Arraz."

Marcus dropped his gun and carefully scaled the walls of the hallway to help guide him through the darkness.

Using Arraz's grumbling as his measuring stick, he used caution not to injure himself by falling through the man-made hole that had been created courtesy of Maxwell.

"Arraz, I'm glad that you're alive again. Are you okay?"

Arraz rose slowly from the ground and rubbed the back of his skull, which had completely healed from the horrendous blast it had suffered a matter of moments ago from the laser shot that had been ruthlessly delivered by Maxwell.

"Just fantastic," he groaned, his head still ringing and pulsating wickedly.

He fully rose to his feet and blinked his eyes rapidly, trying to gain some sort of vision.

"Where the hell are you?" Arraz asked Marcus. "I can't see a damn thing."

"It's still pitch black in here, so don't feel bad," Marcus reassured him. "The power's still out around here."

Arraz looked up to no avail in a futile attempt to see some sort of sign to give his eyes confirmation. "I'll take your word for it. Where is that rat bastard Maxwell, anyway? I've got a couple of scores that I've got to settle with him now."

Marcus couldn't have agreed on anymore with his combustible, gun-obsessed lieutenant. He would have felt the same even if Monica had not be taken captive, but the fact that she was now in his custody only further boiled his blood.

"He's back on the loose, and he's got Monica," he told Arraz as he lowered his voice to the point that he could only hear himself speak. "It's personal now."

Meanwhile, in the basement, Maxwell held on tightly to Monica's right arm as they were about to reach the closed cell door.

Monica squirmed momentarily unsuccessfully to attempt to free herself from his grasp, prompting Maxwell to grab her arm even tighter.

"Don't do that," he ordered sternly, placing the cold barrel of his gun in between her doe-brown eyes. "I wouldn't want to destroy this immaculate face."

Feeling internally frightened by his threat, she remained steadfast nonetheless, refusing to give him the satisfaction of watching her cower in fear.

Thinking very little of her strong motion, he pulled her arm as a non-verbal command to get her to move while pulling the barrel away from her face.

They turned around the last corner and approached the locked cell door that contained the unassuming Rubidoux and Maren behind it.

Peering through the caged square in the middle of the door, the captain smirked while staring at the young rookie navigator who was put in charge of watching Maxwell's extraterrestrial apprentice.

Licking his lips out of starvation of bloody revenge, the captain beamed brightly for the opportunity before him.

"Rube," he serenaded playfully through the crisscrossed pattern of the iron bars.

The hairs on the back of Rubidoux's neck arose upon hearing the voice of his captain, his eyes immediately peering towards the door before meeting those of Maxwell.

"Well, hello there, my little green one," Maxwell gently stated with great hostility while pulling Monica close to him to reveal her face also. "Won't you be a good boy and let me, or rather us, in?"

The rookie's jaw dropped upon the sight out of surprise and disappointment, realizing their plan had taken a most unfortunate turn.

"Miss--Miss Monica," said Rubidoux nervously. "What--happened?"

The smirk upon Maxwell's still-freshly shaved face morphed into a scowl of business.

"That's none of your concern, Rube," Maxwell sharply told him before tapping the cage with his gun barrel to add intimidation. "Now, open the door right now, or I'll put a laser through your brain, as well as hers."

Rubidoux said nothing but valiantly maintained his composure in defying his evil captain.

Surprised by Rubidoux's nonchalance, Maxwell banged the bars on the opening with greater force. "I said to open the door, damn it. Are you deaf?"

The rookie navigator didn't budge upon the captain's abrasive verbal abuse, the backbone inside of him never being stronger than it currently was.

"No," responded Rubidoux powerfully. "I'm just following the orders of my commander, sir. You know--the one who didn't turn his back on us like you did."

The ladder statement sent a wave of anger through Maxwell, his face red as a tomato from the defiance he had received.

Nevertheless, the captain was not about to be verbally upstaged by the rookie. "Well, since you put it that way--I suppose I'm glad to see that you grew some balls, you little son of a bitch, because it only gives me further incentive to destroy you."

He blasted through the caged opening with a laser shot that easily sliced through the caged square and nearly removed Rubidoux's ear in the process.

Taking his armed hand, Maxwell reached through the newly created opening and unlocked the door before kicking it violently and entering, forcing his way through while dragging the helpless Monica with him.

Rubidoux, clearly frightened by the angry reaction, continued to stand his ground, but his valiancy was rewarded immediately with a pistol whip across the bridge of the young man's nose that sent him crashing to the unforgiving ground.

Throwing Monica to the side to free up one hand, Maxwell grabbed Rubidoux roughly by his scalp and pulled him back up before transferring his grip to the rookie's skinny neck.

Maxwell pointed his gun under Rubidoux's chin and could feel the impulse flowing through him to pull the trigger and end the young and underdeveloped life of his young navigator instantaneously for his stupid yet brave acts of defiance.

Rubidoux felt like crying out of fear but maintained his composure against his own will out of refusing to give his superior any further satisfaction.

Monica, meanwhile, could do no more than sit and watch in horror, her body feeling locked out of fear that the young man's life before her was about to end prematurely.

A smirk of approval came over the jailed Maren, who enjoyed seeing his leader taking control once more with the greatest of vigilant force.

Suddenly and surprisingly, Maxwell began to loosen his grip, a curious smile instantly crossing his face. "No, this is too easy and uninteresting. I think I just came up with a much better option for you."

Continuing his rough behavior, Maxwell grabbed the air-depraved Rubidoux unmercifully by his ear and threw his body against the cell bars to further soften him up.

Groaning in tremendous pain, Rubidoux held his ribs gingerly, his breathing heavy while desperately trying to refill his lungs with air.

"Get up and open the cell, maggot," the captain ordered to Rubidoux unmercifully.

"Please, he's hurt," begged Monica. "Leave him alone."

"Shut up!" he hollered back at her while flashing his weapon as a warning to pipe down.

He turned his focus back to Rubidoux and continued his unleashed parade of punishment on the helpless young man by delivering a couple of breath-taking abdominal haymakers with the butt-end of his gun.

"C'mon, I thought you were a big, tough man," he teased the navigator. "You sure talked like you were. But, I suppose that now I see that you're all bark and no bite, pansy."

Rubidoux shrunk against the cell bars, doubling in pain while shutting his eyes to keep his tears of agony from flowing out.

"It looks like you need help getting your sorry ass up," snarled Maxwell before grabbing Rubidoux once more by the top of his hair and pulling tightly upwards to rudely bring him back to his feet.

Despite the overwhelming feeling of pain that consumed him, the bruised and beaten Rubidoux began to bellow a hearty chuckle that struck Maxwell with great confusion.

"What in the hell are you laughing about?" the captain barked at him.

"I--was just thinking about how--you can't win," responded Rubidoux in between breaths. "You--can kill me if you want, but--it doesn't prove anything--to anybody except that--you're a heart-less--and gutless man."

As angry as the statement made him feel, Maxwell once again surprised his rookie with a bright smile and a chuckle.

"You know, you're absolutely right, Rube," Maxwell told him in an upbeat tone. "And it's for that reason, because I'm gutless in your opinion, I'm not going to pulverize the ever-living shit out of you."

He pulled Rubidoux even tighter by his scalp and guided him in front of the locked cell door, which instantly drew Monica's attention.

"What--what are you doing?" she asked.

"Open the cell," Maxwell demanded to the captured rookie while ignoring Monica's question.

"Hell no," answered Rubidoux defiantly.

Maxwell intensified his force and pulled with all of his might on Rubidoux's scalp, which began to feel as if it were ready to peel off.

Rubidoux screamed in agony, the burning sensation on the top of his head becoming unbearable.

"I said to open the cell, you little asshole. Do it before I rip it off."

Realizing the gig was up, the rookie finally gave in to Maxwell's demand and placed his key card above the scanner, which beeped in approval.

The cell creaked open loudly, much to the approval of Maren, who smirked at his captain for granting him his freedom.

Maxwell smiled back momentarily at his right-hand man before kicking Rubidoux in the lower back to add further insult to injury.

Rubidoux crashed to the hard cell floor and lay meagerly on the ground, his body wanting to shut down from the ample pain that pulsated throughout it.

"You see, Rube," stated the captain to the hapless rookie, "because I'm not heartless, or gutless for that matter, I'm going to let you fight for your life. And, best of all, you won't even need to deal with me."

Closing the prison door with all of his might, Maxwell stoically stood with great pleasure, the smile on his face further proving how he felt.

Maren, surprised by the last action of his master, rushed to the front in a panic, his freedom suddenly taken away once more by the most unlikely of sources.

"What is this meaning, sire?" Maren asked with great distress.

"You're going to finish the job for me," explained Maxwell ruthlessly. "I have some personal obligations to deal with, so I'm leaving you in charge of this. If you kill him by the time I return, then I will grant you your freedom. If, for some unexplained reason, you don't, then obviously, you don't deserve to live."

The harsh explanation did little to calm the nerves of Maren, who seemed antsy to be on the other side but insisted on pleasing his master and lord.

"As per the command of your being, sire," he stated submissively.

"Make it happen," instructed Maxwell in a softened tone to Maren, who nodded his head in agreement and turned his body in preparation for pouncing on his wounded prey.

Waiting until Maren threw the first punch onto the seemingly hopeless Rubidoux, Maxwell grabbed the arm once more of Monica, whose face sourly turned in horror.

"You're a monster," she stated to him with tears in her eyes.

Maxwell devilishly beamed even brighter upon her name-calling while roughly escorting her out.

"More than you even know, my dear," he proudly stated.

CHAPTER 30

Still engulfed in the darkness, Marcus stooped from above the open hole with Byers standing below him.

Arraz, meanwhile, continued to try to get all of the cobwebs out in his ever-healing head that still pounded from the slicing lasers that had cut through his skull.

"So, what are we gonna do, Ronnie?" inquired Byers, who could feel the touch of Samia, who had found him blindly and had followed his voice as her breadcrumb trail.

She placed her hand on his back and began to lovingly rub his shoulder blades, a gesture that made him smile and close his eyes for a brief moment of relaxing therapy.

Marcus scratched his head as he tried to rack his brain for a solution. "I don't know. Pray to God that the elevator gets back up here soon so that I can go after the bastard, I guess."

"Well, we're stuck down here," Byers told his friend. "Maxwell made sure we weren't going anywhere. He blew up the elevator panel, so we can't even try to summon it."

"It sure has been a while since it's come up, speaking of which," added Marcus. "I pushed that button, and it seemed like an eternity ago. I wonder where the hell it is."

Byers shook his head over the dismay of the situation but

simultaneously enjoyed the attention given to him by his female companion. He wouldn't admit it to anyone else, including his friend, but he began to feel head over heels enamored for the first time with a woman. It felt so strange, especially considering his first feeling of love was for someone who wasn't even of the same species as him, but at the same time, it felt so right.

He allowed himself to let down his guard completely, her warmness and smile, even in the darkness they were stuck in, shining through brightly.

This was different, he knew. It was different from all of the other women he had experienced in the past and especially different from his own promiscuous nature, which seemed like it had become extinct long ago.

He actually enjoyed, for the first time, the presence and splendor of having a woman by his side as her soft touch scaled every nerve and bone in his body and brought a feeling of joy like no other.

Yes, he knew in his heart of hearts that, for the first time, he was in love and that this new feeling that he had experienced now was real and passionate, unlike anything else he had experienced. It felt wonderful to him to actually understand the mysterious feeling of love, and he couldn't help but fantasize about his future with her if they were to make it out of this perilous situation alive.

Byers took his right hand and placed it above hers to return the affection to her.

Samia beamed upon his touch, understanding his non-verbal gesture as a sign of love, and crossed her fingers between his to give another message of enamor.

I would die for her, he thought to himself. *I would do anything for her.*

While the lovebirds enjoyed their moment to themselves, Arraz leaned his back against the wall, still attempting to balance out his equilibrium.

He was unaware of the love that seemed to be in the air, the darkness in front of his eyes and the cobwebs in his head surviving as his greatest detractors.

Love had also begun to flourish for Jacobs and Jennings, who sat alone in their own corner closer to the elevator and had finally opened up to one another without saying a word.

Jennings rested his back against the wall and sat with his left knee up while Jacobs began to massage around his injured area.

Her touch brought him a feeling of ecstasy that made him feel so alive and, suddenly, more forthright in his own mind.

Now, it's time to go for it, he thought.

His shy nature suddenly disappeared and was replaced by a boldness he had never experienced as he touched her face gently and leaned over to kiss her lips.

The assertiveness surprised the happy Jacobs, who gladly obliged without a shred of resistance as their lips connected together.

Their hearts, both pulsating rapidly, suddenly were beating as one. While both of their fantasies had become a reality in the most treacherous of situations, it was of no matter to either one as they finished their long kiss and smiled at one another out of satisfaction.

Taark, meanwhile, sat in the middle of them all and had fallen asleep with his back against the wall.

It did not matter to him that it may not have been in the most comfortable of positions as he snored so quietly that nobody else could hear him.

While the alien man slept, Marcus, wide awake as could be, ran his fingers through his short hair and continued to wait, unaware of the lovey-dovey activities that were occurring one floor below him.

"This is when I wish they had made stairs on this ship," he lamented loudly. "Of all of the relics we have on this ship, how can we not have those?"

Byers, lost in enjoyment with Samia, predictably had no comment on the matter, as Marcus' complaining fell on deaf ears.

The loving moments between the two couples, however, suddenly came to a crashing halt by the voice that traveled over the intercom that adorned Arraz's body.

"Hello, Marcus."

The commander's blood ran cold upon hearing Maxwell's voice once more, the hatred festering him for his former captain, especially now that he held the woman he loved captive.

Arraz stood silently in the darkness, unsure of what to do, while Marcus peered down into nothing but darkness, his fist clenched as he began to picture himself delivering a roundhouse punch into Maxwell's jaw.

Byers crept closer to Arraz and used Maxwell's voice to navigate himself closer.

"Are you there, Marcus?" Maxwell sang playfully through the intercom.

Arraz did what his impulse told him to do as he cleared his throat. "No, this is Arraz."

"Ah, Arraz," stated Maxwell. "Glad to see you survived again. I just hope that I didn't give you too much of a headache."

His own anger rose for his captain, and Arraz could picture himself going through the intercom to choke out Maxwell. "You're an asshole."

"My, how snappy you've become," said Maxwell sarcastically in between chuckles. "It's almost like you want to kill me."

"Shut up. All I know is that you'd better pray I don't run into you because if I do, it's going to get really ugly for you."

Maxwell took further enjoyment in Arraz's threat. "I look forward to it, boy. But unfortunately, I've got much bigger fish to fry than a guppy such as yourself."

The blood began to boil further inside of Arraz, who clenched the intercom but again resisted the temptation to rip it off of himself, especially considering that the uniform he bore did not belong to him.

"Where is Marcus?" Maxwell asked directly.

"I'm right here," Marcus shouted downward through the hole.

"Ah, there you are. I'm guessing you must still be stuck on the fourth floor, waiting for that elevator. It's too bad that I made sure to put it out of order before any of you could come after me. I do, however, hope that you can at least make this somewhat competitive for me."

Marcus glared back towards the elevator door and growled to himself out of realization that his task had become even tougher.

"Where is Monica?" he shouted towards the intercom.

"Your girlfriend is safe with me. But not for much longer, unfortunately, so I'd hurry if I were you before things really begin to get nasty for pretty Miss Monica."

"Ronnie, please help me," Monica pleaded through the intercom in between sobs. "Please, Ronnie."

The desperation in her voice wanted to bring Marcus to his knees as his heart went down to his stomach. He felt furious with Maxwell for putting her in danger, but also himself for placing her into a bad situation.

Maxwell snickered vilely upon Monica's plea. "Do you hear that, Marcus? I think she wants you to come and get her, and I think that I feel the same way. So, to be fair, I'll let you in on my little plan. Miss Monica and I are going to go on a nice little walk outside by way of the basement hatch because God knows, or, rather, I know, how stuffy it gets in here. So, because of that, we're going to go get some nice, fresh air and talk a bit. Maybe, if you take too long, we'll even kiss under one of the trees for a while before I have my way with her. And then, once I'm done doing that, I think it will be time for her to meet her maker. By that time, however, maybe she'll have an awakening and see me as that maker."

Marcus' rage began to boil over upon Maxwell's sexist and jabbing words. "You can go to hell because that's where you'll be going when I'm done with you, asshole."

Maxwell laughed joyfully over his former commander's

threats. "What a charming statement. I'll be curious to see you back up your words. You're officially on the clock, Marcus, so you'd better get moving. Ciao!"

Monica screamed once more before the intercom shut off into complete silence.

Marcus, meanwhile, wasted no time in hurrying down the fourth-floor hallway and towards the closed elevator door.

Byers heard his friend's footsteps from above and attempted to get his attention.

"Ronnie, what are you doing?"

"I'm going to save Monica."

"How do you plan on doing that? We're all stuck, thanks to that bastard."

"Where there's a will, there's a way, Tommy. And I'm going to find a way, even if it kills me."

Byers stumbled through the darkness, with Samia following helplessly behind him. "That in itself is the problem, Ronnie. He's immortal now, so there's no way you can destroy him. You may win the battle, but he's going to end up winning the war."

Marcus felt the outside of the elevator door and let his friend's latter sentence resonate inside of him. He knew that Byers was right, but he was also going to be damned if he was not going to go down without a fight.

"I'm looking to win both," Marcus told him. "Take care of everyone because you're in charge now."

"Ronnie, no!" screamed Byers in a last-ditch attempt to get his friend to change his mind.

Marcus paid no mind to his friend, who continued to call for his attention, putting his fingers in between the crease of the closed elevator doors to attempt to pry them open. His fingers began to hurt as the heavy doors slowly opened away from one another, but the thought of Monica gave him the strength to ignore the pain.

Jarring the doors open slowly, and the empty elevator corridor awaited him.

He sighed heavily out of relief that he could at least see more due to the small light fixtures in the elevator that never went off, but he sensed his fear of heights come over him while gazing down at the long, empty corridor before him.

Great.

His eyes fixated upon the elevator cable before him, which he instantly realized was his only, yet treacherous, option to get down to where he needed to go.

Doing his best to fend off his fear, Marcus closed his eyes and meditated himself to calm his frayed nerves.

You can do this. You can do this, c'mon.

He opened his eyes as perspiration dewed upon his forehead at the thought of what he was about to attempt to accomplish.

Exhaling heavily, he placed his gun underneath his belt and extended his hand to grab the elevator cable, which offered no sign of extra support or internal comfort to him.

Marcus did his best to pay no mind to the games his own brain began to play on him while he placed his other hand on the cable and leaped from the safety of the ledge and onto the unpredictable cable.

Just don't look down. Just keep going, and you'll be okay.

His hands, clammy from nervousness, offered no extra assistance and forced him to cling for dear life to the cable that began to sway to and fro.

Oh, shit.

Fear now serving as his greatest enemy, Marcus instantly thought of Monica, which gave him all the motivation he needed to continue on.

For once, he was not going to allow his fear of heights to make him a victim, even if his own conscience attempted to tell him otherwise.

Chapter 31

Maxwell hit the red button at the rear end of the basement to open the exit hatch that slowly began to open before his captive and him.

Squirming once more from the tight squeeze applied to her arm, Monica had finally gotten fed up with being the captain's hostage.

"Let me go," she demanded. "You're hurting me."

Maxwell scoffed at her request and rolled his eyes. "Please, this is nothing compared to how you're going to feel shortly. That is unless your boyfriend can come and save you."

She gazed down at her arm, which had begun to bruise from Maxwell's excessive force.

"Aw, would you look at what I did," stated Maxwell sarcastically before rubbing her injured area. "Would you like me to kiss it better for you?"

Disgusted over the captain's creepy suggestion, Monica rolled her eyes in response. "No thanks."

The door finally opened fully as the hatch made a loud, crashing sound against the ground.

Pulling Monica's arm firmly once more, Maxwell forced her

off the ship and officially back onto the extraterrestrial terrain that had become so familiar.

Standing in place with his hostage, the captain took a moment to soak in the surroundings around them, the favorable position he found himself in further sweetening the mood.

Rejuvenated in his newly refurbished and younger body, the sunlight glistened off the dark stubble that began to fester on his face and shadow the baby aspects of his face.

Despite his youthful and well-built stature, Monica felt disgusted by the sight of him and found nothing about him attractive, even though she certainly knew that back on Earth, women would have more than likely flocked to him without hesitation.

Maxwell's infusion of youth meant nothing to her, his internal ugliness clouding her judgment on him. In her mind, she still pictured the vile and disgusting old man who caused great pain to her and the rest of her fellow crewmembers and whose selfishness and black heart would be his eventual undoing, at least in her greatest of hopes.

As much as she counted on Marcus to save her, Monica also realized that she would perhaps need to rely on herself to at least put a damper on Maxwell's wicked plans that he had in store for both her and the man she so secretly loved.

Realizing suddenly that the moment had arrived, she decided to use her charm and beauty to good use to bide her and Marcus some valuable, and perhaps life-saving, time.

Using her available hand, Monica touched the back of Maxwell's head and caressed her fingers through his dark brown mane.

Maxwell's head cocked back in surprise, uncertainty suddenly dominating his emotions.

"What--what are you doing?" he asked her nervously.

Smiling seductively at him, she dialed up the dial on her charm and ditched her honest morals momentarily to distract him.

"My, I never realized how handsome you were until now, Captain," she told him. "Your eyes are so blue in the sunlight. I just love them."

Maxwell, startled by her sudden affection and attention, sheepishly grinned while her fingers trickled down to his five o'clock shadow.

"Re--really?" he asked, his mind clouded with confusion as the blood rushed through him out of excitement. "But, I thought that you--"

She placed her index finger over his lips to interrupt him, his grasp beginning to falter on her arm.

"Shhh," Monica playfully responded. "Please, don't speak. I didn't realize it until now, but you were right. You are absolutely irresistible. We have a moment like you said earlier, so I just want to take you in."

Feeling the bile simmer in her throat, Monica nonetheless did her best to continue to pretend to be sincere without blowing her own cover.

Monica removed her finger from Maxwell's lips, who grinned shyly as if he were a schoolboy.

"Why--the sudden change of heart?" Maxwell inquired curiously. "Is this a trick or something?"

Yes, she thought to herself.

"Don't be silly," stated Monica in a velvety tone. "I want this. Don't you?"

Nodding nervously, Maxwell's breathing began to become as rapid as his heart rate.

Sensing she had the captain on the ropes, she turned the dial on her seductiveness, even more, to further distract him by undoing the top button of her uniform to show a decent amount of her ample cleavage.

"Does this look like a trick to you?" she sexily asked him.

His face frozen, Maxwell appeared as though he was beginning to have an internal short circuit.

"What's the matter, Captain?" she playfully asked him. "You don't like what you see?"

Maxwell shook his head before fumbling out an answer like a malfunctioning robot. "No--no, that's--that's not it. I just--am speechless--and--wow. I never thought--that you--and me--I mean--this--oh, boy."

Monica beamed on the inside, her senses telling her that she was now in control over the micromanaging Maxwell, who, for the first time, appeared lost and confused by the situation at hand.

Deciding to put the icing on the cake, she bit her bottom lip before taking his hand and placing it over her chest.

"Would you like to touch them?" she inquired with a seductive smile.

Maxwell's jaw dropped, his body disabled from sexual excitement.

"Oh--yeah," answered the captain slowly while awkwardly nodding his head. "I--really do."

Smirking sexily at him while being disgusted internally, she continued her act by guiding his hand inside of her shirt, making sure that he wouldn't come close to touching the areas that mattered.

"Are you ready for this?" she asked.

Closing his eyes while biting his bottom lip in anticipation of what he thought he was about to feel, he nodded his head.

Sensing the opening before her, she turned the tables on Maxwell by emphatically kneeing him in the groin.

Grabbing his genitals while tossing his gun in the process, Maxwell's eyes rolled in the back of his head as a result of the excruciating pain he had inflicted as he crashed stiffly to his knees.

Deciding to add a little extra punishment, she gritted her teeth before swinging her right fist into his chin with all of her might.

The pain that radiated from the forceful contact did little to deter from the sweet satisfaction she felt about getting an ounce of revenge as Maxwell's head violently cocked to its side from the momentum and forced his body to crash violently onto the dirty ground.

Acting immediately off of her instincts, Monica ran for her life into the plush, green forest that seemed to eagerly await her to offer greater assistance, her legs never moving as quickly as they suddenly had.

Attempting to get up unsuccessfully before stumbling once more onto the dirt beneath him, Maxwell gritted his teeth and growled at the missing woman who had left him behind.

"You bitch!" he screamed aloud through his disjointed jaw. "You little bitch! You'll pay for this!"

Gaining a good distance from him and running as fast as her legs allowed her to go, Monica's mind began to race. She could only pray to herself in her mind as she could only hope that she had bought enough time for Marcus to save her, along with everybody else, from the chaos she found herself trying to outrun.

As Monica ran for her life, Marcus continued to climb down the cable of the disabled elevator shaft and tried not to look down as he made his way slowly but surely down to the basement.

These have been some of the longest few minutes of my life.

He could feel that he was close as his tenacity and determination began to increase mightily.

The adrenaline that rushed through his body assisted in masking the fear of heights that would have normally stopped him in his tracks.

Even the unsteady wires did little to cease his efforts as his mind focused on the task at hand of taking down his commanding officer, who had been undone by his own lunacy and power.

He was surprised by the evolution of his emotions and no longer felt remorse towards Maxwell, wanting nothing more than to see his captain no longer breathing.

But why do I feel this way?

Realizing that he had no time to ponder over his own question, Marcus shook his head and continued to climb his way down the rickety cable.

A sudden twinge from the wire he relied on caused some concern momentarily, although he convinced himself to keep going by doing his best to pay no mind to the possibly fatal bump in the road before him.

Just keep going. Don't stop.

His bravery was ironically undone in the blink of an eye by a loud snap that echoed throughout the shaft and disintegrated the cable that suddenly fell limp in his grasp.

Realizing his plan had taken a most unfortunate turn, panic began to set in for Marcus, whose body helplessly plunged downward rapidly.

Oh, shit!

With nothing to grab onto but the air around him, Marcus could only hope for a miracle as he realized that his prayers served as his only possibility to escape the death that he was certain was anxiously awaiting him.

CHAPTER 32

———————

His prayers answered, although rather abruptly, Marcus slammed against the top of the boxy elevator, which unleashed a wave of furious pain that quickly jolted from head to toe and ravaged his lungs completely of air.

He couldn't help but feel fortunate that he had survived the fall, and especially that he didn't fall right on his gun, although the bloody murder that his body screamed did little to compensate.

Groaning in agony, Marcus slowly began to peel his body from the roof of the elevator.

Wicked pain shot through his left knee as he rose to a crouch, which felt like somewhat of moral victory considering the fall he had taken.

Marcus felt fortunate that he had somehow survived the epic fall he had encountered and was fully convinced if ever he hadn't been, that there was indeed a God.

And that God is definitely not Maxwell.

Doing his best to ignore the lingering pain in his legs, he slowly attempted to rise to his feet, his breathing dangerously rapid as he attempted to refill his vacant lungs with the air that was desperately needed.

His body exiting its emergency stage with every passing moment, Marcus began to count his blessings for his survival despite the injuries he had suffered as a result.

Gazing up at the area where the wire no longer resided, he shook his head in realization that it probably could have been much worse had he been given the opportunity to take the elevator down.

If we ever make it back home alive, we're putting stairs in, damn it.

Suddenly, his internal body clock once more gave him a hurrying reminder.

You've got to go. You're wasting valuable time to rescue Monica.

Listening to himself while ignoring the discomfort he was feeling, Marcus reached for his gun and fired a few shots at the elevator unit roof below him to create his own exit. And popped his head into the hole momentarily to ensure the coast was clear before preparing himself to jump downward.

He could feel his bones rattle at the thought of his eventual landing from his jump, even though it was a mere eight feet from the floor, due to the residual damage throughout his body still reminding him of what he had just gone through.

This is no time to baby your injuries. C'mon, you've got to keep going.

Taking a moment to deeply inhale and exhale in preparation for leaping onto the elevator floor that would lead him to his final destination and encounter with Maxwell, Marcus closed his eyes momentarily and opened them as he said a quick prayer before leaping downward through the man-made hole he had created.

Here goes nothing. May God hear me out.

On the outside of the ship, Maxwell attempted to regroup himself while on his knees, rubbing the gash on his chin gingerly while massaging his groin, which continued to howl as he waited for his healing ability to kick in throughout his immortal body.

His fury raging violently inside of him, he shifted his focus for revenge onto the lovely Monica rather than his nemesis and former right-hand man Marcus.

Or better yet, as he thought, if things somehow worked out perfectly, he could kill Monica and Marcus at the same time and kill two birds with one stone.

A wicked smirk crossed Maxwell's face upon the thought as he could feel the pain in both his chin and groin begin to decline. His healing abilities had begun to kick in, and he felt like a new man ready to take on the world.

Or rather, in his mind, he took what he felt was his and officially took his place as lord of the ground he felt beneath him.

Maxwell quickly sprang to his feet and cracked his neck as a non-verbal message to Monica that she was next on his list.

Seeing his gun lying on the ground before him, he shook his head but smiled upon realizing that Monica had done almost everything right except take his weapon with her to allow herself to have more of a sporting chance.

"Tsk, tsk, my dear," he murmured to himself. "You may have just cost yourself the ballgame with that error."

Picking up his weapon and glancing toward the open forest before him, Maxwell held his gun high like a commando soldier, ready to go ballistic.

"Unfortunately, it will be your mistake that will be your undoing," he continued to state to himself, "as well as that of your friends."

While Maxwell rushed towards the legion of trees before him like a maniac on a mission, Marcus made his way through the dreary basement and reached the closed hatch door, preparing to open it before a loud bang suddenly chimed throughout the cavernous hallway.

What was that?

Fearing for Monica's life and wanting to ensure that she was not involved, he took a sharp turn towards the cell area, where the sound had been generated, and ran quickly down the slim hallway.

Without hesitation, he flung open the door, which served as nothing more than an obstacle due to its cracked open status, and rushed inside.

Fear struck the valves of his heart upon the first sight of a body that was laid out on the floor and gave the impression that the one who had previously occupied it had seen their last living day.

He began to scan the body from the feet to the head and turned his focus towards the front of the cell block where a familiar face stood, bloodied and badly beaten.

"Rube!" he shouted towards the rookie who rested his body against the hard, iron door while struggling for dear life.

Marcus sprinted towards Rubidoux to get a better look at his rookie navigator, as well as to identify the deceased body of Maren that lay before him.

In disbelief over what he had seen, Marcus turned his attention back to the weakened Rubidoux, who struggled to breathe and seemed to be doing all he could to avoid the same fate as the dead alien man.

He felt overjoyed to see that Maxwell's accomplice was no longer a threat but immediately felt concern over the wellbeing of his young navigator.

"Hang in there, Rube," Marcus counseled to the rookie. "You're going to be alright. Just don't let go."

Rubidoux, through hollow and quick breathing, laid his head against the cold bars and stared blankly at Marcus's concerned face.

"Don't--worry--about--me," Rubidoux bravely advised him, taking pauses in between his words to deeply breathe. "No matter--what--just--make sure--that--you--stop Maxwell. Please--Commander. You--must--save Monica--and--"

Unable to finish his sentence, Rubidoux cocked his head downward, his body appearing as though it were ready to give out.

Marcus, fearing that Rubidoux had begun to fade to his own

death, reached through the bar to shove the navigator out of desperation. "Rube!"

Relief came over Marcus as Rubidoux limply lifted his head to acknowledge his still-living status but could offer nothing verbally to back it up.

"Just hold on," Marcus told him. "I'm going to come back for you, I promise."

Hollow coughing followed from Rubidoux's throat, who fought his inner desires to close his eyes for the final time and end his pain and suffering.

Ignoring his inner desires and continuing to fight valiantly, he raised his voice as much as his body allowed and choked out the only response that he could.

"Go--now."

Marcus, taking the simple command to heart, nodded his head in acknowledgment and ran out of the cell like a bat out of Hell.

Rubidoux, in his critical state, could nothing more than hang his head and pray that his commander would return victoriously before it was too late.

CHAPTER 33

As she sprinted through the forest as fast as her body allowed, Monica turned her head to make sure that Maxwell was nowhere to be seen.

She felt exhausted and out of breath but did not want to stop, fearing that her captain would appear at any moment to do all of the horrible things he promised earlier.

It made her cringe uncomfortably enough to know that she had to fake all of the affection towards him a mere matter of moments ago, and it made her downright sick to her stomach to even know that she had kissed him, even though it was phony and deceptive on her end.

And she couldn't help but realize suddenly at that moment what a fatal error she may have created for herself by not taking his gun when she had the perfect opportunity.

No matter, she thought to herself. *That son of a bitch isn't going to have his way with me.*

Feeling that her lungs had reached their breaking point, Monica stopped to gasp for air while leaning against a large oak-style tree that greeted her upon her stop.

Her survival instinct continuing to flow. She whipped her

head around once more to her left but didn't see her captain anywhere in her sight.

Before she could turn her head the other way, however, something cold pressed up against her exposed temple.

Gasping in horror, she realized that she had been caught.

"All that running, and yet it's all for not, because here we are, my dear," stated Maxwell in a creepy tone, his index finger caressing the trigger of his ready gun. "I have to admit that you got me all heated up back there. But, like they say, fool me once, shame on you. Fool me twice. Shame on me. And, trust me, there will be no fooling me twice. So, I suppose the shame will remain with you, especially once I'm done with you."

Monica could think of nothing else to do but to try one last attempt of seduction to test his willpower, the bile in the back of her throat once again rising.

"But there's so much I have to offer you, baby," she told him in a velvety voice.

"Save it, bitch," the captain replied in a growl. "The only thing I'm going to get from you will be on my terms and not yours. And, if I were you, I would hope that your death will be quick and relentless."

He ran his hand across her right cheek and grabbed her by the throat, the demons in his eyes suggesting he had nothing but the worst of intentions.

"Don't move because you're only going to make it worse for yourself," he told her.

Monica closed her eyes and gulped out of despair as the captain began to sloppily kiss her chin and work his way up towards her violated lips.

Please, Ronnie, she prayed to herself. *Save me, please.*

Marcus, sensing her pleas, stepped out of the open hatch and prepared himself to charge before stopping in his tracks momentarily to look for any sort of clues of which way they had gone.

His eyes quickly scanned the scenery, his focus fixated on the sandy region in front of him that contained footsteps of two people, which suddenly led to a large crater a few feet from its start.

A smattering of blood on the ground dropped his heart from its place and into his stomach, his thoughts telling him that perhaps he had already been too late in saving Monica.

Please, no. It can't be.

His eyes becoming misty from the thought of losing her, he suddenly felt like a failure for not protecting her how he had so often promised himself that he would do.

My God, how did I let this happen?

His sadness turned into anger, he felt upset with himself for not getting to her sooner and rescuing her from the evil clutches of Maxwell.

I never got to experience her kiss. I never got to feel her touch. I never got to know what it was like to truly love her.

An overwhelming feeling of melancholy came over him at the thought of Maxwell taking her life away, his blank gaze stuck upon the blood-splattered area of dirt that had suddenly seemed to turn his life upside down.

I failed her.

His eyes moving for no reason to the side, he suddenly noticed something that immediately picked up his spirits.

Those footprints that lead to the forest--they look like Monica's. Could they be?

An overwhelming feeling of optimism came over him, his heart telling him that she was indeed still alive.

"There's only one way to find out," he told himself before dashing towards the forest before him, his anticipation growing of rescuing the woman he loved and confronting his captain for one final encounter.

In the distance ahead, Maxwell threw Monica to the ground and climbed uncomfortably on top of her, the barrel of his weapon still pressed against her head.

"Get off me," she screamed at him before freeing up an open hand to deliver a feeble punch to the back of his head.

"If this is your idea of being freaky, then keep it up," he horrendously told her while grinning wickedly ear to ear. "I like it rough."

Monica, squirming for her life, felt unable to breathe from the force of his weight while claustrophobia became her secondary enemy and further raised her anxiety.

"Help!" she yelled out of desperation.

"Shut up, or I'll shoot," commanded the despicable captain in a forceful tone.

Tiring of the threats, Monica's bravery bubbled over. "Do it. I'd rather die than live through this hell with you."

He meanly snickered towards her defiant statement and rubbed her battered cheek. "No, you're not getting away that easy, honey. I've still got something really big in store for you and your boyfriend. But who knows? You may just press your luck enough for me to change my mind."

Maxwell bent down and attempted to kiss her warm lips once more on his own terms, but his effort was nailed by a right hook that Monica was able to get across his left cheek.

His head cocked back momentarily as he angrily growled at her defiance and began to raise his hand to threaten her.

"Such a beautiful face," he snarled. "But, I've tired of your rebellious ways, and it's time to teach you a lesson. So, unfortunately, my dear, I've got no choice but to harm it as your reward for bad behavior."

Monica closed her eyes and was prepared to feel the force of his smack before the voice of her hero answered her pleas.

"Get the hell off of her!"

Opening her eyes to the sight of a confused Maxwell, she smiled ear to ear upon hearing the warm tones of Marcus' voice that had arrived right on time.

A grin came over Maxwell, who remained in position and refused the order of his commander.

"I told you to get the hell off of her," Marcus commanded angrily towards Maxwell while aiming his gun in between the captain's eyes. "Don't make me blow your brains out."

Maxwell shook his head and laughed hysterically, amused by the commander's latter statement.

"What's so funny?" Marcus asked furiously, further angered by his captain's defiance.

"I just love your tenacity," stated Maxwell. "Or, rather, your stupidity, I suppose. Whichever it is, your defiance is hollow at best."

Marcus felt insulted by his captain's remarks. "No, you're mistaken. I'm a man of my word, so you'd better believe that I mean what I say."

Maxwell shook his head once more, his smirk never ceasing as he took one step towards Marcus.

"You haven't given this much thought, have you?" asked the captain as he continued to move at a snail's pace towards him. "I am immortal, which means that I cannot die. I'm no longer human, unlike you and your pitiful friends."

Marcus' nerves rose upon the captain's continuing advancement, his trigger finger suddenly as stiff as a board.

"Stop before I shoot," he falsely warned.

The captain paid no mind to his commander's toothless order and continued his zombie pace towards the suddenly listless Marcus.

Monica, frozen in her own tracks with her open shirt swaying briskly in the breeze, felt a slight sense of impatience come over her. "Ronnie, shoot him!"

Maxwell snickered wickedly out of amusement. "Yes, do as she's saying and shoot me, Marcus. In fact, let's try something. We'll take turns, and I'll let you shoot me first. Then, I'll take my turn with you, and we'll see who will be the last man standing."

Marcus realized then that his captain was, unfortunately, right. His will suddenly began to wane from the harsh reality that began to set in.

Feeling helpless, he quickly gazed towards Monica, whose eyes had become softened and begged for any sort of positive action on his end.

"C'mon, Marcus," challenged Maxwell, who was a mere couple of steps from his statuesque commander. "I can almost smell the fear that's stinks from within you."

The wheels in his head spun as quickly as ever, and his mind remained void of feasible options.

Focusing down on his gun, he felt like he wanted to throw it away as if it were a toy.

What good is my gun if he's going to rise from the dead again? We might as well just settle this like men, even if he's going to destroy me.

His latter thought triggered the light bulb in his brain to go off, his pride assisting in his thoughts.

That's it. If I'm going to go down, I may as well do it my way.

Defiantly tossing his gun aside, Marcus held his palms upward towards his immortal captain to tip his hand.

Maxwell, dumbfounded by Marcus' surprise response, stopped immediately in his tracks. "What in the hell do you think you're doing?"

Marcus smirked at his captain's confusion. "I'm challenging you to a duel. We'll let our fists do all of the talking."

Shock curtained Maxwell's face. "You must be joking, boy. Surely, you can't be serious."

Marcus, intent on pushing his captain's internal buttons, continued with his boldness. "Are you afraid to take me on, old man?"

Unappreciative of the cavalier attitude his commander exhibited towards him, Maxwell nonetheless licked his chops over the tasty possibility before him and could taste Marcus' blood on his tongue.

"Very well," answered Maxwell while tossing his own weapon aside. "I gladly accept your offer, boy. There's nothing more I'd like than to have your blood on my hands and personally rip the beating heart out of your chest."

Those are my sentiments exactly, you dirty old bastard.

"Don't get your hopes up," Marcus told Maxwell before raising his fists in preparation for the fight of his life.

CHAPTER 34

Monica was reduced to nothing other than a spectator as she watched Marcus and Maxwell prepare to fight to the bloody end.

"You're going to regret this, you fool," stated Maxwell with a wicked grin across his five-o'-clock shadowed face.

Marcus shook his head and smiled right back, unfazed by his commanding officer's words. "No, I won't because no matter what you do to me, I'm not going down without a fight."

A snarl came from Maxwell upon Marcus' final statement. "You've always been good at running your mouth. Now, let's see how good you are with your fists."

Maxwell took the first swing but missed badly and was rewarded with a kidney shot to his lower back that was delivered by Marcus.

The captain grunted loudly upon the contact but refused to give his commander any satisfaction.

"What's the matter?" asked Marcus confidently. "Did that one hurt?"

Offering no response, Maxwell charged towards him and flung a haymaker towards Marcus' nose that once again whiffed.

Marcus responded with a pulverizing shot to Maxwell's gut that made the captain bow his body.

The commander took the opportunity for another open attempt by delivering a wicked uppercut that shattered the nose of his former commanding officer and sent Maxwell, bloodied nostrils and all, straight onto his backside.

Maxwell, woozy from the last shot he had taken, quickly sat up but batted his eyes in an attempt to get the cobwebs out.

Marcus, enjoying the sight of seeing his captain down, took an open opportunity to chide his commanding officer while taking a quick glance at his sweetheart.

"I'd say so far that I'm doing pretty well with my fists, wouldn't you?" he asked, tease intertwined in his voice. "I'm pitching a shutout so far. At this rate, I'll be the one ripping your heart out."

Little did the gloating and distracted Marcus realize, however, that Maxwell had regained his composure by delivering a momentum-changing jab into the commander's groin.

Marcus groaned in agony and crouched towards the grass, unwittingly giving his captain an instant advantage.

His brain on murderous haywire mode, Maxwell began an unsympathetic rampage by first crunching Marcus' face with his right knee.

Marcus, collapsing to the ground, attempted to get up but was unsuccessful, thanks to a roundhouse punch that snapped Marcus' momentum backwards onto the grass.

Maxwell, taking full advantage of his personal power play, booted Marcus into his ribs before stomping wickedly into his stomach, the latter squeezing every ounce of air that existed in the commander's lungs.

Gasping for air, Marcus attempted to rise to his feet, nonetheless, but was rejected in his try by Maxwell, who grabbed the top of his short hair and sent two devastating haymakers that bloodied Marcus' mouth and cracked one of his front teeth.

A feeble groan was all that Marcus could muster before crashing to the floor and coiling into a fetal position in an attempt to shield himself somehow from the bedlam that had been unleashed onto him.

A smug look adorned Maxwell's face, and he slowly paraded around Marcus' weakened body and took his own opportunity to gloat.

Monica, her cheeks stained with tears of fear, shook violently from her shot nerves.

"Stop!" she screamed with great mercy towards Maxwell. "Please, stop it! Leave him alone!"

Through his blood stained face, Maxwell did little to hide his enjoyment as he peered into her eyes.

"You want me to stop, huh?" he asked her sarcastically. "Well, tough shit, because I promised to rip his beating heart out. And I definitely don't break those kinds of promises, sweetheart."

Gritting his teeth, Maxwell kicked Marcus into the stomach once more before kneeling over and forcing the commander onto his back.

Marcus offered little resistance as pain dominated his body, while Maxwell did nothing to aid his ailments by stepping firmly onto his groin and continuing to apply pressure onto his genitals.

The commander screamed in excruciating pain before beginning to choke on the blood that trickled down his throat, and his breathing labored due to the lack of oxygen in his lungs.

"Well, it appears I've made quite the comeback on you," Maxwell stated to the helpless Marcus. "Now, for my next trick, I will take your remaining manhood before I rob you of your beating heart as promised."

Monica, suddenly unable to take any more of the physical abuse she was witnessing, stormed towards Maxwell, unafraid of the potentially deadly consequences that possibly awaited her. "No!" screamed Monica towards Maxwell. "You leave him alone!"

Her fist clobbered the back of Maxwell's neck, who made the mistake of paying no attention to her screams.

The captain toppled onto the ground and grabbed his assaulted area but rose to his feet quickly to return the favor.

She quickly tried to escape but failed to get far, unfortunately, as the captain grabbed the back of her neck and began to choke her.

"You made a big mistake, darling," he said through raging eyes. "And now, I'm going to have no choice but to break off all of your limbs so you can only sit and watch as I destroy Marcus before you meet the same fate."

Maxwell took her wrist with his open hand and forced her body against the large oak tree that sat behind her.

Marcus slowly began to rise to his feet to save her from harm but felt as if his body was weighted down from the assault he had taken.

Doing everything in his power to get up, he could not get the motivation in his heart to agree with his heavily beaten body.

I've--got--to--get--up.

Fearing that he was going to be too late, his eyes fixated on Maxwell, who began to twist Monica's wrist in an attempt to break it.

Monica screeched in pain, her wrist feeling as if it were ready to snap off from the pressure applied to it by Maxwell.

Marcus, helpless in his battered state, could do nothing else but open his mouth and try to catch the attention of Maxwell, yet not a sound was able to leave his blood-lubed throat.

I--have--to--save--her--c'mon.

Attempting once more to say something but to no success, Marcus fell to one knee, his body and mind not connecting as he realized only a miracle would save both of them now.

Suddenly, in the form of an unknown voice, his prayer was answered.

"Halt!" the voice commanded aloud.

Marcus, shocked by the unexpected turn of events, rotated his head over and saw one of the young village men stand a few yards behind Maxwell.

The captain surprised himself, turned his head behind him

and delivered an angry glare to the man while continuing to anchor down Monica's neck and wrist.

"What--is it, my child?" he asked in a softened tone in an attempt to manipulate the young alien being.

The man, clearly disturbed by what he had seen, did not fall for Maxwell's manipulative attempt. "Sire, my being requests stoppage of this matter. My being cannot allow such behavior from the being of our Excellency."

Maxwell frowned in disbelief over the man's request and let his false front completely down.

"Don't you talk to me like that," stated the captain to the villager, his soft tone turning grizzled and hard. "You give me respect, damn it. I am your master, you unappreciative little shit."

"Negative, sir," responded the man to Maxwell's claim. "For our almighty master would allow no such deviancy such as this."

Maxwell growled like a wild animal and threw Monica to the ground before approaching the youthful-looking alien male in a hostile manner.

"I told you not to talk to me like that," he told the man, pointing his finger while stomping towards him violently. "You must bow to me. And if you do not, I will take your pitiful life for your insubordination."

"Negative, for your being will not," said the voice of another villager, this time in the form of one of the young women who approached from behind a tree. "Our Excellency does not embrace the responsibility of death as your being has. It is for that reasoning that your following is non-existent towards our beings."

Turning his attention to his new enemy, Maxwell's berating continued onto her.

"You will suffer the same fate as your friend here," he warned her crudely as he pointed now towards the ground. "Bow down and worship me now, or pay the price!"

"Negative," responded another village man who had suddenly emerged. "For there is no worship for beings embedded with evil such as that of yours."

Maxwell had tired of the rebellious nature of the three villagers who had approached him. "You will all pay for this. First, I will destroy these two, and then your asses will be next. Five against one is nothing for me."

Much to the captain's dismay, however, the rest of the villagers emerged from behind various trees and lumped together to stand in unison against Maxwell, refusing to put up with his terrorizing ways continuing any longer.

Monica stared at Marcus, who finally found an ounce of strength to rise to his feet and observe what was going on through his beaten eyes.

Maxwell stood in stunned disbelief, the reality setting in him that his reign of power over the villagers had officially ended.

Marcus, leaning his tired body against the closest tree to him, found joy in watching his captain fall flat.

"You abused your power, John," he was able to muster up to Maxwell. "They no longer respect you, much like we don't. You have failed as a leader and a man towards us all. And now, it's time for you to face the music and give up."

His heart filled with hatred. Maxwell turned towards Marcus once more and delivered a deadly stare. "Say what you will, Marcus. No matter what, I am immortal, and I will rule this planet. And it is for that reason that I will completely obliterate all of you. And I will start, with great anticipation, with you."

Maxwell charged toward Marcus like an angry bull, while the feeble commander could do nothing more than prepare himself for the incoming train that was on track to hit him.

Maxwell's attempt, much to his own surprise, came up short courtesy of a laser shot that pierced through his heart and sent his momentum backwards.

Marcus, shocked himself by the force that failed to reach him, searched eagerly around to see who had fired the shot.

His eyes caught onto Monica, who nervously held the gun outward through trembling hands, her wide eyes giving away her own surprise over what she had done.

Maxwell, through heavy and labored breathing, stumbled around and gasped for air as blood stained the chest area of his shirt before he grabbed onto the first plant that met him.

"I am immortal!" he screamed, choking on his own blood. "You cannot kill me, for I will come back and destroy you all!"

Unbeknownst to Maxwell, he had grabbed onto the wrong plant, and it suddenly began to shake and grow bigger.

Marcus, still trying to capture the missing breath from his lungs, cracked a half-grin upon realization of what Maxwell had just gotten himself into with the alien plant he himself had gotten all too familiar with earlier.

Ludan, as angry as ever, came to full life and hovered behind Maxwell, who felt the incredibly large presence behind him and turned around to the surprise he had awoken.

"What--what the hell is this?" he asked, his bulging eyes still taking in the giant before him.

Ludan growled upon the captain's mistake. "You have dared to disturb my slumber, creature. How does your being explain?"

Maxwell's cavalier attitude refused to fade even in his grave condition. "I don't need to explain anything, especially to a thing like you. You will either bow down to me or die."

The sewlet did not take kindly to Maxwell's words and responded by grabbing him by the throat with both of its branched hands.

Marcus, Monica and the villagers watched in wonder as Ludan began to squeeze tightly on Maxwell's throat and lift him from the ground like a ragdoll.

Maxwell, suddenly in a helpless state of his own, weakly attempted to pry the poisonous grasp of the sewlet's leaves that vacuumed against his neck.

"Negative, foolish creature," Ludan strongly told the arrogant captain. "The bowing will come from your being."

Poison began to filter through Maxwell's veins, who could only harmlessly kick his legs in a feeble attempt to free himself from the vice-like grip of Ludan.

Marcus, grinning ear to ear at the sight of his commanding officer struggling, enjoyed seeing the shoe on the other foot.

Karma's a bitch.

Maxwell could do nothing more than groan as the venom from Ludan slithered through his blood like a snake and turned his once immaculate skin to an unhealthy purplish hue.

As the venom reached his heart, Maxwell choked loudly in a last gasp effort to breathe before his eyes rolled back into his head as his soul left his listless body.

The sewlet growled in approval over his accomplishment before throwing Maxwell's dead body onto the ground, which crunched loudly as it bounced roughly off of the grass before settling in place.

Marcus stepped slowly towards Maxwell's dead and broken body and summoned Monica over to join his side.

She happily complied as she rushed to his side and handed it over willingly.

Readying his gun and aiming it towards the skull area of his dead captain, Marcus felt unsure of what to do, feeling the need to prepare for Maxwell's pending resurrection just in case.

His trigger finger, however, suddenly began to relax upon the sight of the change that began to occur in Maxwell.

The captain's flesh, once young and tight, suddenly began to sag while his face quickly faded from youthful to aged and wrinkled like before.

"What's happening?" Monica asked Marcus out of confusion while Ludan began to shrink back to his normal state.

Marcus shrugged his shoulders, unsure of the accurate reason. "I don't know."

The male villager who had first approached Maxwell shuffled toward the dead captain's body and knelt on the ground over him. Using his open palm, he gently brushed Maxwell's forehead.

Marcus, worried over the immortal status of Maxwell, felt the need to warn the brave village man. "Be careful. He may come back to life at any moment."

"Negative," responded the man calmly. "His being has expired."

Marcus' shock value rose upon the man's words, but disbelief also ran through him as he couldn't take his latter statement as face value.

"No, that can't be," he stated while shaking his bloodied head. "I mean, he's immortal, so he can't die, right?"

A village woman walked towards them and stopped at the side of the man, which Marcus assumed to be his wife.

"Our ancestors created a legend of such prophecy," the woman chimed in. "In the possibility that our Excellency contained hatred as a majority, the falling of his being would be timely. If his being was to contain harmony, immortality would belong to his being. It is of the utmost appearance that the venom of Ludan and the hatred his being contained was fatally coupled."

Marcus appeared confused by the usage of language, a raising of his eyebrow helping to state so.

Monica, however, nodded her head as she seemed to at least have an idea of what she had stated. "So, you're saying that because he had evil in his heart, that, combined with the poison, was what destroyed him. Is that correct?"

The man and woman both nodded their heads in unison.

"That is positive," the woman answered.

Marcus was impressed by Monica's interpretation skills. "You're good," stated the commander understatedly to her while cracking a bloody smile to her.

Monica turned her head and winked back at him. "I'm better than good. I'm great."

Marcus, sensing that he was once again getting entranced by her, cleared his throat to get himself back into business mode.

"So, does this mean he's permanently dead?" was his inquiry to the alien couple.

"Positive," answered the smiling man, who himself appeared to be extremely relieved that the brief yet terrifying reign of Maxwell had officially ended.

Marcus smiled himself out of relief but couldn't help but stare at his now officially deceased captain, whose skin tone began to fade from purple to pale white as the blood officially stopped pumping through his body and rigor mortis began to set in at a snail's pace.

He felt satisfied to know that Maxwell had officially been brought down but couldn't contain the slightest feeling of sadness over seeing his one-time mentor perish the way he had. It felt odd to see Maxwell dead on the ground and bittersweet to know that he would never deal with the feisty and bossy nature of his captain ever again.

Monica, peering over at Marcus and noticing that he appeared lost in thought, felt the need to check on him.

"Ronnie?" she asked to break him out of his internal trance. "Is something wrong?"

"No," he slowly answered while gazing into her eyes, feeling free for the first time since he joined SAGE. "I couldn't be any better."

Even despite her gorgeous smile that beamed back at him, he did his best not to let his romantic feelings gush over at this moment and time, which was further assisted by the fact that his dead captain resided only a few feet from them.

And, the fact that his mouth had been bloodied definitely prohibited him further from giving her the first kiss he so badly desired.

In due time, hopefully.

Choosing to play it cool yet again, he grinned sheepishly back at Monica before turning his gaze towards the villagers, who eagerly awaited one of them to speak.

"Thank you," he simply told them. "I truly thank you all for your help with this."

"It is of the greatest pleasure of our beings," answered one of the men. "Is there more assistance that is required?"

Marcus shook his head and felt relieved to know the adventure they had been forcefully made a part of was coming to an end. His brain suddenly clicked, however, and gave him a stern reminder that work still needed to be done immediately.

He thought instantly about Rubidoux, who he was hoping had not died on him before he had the opportunity to return.

"Yes, please," he politely stated while nursing his various injuries. "My friend back on our ship is in need of dire medical help. He may die if we don't hurry and help him. And I have others, along with two of your own, trapped in the dark on our ship. Will you be able to help us?"

"Positive," responded the woman with a polite nod of her head. "It would be of the utmost pleasure to assist. Our mission will consist of aiding the deceasing friend. Our beings will proceed to our residence urgently."

"Thank you so much," Marcus gratefully said. "But, please, hurry. I'm not sure how much longer he has."

A simple nodding of the head came from them both before they hurried towards their village.

The remainder of the villagers stood behind as they waited for Marcus to lead the way.

The commander turned towards Monica, choking back the pain he was experiencing while remaining focused on the next task at hand.

"We've got to hurry," he quickly instructed Monica.

"Right behind you," she simply stated.

Marcus, with the others following behind, limped quickly towards the ship, the pain in his body becoming almost unbearable, yet his concern remaining solely on saving the young Rubidoux from death that waited on the doorstep.

Chapter 35

Marcus hurried along with his followers through the corridor and into the cell block that was occupied by Rubidoux.

Thrashing open the door, his sight was instantly met with that of the rookie lying flat on the ground, his eyes shut with no sign of breathing or confirmation that he was still alive.

His heart dropping from fear that he was too late, Marcus stumbled over to the cell and fumbled around for his key card to open the cell.

"Rube!" he shouted towards the rookie, but no response was given. The commander's hands violently shook as he struggled to take out the key card from his belt needed to open the jail.

Monica began to sob at the sight, her anxiety reaching its maximum point.

"Rube!" she cried out in despair. "Please, open your eyes!"

The rookie's body remained limp upon her final plea while a dead silence filled the air that only heightened the intensity.

Marcus, battling his nerves, finally detached the card and clumsily placed it above the scanner before pulling open the door.

The villagers who came with them sat in stern silence as they observed what was happening before them, and the concerned expressions on their faces were simultaneous between them all.

Marcus rushed towards Rubidoux's body and knelt quickly before him.

"Rube, open your eyes," he commanded desperately before placing his hand over the rookie's chest to see if he could feel any sort of heartbeat.

A faint pulse existed but did little to ease the commander's worries.

Monica, overcome with emotion, placed her head in her hands and cried loudly out of fear that they were too late.

Marcus, an internal emotional wreck himself, felt as if he wanted to do the same but resisted the urge to remain strong for her.

"C'mon, buddy," pleaded Marcus to Rubidoux. "Give me some sort of sign here, please."

The alien man and woman rushed through the open door like doctors and were a welcome sight to both Marcus and Monica, who raised her tear-stained face from her hands and choked back on her tears.

"Thank God you are both here," Marcus proclaimed while continuing to stand closely by the side of Rubidoux. "Do you have the remedy?"

"Positive," responded the man, who joined the side of Marcus and knelt down before the body of Rubidoux.

He placed his hand over Rubidoux's forehead, concern apparent over his youthful, bearded face while he shook his head slightly.

"What--what's the matter?" Marcus nervously asked.

The man only continued to shake his head momentarily before speaking what was on his mind.

"The fear of my being is that your friend will have expired prior to the assistance our beings can offer."

Marcus' jaw dropped violently. "What do you mean? All that we need to do is give him the remedy, and he'll be fine, right?"

The woman knelt down herself by Rubidoux's body, an expression of grave proportions etched on her beautiful face.

"Negative. Once your friend has expired, the remedy is of no importance. It is the fear of our beings that your friend will be of deceased status before the remedy reaches the internal matter of his being."

Marcus stared blankly, the air in his lungs feeling as if they had been robbed by the woman's proclamation.

Biting his bottom lip, he turned his head toward the dying body of Rubidoux and deeply inhaled and exhaled to attempt to regulate his breathing and slow down his rapid heart rate.

"So, is there nothing that can be done for him?" he asked them desperately.

The man and woman peered at one another as if to decide who would speak next.

"There is one option of possibility," the woman finally replied. "It is a decision of hardness for your being."

Marcus' curiosity rose instantly. "What is it?"

The woman dramatically paused before finally answering. "His being must drink the sacred liquid of our beings and become of immortal stature."

The proposition instantly stumped Marcus, who began to weigh the pros and cons while turning his head towards Monica, who herself appeared uncertain of what they should do as the life of the young man suddenly lay in their hands.

Marcus turned his attention away from her and gazed towards Rubidoux's body, his mind pondering over what decision would be the best for the young man who battled for his life before his eyes.

An uneasy feeling came over him as he quickly considered the pros and cons behind each decision.

If he drinks the liquid, he lives, but as a young man for all of eternity. If he doesn't, he dies in front of us valiantly yet doesn't live the full life he deserves.

"My pardons," intervened the man, "but this is a hurried matter of deceased or living status for this being."

Marcus broke from his momentary emergency meeting with

himself and stared upwards at the man and woman, who anxiously awaited his decision.

He turned once more towards Monica, who nodded her head in assurance that she believed that he would make the right choice.

He paused and gulped heavily before giving his answer.

"Do it," he whispered loudly to them.

"Are your being positive?" asked the woman.

Marcus hesitated briefly before nodding his head gently.

"Yes, I'm positive," he answered quickly before turning again towards Monica.

She said nothing as their eyes met each other, but gave the approving look in her eyes was all he needed to know that he had made the correct choice.

The woman reached inside of a brown pouch that she carried on her and took out a wooden vial.

She popped open the cork cap that fit perfectly into the opening while the man placed his hand under Rubidoux's head and held it barely above the ground.

Braving the blood that was spattered throughout Rubidoux's face, the man took his other hand and manually opened his mouth.

The woman, meanwhile, took the vial and placed it above the navigator's open mouth before pouring the liquid slowly inside.

The stream that flowed from the vial glistened in the dimness of the cell until the last of the liquid dripped from the opening of the vial and ran empty.

Monica joined Marcus by his side as they both could do no more than watch inquisitively while the two village strangers they had placed all of their trust and hope in tended to Rubidoux.

The man cocked Rubidoux's head up slightly more to further ensure the liquid would flow down the dying young man's throat.

"So, what happens now?" Marcus asked curiously. "Is he going to make it?"

"It is of unknown value," the man answered. "Patience is now required. It is of great hope that it is of success."

Silence was met with the man's statement by the two Earthlings, who could do nothing more than to see what would come of their comrade.

Their eyes never left the body of Rubidoux as they simultaneously prayed internally for their navigator to pull through.

C'mon, Rube. I know you have it in you.

Much to their relief and happiness, Rubidoux slowly began to open his eyes.

Monica gasped and clutched Marcus' uniform top while tears of joy began to flow down her cheek.

Marcus' eyes also began to water with happiness as the young rookie opened his eyes fully and took a choppy yet refreshing breath.

The man and woman smiled down at Rubidoux, who blinked his eyes before gazing up at them both with confusion as to who they were.

The rookie lifted his head and had his eyesight met with the presence of Marcus and Monica, who smiled joyously together at their resurrected patient.

"Where--am I?" Rubidoux asked in a whispered tone.

"You're in the cell on the ship," answered Marcus happily. "And I couldn't be any more pleased to announce that to you."

"Oh," he answered simply before turning his attention back at the mysterious man and woman who hovered above him. "Who are you?"

"They're our new friends," stated Monica while staring at the alien man and woman, who gazed back at her and smiled. "And they're the ones who saved your life."

Rubidoux sheepishly grinned at the man and woman, feeling indebted to them both.

"Thank you," he softly told them.

The man and woman simply nodded their head back and smiled to acknowledge his gratefulness.

Rubidoux turned his focus back towards Marcus, who still hid his tears of joy from overflowing from his eyes.

"Maxwell--is he--dead?"

Marcus grinned strongly towards his navigator. "Yes. He's dead."

A nervous smirk came across the rookie's face, who stared into the ceiling above him. "I guess so much for being immortal then, huh?"

Monica glanced over at Marcus and met eyes with him once again in an attempt to encourage him to tell Rubidoux about his newly minted immortal status.

Understanding the look she had given him, Marcus cleared his throat to allow himself a brief moment to find the right words for a proper explanation to Rubidoux.

"About being immortal," Marcus began to explain slowly. "Well--we had to make a decision with you in order to save your life."

Rubidoux's gaze immediately left the ceiling and fixated on his commander with great confusion.

"And, well--you were dying--you see," Marcus continued to explain. "So, because of that--our friends here gave you the liquid so that you--wouldn't die."

The rookie's eyes, large from anticipation, picked up on where the conversation was going.

"So, you mean--"

Marcus halted for a moment to compose himself before finally completing Rubidoux's sentence to cut the deafening silence in the cell.

"You are now immortal," Marcus told him directly.

Monica and Marcus, peering at the stunned Rubidoux, worried over how the young man would take the earth-shattering news.

"So--I'm going to live--forever?" he asked sullenly.

Marcus nodded his head. "Yes, I'm afraid so."

"And--I'm going to look like this--forever?"

"It appears that way, Rube. I'm sorry."

Rubidoux's face did little to change as he continued to soak in the reality.

His silence worried Marcus and Monica, who were afraid that he was going to take the news harshly.

"Damn," he finally answered after a few moments of quiet with a half-smile. "I guess that I'll never be able to grow a mustache then, huh?"

Marcus, taken aback by the rookie's response, sat in stunned silence, waiting for the other shoe to drop.

Monica, equally as surprised, joined in a smirk.

"So, you're not upset, then?" asked the commander.

The rookie's bottom lip engulfed its top companion while he shook his head. "Nah, not really. I mean, I don't know how in the world I'll eventually tell my family, but maybe in time, they'll understand."

Marcus, finally feeling at ease, grinned upon Rubidoux's remark. "Yeah, I'm sure they will."

The commander, at an all-time high from the positivity, glanced once more at the alien man and woman, who both beamed brightly upon sharing in the special moment.

"Thank you both again once more," Marcus told the two of them. "I apologize because we never asked you, but what are your names?"

The man and woman turned toward one another before turning their focus back to Marcus, surprised by the question.

"It has been ages since an introduction was necessary," stated the woman. "The name of my being is Allea, and his being is Prat."

Marcus smiled at them both warmly. "It's a pleasure to meet you both."

The aliens and Earth people shared in a warm moment as the ice was officially broken on their new kinships.

Chapter 36

The liquid began to galvanize throughout the newly immortal Rubidoux, who rose from the ground like a phoenix from the ashes.

The blood on his face remained, but the bruises and cuts had fully healed under the coat of red.

"You alright?" asked Marcus out of concern to the rookie.

Rubidoux smirked upon the question. "Never been better, Commander. For being immortal, I feel pretty damn good."

"Well, you look great sans the bloody face," joked Monica. "As soon as that gets cleaned up, you'll be back to your sexy self."

Rubidoux chuckled heartily upon her statement, his face blushing under the red while he peered behind him and stared at Maren's cold, dead body that remained sprawled on the ground.

"What will become of him?" he asked, focusing his attention on Allea and Prat for answers.

Allea shrugged her shoulders at his question. "It is of unknown value. It has been many cycles since a being of ours has deceased."

"So, you mean that he won't be coming back from the dead?"

Prat shook his head gently to intervene. "Positive. Our beings are not of immortal value such as that. Our beings are not sufficientfor aging. However, the bodily matter is capable of deceasing such as yours. The bodily matter of Maren will engulf into the soil throughout the changing moons."

"Oh," Rubidoux said simply as he nodded his head in acknowledgment and began to finally take his first somewhat wobbly steps since resurrecting.

Marcus and Monica watched Rubidoux with precaution, prepared to catch him if he was to have fallen, but it seemed to be unnecessary as the navigator made his way out of the cell block without a moment of peril, his stomach beginning to growl loudly.

"Pardon me, I'm just feeling hungry."

Marcus smirked at the odd timing, remembering at the same time that Arraz felt the same following his resurrection.

"I don't have any food pills, Rube," he gently said. "Sorry about that."

Rubidoux offered nothing other than a shrug of the shoulders towards his commander's response.

Turning back to the dead body of Maren, Marcus scratched his head and further pondered the next move before glancing at Allea from the corner of his eye. "Should we do anything with the body?"

Allea simply smiled and shook her head. "Our beings will take the bodily matter."

Marcus' bottom lip engulfed the top while he nodded his head. "Very well. In that case, let's head on to the elevator shaft so I can show you our next dilemma."

He waved his hand and led the charge with Monica, Rubidoux, Allea and Prat in order as they exited the cell area.

Prat turned behind him and summoned the remaining villagers, who had lurked by the open hatch until further command had been given, with his own hand signal.

Making their way through the basement, they reached the open elevator door, where the busted elevator remained grounded. "What is of this area?" Prat inquired curiously.

"This is our shitty elevator," answered Marcus underhand-edly. "It's supposed to take us up and down, but as you can see, it's not really going anywhere."

He pointed upwards at the manmade hole at the top of the elevator, which he had made exclusively.

"There's usually a cable that pulls the elevator up and down, but it broke as I was climbing down it, and because of that, we can't get to the area above where our friends, and a couple of your friends, are stuck. So, we need to find a way to get up there."

The extraterrestrials stared in awe upon the sight before them, their eyes never previously being exposed to such technology.

"Remarkable," exclaimed Prat. "It is of the upmost pity it is not of functional operation so our beings could further examine. Possibly an idea of simplicity is of greater importance for a future date?"

A nodding Marcus couldn't have agreed on anymore with Prat's comments. "I think you're on to something brilliant there. It's amazing that aliens such as yourselves can acknowledge that, and our own superiors cannot."

Prat paid no mind to Marcus' compliment and complaint. "I have accomplished an understanding of the dilemma your beings possess. Allow our beings the opportunity for assistance. The answer has come clearly."

Monica, Marcus and Rubidoux had no idea of what Prat was talking about, but all three simultaneously turned their heads and waited to see what the young alien man would do next.

Paying no attention to the fact he was being watched, Prat turned to the other villagers and simply cocked his head up and down with a quick nod.

The villagers responded by rushing out of the elevator, through the basement,, and out of the hatch, which led them back outside without a peep.

Prat and Allea stayed behind before turning back and being met with gazes of curiosity and amazement on behalf of their

Earth counterparts, who were intrigued yet unsure of what exactly was occurring.

"I'm taking a guess that you have a solution to our little problem?" Marcus asked on behalf of all three of the Eartlings.

Prat nodded his head and smiled. "Positive. Allow our beings a yarber."

"A--what, I'm sorry?" asked Monica politely out of confusion. "Did you say--a yarber?"

"Positive," Allea answered. "Are your beings aware of the definition?"

All three shook their heads, but Rubidoux took it a step further and shrugged his shoulders greatly to show his confusion.

Allea, surprised by the response, turned towards Prat, who himself seemed unsure of how to describe it to their visitors. She thought for a moment before attempting to explain to the foreigners before her.

"Defining yarber," Allea slowly began to explain, attempting to find the right words to be clear to the three Earth people. "Yarber defines the formatted statement of measurement of time broken into units. Such as, see your being in a yarber."

The light bulb went off in Marcus' head upon her explanation.

"Oh, you must be referring to a second," stated the commander, who felt on board despite Monica and Rubidoux not feeling the same. "I get it. In our language, we call that a second."

"A--second?" Prat said in confusion. "Interesting, yet curious, wording for your beings."

Yeah, look who's talking.

Marcus, cracking a smile, decided to get somewhat playful with his new comrades. "We will gladly grant you a yarber."

"Appreciation for the granting of a--second," Allea responded with a grin, picking up on what Marcus was doing and deciding to play along.

Their yarder, or second, was indeed that as the villagers returned quickly with their arms full of supplies.

His curiosity rising, Marcus gazed at the vine-like stems and branches that they carried closely to them.

"Wow, that was quick," he stated in amazement to them. "But, what is all of this stuff for?"

"Observe," Allea simply stated with a nod.

The villagers put down their supplies on the ground and began to dig through them.

Singling out the branches that contained yellowish leaves, they began to pluck the leaves away from the grasp of the branches, throwing the branches to the ground once they were left naked.

Four of the villagers began to ball up the leaves and rubbed them rapidly through their palms.

The other villagers, meanwhile, continued to pluck more leaves and formed a pile onthe hard floor.

Completing their strange leaf rubbing techniques, the four villagers let the balled-up leaves fall to the floor and stomped their worn shoes onto the helpless leaves that had flattened into the floor.

While the four villagers continued to move their feet violently, the others took the vines they had carried with them and quickly began to form a long rope by fastening each end and tying them tightly together.

Working like maniacs, they formed a lengthy vine in the flash of an eye.

The three Earthlings stood in wonder upon the sight of the well-oiled machine of an organization that had moved in a flash before their eyes, curiosity arising over each of them in wondering what was about to happen.

The four villagers, remaining focused on the task at hand, each took hold of the vine and approached the open area of the elevator.

"Our pardons," said one of the village men as he, along with the other two village men and one woman, stepped by their Earth acquaintances and began to climb the rough exteriors of the wall with their sticky hands and feet like spiders.

Climbing in a single-file line, they each carried the vine through their teeth to efficiently multitask.

"Wow," stated Rubidoux in awe. "This is amazing."

The splendor in their faces delighted Allea and Prat, who stood with them in unison and joined the observers in watching the traveling villagers, whose bodies quickly disappeared into the darkness.

"We didn't even get a chance to tell them where to go," Marcus told Allea and Prat.

Prat appeared unfazed by Marcus' concern. "No worrisome existence. Their beings contain the knowledge necessary."

Marcus felt surprisingly comfortable with putting four strangers in charge of rescuing the rest of his crewmembers, his trust level with them extremely high.

It dawned on him at that moment that it was indeed his crewmembers and that he was now the highest commanding officer remaining on the ship thanks to Maxwell's death. He was officially in charge, free from the mental shackles that had been placed on him for so long by his captain.

I'm in charge now. This ship, damaged or not, is mine.

While the captain-by-default pondered away, the climbing villagers reached their destination and cornered the rectangular doorway.

A woman who took up the rear flung the vine through an open socket and securely fastened it through a loophole that was implanted in the dead center.

"Release," she commanded to her village partners, who followed her order and dropped the vine that rapidly fell down the chute and snapped against the wall.

The manufactured rope came to a halt at the chest level of Marcus, who gazed upwards and smiled at the accuracy of the assisting aliens.

"Well done," an impressed Marcus told his extraterrestrial equals who stood with him. "Well done, indeed."

CHAPTER 37

With the majority of his entrapped crew officially free and back onto the deck, Marcus stood with Taark in the cell of the basement area, his eyes fixated intently upon the dead, cold bodies of Maxwell and Maren while his mind couldn't help but to run wild of any outlandish ideas.

Stay dead, you bastards. Don't even think of coming back to life.

Two male villagers, who had placed Maxwell's cold body onto the floor next to his dead accomplice, left the room before patting the back of Taark, whose sad, misty-eyed gaze fixated upon that of his deceased son.

Marcus, sensing the devastation from the alien man, cleared his throat before attempting to act as a brief counselor. "Are you doing okay, sir?"

Taark closed his eyes to try to hold back his tears. "My being is of unstable emotional health, but it is of realization of my being that a result of this magnitude was of great necessity. The seed of my being was destructive and caused great agony and distress. It is of great misfortune that a result such as was of necessity."

Unable to hold them in any longer, the alien father knelt down and caressed the cold face of his dead son.

"Your being contained hatred," he quietly whispered to his son, "but the feelings my being contains remain for that of your being for eternity."

Abruptly rising to his feet and his emotions overflowing, Taark rose to his feet and turned his attention back to Marcus, his poker face not letting on his true emotions while the tears streaming down his face picked up the slack.

"My being is of great gratitude to that of your being and Earth companions," he told Marcus quickly. "The body of the seed of my being is a gift to that of your beings for observational purposes. My pardons as my being must depart."

His emotional bucket finally running over, Taark stormed by Marcus out of the cell, his tears flowing freely as he set foot back onto the soil of his planet and past Samia and Byers, who turned from each other's gaze and onto that of the distraught alien man.

"Is your father going to be okay?" Byers asked Samia with real concern.

Samia shook her head, her eyes still red from crying but, for the moment, defunct of tears. "It will be a great struggle for both his being and mine. My being will miss that of my brother, but it was of expected nature due to the behavior of his being."

"I'm here for you," he told her while placing her small hands inside of his.

A half-smile came over Samia, who massaged her palms inside of that of Byers out of appreciation.

Feeling the love with her, Byers felt more than prepared to take it an uncharacteristic extra notch to show how serious he was about her.

"Come with me back to Earth. Your father can come also if he wants. You both can start a new life there."

She shook her head over his offer. "It is not of logical sense. It is of the greatest desire of my being to concur. My being belongs home with my father and our beings, especially past a tragedy such as that of the being of my brother."

Byers held her hands tighter, his heart further longing due to her rejection.

"Please," pleaded the lieutenant to her as she tilted her head down. "I will make you so happy, I promise. I just can't, and won't, picture my life without you. I want to take you home with me to my mother and see where this can take us. I've never wanted something like what I want with you. I want to grow old and gray with you."

She turned her head up at him curiously upon his latter statement with great confusion.

"Well, I mean, I'll grow old, and you'll look amazing forever," he said, correcting himself upon realizing she would not age. "The point is, I can't see myself being with anybody besides you, and I want to give you everything and treat you like my queen for as long as I live."

"It is of great desire to my being to concur to this request," said Samia, who continued to hold hands with him and gaze into his dark eyes. "It is of great misfortune that this is home to my being. Leaving is not of a valid option at this moment in time."

Feeling his heart further sink from her second rejection, Byers tried to pull out every trick he could think of to get her to change his mind.

"I'll stay here, then," he stated as a second option out of desperation. "I can tell Ronnie right now to just take off without me so that I can live here with you. This planet is beautiful, and I can see this being my home as long as I'm with you."

Samia shook her head once more, her bottom lip quivering from having to reject him once more. "My desire to be for such a request is great. My being cannot be of allowance of such a demand, to great misfortune. It is a great desire to have your being with mine, but it is also of greater desire to be here with the being of my father as our beings grieve. Such a desire would be of selfish nature for my being."

Byers, realizing he had reached the end of the road in terms of options, glared away to try to hold back his own tears.

"I just--want you, Samia," he told her, his voice trembling. "That's all that I want."

"It is of the greatest desire of my being also," stated she. "It is a possibility in a future setting. It is not a valid possibility of this state at present time."

Byers nodded his head in agreement, realizing there was nothing further that could be done on his end. "You're right. I want you so badly, but I understand what you're saying."

Samia, sensing the curtain on their brief yet passionate relationship was entering its twilight, could feel her sadness engulf her further as she closed her reddened eyes and managed to squeeze out a couple of more tears.

"Pardons of my being to yours," she whispered to him.

Placing his hand over her face, Byers wiped a tear from her eyes and stared at her to take in her beauty for one last good look at her perfectly beautiful olive-toned face before having to say goodbye.

Marcus, who stood in the opening of the hatch, hated to intervene at the moment but knew he had to say something, even though in his heart of his hearts, he hated having to interrupt them.

"Tommy, I'm sorry, but we need to get ready for take-off."

"I'll be there in a minute," Byers responded while getting lost in Samia's eyes.

Samia touched his cheek and gazed lovingly into his eyes. "Depart," she softly advised.

Summoning up all of the inner strength he had to keep himself from bawling his eyes out, he took his thumb and rolled it softly down her bottom lip, his heart ready to tell her how he truly felt for her.

"I love you."

Samia's face softened upon his statement of amour, as she did not need any sort of translation to understand what he had just told her.

"My being also loves yours," she told him in her own way.

Byers smiled before leaning towards her to give her a passionate kiss of remembrance.

She closed her eyes, and he followed her lead as they locked lips, their hearts beating rapidly together in love.

Realizing that reality had set in, Byers separated first from Samia and held her in his arms, his mind searching for the right thing to say.

Samia, beating him to the punch, simply said one word to put a close to their romance. "Depart."

Nodding his head, Byers stepped away from her and backed up until he reached the opening of the ship.

Her eyes full of tears. Samia moved away backward from the ship and watched as the hatch had nearly closed entirely.

Byers' eyes began to dampen once the hatch engulfed his view of her and crashed with a closing sound that echoed through his heart valves, a harsh reality coming over him that his brief romance had come to an official end.

Samia bowed her head in sadness, her passionate longing for him already overwhelming her as she burst into tears.

Byers, meanwhile, placed his hand against the hatch and closed his eyes as he ditched the tough guy act and began to sob loudly to himself.

Marcus, a mere few feet behind his friend, could sense the melancholy steam from Byers' body as he slowly approached him and placed his hand on Byers' shoulder.

"I'm sorry, Tommy," Marcus told him softly. "I'm sure this has to be hard."

Sniffing loudly, Byers tried to choke back his tears and toughen up his exterior. He felt as if he wanted to bawl his eyes out in front of his best friend but instead elected to play it cool.

"Nah, I'm fine," he flatly answered, staring at the ground to avoid Marcus seeing his tear-stained face. "I'll be just fine."

Marcus, who knew better than to take the false front, patted his friend on the back. "If you ever need to talk, I'm here for you."

"Thanks," he loudly whispered, rising to his feet as he

suddenly did not feel ashamed to let Marcus see his emotionally wrecked face.

Wiping his eyes, Byers attempted to pick up his fragile pieces and get on with the business at hand. "Let's--go home."

Offering no response, Marcus put his arm around his best friend as they walked side by side towards the elevator opening in preparation for climbing back up to the deck.

Before they reached the vine that awaited them, however, Jacobs' voice sharply through the intercom of his uniform that had been exchanged back to him courtesy of Arraz.

"Commander, we're ready for takeoff," she stated. "However, headquarters is on the line waiting to speak with you, sir. They are requesting a status report."

Marcus gulped heavily and peered at Byers, realizing he was about to deliver them shocking news. "Plug them through and begin takeoff."

"Commander," the deep voice of Admiral Raymond Kim intervened. "We are so happy to finally hear from you all. Is everything okay?"

Marcus' mouth opened, but no words immediately escaped from his ajar portal, his mind unsure of what to offer his superior.

"Yes, we are okay, sir," he finally responded nervously.

"We are pleased to hear that. Why are we speaking with you and not Captain Maxwell, however?"

Realizing it was time for him to deliver the verbal goods, Marcus bit his bottom lip and exhaled deeply before giving the news he was certain was going to send immediate shock waves back home.

"Captain Maxwell--is dead, sir."

Chapter 38

Three days had passed as the crew aboard the Beso de Maria had finally arrived home safely on Earth.

Time was of the essence, however, for the sleep-deprived Marcus, who wasn't given time to relax back at home, however, as the commander found himself uncomfortably reclined in the cozy chair in Admiral Kim's office thanks to an emergency meeting his commanding officer had called upon hearing the news of Maxwell's death.

Kim, a slender man in his late 40's with not an ounce of gray in his hair, sat silently in his office with his hands folded on his dark granite desk while Marcus began to dive into the entire story of the hellacious journey he and his crew had just endured.

The admiral, offering not a peep to even question any part of the story or clear his throat, sat stone-faced at his desk and remained still through the commander's nearly two hour long monologue of a story, the blinking of his eyes being the only give-away that he was still alive.

As painful as revisiting some of the memories was to rekindle and rehash, Marcus couldn't help but feel as if he were also enduring a free therapy session to help further clear his mind and heart of the toxicity he had just survived.

The light afternoon skies through Kim's window that oversaw the South Angeles valley in the beginning of their meeting had begun to fade into darkness as the evening officially took command of the remainder of the day.

The lights that automatically shone in the room did little to alter the admiral's statuesque manner, his spectacled eyes remaining glued completely on his speaking commander.

Sighing heavily while finally beginning to wind down his lengthy story, Marcus felt relieved to tell Maxwell's own commanding officer what hellacious activities the dead captain had made them endure.

"It was all just so horrible, sir," Marcus concluded. "I never in a million years would have guessed that something like that would have ever happened. I just thank God that we all made it back home alive."

He gazed up at Kim and was met with the same silence he had given throughout.

The admiral, for the first time in a couple of hours, finally showed a sign of life by blinking his eyes towards the commander, yet did not offer any sort of immediate response other than removing his black-rimmed sleek glasses from his face and rubbing the corners of his eyes.

Blinking his eyes greatly once more after rubbing them for a moment, Kim placed his glasses back in their respective spot on his face before rising from his chair and running his fingers through his parted, short raven hair as he peered through the window behind his desk and outward into the darkened valley before him.

Marcus, confused by the admiral's immediate response, waited in wonder if he, his commanding officer had anything to offer. "Sir? Do you have anything to say?"

His eyes were still fixated outward, and Kim exhaled a giant before hanging his head.

"I cannot apologize enough for what has happened to you all," said the admiral, finally breaking his silence while he folded his arms behind his back, his strong voice cracking in between. "I--can only imagine what you all had to endure."

The admiral lifted his head and continued his blank stare out towards the night-washed land. "When we hadn't heard from you all for a few days, we knew that something was wrong. But none of us would have ever imagined something like this. I--can't even tell you how truly sorry I am for the hell you all went through."

Marcus shook his head at Kim's sincere apology. "No need to apologize, sir. There's no way that anybody would have known that something like this could have happened."

Kim turned his attention downward to the ground. "No," he stated while exhaling deeply before delivering the heavier part of his statement. "But, I'm sure that we didn't help matters by informing him before the mission that we were placing him on early retirement."

"What?" Marcus questioned, his jaw dropped to the floor over what the admiral had just informed him of. "You put him--on early retirement? Why--would you do such a thing?"

Kim cocked his head back upward and gazed back out towards the night-curtained valley speckled with street and home lights. "Indeed we did. Looking back, it probably wasn't the best timing on General Diaz's or my part to make such a major decision, especially the day before this past mission. Maxwell, as you can imagine, didn't take the news well at all, and he had no problem letting us both be aware of that, of course."

Finally able to face the music fully, Kim did an about-face and turned towards Marcus to see him eye-to-eye. "We just never thought that he would stop to do such horrible things as he did. I suppose we are partially responsible for what occurred."

"But--Maxwell had told me that he was going to retire because of his family," stated Marcus. "He gave me a complete heart-pouring story about how his job cost him his marriage and his relationship with his kids."

Kim shook his head and ran his fingers once more through his dark hair. "I'm sure he wanted you to believe that. He was never one to admit defeat, as you know. I guess that was his eventual downfall, now, wasn't it? It's too bad that, even in his advanced years, he never learned to check his ego and just admit to his own shortcomings as a man. We offered him vacation time on numerous occasions, only to see him turn us down every time. He had a wonderful family that really loved him, but it just didn't seem like he put the same effort into them that he did here. So, we figured we would make him take time off--permanently."

Marcus scratched the back of his neck, still trying to take in all of the new information he was being given. "So, if you don't mind me asking, sir, why did you let him lead us on this mission after that?"

"I suppose we could chalk that up to loyalty more than anything," answered Kim, who floated back to his desk and sat back down in his plush chair. "Despite his fiery and, frankly, difficult personality, he honorably served us for over thirty years, and we thought that we owed it to him to at least give him one last mission as a proper sendoff. I guess our loyalty was indeed over-rated when it came down to it, in hindsight, since he clearly defied us all."

"I suppose it was," Marcus agreed downtrodden. "But--I still don't understand, sir. I mean, I know that I I felt loyal towards him, but for you all to put us in the line of danger like that- well, I find that borderline unacceptable, if you don't mind me saying, sir."

Kim's face remained straight upon the bold statement made by his underling.

Marcus, who suddenly began to regret his choice of words, felt nervous by the silence that was offered in response.

Oh, shit. I think I overplayed my hand.

Picking up two metal stress balls in front of him at his desk, Kim began to fondle and play with them in his palm while he sat back for a moment and curiously stared back at his ballsy commander, who awaited his response.

"I suppose that overall I cannot disagree with you," slowly

stated Kim while stopping the movement of the balls in his hand. "I applaud you for your honesty, by the way."

Marcus exhaled deeply to himself, glad that he had not infuriated the man who now directly oversaw him.

Kim, meanwhile, stared directly into Marcus's pupils and began to fiddle once more with the stress balls in his hand.

"In retrospect, we should not have allowed this to happen," he continued. "But frankly, things happen that we sometimes don't expect, Marcus, and this is something that we will not allow to happen in the future. Rest assured. I do want you to know, however, that we did put thought into this mission after we met with Maxwell. While our decision ended up backfiring, we also originally considered replacing him with you, and we made him aware of that. We, perhaps, looking back, should have taken the former decision over the latter."

Marcus' eyes grew larger upon the last part of Kim's statement. "Wait, you were actually considering replacing him with me? How did he take that, if you don't mind me asking?"

"Not well," answered Kim before stopping the movement of the balls again and placing them back on his desk. "He thought we were making a mistake, and he told us we'd regret it if we did that. But again, as I stated earlier, we went with loyalty, and it did us a lot more harm than good, as you can see. Or rather, it did you all more harm. But, once again, I cannot offer any sort of apology to match what I really am feeling."

Marcus had no reaction to Kim's latter apology but continued to sit in his chair, breaking away from his admiral's direct stare to gaze out of the window momentarily and take a look at the quarter moon that seemed to be smiling back at him.

He stared back at Kim after a brief change of scenery and leaned back, exhaustion surprisingly not hitting him yet as he felt as if he were ready to discuss business with his superior.

"So, where do we go from here then, Admiral?" asked Marcus seriously.

Kim, taken aback by the question, shook his head at Marcus.

"Perhaps we should discuss this later once you have caught up on your rest," he suggested as he appeared as though he was attempting to close the one-on-one session quickly.

The admiral's suggestion was to no avail as Marcus carried on. "I would like to know what's on the horizon, sir. I think you owe that much to me, don't you?"

Kim's silence said it all to Marcus, his eyes suddenly becoming as serious as the new frown on his face.

"Very well," he answered, his elbows resting on the desk as his fingertips touched the bottom of his chin. "I suppose the least I can do is to let you in on what's going to be happening soon."

This ought to be good.

Kim stood from his seat once more and began to slowly approach Marcus. "First off, we will need to refurbish the Beso de Maria entirely before your next mission," he started as he began to circle around Marcus. "It's going to take some time, so be prepared for some land labor until it is completed."

"Why can't we just get a new ship, sir?" he asked fearlessly in an attempt to barter.

Kim chuckled at the question and completed his full circle around the seated Marcus before making his way back to his chair.

"You must be joking, Marcus. In case you haven't noticed, we're not exactly rolling in dough here. SAGE may be funded by the government, but they still are placing somewhat of a financial vice on us. We're not the military, and we are still trying to make our mark to have future expansion approved, so until we actually do, that will be our best and only option I can make available."

Marcus stiffened his chin upon the initial rejection but felt the need to continue to negotiate. "In that case, I have one request: Can we only go that route? I want that elevator replaced completely, and I want stairs put in for emergencies."

Standing over his desk, a smirk snuck onto Kim's face upon Marcus' demand.

"Your archaic request can be arranged," chuckled the admiral out of amusement. "It will take an even greater amount of time, for sure, but I'm sure we can pull the necessary strings to make that happen."

"Very well," smiled Marcus upon getting his wish. "Now that that's settled--what's on the horizon for me?"

Kim's grin only expanded upon the question. "I'm glad you asked. Our plan has been, and now especially, to promote you to the ranks of captain. We have seen the way you have interacted and grown with your crew over time, and we feel that you are ready to take the next step. That is, assuming you pass the necessary requirements and tests, of course."

The commander slyly smiled upon his admiral's verbal challenge. "That shouldn't be a problem, sir," he stated with confidence. "I'm not too worried about that."

"I don't have any concerns about that myself," the admiral replied in agreement while sitting back down in his seat.

Marcus, feeling the need to take advantage of as much as he could while the going was good, had one more question up his sleeve.

"I also request that Byers be promoted to be my commander once I am promoted, sir."

Kim's smirk disappeared instantly upon Marcus' request. "That one I'm not so certain about. Sure, he's been here quite some time and given some great service overall. However, in my eyes, he's got an awful lot of growing to do to take on that extra responsibility. I have seen nothing on my own end since I took this position that impresses me about him, so I'll leave that up to the two of you to change my mind. That is if he takes it seriously enough."

"I'm confident that he will," Marcus stated in a stealthy manner.

"We shall see," the admiral sharply responded. "Because it will also be on your head if he fails."

No pressure.

Kim, visibly displeased with the notion of Byers, exhaled

before changing the subject. "With that being said, is there anything else of importance that I should be aware of?"

Marcus debated for a moment, deciding to keep confidential the eternal statuses of Arraz and Rubidoux to respect their privacy.

He doesn't deserve to know anyway.

Deciding to at least show his admiral their important find, he undid his bag to reach for the discovery. "Yes, sir, I brought something of extreme importance back with us."

He reached down into his backpack and began to fumble through it to find the vial of liquid he had brought back from the alien planet.

Kim sat back down at his desk and raised his head curiously to see what his commander was up to.

Finally feeling the vial in between his fingers, Marcus pulled it from the wreckage of junk inside his bag and lifted it in front of his face.

"This liquid is what transformed Maxwell into his youthful, immortal state."

Kim's eyes locked onto the vial in wonder as he reached over and grabbed it from his commander's grasp.

His stare, deeply lost in curiosity, never left the encased liquid. "So, this is the eternal liquid you told me about, huh? It looks unremarkable like it's nothing more than water."

The commander grinned at his admiral's somewhat naïve statement. "Don't let its looks fool you. There's an eternity of youth in there."

The admiral snickered upon Marcus' response like a schoolboy.

"My God, Marcus," Kim softly said to him. "If it's true what you say, then I can only imagine the possibilities that this little vial could contain. We'll have to deeply research this, for certain. The planet that you got this from--what did you say its name was?"

"It didn't have a name," answered Marcus. "Not even the aliens that lived there had a name for it."

Kim's eyes remained focused on the vial, which he scanned from a variety of angles to take in the simple awe he held in his hands. "Fascinating, but perhaps we should come up with a name for it. Since you are all basically the pioneers of finding it, even if by force, why don't you come up with one on your own?"

Marcus paused for a moment to think of the perfect name before saying the first thing that came to his tired mind. "I was thinking 'Divinity.' But I haven't really discussed it with anyone else, so I'm just putting it out there."

The admiral's eyes left the vial and focused on his commander, beaming widely to show his approval.

"I have no objection to that name," stated Kim. "I would advise discussing it democratically between your crewmembers, however, to avoid any sort of potential hard feelings."

"Yes, sir."

"Is there anything else that merits discussion at this moment?" asked the admiral.

Marcus thought for a moment about telling his superior officer about the change of statuses for both Arraz and Rubidoux but once more resisted the urge.

"No, sir," he answered, deciding to keep what had happened to them both a dirty little secret, at least for the time being.

Let's just hope it stays that way.

As much as he knew he probably should have confessed what had happened to them both to Admiral Kim, he thought better of it to keep it between his crewmembers only, and he could only imagine how tough of a secret it would be to keep, especially once the bodies of the two young men declined the usual aging processes down the road.

I might be putting my ass on the line, but I guess we'll cross that bridge if and when we need to.

Kim nodded his head in approval, his body language suggesting he was ready to wrap up their lengthy meeting. "Very well, then. In closing, I am granting each one of you an indefinite leave effective tomorrow. You may all go home, on vacation, or wherever you need to mentally and emotionally recover from this disaster. We will also be setting up counseling visits with our psychiatrist for those of you who feel it is necessary. It's the least we can do for the hardships you've all had to endure."

"Much appreciated," Marcus thankfully said as he nodded his head in acknowledgment. "I can speak for us all when I say that we could all use a break."

Kim leaned back in his chair but remained fixated with the vial in his hand. "I can only imagine. Well, if there is nothing more on your end, then that is all, Commander. I took the liberty of having your crew informed before the two of us met, so I'm sure they are all sleeping tightly in their quarters by now. In the morning, you will all be officially dismissed until you have all been deemed mentally fit to return."

The admiral stood up from his chair and placed the vial down on his desk, extending his arm outward to shake Marcus' hand.

"You are dismissed, Commander," he told Marcus.

The commander joined his superior officer and stood before approving the handshake request with his admiral with a firm response.

"Thank you, sir," smiled Marcus, the visions of his own bed in his quarters beginning to formulate inside of his head.

Freedom!

Turning away from Kim, Marcus began to walk towards the door before the admiral stopped him in his tracks.

"There is one more thing, Marcus. We must keep all of what we have discussed confidential to the outside world," he sternly ordered.

Marcus, gritting his teeth from his slight delay to slumber, cocked his head sideways to listen as intently as his tired mind allowed.

"We must especially keep quiet as to what really happened to Maxwell," Kim continued. "We cannot let the media find out what truly occurred on that planet, nor can you allow your families and loved ones to know the truth. It could be potentially fatal to this organization, and I need you to understand that. Have I made myself clear, Commander?"

Marcus nodded his head. "What about the captain and the alien man's body? How are we going to explain that?"

"Maxwell's body will be kept in preservation here, and his family will be allowed a private funeral to say goodbye," Kim answered. "As for the alien, we will also preserve his body and perform a series of tests under extremely classified conditions to further understand their species. I am particularly counting on you to keep this all a secret, Marcus. You must."

Feeling uneasy by the admiral's request, Marcus turned to face Kim. "I understand the whole part about the media, but what do we say happened to Maxwell then, sir? What do we tell our families who want to know?"

"We tell them that he suffered a heart attack," Kim answered robotically. "If we say that, there will be no more questions from either your family or the media. In their minds, he will have died bravely and honorably. By doing this, everybody wins, especially his family, and our organization remains untainted."

Shaking his head in disgust, Marcus was unafraid to take his admiral to task for his logic.

"Yeah, everybody wins except for the ones who knew what truly happened, right?" he responded matter-of-factly. "But, hey, it's like you said, sir. Everybody wins because SAGE is untainted, right?"

Kim, speechless and surprised by his commander's boldness, stood in place like a statue embedded in cement.

"Marcus, I simply require that you understand--"

"Don't worry, sir," interrupted Marcus. "We'll all put on a happy face for you, so no need to be concerned on your end. Therefore, as you said, everybody wins."

He smiled falsely at his admiral before sharply turning away from Kim and storming through the open door that had quickly slid open in front of him.

Kim, still standing in stunned silence, could do nothing more than remove his glasses and rub the inside corners of his eyes once more, a realization coming over him that he may have

Marcus, unafraid of any potential repercussions, reached the hallway and continued towards his quarters without turning back, his mind solely on that of his bed, which awaited him a mere matter of doors down.

The door to his quarters was sealed in front of his face, and Kim placed his glasses back on his face and glided back to his desk.

Sitting down in his comfortable chair a moment later, Kim picked up the vial once more and examined its contents once more.

Feeling somewhat awful for what he had just told Marcus, he began to fondle it between his skinny fingers and exhaled deeply.

His bad feelings, however, proved to be brief thanks to the wondrous find before him, his mind beginning to suddenly fantasize at the possibilities that existed in the palm of his hand.

"Divinity," Kim said to himself with a guilty smile.

Chapter 39

Following the best night of sleep that he had experienced in over a month, Marcus felt refreshed and reenergized on his day to go home.

Despite the insanity of the entire mission he had experienced, along with the awkward and uncomfortable ending to his evening meeting with Admiral Kim, he wasted no time in packing his bag with some of his personal items as he sipped on his half coffee, half French Vanilla cream concoction that was his personal treat for a job well done.

There was no place like home indeed for Marcus, who smiled upon every sip of his sweetened morning drink that counted towards one of the several things he had missed during his long and emotionally draining mission that he felt blessed to have survived.

Various items of interest went through his mind, but especially that of Monica, who he was hoping to catch before they all went their separate ways for their hiatuses.

The thought of her alone made his morning even brighter, but the thought of carrying out the personal goal he had set for himself still frightened him, his mind still unsure of how to approach her strongly yet with great kindness.

He put down a couple of shirts that he had folded and placed them on the dark green comforter of his bed, his imagination suddenly taking over to assist him in his dilemma.

"So, Monica," he said smoothly, pretending that she there with him. "I just wanted to say that I think you're awesome, and I'd like to know if you would like to go out sometime."

Marcus shook his head at himself upon his primary imaginary approach. "No, c'mon, you've got to say something better than that."

He strayed from the edge of his bed and floated in front of the mirror to his left, smoothing out small wrinkles he thought he could see on his charcoal gray t-shirt.

Running his fingers quickly through his close-cropped dark hair to give himself an imaginary makeover, he began to smile at his own image, pretending as if the woman of his dreams were there instead.

"Hi, Monica," began the commander once more in a slightly deeper and seductive tone. "I think you're beautiful, and I'd like to make you feel beautiful every day if you give me the chance."

That's lame.

"Stupid, man," he unmercifully told himself, shaking his head at his own reflection before closing his eyes to compose himself.

C'mon, man, you've got it somewhere inside of you.

He reopened his eyes and gazed back into the mirror, ready to take another crack at his imaginary approach.

"Hey, Monica," he started, trying to maintain his confidence throughout. "I wanted to let you know that I think that you're very nice, and I'd like to know if you would like to--"

Lost in his own world, Marcus didn't even notice Byers walk through the sliding door that had been left unlocked.

Realizing instantly what was going on, Byers grinned ear to ear and crossed his arms, keeping quiet to see his friend finish out what he was doing.

"--go out with me for dinner."

"After that, I know that I sure would like to, Casanova," Byers stated jokingly through snorting laughter.

Marcus, who nearly had a heart attack over being caught in his daydream, turned around and stared at the amused Byers in embarrassment.

"How--how long have you been here?" he asked Byers.

"Long enough to see you ask yourself out in front of the mirror. I've got to say, after that, I would go out with you."

Marcus shook his head and covered his face. "How in the hell did you get in here?"

"You left the door unlocked, you idiot," he told Marcus in between his insane laughter. "I wish there was a camera in here so that I could have recorded all of that. It would have really come in handy down the road."

"Whatever. What are you doing here, anyway?"

"Well, I thought that I would at least check in with my commander and friend before I take off on my, or rather, our, mandatory vacation. But after seeing what I just saw, I've got to inquire first if you're going to be asking Monica out."

With a simple shrug of the shoulders, Marcus attempted to brush off the question by feigning ignorance. "I don't know what you're talking about. I was rehearsing lines from an old movie I saw."

His friend and lieutenant shook his head and chuckled loudly. "Who do you think that you're trying to fool? I've known you for almost my entire life, and you don't think I know when my brother from another mother has feelings for someone?"

Byers shook his head while peering at Marcus' reflection in the mirror.

Marcus, standing erectly like a statue, began to once again smooth out the wrinkles in his shirt with his open palm and attempted to pay no mind to the stare from Byers he saw in the corner of his eye.

"Just ask her out, Ronnie," advised Byers, the tone in his voice getting more serious while his gaze caught the reflected attention of his pal. "Be yourself, and you should be fine. And if she says no, what's the worst that can happen? No matter what, at least you'll know where you stand. You'll never know if you don't ask, right?"

Amazement rocked through Marcus upon Byers' surprisingly inspiring and true words, who realized that it was time to stop pretending.

"You're right," he concurred while turning towards Byers. "Who am I fooling? I'll never know if I don't try, so I guess I'll just give it a shot and see what happens from there."

"Atta boy," said Byers, who pumped his fist in the air to applaud his statement. "You see, your friend is wiser than you think. You listen to me some more, and you just might go places."

Marcus chuckled upon Byers' latter statement and held his palms upward towards him. "Let's not get carried away here," he told him as they both laughed at each other's friendly ribbings.

Resuming what he had been doing prior to his mental break, Marcus picked up his shirts and began to stuff them into his mostly full bag.

"So, what about you?" he asked Byers. "Are you feeling alright?"

Byers stuffed his hands into his jean pant pockets and walked gingerly at a snail's pace aimlessly around the room, his face turning suddenly serious from the question.

"Yeah, I guess," he answered dourly. "I mean, there's not really much that I can do, right? It is what it is, I suppose."

"Does that mean that we're going to be seeing you back at your old tricks at the clubs around here soon?" asked Marcus.

Byers shook his head upon his friend's question. "No, I don't think so. I'm going to go home to see my mom and then probably go somewhere for a while to clear my thoughts. I feel that I need some personal time to think some things over in my life."

Plopping his already stuffed bag onto the bed to fill it up some more, Marcus focused on his friend, his face refusing to hide his surprise over Byers' grown-up statement.

"What? You mean no more one-night stands?" he asked.

Byers shook his head straightly. "No, no more of that. I think I kind of want to be alone for now and gather up my thoughts, you know, so maybe I'll be ready to actually jump into a real relationship when it's all said and done."

Shock escalating throughout him, Marcus blinked his eyes rapidly and playfully grabbed at his chest. "I can't believe what I'm hearing right now. The self-proclaimed bachelor admits he may want to be in a relationship soon. Stop the press on that, people."

Byers held his palm upward like he was halting traffic to interrupt his friend's proclamation. "Hey, hey, let's not get carried away here. I didn't say soon, so let's just at least get that part straight."

Marcus shook his head and smiled. "Alright, I guess it'll be baby steps with you in that regard. But it's progress, nonetheless."

"I appreciate your understanding," Byers stated while sitting on the edge of Marcus' bed and watching him put away the last of his stuff in his bag. "So, how'd the meeting go with Admiral Kim?"

"Interesting," Marcus answered carefully after taking a moment to decide the appropriate word. "There are a lot of things that I'll go over with you, but not right now. We'll get together sometime during our sabbatical and talk things over. The only thing that I can advise is to not talk to the media or your mom about what happened on our mission and to keep everything about Maxwell hush-hush."

"Well, considering how much of a media whore I am, I'm not sure if I can do that," sarcastically stated Byers. "But I can damn well guarantee you that I'll do my best. As for Mom, well, that's a whole other story."

"Whatever," Marcus said while closing his bag. "Well, like I said, just keep it zipped, even with your mom, alright? Oh yeah, and before I forget, I meant to tell you that I gave my recommendation to Kim for you to be my commander. Now, of course, I also forgot that you told me last week that you were thinking of leaving SAGE, so I just wanted to let you know in case Kim or somebody else talks to you before you go."

Byers placed his hand on the wall and leaned towards the open door. "Well, about that. I debated that issue and gave it a lot of thought on the way home, and I decided that I was probably going to get my service out some more. Especially with Maxwell being gone, I figured, why the hell not? I've got nothing else to do outside of this, so maybe I'll hang around for a bit longer. That is, if that's okay with you, Commander."

Byers saluted his commander jokingly, a large smile implanted on his face.

Joining in on the fun, Marcus playfully saluted his friend back. "What other choice do I have?"

"Glad to have your approval, sir," exclaimed Byers, who put extra emphasis on the last word and put down his salute. "Now that that's been settled, I'm going home. Will I be seeing you back in the neighborhood soon?"

"Considering that I'm going to see my mom too, I guess I'll be seeing your ugly face again very shortly," he answered, sending the two men into hyena-like laughter before they both hung an arm over one another for a masculine half-hug.

"I'll see you back in the neighborhood soon," Marcus told him.

"You got it," said Byers. "See you over there soon."

Byers turned and began to make his way out before his friend stopped in his tracks underneath the doorway.

"Tommy--I just wanted to say--thanks. For the advice, I mean."

Byers nodded his head to acknowledge his gratefulness. "That's what friends are for, right?"

Marcus nodded his head back and smiled, a feeling of gratefulness coming over him for having a friend like that in his life.

Byers, unable to stay serious for too long, couldn't resist the urge for one more parting shot.

"By the way, your Night Watch reign ends when we come back. You know that, right?"

Marcus shook his head and grinned at the opportunity for smack talk. "With how sorry you are, I feel pretty good about my streak going to a dozen, Granny."

The lieutenant chuckled out of appreciation and held up his hand to wave goodbye for the moment before heading out of Marcus' view and down the hallway to make his way back home.

Marcus, watching as the door slid back closed, chugged the last of his coffee drink before picking up his bag and gazing around one last time to make sure he didn't forget anything.

Seeing that everything he owned was properly accounted for, he flung the bag over his shoulder and threw his empty coffee cup into the environmental-friendly trash can to his left ,instantly dissolved the waste.

"Lights off!" he commanded aloud to turn off the lights that instantly followed his command and flicked off once he stepped onto the hallway.

He froze outside of the door to give one last command. "Close and lock!"

The door, identifying his voice, automatically followed his order while he turned to his right and began to head down the hallway to take him to the outside of the building.

It was no coincidence, at least in his mind, that he was going to pass Monica's room before hitting the lobby and exit, and his only hope was that he was not too late to tell the woman he cared about how much he truly did.

Before he could make a move, he was halted dead in his tracks by a shout.

"Commander!" a male voice called out.

Marcus gritted his teeth and wondered who had interrupted his intentions.

He turned and was met face to face with Jennings and Jacobs, who stood closely to one another and were touching fingertips together, appearing to try to be as secretive as possible about it.

"Doctor Jennings and Jacobs--what a pleasant surprise," he said, smiling falsely while attempting to sound somewhat excited to see them both.

"Commander, we just wanted to thank you," stated Jennings. "I mean, without your little extra push, I--well, us, would not actually be doing out on a date together."

The commander grinned upon hearing this but still hoped that this conversation would not take much longer to complete. "That's great, guys," he rushed. "Well, update me on your relationship status when we come back, and good luck to you both."

He attempted to turn around but was stopped by Jacobs, who grabbed him by his arm carefully.

"Commander, I, like Desmond, can't thank you enough. And I can't believe that you never told either one of us that we both confessed our feelings for the other to you."

"Well, you know me," Marcus said, shrugging his shoulders while attempting to wind it down. "I'm good at keeping secrets, I guess. Well, again, thanks to you both for your great work and--"

"I just--really like her," Jennings interrupted Marcus, smiling brightly from getting to finally no longer having to hold in his feelings for Jacobs. "And it's great to know that she feels the same way about me. We really both couldn't have done this without you and your great advice."

Marcus nodded his head and attempted once more to get away cleanly. "My pleasure to be of service to you both, but really, I--"

"We should get together sometime during our hiatus so we can take you out to dinner," intervened Jacobs before Marcus could finish his sentence. "It's the least we can do to thank you. What do you say?"

Marcus' jaw hung open as he tried to find the most appropriate response to the two lovebirds, who anxiously awaited his answer.

Saying the first thing that came to his mind, but trying not to be overly rude, he knew he had no choice but to be direct.

"I've got to go," he told them before turning quickly and rushing down the hallway toward the lobby and Monica's quarters.

Jacobs and Jennings stood in confusion upon their commander's rapid reaction.

"Was it something we said?" Jennings asked her.

Clearing the unexpected hurdle that had come up, Marcus rolled down the hallway with a head of steam, determined as ever to reach his desired destination and confess his love for Monica. Nothing in his mind was going to stop him now as he felt as prepared as ever to tell her how he really felt about her, especially once he made the needed right turn to get even closer.

His readiness, however, was further delayed by another male voice screaming for his attention.

"Commander!" the voice yelled.

Shit!

Skidding in his tracks once more, he turned around and saw Arraz chase him down, his hand in the air as if it would help in stopping him from going any further.

"Arraz," mused Marcus, who attempted to hide his annoyance. "What can I do for you?"

"Sorry if I caught you on your way out," started Arraz, "but I just wanted to thank you for your leadership and taking care of me, and mostly, to tell you how sorry that I was."

"What are you sorry about?"

"That I put myself in that bad position out on that planet when we first arrived," said Arraz, who, for once in his life, had decided to take accountability. "I should have listened to you in the first place. If I had, I wouldn't have--you know, died. And if I had listened, I wouldn't be stuck having to live an eternity to think about it."

Marcus once more felt the need to cut off the conversation for his own selfish reasons but couldn't quite come to grips with doing so due to the genuine nature of Arraz's words.

"Well," Marcus began, still trying to avoid being a jerk for that particular moment. "I wouldn't feel too bad about it. I mean, I guess if you look at the bright side, you'll always look and feel young, right?"

"Yeah, but I just don't know how I'm going to explain it to anybody. Does Admiral Kim or anybody else with SAGE know about Rubidoux or me?"

Marcus shook his head. "No," he answered quietly. "And let's just keep it that way, for now, at least. As for your family, just tell them when the time's right, I guess. I'm sure everything will be fine."

"I guess so," agreed the immortal lieutenant. "Thanks for not telling anybody here. I really appreciate it."

"You bet," said Marcus, who saw the opportunity to wrap up the brief conversation. "Well, great work again on the mission, and--"

His plan was once again foiled as Arraz failed to get the hint and interrupted him in the middle of his goodbye.

"I just wonder what to tell my family and friends," he stated with worry intertwined in his voice. "I mean, to tell my folks what happened especially, and not to mention my sister, who's a huge crybaby, how do I even go about doing that, Commander?"

Marcus, feeling like he was trapped, rolled his eyes internally. "I'm sure you'll figure it out. You're bright. I've got faith you will be able to do so in time."

"Thanks. But, really--what should I do?"

Marcus, standing in front of his lieutenant with a wide open jaw, was once more unsure of what to say.

Going strictly on impulse, he said the first thing once more that came to his mind, hoping that it wouldn't quite come out as badly as it did with Jacobs and Jennings.

"Go talk to our therapist here," was his unintentional cold recommendation.

Marcus patted Arraz on the shoulder as a means of support before scooting past him down the hallway once more, leaving the vulnerable immortal being there by his lonesome.

Confused by his commander's strange suggestion, Arraz blankly blinked his eyes while attempting to process what he had just been told.

Another quick left turn brought Marcus one step closer, who strode briskly, making sure not to run too fast to avoid running over somebody.

His heart, racing at an all-time high, could sense how close he truly was, with only one more quick right turn remaining as an obstacle before he hit the straightaway lane to Monica's room and the exit out of headquarters.

He took the right turn but felt his momentum suddenly take him backwards thanks to a nasty collision he took with somebody else head to head.

His bag was sent flying a few feet behind him. Marcus rolled over in pain and rubbed the top of his forehead before rising to his feet to see about the other party he had injured.

"Sorry about that," apologized Marcus, who went back to pick up his bag and continued to nurse his own injury to the fallen man. "Are you alright?"

"I'm okay," said the young man, who now picked up his head to put an end to the brief John Doe mystery.

Marcus exhaled upon seeing who he had unluckily rammed over.

Oh, great.

"Oh, Commander!" the now identified Rubidoux gleefully stated. "Sorry I ran into you, but I am glad to see you because there was something that I wanted to talk with you about before we go."

Oh, hell no!

Marcus shook his head to further rid himself of the cobwebs in his brain and to also refuse the young Rubidoux's request. "Sorry, Rube," he said, trying to be as sincere as possible, even though his patience had officially run thin. "I can't really talk now, but we'll catch up later."

He picked up stride and sprinted by Rubidoux, who

remained down on one knee, still recovering from the shot he had just taken.

"Wait," requested the rookie to nobody in particular, as his commander had already left the scene.

His heart beating rapidly upon the sight of Monica's door, he stopped in front of her room and began his nervous habit of brushing his shirt to smooth out the wrinkles once more before running his fingers quickly through his hair in preparation for spilling his guts to her.

Clearing his throat loudly, he knocked on her door gently.

Here we go.

His attempt, however, was met with neither a verbal response nor an opening of the door.

Failing to let that be a deterrent to his efforts, he pushed the doorbell button to the right of her door, hoping that perhaps she was just unable to hear his initial knock on the door.

A nervous tick went through Marcus, who waited for a response of some sort.

Gazing at the electronic telecommunication receiver next to her doorbell, he was met with nary a voice over the speaker or a face on the screen to greet him.

He turned his attention towards the door, which remained as sealed as before and seemed to generate no kind of hope on its own end.

"She's gone, Commander," the voice of Rubidoux said suddenly while he began to walk slowly towards him while rubbing his forehead. "I saw her walk out."

No, it can't be.

Marcus' face and heart fell to the depths of beneath upon hearing the devastating words from his rookie navigator.

Feeling the cockles of his heart begin to deteriorate upon Rubidoux's confirmation, he bowed his head downwards and gritted his teeth in frustration.

"She left a few minutes ago," Rubidoux continued, who had known all along from his own hunches about his commander's feelings for the beautiful Monica Brackenridge. "I'm sorry to tell you that. Maybe you can talk to her next time."

The apology did nothing to rid the salt from Marcus' internal wounds as the commander swallowed the elephant-sized lump of heartache that he felt inside of him.

How many more 'next times' am I going to allow?

"Thanks," Marcus choked out to Rubidoux before dejectedly making his way to the lobby area, which, although only a matter of yards from him, seemed like the longest walk of his life.

Rubidoux discontinued nursing his injury and felt the pain of his superior officer as he could do nothing more than be a spectator in the tragedy he saw before him.

An older male security guard who attempted to give his own goodbye was not even acknowledged by Marcus, who dragged past him like he wasn't there and had his body scanned for identification before walking through the sliding glass exit door and underneath the entrance overhang.

Crawling away from the exit and towards the pick-up and drop-off area, he held up his hand and landed a small bit of fortune in flagging down a taxi that just happened to be at the right place at the right time.

At least something went my way, huh?

Reaching the hovering vehicle that awaited him, he opened the door and threw his bag, a sulking attitude behind it while he sat firmly down on the seat.

A final look at SAGE headquarters was his final goodbye as he exhaled deeply out of sadness and slammed the door roughly shut.

"Where to, Mac?" the smoky-smelling, high-pitched voice of the taxi driver asked.

Marcus took a deep breath inwards and outwards, attempting not to snap at the driver, who had nothing to do with his own bitter frustration towards himself.

"23rd and 2nd," he quickly responded.

"Need your thumbprint," the driver stated for both a method of payment and usage of identification.

Marcus obliged and placed his thumb on the small scanner, a bright green light and somewhat happy-sounding chime signifying approval.

The driver, hearing all he needed to, began to float away from the curb and into the traffic that stood in front of them.

An uneasy feeling came over Marcus, who closed his eyes momentarily and continued to beat himself up for not being quicker to the punch with Monica.

He wished that he had listened to the advice he had given Jennings about telling her how he felt, and fantasized about what could have been while regretting all of the moments of opportunity that he had not taken advantage of and all of the delays he had given himself.

You blew it, you idiot. You've got nobody to blame but yourself.

Gazing out of the window to try to ease some of his tension, Marcus took one last gander back at headquarters and felt like his eyes began to play tricks with him as a woman, who looked a lot like Monica, walked out of the building.

Marcus shook his head in disbelief, thinking that his mind was messing with his vision.

Feeling the need to verify that he was indeed hallucinating, he peered out through the window again but was surprised to see the woman once more, who now held out her arm to try to hail a taxi of her own.

The color of her skin, her long dark hair, and the smile on her face were all of the confirmation that he needed to realize that he actually was seeing Monica and not a figment of his imagination.

His once dormant heart was now filled with joy, and he waved his arms to try to get the driver's attention.

"Wait, stop! Go back and pick up that young woman, please!"

"No can do, Mac," responded the driver to his command. "I've got places to go and people to take, and you ain't the only one who needs a taxi in this town."

Marcus quickly thought of anything that he could do to change the driver's mind.

"I'll pay for her fare--and give you a tip of five-thousand dollars," he desperately offered, even if it financially drained him.

The offer was more than sufficient to the driver, who quickly applied his brakes and stopped on a dime.

"Backin' on up," said the money-hungry driver, pointing back with his open thumb to the vicinity of the thumbprint scanner. "You know what to do, Mac."

You're damn right.

Marcus wasted no time following the driver's instructions. He quickly placed his thumb back onto the scanner and felt relief as the green light and jingle once again confirmed that the transaction had gone through.

It was especially sweet music to the ears of the driver, who smirked in approval while twisting his head towards Marcus to prepare himself in backing up the vehicle.

"That's what it's all about, Mac," the driver said before humming a sweet song aloud for the extra money he had just made.

The taxi rapidly began to back up and stopped in front of Monica, who put her hand down and appeared overjoyed to have gotten a ride sans a long wait.

Marcus' heart pounded in his chest, the moment that he had longed for finally arrived.

Nice and easy, man. Nice and easy.

He felt nervous about what to say but gave himself little time to ponder it over any further as he swung open the door and said the first thing that came to his head.

"Do you mind sharing a taxi with me?" he asked while stepping out and flashing a cozy smile at her.

Monica grinned shyly from his question and tilted her head downward out of embarrassment.

"Not at all," replied the beautiful young woman, much to Marcus' delight.

Marcus' nerves, ever-so-present as could be, did little to

disable him as he approached her with all of the confidence that he could muster.

Taking her bag from her grasp and placing it on the ground to get it momentarily out of the way, he held her smaller, soft hands inside of his, unafraid of any possibility of superiors possibly seeing the nepotism that was occurring.

Caught-off-guard but offering no resistance, she brightly smiled upon his symbol of affection, which appeared to be mutual.

"Miss Brackenridge," he confidently began, despite the butterflies that fluttered rapidly in his stomach. "I've had something I've wanted to ask you for so long."

His nerves flickering again inside of him, he exhaled once more before saying the first thing that came to his nervous mind.

"I'd like to know--would you do me the honor of going out with me for some good conversation over dinner and wine?"

Monica coyly gazed down at the ground and giggled nervously but continued to smile.

Raising her head after a brief moment, she gazed into his eyes with great warmness that flooded his once tough interior.

"I would love to."

They smiled joyously at one another, the sparks in their eyes apparent while their feelings for one another had finally become known to each other.

Marcus' hand never abandoned hers as he picked up her bag with his open hand and escorted her to the taxi.

Gently placing her bag on top of his on the seat, he stood by the open door to wait for her to enter first.

She ducked into the taxi and thanked him for his gentlemanly act before he followed her inside and closed the door behind them so they could both officially head home.

The taxi pulled away recklessly from the curb and onto the street, its driver once again not checking for ongoing traffic.

The couple it carried, however, paid no mind while they

stared deeply into each other's eyes and began a conversation that was the start of something divine.